CHEAT CODE

AFTEN BROOK SZYMANSKI

Immortal Works LLC
1505 Glenrose Drive
Salt Lake City, Utah 84104
Tel: (385) 202-0116

Cover Art by Ivan Zanchetta
www.bookcoversart.com

Formatted by FireDrake Designs
www.firedrakedesigns.com

AISN B0793F2K2J (Kindle Edition)
ISBN 978-0-9990205-7-9 (Paperback)

If it weren't for the men in my life constantly laughing at my gaming skills, I might never have written this book.

Who's laughing now?

1

'WELCOME DONORS'

The illuminated words in bright green letters light a path where an EXIT sign should be. The words are the only source of light in the room. I stare up from the dark entry, unsure where I am or how I got here. Or who I am, for that matter. Not feeling the whole 'welcome' vibe at all. Yet, it's not particularly weird as people press around me in a direction toward the sign. Nothing pricks my 'no worries, this is normal' nerve, so I don't follow. I also don't run.

I might be an idiot. Right now, I'm guessing I'm a total-amnesiac-moron.

Lack of light isn't the only sensory hole in this space. Sound *shuffs* away into the darkness like an anti-chamber.

Instead of shutting off my senses, I'm on fire, desperate for information. I seek out the light bits and sound parts for guidance and security. All around me people behave with pattern-like confidence, moving toward the lighted words, shuffling samely together. The little sparks of sensory information, all too eager to lead me along with the rest, offer no alternative to 'welcome'.

The phrase shines seductively, directs me forward. It casts distorting shadows over the people packed around me. The difference between them and me is they walk like they know where they're going and are eager to get there. I have no idea what's ahead. And I'm not at all thrilled about the word 'donor'.

Illuminated arrows diverge from the greeting, leading people in two directions. 'Ads' one way, 'Game of Life', the opposite. The rest of the group presses forward, like they've studied for this decision.

How am I without a plan? I'm a girl of action—*that* I know. Or a girl not of dis-action. Alright, I know close to nothing about myself and I want to believe I'm awesome. *Please, be awesome.*

I stand, dividing the crowd that presses toward the lit words. I don't know which way to go, but I do have an overwhelming urge to bite the person nearest to me. It might be an overreaction. It's hard to know in a room full of strangers when I can't even remember my own name. Then again, biting people might be my best course of defense. I don't yet know …

Stop. Before I sink my incisors into some dude's arm. *Don't be a psychopath.*

Someone bumps me, jamming my right shoulder forward. I smack my left hand against my hip expectantly, but whatever I hope to find attached to my belt isn't there. I want to go back to before here, but I can't remember where. Or what it was. None of these idiots seem concerned.

I turn back hoping to find the 'EXIT' lit in the same neon green as the other illuminated words, but find only more people with their eyes set on the bright letters shining above, like it's some kind of goal line.

Reaching out a hand, I stop a girl near my age moving toward the 'Ads' arrow. The girl stands symmetrically perfect, having both curves and height. It seems unfair considering I feel mismatched when it comes to my limbs. I can't help when a little scoff escapes.

The girl stretches her back to her full height, demonstrating the real difference between the two of us—her poise and my edge. And the fact she makes the formless dress look good. I'm wiry to the point of being lurpy, with electrified nerves to match my lightning blond hair.

"Where are we?" I ask without excusing myself for halting her progress. It earns me an up-down judgment glare.

"Did you need something? I don't want to miss the next ads audition," the girl says.

Purple streaks, the color of her lips, take the edge off her black hair. Everything about her screams confidence. I feel like her complete opposite, lost in a crowd.

Forget that.

I push into her personal space, forcing her to step back. "Do you know what's going on?"

She leans away from me even more. "Of course. My agent worked his tail off to get me on the donor list when they found out I was terminal." She squints at me. "What're you? Some kind of pre-assessment?"

I roll the words 'donor list' silently around in my mouth, tasting them. I don't like the flavor.

'Terminal' and 'pre-assessment'? No time to dwell on that.

She holds her forearm up to my eye line. "GenE247" appears burned or inked into her skin in black block letters. It's weird. She folds her cream-colored sleeve down several times, covering the markings.

"I'm cleared for Ads." Her superior attitude melts into a softer, sweeter girl with sparkling eyes smiling along with her full mouth. "I know only Entertainment and Marketing Gen can audition."

"GenE247, you're holding up the line." Someone in a white coat with a clipboard appears from the point where the Ads line bends around a corner. It's impossible to tell if it's a woman or a man, but they definitely have the stance of 'authority figure' down.

"Coming." GenE247 hurries away like a misbehaved child. I step backwards—away from the white coat—and hide in the flow of moving people while observing GenE247. *Don't look at me, person holding the clipboard.* Why do they keep looking this way?

When GenE247 reaches the person in the white coat she lifts her left arm again. Her purple streaks shine under the lighted lettering. The authority figure places a black device at the crook of GenE247's elbow and drags it the length of her entire forearm. A beep of approval chirps from the black object as the girl rounds the corner. The white coat person disappears behind her with the black device still in hand.

The people around me continue to move, jostling me so I have to shove them forward in order to keep my distance from the glowing words and their blind corners. Everyone pushes their left sleeves up as they advance in their respective lines. I look at my left arm and fold back my sleeve. There's nothing but skin. I'm not sure if that's good or bad. GenE247 appeared proud of her branding.

Craning my neck as people filter forward, I look for exposed skin of left arms. 'Gen' follows a letter and number sequenced tattooed on their left forearms like a VIN number. I brush my hand over the clean slate of my bare flesh and hold it there, waiting for a mark to reveal itself.

People continue to pass me. No one steps out from behind either corner to beckon me forward like they did for GenE247.

The crowd thins to a trickle. Most head toward the arrow indicating 'Game of Life'. I wait until I'm the only one standing in front of the 'Welcome Donors' sign. At my back, blackness. No exits anywhere. There's a fine line between taking action and being rash. I need a plan. My mind wipes of information I need to form such a thing.

A door slides across the open bend of the 'Ads' hallway. The mechanical grinding and sucking-pull of air from the door cuts me off from joining Ads. The path seals. The lighted arrow flickers once, momentarily revealing the emptiness inside what were shadowed corners, then goes out.

The 'Game of Life' pathway remains lighted. The thought of being cut off, left in the haunting glow of the welcome sign alone, sends a chill across the tops of my arm hairs. Each one stands on end.

I race to the bend in the hall where the arrow points forward. No one in a white coat waits for me. I don't know if I miss them or if the black scanning device waits ahead. Keeping my right hand pressed over my left forearm, I continue walking until the lighted arrow sizzles once then goes dark.

"Hello?" I call.

There's no answer. No sign of anyone. All the masses of people before me are gone. A sliding door slams shut from where I entered this space, trapping me in my decision. I again reach to my hip for something with which to defend myself. My fingers throb at having nothing to grasp. I pop the knuckle of my index finger to release tension in the tiny joint.

My stomach jumps into my ribcage. I'm trapped. My eyes strain to make out the room, but it's all dark. Extending my arms, my fingers brush a narrow chamber. The walls sting with cold. No shifting air seeps under gaps in doorways or down corridors. I slap both palms against the wall.

A tinny clap echoes back, muted by the pounding of my panicked heart. "Let me out!" I kick the same wall, jarring my shin in the effort. I could kill that wall right now if I had a weapon, but I'm too busy hopping on one foot because the sting of the unmovable metal still rings up my calf.

This time there's an effect. A vibration rings under my toes. The pads of my feet go numb as the shaking climbs my legs and settles into my knees. The floor disintegrates around my feet. I sink through crumbling metal which has become something like sand.

"No, no, no..." I say, lifting one foot and not finding solid ground anywhere. "Go back," I say, motioning my hands to steady the floor. "As you were."

The sand of the floor bites up my ankles, each grain picking higher and higher up my leg to cling and suck me down a millimeter deeper.

"Open the door," I shout. What was so horrible about the welcome sign anyway? It was at least... welcoming. Not like this. I'm being expelled, digested through the bowels of a hallway.

The sand pecks at my knees. I slip further and further inside, unable to feel any part of me that's disappearing into the grains surrounding me. Holding my arms high above my head, I worry if I touch the sinking sand with so much as a finger, I'll sink faster.

"Help!" I want to bite back the word. Besides, there's no one else in this space to answer my call. At this rate, I won't be here for long.

Help doesn't come and I'm running out of time. Wherever the people in the white coats have gone, they're not coming back for me.

Opening and closing my upstretched hands, I hope for a ladder rung to magically appear in my palm and lift me out of this mess. Maybe if I concentrate hard enough, I can will an escape option. Mind over rapidly-shifting-matter. I mean, if a solid floor can change into sand, maybe it can turn into a stairway.

A light crackles to life above me. I've done it. I've activated a way out. But it's not a hand reaching down to rescue me or a walking path out of this hell-hole. It's an illuminated phrase far out of reach.

'Have a Nice Game.'

"Screw that," I say. "Pull me out." The sand races toward my neck and face.

Without enough time to suck in one last breath before my mouth and nose are covered, the neon phrase changes to 'Good Luck' and I can't help but feel the room mock me. It might as well be a giant bird icon for how much I'm being given the finger. Raising my middle finger in reply, it's the last thing consumed by the microscopic grains of glass.

2

L ight bursts against my eyelids like it's pressing in, even though I'm squeezing them shut as tightly as I possibly can. Then I realize I'm still breathing.

"I'm alive?" I blink away the sting of sunlight.

Everything flips from right-side up to upside-down and back again. Or maybe I'm simply disoriented. Which turns out to be the case as I take one step and fall to my hands and knees. My hands are buried in sand. I pull away from the clinging stuff and brush the dirty grains from my arms, anticipating the floor to suck me in once more. The sand stays put around my calves and feet.

Air fills my lungs in the same urgency of feeling like I've already wasted my last breath. I keep sucking in oxygen, terrified I won't get enough. Gulping in air brings salt with it. I cough until it hurts.

Looking in every direction, all I see is beige sand. Except where the gleaming blue sky above me presses in, curving and closing around the edges of the sand. I run toward the curve of the sky.

Slam.

My head spins, as if the object I'm trapped in had been spinning and came to a stop before my brain could cease sloshing inside my head. It's a bubble. No, a dome. I'm in a sand-bottomed dome. Like I'm the focal point of a snow globe, but with sand. Pounding the barrier holding me in with the sand does nothing but reverberate the effort back toward me. Vibrations of my fist against the structure wobble back to attack my eardrums. I cover my ears.

I follow the edge of the dome around in a circle. In no time, I'm back at my own scattered tracks. Saline settles on my skin like filmy dew. I stick my tongue out.

There's moisture in the air, a humid fog. I press my face against the bubble sky wall. It's see-through. Below my enclosure stretches a half-built, blocky land. I'm somehow floating far above everything.

People bustle about below me, pushing, dragging, and stacking huge chunks of materials.

"What's the point of that?"

As expected, I get no answer. Slamming the glass doesn't draw attention like I hope.

"What are you doing?" My words bounce back to me, echoing within my dome. The people below act like I'm not here. "Am I supposed to get down there?"

The people below behave similar to the people in the entry space from before. They all seem to be on autopilot.

"Bunch of morons. Just doing what everyone else does," I

holler to them with my hands in the air to draw their attention to my insult. My words bombard me from all sides, reverberating off the dome. "Look up, at least." I slam the dome wall again. "Get me out of here."

I can't figure out if it's better to stay where I am or find a way down to where the rest of the people are. I shift my focus and search the sky beyond my cage. In the not-far distance another dome levitates. Except, it's not a dome. It's a sphere. There's hundreds of them suspended without strings or cords or anything, filling the sky. I step back and look at my feet. Am I in a sphere too?

Pressing my face against the bubble again, I strain to see what, if anything, the other spheres hold. A person standing upright, like me, has their hands pressed against the side of their own bubble. "Hey." I pound three times against the glass to get their attention. They do the same.

I startle and push away. So does the other person.

"Am I seeing myself?" It's not the weirdest idea, based on how things are going.

I press my face back against the barrier to see. The other person doesn't match my movements. It's not a replica of me, it's another trapped person. At least I'm not the only one. The opposite half of the sphere also has a clear bubble. With one difference. The downturned half of the sphere is filled entirely with water, magnifying the distorted image of a person floating inside.

An unmoving person. Drowned.

I'm staring at a dead body.

Stumbling away from the glass, I cover my mouth with my hands. I lift one foot off the sand, and then the other, like that will make it less possible I'm standing on top of someone else's watery grave under my sand. What if I'd materialized in the water side of this sphere?

My dome shifts.

"Oh, come on. I take the question back." I cling to the side of the dome, my hands squeak against the glass as the sphere continues to tip. "I'm not asking because I want to switch sides." I try to appease whatever force screws with me. "This one's good. It's fine."

Sticky air soaks my dress. The cream-colored cloth of my uniform bleeds with moisture, clinging to my skin beneath. A puddle forms at one corner of my dome. The structure tilts toward the growing collection of water like it's being weighted in place.

Droplets stream along the glassy sky, hit the bubble, and slide in huge streaks toward the puddle, weighting my dome even more, so it's off-kilter.

"No!" I jump on the opposite side of the growing puddle, trying to level out the tipping that's happening faster and faster. I dig at the sand hoping to dam a safety zone between me and the ever-growing pond.

"You've got to be kidding me." I keep digging. My finger-nails cake with dirt. I can't conjure anything else to do and there's no way I'm going to waste time thinking about it.

My side of the dome rises like the high end of a teeter-totter. I don't want to find out what happens when I pass the halfway point. It's already all I can do to dig a mound of sand so I don't slide into the lake at the other end.

Humidity saturating the globe makes breathing difficult. I

stop to peer out toward the nearest sphere. It too tips, turning the other person's world upside down. The person on the same sandy side as me has already fallen into the water. Wild splashing follows pressed palms against the glass, the desperate last plea for escape. I feel it already. How soon until that's me?

It'll never be me. I, for one, wouldn't stand there with my hands on the glass if there was something else to do. Like digging.

My feet slip against wet sand, reviving me to my state of emergency. I can't save the other person.

"Dig, dig." Not like I'm not digging already. I cup my palms to shovel back more ground at a time.

My hands plunge into liquid sand. "What? No. Be dry." Find an air pocket or something, like I can dig to the other side where the air will go, to escape to while this side floods.

Water bubbles at my knees. I stand, almost falling backwards because of the angle of the ground. In order to correct my balance, I step into the water burbling from where I dig.

What can save me if water comes from both ends of my side of the sphere? I look behind me at the water still growing, heavy with salt. Gurgling, bubbling liquid continues to pop at my shoes. Everything ticks toward the lake of salt water collecting at the far edge.

My hands grip the hole I make. The tiny particles melt beneath my fingers, my grip useless. I grasp over and over at the evaporating sand and slam my head into the clear material holding me inside this puzzle ball.

The sphere nearest me, beyond my own trap, has still water.

The person inside no longer flails. They're only a body floating in the heavy end of the dome.

"Survive," I yell, thrusting my head against the barrier again and again, like I can break out using my thick skull instead of my wit. My fingers lose grip. I slide farther in the direction of suffocating water. I spit into the air for no other reason than to get any and all liquid away from me.

Unsure if I'm making a wise choice, I resume digging into the burbling water-hole of sand like my life depends on it, strongly of the opinion that my life, in fact, *does* depend on it.

The sand disappears like sugar in milk, revealing a large gaping well pouring liquid into my dome. Everything fills faster. I'll slide sideways soon, leaving me no chance of survival.

There's no more time to decide what to do. I suck in a deep breath, clasp my hands in a bladelike grasp above my head, and dive headfirst into the hole I've dug.

My hands thrust through the hole into the opposite side of the sphere. Water presses me on all sides. The pressure of it wipes me. My lungs flatten under the crushing weight of too much water. My blood will boil from oxygen forced out of my lungs. Veins are already filled to slam-capacity. Everything heavy or bursting.

I continue slicing through the water in the direction I dove. There's no light. Then bubbles race at my sides. Air from my lungs bursts through my skin. At least, it tries. I want to breathe, but don't dare open my mouth. The bubbles push me faster through the water. And a body, which had been completely submerged opposite my side of the dome, slams against my fingertips, jarring them.

Opening my mouth to breathe doesn't help at all. I force my hands against the current to cover my mouth in an effort to keep air in, not out, of my lungs. My feet tumble ahead of my arms. Fighting the water sends me head over feet, and feet over head, I twist and turn in a tirade of falling water. I'm falling with it.

I open my eyes to discover the sphere isn't holding me inside any longer. I've been dumped headlong onto the half-assembled land below. My mouth opens and fills with sweet air. Okay, it's still salty, but I can breathe and that's sweet. I choke and gag, coughing up water and bile together, no less sweet because all of this means my insides aren't giving up either and I'm good with that.

Next to where I've landed, lies an unmoving body. A person. A male. I assume he and I belong to the same broken dome trap. I scramble away.

Because he's dead.

He drowned below me. I've never been this close to a real life dead body. Out of curiosity, I move closer and bend an ear to his chest. Nothing. I knew it. Totally dead.

Still. Unwilling to let this place tell me what's what, I push my sleeves up and compress his chest again and again. The hard lines of his face and worn look of his hands indicate he isn't a stranger to fighting his way through obstacles. He's not weak. He couldn't break out of the dome?

Nothing happens when I compress his chest. No *gasp*, 'I'm alive. Thanks stranger, here's a hint on how to get out of here', the way I picture things going. Not even a, 'get your grubby hands off me, I'm fine.'

I stop long enough to wipe my arm across my forehead and

take in his youthful face, marked with hardness in lines around his eyes. So far everyone has had the look of no worries, but this person seems aged with anxiety. More man than the young adult he appears to be, like a thirty-something actor cast to portray a brooding eighteen-year-old. I stop analyzing his looks and continue compressing his chest.

My muscles burn. Every second's tick comes with a 'you can stop now,' and still I don't stop pressing, pushing, shoving, pounding on this stranger's chest. And then a horrible thought breaks through—*just break his neck, then you can stop.*

But he's already dead, weirdo brain.

He coughs and gags. It takes me a minute to realize it's worked. He's yacking on his own. I really can stop shoving his ribs into his lungs now. His eyes are the color of mud when he opens them, not the crystal blue I imagine, but I can't hold that against him. He's alive. I want to jump and high-five someone. I did it. I saved the hot guy!

Except he doesn't award me the grateful smoldering gaze I hope for. His eyes open to me bending over him, then widen beyond what's natural. He does a full roll so he's no longer directly under me, as if I, the person who forced air back into his lungs, am a threat.

There's nothing congratulatory about his reaction to me saving his moron life either.

Crack

He clocks me across my cheekbone with his muscled fist, forcing my face sideways before my neck, along with the rest of my head, can do anything about it.

3

I'm knocked from my knees and land on my butt. My hands, which already ache from compressing his life back inside him, hold my face together. It feels like my whole head needs to be reassembled.

The dude gets to his feet. He swipe-slaps the sand off his hands, then moves to brush off his knees. His eyes watch me below scruffy hair cut to hang well past his brows, like some nonchalant stand-off. He mutters something unintelligible under his breath, cocks his head to the side, looking up toward the sky-spheres at an angle blocking the sun from shining in his eyes.

"You broke my face!" I scream through my hands still patting to determine the extent of the damage. On close inspection, I only have a fat lip.

"What are you doing?" he asks, beating me to the affronted interrogation role, leaving me nothing but in the wrong.

I push my feet into the wet sand, sliding back on my butt, increasing the distance between us by maybe an inch and a half.

"Why didn't you lead with the question and punch later?" My jaw clicks when I move it. I roll my chin so it catches below my ear, where things come together. One loud pop and the click goes away. I popped my own jaw back into place. I'm certain I can just as easily dislocate this dude's confidence.

"You didn't answer my question." He keeps his eyes on everything at once. The shuffling people, me, his own fist, me, materials nearby, me, the sky, me, the watery mess surrounding us, me, me, me.

"I saved your life, moron." My insult comes out neutered by the fact I'm sitting in the muddy sand while he casts a broad shadow over me. I think I've earned the right to be the one demanding answers.

"Why would you do that?" he asks. I can hear he's working at keeping his words even and calm. He's breathing heavy. How did I miss this earlier? He's playing at having the upper hand. But he's shaken.

If I had a knife in my belt, he'd have a slash to remind him not to right-hook-hello.

We're both covered in salt and sand. I shake my hands of loose dirt and ring out my hair. "I'm wondering the same thing."

"I know how to get out of Castaway Island without help."

I assume the sphere things are what he means by 'Castaway Island'. And for the record, he sucks at it. I stare up at the spheres floating in the sky. Some are horizontal with the bottom half water-logged and the top half a fog. The others are at different degrees of tipsy with a single body either floating or treading water as the dome fills on one side and empties on the other.

"I hate to tell you this, but you drowned."

He stares at the inches of water surrounding us. He kicks the standing water away from him. "I had things under control." His face darkens in thought. "Do you know me... who I am?"

I shake my head no, and hope it means I'm not so much of an outsider instead of the only person who doesn't know the answer to identity questions. "You're welcome," I say. "You know, for saving your life."

"I don't owe you," he says, which isn't exactly what I meant to imply, but now I sort of *do* feel like he owes me.

Darkness rolls overhead like a fast-moving night sky. I startle.

"Day cycles." He catches me visually trail the line dividing the light. "Night goes fast. We don't need sleep, so daylight lasts longer. It messes with the mind, if there's no night." He points to the sky like he's doing me a favor explaining stupid crap like day and night. "So they threw that in."

I stand and press water out of my skirt before remembering my clingy dress. I cover one hand across my mid-section. He continues to look at and then away from every move I make.

"Could you at least stop staring?" I say. "So I can walk away from you with some semblance of dignity?"

His jaw drops, as though my request takes him by surprise. "What?" The blocks in the distance call his attention now. "It's not..." He stops trying to explain and lets out a long deep breath, collecting himself. He doesn't manage to cease the quick stolen peeks in my direction. There's nothing leering about his expression though. I can't decide if he's amused at my discomfort or if he's distressed by my appearance. "Sorry I hit you."

"You punched me."

His lips become a thin line of what he wants to say, but keeps bottled in. "What's your code?" he asks, nodding toward my left arm.

"My code?" More than anything, I wish my arms were both behind my back, but I kind of need them to stay right where they are—hiding my exposed underthings.

He raises the sleeve of his soaked white shirt, exposing a number similar to GenE's. His code stretches long. GenAK972319357 fills the entire length of his forearm. GenE's tattoo covered less skin, a much lower number in her sequence. I stare at his arm and nod. His eyes are on my left arm, like he's waiting for me to reveal my number. There is something about how he's staring. It's like he can't decide if he knows me. An almost familiarity, but he keeps a distance. As though, if I'm who he thinks I am, I'm dangerous. I keep my arms tight to my side, because maybe I am who he thinks I am.

He suddenly curses, punctuated by dropping his head forward, no longer staring in that *'don't I know you'* manner.

I panic when I hear the faint curse escape him like he guesses I'm a liability or threat. "GenE247," I say hoping to not expose the truth about me. My sleeves are made from a thin material. I try to remember to keep a twist at my wrist as I cross my arms so GenAK isn't staring at the virgin skin of my forearm. No tattoo, no code. Don't advertise those facts.

"GenE, huh? Okay." He points to my arm, causing me to flinch away like I've been found out. "It'd have to be a lower number," he says. "It doesn't stick out the base of your sleeve. Where'd they inject you? Below the elbow?" He flinches slightly, as if he'd been bit on the ankle. I look down hoping the distraction of an insect will save me from answering. I'd let it bite my whole arm off at this point.

I have no idea what he's talking about, but nod like he guessed right. "You're good."

His tongue rolls along his teeth. "A GenAK who can't pass Castaway Island? Yeah, I'm a real genius." He stands next to me. He's tall and broad. His wet hair hangs forward in his face. He leans to the side when he stands, or perhaps he's just keeping more distance between him and me. Everything about him says 'I can kick your face in with my pinkie toe'.

"AK? What's that, military or something?"

"Are you kidding me? I mean, I know GenE's aren't the brightest, but come on. At least fake a little intelligence." He starts walking toward the section of land where people are working to stack a building structure of some kind. "You coming?"

I rub my jaw and look behind me. Nothing but water running off the edge of a falls. "I guess."

"There's probably not much time before we have to level up. Best not waste it here." He walks away at a fast pace, his back square to me. His brisk walk and cold shoulder have 'I don't want you following me' stamped on them. But he keeps checking over his shoulder with his eyes squinched to see if I'm close.

Around us, people move massive blocks made of all kinds of different materials—crystal, steel, wood, copper, and something yellow—toward other massive blocks. The objects are stacked poorly. From above, in the sphere, the ground looked like a blue-print of buildings.

From down here, it's ruins. Littered all over the ground are white packs with red crosses painted on the outside. There's nothing inside. Whatever had been has long been looted, but no one took care of the cases. The cases trash the landscape as much as the poorly designed giant building blocks. GenAK doesn't pause to search out cases, nor does he join anyone struggling to haul large squares of material.

I jog to catch up because if there's something to this 'leveling up' he's talking about, there's no way I want to miss it. And the rest of the people on this level don't appear to be accomplishing anything. No more 'trapped in a room with a floor crumbling out from under me' nonsense. One of the block-movers leers when I pass. It's a long stare with lots of eyebrow. No way do I want to start a conversation with him.

"What about those guys?" I indicate the weirdos sweating while pushing on man-sized cubes.

GenAK turns his head long enough to make eye contact with the dude giving me the stare-down. The glarer suddenly develops intense interest in his task, while GenAK doesn't veer off his chosen path. "Sheep." He nods to several more workers, busily sweating over various materials. GenAK kicks one of the empty cases, causing all the workers to jump, follow the container with their eyes, and gasp when it falls, as though they expect something to fall out of it. It's nothing but an empty white case with a red cross on the outside when it comes to a halt. The same thing it always was. They go back to their task. "All of them. Sheep."

None of this makes sense.

GenAK isn't the chatty type. If I can't get him to divulge all he knows about this place, maybe I can get him to tell me something about himself. "Seriously, what is GenAK? What does it stand for?" I ask, closing the gap between me and GenAK, while widening the distance from the glarer and sheeple.

He stops and fills his lungs. He holds his breath in a moment, like his next words are going to hurt. "I'm a war hero," he says finally. Not much pride in his voice. He lowers his head, obscuring the chisel of his face like the word 'hero' is incongruous with defined muscles.

Pfft. "And you can't figure out the hourglass sphere thingy?"

"Don't talk to me right now." He shows me his back again. I hadn't realized he'd swiveled my direction until he turns away. "We have a task to complete."

"Fine with me." I put a hand to my still sore cheek. He seems to know where we are and what we're doing and I don't. "I never wanted to talk to you in the first place." Except I do want to talk. I'm apparently the only person who has no clue how to escape this nightmare.

GenAK stops, turns, and puts his hands on my shoulders. The weight of his hands is unreal. No wonder it felt like he broke my face. The man has bear paws. "You're going to die out here if you're not prepared."

I lean back, rolling my shoulders, no longer under the pressure of his hands. It also throws off my balance. "So far, I've saved *your* life. So can you please put aside your judgy stare and get me the hell leveled up?"

"I'll tell you how to level up," he says, stepping wide and extending his arms. I don't quite know what to expect here, but obviously some kind of show. He changes his voice as if he's addressing an entire arena filled with me. "You've made the donor list. Congratulations. Live long enough to prove your intelligence, survive all levels of the Game, and win immortality." He ends with a salute.

"Immortality?" *Pffft some more.* "Yeah right."

GenAK relaxes his stance. "Everyone here is an intelligence donor. We're competing to be the brains inside artificial intelligence units." His eyes drop to my arm again and I flinch to check it's covered. It is. "We're in a competition right now. One we'll fail if we don't complete our task."

That's interesting. Everyone here competes for the same goal. I fold my arms and nod, not wanting to give away my ignorance. Him not knowing what I don't know benefits me. I hope. In truth, I'd like to hear more about the donor list. It sparks something in my memory. I'm not on a list. Should I be?

"I'm not after immortality," I say.

"You better start wanting it. It's live forever or die immediately around here. That's what the Game of Life means. Death. It's a test. Prove our trust while teaching us how to process thoughts circuitously. If you're not at least trying to win, you won't make it far."

Whatever. *Circuitously?* So not a word. "Why wouldn't we be trusted?"

"For the AI." His opinion of me hangs heavy in the air. It's poor. I don't *opine* too highly of him right now either. "Artificial Intelligence has to be supplied by human intelligence, proven to retain human thought, motivation, and loyalty under the least favorable circumstances for those qualities, while operating through computer circuitry."

Donors. Like organ donors?

"Wait, we're *dead*?" So that's what the 'Donor List' consists of? A bunch of terminal losers gambling to beat fate? But, instead of some human patient receiving my liver or heart in a transplant surgery after I die, a computer receives my brain-waves. Someone's most likely walking around with my heart and liver and any other working organ right now? I have to stop and process this for a second. "… 'Donor List'? …We're not real?" I stare at my hand, opening and closing my fist. It's all working together. But I don't have a real-life hand. Bunches of binary nonsense move in front of my face. It just looks real.

"Yes, we are." He puts a hand over my fist, forcing me to stop opening and closing it. "Don't do that."

I'm nothing more than electrical charges that once powered a human body. "Right now, where am I?"

"In a program. You're code. We're code." He pauses. "In a program."

As if on cue, a thin band of light strikes the horizon and climbs, filling the artificial land with color of sunrise. *Good morning, fake-ass me.*

I stop walking alongside GenAK. If everyone with a code on their arm is a donor… what happened to my code? I run to make up the distance between us. "Code? Like human blips and dashes, ones and zeroes? That's it? Freaking coded intelligence from a formerly alive person?"

"It's too dangerous to have machines working alongside humankind, undistinguishable from the rest of us, but with machine sourced thoughts."

"I'm dead." I sit down to let the idea settle in my fake, programmed, simulated bones.

GenAK grabs my arm and pulls me back to my feet. "You will be, if you sit down. This is your second chance. Not everyone gets this."

I'm in the program. I'm playing the game. I'm competing for the prize, or I die.

I stomp past him. "What happens if you don't 'level up'?" I use air quotes on the term he used earlier.

GenAK almost trips over a concrete barrier he crosses and chokes on a laugh. "It's over. Nothing else happens. Ever." He pushes his hair out of his eyes.

"How'd you get on the Donor List then?"

"I'm a hero. Developed software which won the intercontinental civil dispute." He says this like it's common knowledge. "Minutes after I hacked a computer and unmasked two moles in our unit, a kid walked into the tech base and blew himself up."

GenAK licks his lips like he can taste the memory in the salty air. "A kid. Younger than my little sister." He looks up and sniffs, the wiping a running nose kind of sniff, not the hiding emotion sort. When I check his face to be sure, there are no tears, no shaking iris, no perspiration around the edge of his hair line. He clenches his jaw and keeps walking. GenAK is as artificial in his interactions as it sounds we are in this program. "I got on the list because I was the shortest living hero in history."

"You must be so proud," I say like a seasoned terrible liar.

"Had to learn the outcome of the war through ads." He points to a billboard in the distance. I squint, expecting to see GenE. The real GenE. The one I'm impersonating. Even from far away, I can tell she's not the blonde displayed on screen. I stop squinting to avoid drawing attention to the ads.

I've never heard of him or the intercontinents and their supposed dispute. I nod like 'Oh, now I remember,' and change the subject because we've arrived and if I say anything else it'll be snarky and probably earn me a black eye to match my fat lip.

The clouds collapse around the edge of the horizon, like the entire world domes and the clouds have reached the bubble barrier. Greenish brown gases rush down the edge of the invisible wall and plume back toward us in the center of the city, or the center of this strange domed-world.

"That's not good," I say.

"Very not good," GenAK agrees, still pressing toward the platform. "We're not dying here." He picks up speed. I can't keep up.

"GenAK!" I holler. He doesn't look back. I'm almost certain he pushes himself faster.

Instead of being tipped into a water coffin, we're about to be gassed. He gets one foot on the level pad, stepping past the large letters spelling 'Level Up' across the expanse of rubber covering, and reaches a hand back to me. The instant my fingers contact his, he hurls me—arm, shoulder, and the rest of me in a whiplash lump. Mere seconds later, the gaseous cloud bounces off the border of the platform.

An invisible barrier, lucky us.

"I can't take the anxiety of this. I'm not a gamer," I say.

"There's worse things than anxiety." He nods to the barrier, to what's on the other side.

That's when the screaming registers. It claws into my brain and sets a foot against the cord running down my spine. Kids outside the platform barrier are enveloped in fog. Their skin melts away until nothing but black and green coded lines are exposed. The black marks on their arm shine against the green cloud and then all that's left is... nothing. They're gone.

I can't look away, but I can't stare either. GenAK's arms wrap tight around me. "Don't look, Jilly."

I push away, wanting to run back to the programmed world beyond the pad. "It's GenE," I say.

GenAK opens his mouth in the same embarrassed way he did when he mentioned he was a war hero. He shakes his head, pushes his hair away from his eyes, then closes his mouth before turning away from me. Is it really that hard to remember someone's stupid code-letter combo thing?

People run for the barrier from the acid rain, melting with every step. Some manage to make it through the invisible divide and launch themselves at those standing on the platform. The melting reaction takes hold of anyone it touches, even the people previously safe with the barrier between them and the flesh-eating storm. Everyone crowds tight together in the center, trying to be the farthest from those half-dissolved persons tripping toward us.

Forget personal issues and difficulty recalling names, I run close to GenAK and grip him like he can save me from what's happening on the platform. He doesn't push me away. He doesn't pull me in either.

"Pad is clear of failure. Prepare to level up," a voice announces over unseen speakers echoing along the edges of the platform.

4

Burning buildings are our first hello to a new game-scape. I look at my fingers, my hands, my arms. Not melting away from a rot-virus. Still no code on my left forearm. I quickly slap my left arm tight to my side, hiding its bareness.

Rushing waves of water, which seem to be generating out of nothing, have no effect on the fire that is this new world, except to put pasty ash in the air. It settles in my hair and on my clothes. The waves crush buildings and lift cars like they're nothing.

"I'm getting a real water complex," I shout over the roar of destruction. There's no time to orient to the new level or its objective. I'm not sure if something is wrong with the program, or if this unprepared sensation is another indicator of something wrong with me. That insecurity is the only thing preventing me from yelling out for it all to stop and make sense of itself, or at least give me a second to breathe before threatening 'failure' at me.

GenAK reacts fast to the new landscape, like he's trained for decades how to respond to hypochondriac-nonsense-level natural disasters. When I finally locate him, he's fifteen yards from me and crouching beneath a cement bench. I opt for different cover.

I'm on a rooftop, I think. The longest stretch of rooftop I've ever seen. It's almost ridiculous. The space stretches out so I don't know how far up we are except there are taller buildings and shorter ones all around.

A boy at my side turns his head toward me. His wide-open eyes scare me more than the fact he's dressed as a sad clown, only fat on the bottom half of his body. The crown of his head is bald with white powder and spikey yellow tuffs of hair circling it. He doesn't move toward me, but keeps his gaze dialed in so that when I lean forward his eyes shift to follow. "GenAK?" I move backwards away from the clown, closer to GenAK and his stupid bench cover.

Other weird or creepy items add to the scene. Wooden podiums litter the roof as well as multiple hangman's nooses set at random. One person runs screaming, his head catches in a noose as if he didn't see it. His feet fly out from under him as he's clotheslined by the rope. The ground falls away beneath him and he flails in a useless attempt to free his neck. The roof continues to disintegrate in chunks getting closer to where I stand. The clown boy's arms reach up to the sky as if he's expecting help before he tumbles backward into the dark interior of the building. Not once did clown-boy move his feet.

I could have reached him. If I had made up my mind it was a safe, strategic, or neutral move to do so. He would be standing where I'm standing. With me. But there's no way I'm trusting a clown in this place.

GenAK smacks my arm. He doesn't have to say anything. I know to run. We crouch behind an abandoned podium. Like we can lose pursuit of the insane terrors at our heels by being out of sight. "Because, of course, hiding from eroding roofing will save us," I huff under my breath at GenAK, demonstrating I'm also afraid the sound of my voice will give away our position to the growing hole.

Deep scratches mark wood on the stand. Index cards labeled 'talking points' fill a shoebox on the slanted tabletop. That's weird. A girl approaches the podium and lifts the box to select a card. Tears stream from her eyes like she's being forced to speak while watching a loved one be guillotined.

I'm pushed out of someone's way as they barrel past where GenAK and I crouch. Several more players run, eyes wide with terror. "What's wrong with these people? They look and act like lunatics." Is there something in the air? I hold my breath, just in case.

"Look for something to let us know what this level is," GenAK says.

"Where the hell are we?" I shout as we pass by fellow lunatics. No one answers. It's definitely hell. More people run by —only one of whom tumble into the growing roof hole. "I'm pretty sure the challenge is to run."

Looking across the roof we're on, I spot a massive billboard with the words, 'Agoraphobia. Fight your fears in order to survive.'

I point a thumb to the sign. The sign changes to an ad then morphs back. "That explains a lot." It doesn't curb my desire to take a swing at the players behaving like terrorized children. Some of them *are* children. "Why are there kids here?"

GenAK adjusts his shoulders like he's preparing to leave me behind. "Donors are all ages, but there's no way to tell anyone's real age. A person could be ninety but have the mind of a seven-year-old. That's what you'd see here. How they are in their mind." His voice drops lower. "How they see themselves. Or want to see themselves."

It's confusing how perception defines reality here. Apparently a lot of people see themselves as young adults. Also, GenAK sees himself as ripped.

"Age and appearance could also be a trick of the mind in this place," he says. GenAK steps away from young gamers. "Children don't belong in war." As he says it, one of the boys in the center of the group opens his vest, blinking red lights flash. "Do it now," he says, not indicating what he expects me to do. A bright white burst knocks us on our backs. The crowd is gone. All the children vanish in the explosion, but no carnage remains on the roof. None of it was close enough to damage either me or GenAK beyond falling back from the heat wave. It must be a trick. Another twist in this game meant to unsettle us.

GenAK's breath rattles. His hands shake when he stands. He smooths his palms over and over along the sides of his legs like he can iron the tremors out. The way he behaves, I question if I should be shaking.

"Are you afraid?" GenAK asks once he's finally under control.

I nod vigorously.

Hordes of players rush the edge of the roof. Bugs the size

of skyscrapers appear from over the tops of buildings around us. Great. Giant insects. The insects are gross and not something I want to challenge, but I don't have the irrational fear I assume comes with the things I'm truly afraid of. "They're just large, right?" I ask, not really expecting an answer. "Not so scary."

The nearest creature, a cricket type thing with a stinger attached at the back, plunges its stinger through the speaking girl's skull. Right in front of us. The notecard crumples in her white knuckled grasp. That's not meant to just unsettle us.

It's damn disturbing.

This time there's blood spatter and screaming everywhere. I'm screaming.

Both of us turn and push people out of our way as we run away from the creature. Glancing back, I witness the same bug expose dripping fangs and use them to pierce the abdomens of three people at once.

The intensity level from one game to the next isn't right. There's no progression. We go from a physical labor challenge to 'run for your life'. "How is 'let your fear run you to safety' a skill we need? Does fear prove we're a compatible intelligence donor for AI?" I yell to GenAK. "This has to be pretty advanced, right?" I push slower people aside as I run, caring little for their fate over mine. "Maybe we rose to the top of the game levels and we're almost out."

There's still a lot of roof ahead of us. The building seems to go on endlessly, yet GenAK stops. I don't put on the brakes for several more strides. He waits for me to go back to him, even though the insect isn't far enough away for comfort.

"We need to keep moving," I pant. "Get far away from those things."

He looks into my eyes, his gaze shifting between my pupils. "We're so far away." He's panting as though he wasn't made of code, but worn muscle and punctured lungs. It frustrates me to have to deal with whatever issues he's got when our lives are on the line.

"We don't have time for melodrama. That thing can jump. We're not far at all."

"From the end," he says. "The end of the game. It's a looping puzzle." He drops his head like he's giving up right there. "It's impossible to get to the end."

We've barely started and he's already acting defeated. A quitter. "Yeah, with that attitude, I'm sure. But we're only on level two. Pull yourself together. The bugs are getting closer." The age lines around his eyes match the cowed version of himself.

How long has GenAK been playing this game?

He rubs a hand across his eyes, showing no sign of moving. Massive killer insects continue to slice anyone who finds themselves on the roof and is dumb enough to scream, pulling attention to themselves. "But the bugs…" I whisper.

"It's not my fear," he says, like it sponges out all the blood caused by the beastly insects.

It's not my fear either, but someone sure as hell fears a bug slaughtering a bunch of bystanders. I don't want to be the victim of someone else's fear. My options are to run from the bug alone or stay with GenAK. "We need to move." I grab his arm.

"Or get off the roof. It's only attacking in the open." Dude has a point.

We push our way to the edge of the building. The ground, which was already far down, falls farther away. Huge chasms open, preventing us from reaching safety. It's like the game can read my mind regarding anything preventing successful escape. The side of the building offers no refuge.

"I want to stay on the tower," I scream at GenAK over the sound of ground breaking, people screaming, and thick darkness rolling up from the crack in the earth. "We won't be able to see where to walk, what to run from… anything."

"I think that's the point," GenAK says. "Are you afraid of the dark?"

If I wasn't before, I am now. Here, on this level, fear dominates. "Maybe I am."

The blackness rolls up the building as well as the open expanse of roof ahead of us, as if it's anticipating where we'd run. I step back from the ledge, not wanting to get too close. GenAK walks toward the thick black vapor.

"What's our goal here? How do we level up?" I yell. "Running sounds a lot smarter than walking into *that*."

"Trying something different."

I grab his arm, not letting him leave me behind. No way am I willingly going into the fog.

"It's different every time," he says, like he's been here before.

The dark cloud yawns closer. People run from it screaming. We don't run. The chill of a cold front settles over us.

"Any idea how long we have until the next siren raid?" I hope he knows I'm talking about the siren-like announcement signaling the pathway to a new level, i.e. escape.

"From the looks of things…" He sidesteps a child running hand-in-hand with an old man. They don't vary their path to avoid him, fatigue making every effort of running a straight line too much to continue. "Not long."

GenAK lowers his brow, like he's going to head-butt the mist with his forehead.

"Why are you still going toward it?"

"Because they're not."

I keep a grip on his arm. "They've been here longer. Maybe they know something you don't."

"This level is named after fear. Their eyes are filled with it." He motions to the running, screaming masses. "I don't think they're winning."

Looking again at the faces jumping from buildings, running past, and crouching in hopeless terror, I hope he's right. The ledge reveals those who jumped while screaming and flailing landed hard on a platter of binary and green black strings of code.

"Maybe not that way," I say.

The cloud of pure black closes around us. The weight of it presses my will to fight to mush. The silence kidnaps my words before they reach my own ears. On a positive note, I haven't seen a massive bug come out of it since it overtook them.

"A door." GenAK walks briskly toward a typical roof access, not running. It wasn't there before, like it popped out from his mind. If everything here materializes based on fears, what about a door scares GenAK? His face is set on escape. "There. Come on."

I copy his expression, although my insides shake and my

confidence wilts. But what's happening with my insides isn't what other people see, and lies give me courage. "Good. Right. A door. Of course." I nod.

He glares sidelong at me and I close my mouth. Threat of abandonment from my military escort cures me of all things terrifying. He can't leave me behind. I won't let him.

A girl drops to her knees seconds before the cloud covers her. My step quickens toward the door. I don't want to lose sight of it. GenAK steps in front of me, forcing me to slow my pace.

"We're not running away," he says. "Remember that."

I nod. No words come out of my mouth. I repeat, *not running away*. But my feet are dancing side-to-side while we're paused there, waiting to move forward again like a child in desperate need of a bathroom.

Cold nips at my heels, crawls up my calves, and picks at the hem of my skirt. The cloud vapor cuts like ice razors on my skin. Muteness cloaks the dark, like a blanket of quiet lying over the top of madness. Lack of screaming scares me. I smack my tongue against the roof of my mouth so there's a noise, but the sound doesn't travel beyond my mouth. The air has a metallic taste with hints of ammonia, like too many animals tried to mark their territory here.

My mouth stays closed in the blackness. I don't want to taste this air. Ideas color the images black with death, hiding in the dark. GenAK's hand gently pulls me closer to him. A calm spreads from his touch, out into my limbs, not quite reaching the 'murder' threat hiding in the corner of my brain. He whispers, "Don't give thought to your fears."

My eyes remain closed, which really isn't helping in this situation because my brain keeps conjuring up slinking skeletal arms reaching out, unseen and rotting faces screaming my name, then gurgling hisses of "mord." I have no idea what it means, but the computer programmed skin of my arm raises into tiny bumps. "I'm scared," I admit in a squeaky voice.

"What you think, it becomes," he says.

How does he know this? Frustration takes over where fear had hold. How does everyone know more than I do? Someone bumps into me and their skin melts away from their bones. Before their lips are gone, the person speaks, "Poison gas."

I gasp. And choke. Gas fills my mental spaces. Poison gas. I let go of GenAK to claw the picture from my mind. My eyes go wide and smell returns to my nose. It's burning, melting flesh and smoke. It's in my throat.

My head slams against the door. I close my mouth and shut my nose with one hand, fumbling for the knob through the blackness with the other. The door won't open.

GenAK brushes my fingers aside and opens the door. I elbow him out of my way even though he's helping. His fault for being calm all up in my face.

"Get off." I slap a hand back over my mouth, coughing instantly because... poison gas!

He pushes me inside, the roughness of the move totally uncalled for, then steps through and pulls the door until it clicks. He continues to pull the doorknob tight, shutting the dark cloud out, only stopping when sweat causes his grip to slip from the metal. "I told you," his voice shakes. "Don't paint your fears."

"I'm trying not to."

He turns to me. I'm still choking and gagging back the acid. Vomit rises in my throat and I spew it out in heaving gargles.

"You're okay," he says at a distance, probably not wanting to get too close to the puke puddle.

"Back off," I gag between heaving fits. He's not even close to me, which is partly why I'm upset. I'm angry with myself because I wouldn't mind if he bent down and put a hand on my shoulder, making sure I'm alright. Weak on me.

"We keep moving."

I get it. We're on a mission, one we don't even know yet. But the thing that's bothering me most is GenAK seems to know more than he lets on. He has some weird balance of 'I'm the sole survivor' in combination with 'we're all going to die'. I can't figure out if he's confused on where he falls on the spectrum or if he's faking internal conflict on the matter. He did tell me everyone has an agenda. I have to assume that includes him. I'm not an idiot. He's probably using me.

Stairs lead in a square pattern down endless flights and landings. The black cloud remains outside the stairwell we're in. It didn't follow us. The second I envision the cloud, black vapor slips through the seal at the bottom of the closed door. Dangit!

"Stop that," GenAK says. He points to the smoky wisp and turns his finger on me. "Don't let it in." He taps his head. Honestly, he looks crazier than I feel.

Telling me to *not* think about the black cloud puts the image of billowing smoke at the forefront of my mind. *Think of something else.* Fire! A pillar of flame bursts on the landing below us. Now we're trapped between cold smoke and hot fire.

"Jilly!" he shouts, or maybe he says, "GenE!"

The name reminds me of the girl with purple streaks in her hair. Is she here? I look around for her. Maybe she can help us. She's surely angry I claimed her identity. When I look at the door, her face reflects silver in the round knob. I step away, closer to the climbing fire.

"Control your thoughts." GenAK grabs my shoulders and I realize he's calling *me* GenE.

I squeeze my eyes shut, hoping he doesn't notice I'm a fake, a fraud, a thief. There's no way to control my thoughts, not like I need to here. I'm giving too much away. Sweat drips from my face and sizzles on the hot steps.

Water. That's how I can gain a little control here. Focus on fear of water to put out the fire. Manipulate the system. This place only makes what I'm afraid of. Having been trapped in a water-sphere for the first level, it's not hard to conjure a fear of water, of drowning. *Don't take the thought too far.* It works, but once the fire smolders, more nightmares fill its place.

Too many terrible ideas vie for space in my mind. An endless pit of stairwell, doorways hide assassins coming to cut the blank skin from my arm and drop a lopped off portion of someone else's coded arm in the same place, weirdly vivid.

"No!" I cover my arm, but blood sneaks out from under my fingers. My eyes go wide. I'm doing this. When I lift my face to GenAK, we're both panicked. He looks at me and says nothing. My arm bleeds spontaneously and he's not telling me to calm down. Believe it or not, that's worse than when he told me to pull it together.

Fear of worst death possibilities shines from my eyes. GenAK reaches down to me, holds both his hands against my jaw. The temperature of his skin is like ice sliding up my cheek. For a second, I worry I'll melt him, but then it's me that's melting on the inside. GenAK tilts my mouth toward his, and closes his lips against mine. A brief and simple kiss. Everything sharp, all the pieces I hold out against the insanity of this place, dull and bend like plastic in an inferno.

GenAK breathes a word while he's still frighteningly close, so quiet I can't make it out. It's strange and melodic. Not like code. It's a name. Something no one has here. I want to ask him to repeat it, so I can capture the magic of identity found inside something so rare as a 'name'. Before I can speak, he pulls away. His eyes close along with his fists. No part of his frozen skin contacts mine, leaving an icy-burn in his wake.

I'm made a fool as I stand there without words. Processing what the hell that was takes more energy than pretending to belong in this nightmare. Romance ranks last in the list of pressing emotions this moment, but I feel something bigger than this being a random dude I chest punched to life. Still. We're absolutely going to die.

A red light flashes to life below us, the exact tone I envision my skin being. I've been exposed. My hands drip, covered in my own blood, I wipe one palm across my face, more comfortable, more hidden. Dang this place. Even a kiss frightens me.

GenAK offers no explanation. He doesn't address me at all. Won't even look at me. He descends the first flight of stairs toward the flashing light far below. I draw my other hand through my hair and let it smear lengthwise down the left side of my face before I nod, because nothing makes sense here, and follow him deeper inside the guts of the stairwell.

5

The stairwell goes down for so long, it's all consuming. *Don't think about it.*

I'm totally thinking about it.

"We don't get tired?" I say, dragging my hand along the banister and huffing from exhaustion. Being winded obviously isn't exempt.

"Nope."

"Don't have to eat or, you know, relieve ourselves?"

GenAK turns toward me, a small laugh in his voice. "We're real, but not *that* real."

Everything inside this tower echoes. So I whisper, "We can smell and taste, but not eat… What's the point?"

GenAk stops in his tracks. I wait for what he has to say.

And then he's running down the stairs away from me. I look behind me for a threat. Nothing behind me.

Every effort goes into wiping my mind of creating 'what

might be' in the shadows and trying to let what truly hides present itself. "What is it?"

"You're acti—infected," he says in a low voice.

"I'm what?" I pat my face, half expecting my skin to melt or something horrible. No.

But I'm not fine either.

Something is wrong on my face.

My shoes clap against the stairs as I rush ahead of GenAK in search of a reflective surface. Reflection.

Every window seals with wood. I touch the wall, sliding my hand along the rough surface. The banister. It's silver. Using both hands I smooth over a section as if polishing it.

I search for my face in the banister's reflection. Rubbing my sleeve over the surface, I search again. Infected. I'm infected.

"No." My face... It's gone.

Everything smooth; bumps protrude where features used to be. No nostrils, no mouth. My voice works, but I don't have a mouth. And my eyes. Skin dips where my eyes should be. My reflection in the banister can't be real—a faceless version of me. An eyeless face.

My hands, my hair and my skin, they're all there. I conflict with my reflection. But, my face, the features of it, is gone, missing, absent entirely.

"Infected?" I look back toward GenAK, my voice shaking. "What is this? Infected with what?"

GenAK rushes to me. He puts a hand out, but doesn't touch me with it. Not yet.

"It's this place," he says. His hand closes the inches between us, but I can feel the pressure it takes for him. The space around us is tense, full and thick and heavy like our insides.

"My face..." My hands return to search the smoothed out dimples where features used to be.

GenAK takes my hands away from my face. "It's not real," he says. "It's an illusion and an idea. It's fear."

"It's fear," I repeat it. My face will come back. My features under my skin. *Where's my knife?* I'll cut features in my skin. *I don't have a knife.* Dang again. "How could this happen? I wasn't afraid of being infected."

"It's what I'm afraid of," he says. "It's not real. You're fine, you're fine, you're fine..." He keeps saying it. "You're fine..." He's convincing himself, or trying to. It doesn't help me at all.

I slap him across the cheek. "You wiped my face! Stop chanting like a monk and change it."

"Sorry, GenE." When he says my name, it sounds so much more like Jilly than GenE.

When I hear the name I know it's not my real name and I hate wishing I own an identity. Nothing about me is real. I'm a dead girl with a fake name and no face. Not even a number on my arm. I'm no one. I'm pretend. But my fear is real, maybe more real than any other part of me. GenAK steps close enough I can smell him. He smells of burnt dust. Not great, but not the worst ever.

GenAK looks deep into the indents where my eyes should be. The person I want him to see reflects back at me in his eyes. When I reach up to feel my lips, they're there. Real and truly. But that's not all. A smooth featureless face hides below the surface. It's not gone. I'm still infected. Does GenAK know I'm wearing a mask of features? "What infection does that?"

"Nothing," he says. The tension in his shoulders, the twitch in his jaw, and the pull along his hairline all say he's holding everything alert and back.

A scratching from the outside of the building drags along the siding and bumps over the wood boarding up the windows. Soft chirping clicks against the other side of the wall. This place isn't made for winning. Why must we respect fear to qualify as an AI donor? Manipulation of others' fears will stay with me beyond this nightmare. I just know it.

"Keep moving," GenAK says. "We have to survive longer than what we're afraid of."

6

Crying echoes from somewhere below. It's the cry of a young child, the kind making me want to hug something until the sadness ends. That or stuff a sock in each ear.

It's a trick, it must be. My chest tightens, as if it's testing if I know it's a trick. GenAK stretches an arm across the corridor, blocking our progress. His skepticism is electric in the air, saying 'trust nothing'. The sound whimpers, turning to crying. We move closer to it, taking each step more slowly.

Two landings down, a male child crouches in the corner. His arms are wrapped around his knees and he's resting on both his bum and flats of his feet. His head curls low into his crouch. He shakes, whines, and twitches with the slightest rise of his head.

What will his face look like when he lifts it? Will he have a nose? Will he look gashed and gnarly, half alive and hungry?

"Don't put anything on it," GenAK says tapping his brow, and looking at my forehead. "Let him show us."

I know what he means. Don't think. Don't think a dang thing.

Basically, if the kid's a monster, it's because I'm afraid. This world promises the worst of everything and I'm good at populating it.

The kid looks up. His face is soft, round, and young. I let out breath held inside me for so long it's molded. "It's just a boy," I say, relieved.

The child looks five, maybe six. His eyes catch mine. There's no glint or shine to them behind thick-framed glasses. Soft curls cover his head. I bend toward him and GenAK lays a cautious hand on me. "What's your Gen?" I ask gently.

"I'm an ED."

I stand and look at GenAK. "Academics. Scholars," he says, filling in what I don't want to ask.

"Authorities in their field of study," the child corrects in his mini voice.

"But you're a child," I say.

"That's what I'm afraid of," the small voice says. "Being unimportant, a nobody. A child." His fear isn't life threatening or scary. Does it even qualify as a fear? "Can I go with you?" the child requests. The pleading in his voice is innocent and small. He needs looking after, protecting.

"You know how this world works?" GenAK asks him.

ED nods. "What's your code?" he asks with a sniff.

"I'm an AK and this is GenE247." GenAK doesn't bother repeating his long number. I guess it's common for the AK's to be littered with numbers.

"I'm GenED92," he says.

ED boasts a number below the 100 mark. If, as a scholar, it indicates his IQ, maybe it's good we found him.

"We could use you," GenAK says. "Whatever you know from before donorship might help."

The eyes of the child deepen, sharpen, and age. Only his eyes.

We set out again. For all the strides we make, we never seem to get anywhere. ED, me, and GenAK, who doesn't take my hand back once we find ED. My arms swing. I don't touch the railing again, afraid my blank features will return. *Don't conjure dumb things to be afraid of, dangit!* We're not going anywhere, or getting anywhere. All our focus stays on not running, not jumping, not screaming. Being not afraid.

ED grabs my fingers and crawls his little hand finger by finger higher into mine. My palm engulfs his hand and I smile the way I smile at a child. His piercing eyes disturb me. He's a child and things inside me are sparking in a way they shouldn't. Somehow ED looks taller than he did a moment before. When I look at our hands, his outgrows mine. The fingers of his free hand wiggle in some silent calculation. It's some sort of twitch or habit of comfort by the manner of it.

I check behind me. GenAK walks a few paces back. His eyes are on my hand, the hand holding onto ED. I flush pink and gaze forward again. GenAK is jealous, perhaps. Our meager shared moments bond us and no child-fearing scholar has claim on that, no matter how adorable his pudgy cheeks. The only thing more dangerous than fear is jealousy.

The wall ahead of me shimmers as a projection covers it. Billboard images scroll the wall with another list of ten codes.

The current standings.

GenAK has climbed the ranks, now at number seven instead

of number nine. The list in front of me comprises mainly three code types: GenB, GenED, GenAK. There's one GenTECH in the mix, but absolutely no E's.

Once again the images shift to reveal a scene of actors. Family members of a donor gather around a metal corpse, waiting for movement. The mechanics of the hand produce a jerking hydraulic motion to which the family embrace each other and reach out to touch the cold metal shell. It responds as though it can sense the warmth, a glow radiates from inside the eye sockets once they blink open and the metal person endures wet tears falling from its pretend family.

GenED flinches next to me. This scene playing out has an impact on him much different than the fear of being an insignificant child. He coughs and wipes at his face concealing his eyes, an attempt to hide his reaction. I pretend to not have noticed.

A siren sounds. Change comes with it. I feel it in my core. A change. But it's wrong. Very wrong. I don't know what's off about it other than I know there's something I'm not prepared for ahead. Like a sting pulling against my spinal cord, yanking through my entire system, and adjusting the dilation of my pupils.

Then everything stretches and the world changes.

7

The foreboding feeling from the fearscape stays behind once I configure in the new level. It's impossible to guess what new challenge awaits. One good thing is I have a new outfit, complete with leggings and a belt around my shirt. My hair falls past my shoulders in fashionable blond waves. *How cool is this?* All fresh and prepped to dominate a new challenge. *Better than the start of last level.*

ED is, in fact, a handsome man. Super handsome. I say man because he looks older than a teen, but not old-old like someone who teaches college. If he's a scholar, he's the youngest version such a distinction comes in. His thick frames weigh on his nose. When he pushes them up, he includes a lift of his chin in an 'I'm smart and I know it' manner. The boyish curls that had been present moments before, replaced with short hair cut too close to wave.

His brow sharply shrouds his eyes, giving him a hawk-like presence. If not a hawk, a definite bird of prey. ED visibly calculates. His mind turns things over to gauge how to use us, GenAK and me, to his best advantage. Sucks for him. We're barely advancing as it is.

"I didn't think I'd make it out of there," ED says to me. I don't expect his voice to sound so sincere. It's disarming. Aside from the fact he neither thanks nor acknowledges GenAK.

Highway sounds dominate the air. Honks, tires screeching, and the thrum of wheels against paved road seams, a constant peal of noise. The landscape reveals multilayer highways, parking lots, massive garage structures. A speed limit sign has the words 'Race, Chase, and Stockpile' where the numbers should go.

"That sounds easy enough," GenAK says.

I can't tell if he's being sarcastic. Up to this point, he's so intense he teeters on melodramatic with his silence.

"Objective. Obtain assignment from a phone box. Complete assignment. Earn minimum payment required to level up before time runs out," a sky voice says.

Phone box? What's a phone box? "That's new," I say.

"It's automated to play whenever a new player arrives in-world," ED says like he's experienced it before. He's pointing across a raised highway.

A group of five players stand together and stare up at the sky as if listening to the same thing we heard. The group reacts in unison. Everyone across the roadway searches for a location to obtain an assignment. One girl points toward a phone booth near my little group of three. Ah, phone *booth*. Of course a program doesn't know the difference.

"Come on," I say. "Let's get there first."

GenAK rolls his jaw to one side. "I don't see the point of racing."

ED lifts a hand, like a student in class, not an authority figure. No one calls on him, but he speaks anyway. "I studied the donor program before I ever made it on the list. I know almost everything there is to know about it. So, if you're wondering, or if you ask, I'll provide an answer." ED's mouth remains open, like he has more to say but thinks better of it. Except then this comes out, "It's not just racing one team."

"Excuse me?" GenAK says.

They each regard each other like they're ready to butt heads, literally. Their brows are even lowered so the flattest portion of their foreheads mirror each other. "We need to move faster in order to beat the other group to the phone box," I say, trying to cut short the fight building between ED and GenAK.

"The test measures your ability to assess important details and achieve a goal under pressure," ED says.

"I can follow directions," GenAK says.

"That's not what I said," ED argues.

"I said we need to move. Now," I grab their arms and pull until they both pass me, running for the phone box. Actually, they're racing each other, not passing me. GenAK reaches the phone box first. ED and I are seconds behind.

"Doesn't prove anything," ED says, shoving GenAK away from the booth's bi-fold door.

The group of five persons approaches from across the road in the opposite direction from where we ran from.

"Hurry up. We need to get our objectives too," one of the

group's non-stand-out members shouts from inside their small crowd.

Up close and personal, the other group consists of gadget-wielding, number-crunching, narrow-eyed persons. One male, one female and three of their group I'm unable to categorize by gender. The more I think about it, the game world is dominated by persons, not he's or she's. The non-distinct persons all have a similar short cut to their hair—not too short, but not long. Their features are something between sharp and soft, lacking any clear masculine or feminine edge. It's amazing how a person can be so clearly 'person' without claim on gender.

"You can reuse the same booth?" I ask.

The five chuckle like I'm the least smart person ever.

"Not adding much to the team is she?" one of the persons asks GenAK. "We could use an AK, if you want to switch teams for one sure to level up."

"We're doing fine," GenAK says.

I smile and catch his eye.

ED steps forward. "What's your team dynamic?" he asks.

"We've got three GenTECH, a GenS and I'm B," says the person acting as leader.

GenAK flinches when those coded as GenTECH are mentioned.

The female on their team presses her shoulder to the front of the group and stands in front of GenAK. She has spiked rainbow hair and a stance that could put your eye out with her hip. Everything about her is opposite of me. Naturally I want to destroy her from off the face of the program. "You got a problem with GenTECH?"

GenAK's attitude changes when he notices her well-formed stems and the full scoff of her petal pink lips. "I didn't say that."

I step out from behind ED. My grand entrance is the lurpy, blond opposite of TECH-chick, who should be the poster model for scary-smart computer chicks. She manages to keep her eyes on me without moving her head, like a creepy painting that follows you through a room. "Let us get our objective and we'll get out of your way," I say.

"What is this?" One of the TECHs in their group grabs my arm and lifts my sleeve. I pull back before they can expose the blank flesh of my forearm.

"GenE247, thank you very much," I say. The person releases my arm. "You could ask." I hold my arm behind my back. Until I know what it means, I need to stay alert in hiding the fact I have no code. Several from the new group chuckle. TECH-chick clicks a device low at her side without looking at what she's doing, like she's sending unflattering messages regarding my group, except we don't have phones and social media here. She's doing it to annoy me for noticing her creeper-stare, is my second guess.

Cars jump the lanes behind us. The commotion doesn't ease the tension of our two groups facing off in front of the booth. The sky brightens with gold numbers, scores following teams and individuals.

"Your team makes no sense," the guy with GenB on his arm says, ignoring the car chase fast approaching. "You have an E? What good are they?"

ED straightens his tie and narrows his hawk-like eyes at the bland individual. "You've got three TECHs. They're the most

54

prone to virus. You're the ones risking more."

GenAK averts his gaze from me when I search him out at the mention of virus.

"That's a rumor," one of the TECH Gen says, stepping further into the middle of his own group instead of stepping forward like the rest of us.

ED slides into the phone box and closes the door.

"Should we be in there with him?" GenAK asks me with a hand directed toward the booth, no longer assessing his opinion on TECH-chick's virtues in the game. "Do you trust him?"

I trust none of them. Including GenAK.

The time for my response passes without my having spoken.

"The only thing I know about him is he's afraid of kids," he says in a tone that makes me suspect he is the one who is actually afraid of children.

"He's afraid of *being* a child," I say to GenAK. Under my breath I add, "There's a difference."

Crossing his arms, GenAK stands in the way of ED's exit from the booth, in front of the GenB guy, who sidles his way between GenAK and the door at a thin awkward angle.

I lean toward GenAK and speak low. "What's an S?"

"She doesn't know what an S is? What are you, plants?" one of the TECHs asks. Arms go up defensively. It's as if I've drawn a weapon by asking a simple question.

The air electrifies around us. It's like we're charging each other in a polar friction, bound to explode at any moment. Except, when I look at GenAK, he lingers gazing at the female TECH. The expression on his face, a different kind of electric, sends my fingers to my mouth, in order to hold onto something like a memory I'll never get back.

I hate the rainbow-haired TECH-chick.

"Subservient Generation. Laborers," ED answers as he exits the booth. Not soundproof wood, I suppose. Except I didn't hear anything on ED's side of the door.

We're all so busy sizing each other up and judging one another, too distracted to pay enough attention to ED before he's out of the booth. I notice the one identified as GenS shaking his head like ED's full of arrogance and probably defined the Gen harsher than it's generally referred to.

"One of us next," B says, stepping up.

Putting a hand out, GenAK stops B and steps through the instructions gateway. "I need to know if ED can be trusted."

ED doesn't take the general announcement well.

"Scholars are the best liars, aren't they?" GenAK pokes the tips of GenB's fingers out from the small gap remaining between the door and a sealed close. "Maybe we each get our own task, not work as a team." The opening clicks shut.

GenB kicks, then slaps the side of the booth. "You're intentionally holding up the booth. We're all on the clock."

One of the TECHs looks at ED and me in turn. "No one outplays gamers at donor-life."

I'm guessing the TECH dork thinks of himself as a 'gamer' in and out of this place.

"Then why do more gamers succumb to the virus than any other Gen?" ED says. When all the TECHs' heads turn toward him he raises his hands. "I study. It'd be insane to get into the donor program unprepared. What chance would you have?"

All eyes turn toward me. Like I have an answer to that?

"I failed ads auditions." My shoulders hunch up. They all measure me up and down like I'm an idiot with no chance of winning this thing. They're probably right.

"Didn't know you could switch tracks," the TECH-chick says. "Maybe you could try again. I bet they didn't think you'd make it this far. How many levels have you upped?"

"Lots," I lie.

ED stays too quiet at my side. His attention on the TECH-chick still, he twitches in my direction when I shift my feet. Listening to my movements, calculating my responses. He's already playing this level and he hasn't informed me what our objective is. GenAK might be right not to trust him. I want GenAK out of the booth. There's something about ED. Something glitchy.

GenAK comes out and grabs my arm. "We have to go," he says.

The members of the other group all shift weight in unison to learn what changed in GenAK's urgency.

"Was your guy lying? Is it every man for himself?" B asks.

A car skids on the highway. No one gives much thought to the screeching brakes or crunching metal sounds of the road until sparks come toward our knoll. The car careens directly for the most concentrated pocket of persons standing around.

Us.

"What the heck?" GenS says, covering its head with its hands. Like that's gonna help.

Still gripping my arm, GenAK pulls me toward a parking garage. "We have to go," he repeats.

"You knew a car was going to come at us?" GenB screams while running from the smashing vehicle. It crashes into the booth, sending wood splinters and glass shards spraying outward. "I'm not wasting time finding another booth," B says.

"It's group points," ED announces behind us, running in our wake. He points accusingly to GenAK. "That guy's a glory hound. You can't trust a thing he says."

Another car driving on the highway gets within short range of the group and makes a sharp turn toward us.

"I'm not sticking around waiting to be run over," the TECH-chick says. "All TECH might be firewalled from hacking, but I don't need to be able to program to get off this level."

Firewalled? All TECH source code have been blocked access from messing with game programming? That's the smartest thing I've heard all game. I'm suddenly feeling much more optimistic about my surroundings, knowing she can't sabotage me with her binary know-how. Though she's working a whole different angle of sabotage at the moment. I glance at GenAK and ED. Both sneak assessing stares toward TECH-chick and her elegantly stretched curves.

Our two groups merge into an ineffective escape mass.

The murderous driver manages to clip GenS and both non-distinct TECHs from the other group. Their game image flickers green and black. We pause to witness the transformation, more out of curiosity than reverence. Strings of code convert to coins and fly into the air, adding to a number floating above the other vehicle. The car shifts to reverse and the engine revs for a second ramming.

"They get points for hitting us? The other gamers?" TECH-chick asks, slapping the device she's been clicking at as though it's misbehaving, and half turns in a dance-like move of frustration.

"So do we," GenAK says in the lead.

My feet can't move fast enough to keep up with him. Three of my strides equal one of his.

"Why didn't you say anything?" I yell to ED.

He rolls his eyes, seeming more childlike now than when he was afraid. "Because I figured we'd run them down while they were getting instructions. I didn't want to tip them off," he says.

"You what?" TECH-chick's voice goes high pitched.

I can't help but admire his moxie. I'm not entirely opposed to his plan either. I mean, that's the game.

"There were five of them," ED says. "It would have been a decent start."

"I'm going to level you." B gains on ED and punches him in the back.

The car following us gains speed.

"Stop it," GenAK says. "Points compound by how many are in your group. We need everyone we can get."

"Yeah, right. You were going to back over us the first chance you got," TECH-chick says, her hand pounding the pant pocket where her device is stowed, as if she's administering some kind of hacker's CPR for malfunctioning handheld tech. "We didn't even go in the booth. We're supposed to trust you're not lying to us right now?"

"Find another booth. What do we care?" ED says.

A speed bump connects with the undercarriage of the car chasing us. Sparks fly as a piece of metal bounces off the pavement, hits the fuel line, and rips the bumper from the back of the vehicle. Not two seconds later the entire thing bursts into flames. The explosion pushes my back ahead of my feet. My hair burns with fire. Leggings melt in ribbed patterns against my calves. Do I turn into strings of green code? It hurts.

My knees hit the grass first and the rest of me skids to a stop, my shoulder deep in the dirt. What happened?

GenAK stumbles twenty feet ahead. He walks back toward me holding his ear. I lift my head. The ear facing the burning car rings. My other ear, the one against the dirt, catches sound as if from inside a tunnel and rolls it around several times before passing the information on to my brain.

"We lost B." GenAK's mouth makes the sounds, but I can't be sure that's what I hear.

The carnage of the burning car, the mangled body of GenB, and the four people belted to the wreckage turn to green strands. They circle back on themselves as the strands rise in the air. The circles change to gold and fill in as coins, which become numbers hovering centrically above our group. B's score adds to our number.

"No way!" TECH-chick says. "You can't take B. It's not yours to take."

"We didn't do it," I say stepping closer to her. She's the only one from her group left.

"Wait." ED points to the flames and popping metal of the car. "They still have a number up there." The sky above the vehicle has a high golden tally. The number includes a comma. ED walks slowly toward the passenger side, grabbing a long pipe. The pipe scrapes and bumps along the ground behind ED.

"No!" GenAK shoves me over as he tries to reach ED. His objection is possibly a blanket reaction to anything coming out of ED's mouth. Or he's genuinely opposed to killing the people who tried to run us over.

"That number is ours," ED says, not listening to GenAK's protest.

TECH-chick catches on to what is taking place. She snaps what's left of a seatbelt, which she must have pulled from the ground. ED turns toward the sound. His face reddens as if he's calculating her attack and his victory. "Who's your target? Me?" The hand not holding the pipe points toward the smoldering car. "Or them?"

TECH-chick takes a moment and a step closer before answering, her hand never far from her pocketed device like it's a security blanket, or detonator. "I'm part of your team now, aren't I?"

"Are you?" ED puts both hands on the pipe.

"Stop," GenAK says.

"I thought you were military? Don't AKs like violence?" TECH-chick snaps her belt once more, as if she's clacking the binary version of Morse code. Translation: get out of her way. Would it be so bad if we chose her point value over her team member value?

With everyone distracted, I run to the car. I can't hear what's happening behind me because of my damaged hearing from the explosion. I hope GenAK can keep the warring away from me long enough to get the people left in the car out. I'm not against ED's plan with the pipe, but if GenAK doesn't like it, I want to learn why.

Both passengers in the front seat are gone, turned to coded

strands and converted into game points. The backseat has one player still struggling with the belt. It's a boy, badly burned and choking.

"Stay with me," I shout over the rumble of vehicle parts still settling after the crash. The front of the car burns hot. I anticipate a second explosion any second. Isn't that what happens in this type of situation? "Can you unbuckle?"

The boy shakes his head. "Why are you helping me?" he coughs. "Just so you can kill me?"

"No! What's wrong with everyone?" I ask.

"The game," he says. "We have to take points from others." He pauses to cough up blood. Not a good sign. "It's the only way to win." Upon closer look he's not a boy, but a young teen— perhaps around thirteen years old. His arms and legs hold together at knobby joints twice the thickness of the bones they connect.

"Then the game sucks," I say.

"I'm gonna live forever." The boy gargles and spits something solid along with blood. He wipes his sharp angled face, leaving red smears in the wake of the back of his hand. He has thick, grease-colored hair and no apparent understanding of what 'near-death' means. By the set of his jaw, I'd expect he could run the entire state of Rhode Island singlehandedly, mob style.

I crawl into the heated metal through a broken window. The belt sticks. I can't budge anything by pushing the release button or yanking on the strap. Every yank makes the young teen wince.

"GenAK, I need you." I notice something shiny on the floor mat of the damaged car and rifle for it. Maybe it's sharp. A key. It's flat on its end, but I can still saw at the belt with it. Using the straight end, I fray the side of the belt. The key doesn't have a serrated edge. It's more of a digitally coded strip of metal. It makes sense for the gaming realm.

GenAK must not have heard me. He doesn't answer. I manage to fray the entire width of the seatbelt without the car exploding a second time. When the polyester belt snaps I hear a crackle of skin where the thing has fused to the young teen as it breaks free.

"Hurry, get out of here," I say to him.

His hand touches my left forearm as he leverages his feet loose.

I pull back and cover my arm with the key still in my hand. If the kid wasn't curious before about my arm, he is now. "I can't protect you from the other players," I tell him. What I mean is for him to get out of here and forget about my arm. "They're coming, and they're armed." Don't mention armed. The kid rubs his blood smeared jaw, eyes on my key, while TECH-chick, GenAK, and ED close the gap on my distraction. Except they all hold weapons on one another as well as swinging an object wide in a more general threat. Idiots.

Does the kid not see the three people with makeshift weaponry headed his way? ED's pipe is ready and waiting to splatter the kid's source code. I try warning him off again. "I don't know if it's safe. If you want to level up, run."

"I won't make it." He's right. He won't make it on his own. Not now. He could have three minutes ago, if he would have listened to me in the first place.

"Hold on." I back toward the three-way standoff. ED and

TECH-chick against GenAK. Everyone looks like a cornered animal. "It's a kid," I holler before getting too close.

ED turns to me and startles. I must look a mess. His pipe hits the asphalt. TECH-chick takes it as her cue to jump me. She runs for me with the belt at throat level, screaming. Her legs stretch long between strides, and I'm frozen in place, unable to convince myself to react. While she runs, she shifts her attention from me —her unfortunate target–to the mangled vehicle. I turn my head to signal the kid to find cover, but can't catch his gaze. The kid shakes his head side to side, in a controlled manner unbefitting a traumatized car crash victim. He does this while locked in some visual spar with TECH-chick, which doesn't slow her attack against me, but sure as hell distracts me from defending myself. I duck with both hands over my head, protecting my throat.

"Stop," ED screams. "The numbers." He's pointing to the sky. "They've attached to GenE."

GenAK stumbles where he stands, but still manages to look up. "Is the boy with you?"

I look over my head. The large number previously hovering directly over the wreckage now centers between where I stand and where the car smolders, like it's tethered at a perfect balance between me and the kid. "Yes, but he's not doing well. He needs help."

"Well, let's help him," ED says, ambling toward me. When he gets close enough, ED whispers, "That score is mine."

GenAK hobbles forward as well. He moves quickly, not letting ED alone near the lone survivor of the car accident. "Wait." He points toward the numbers in the sky, like he's puzzling over them and it's uncomfortable.

ED rolls his head on his shoulders, joins GenAK staring up at the sky and his fingers wiggle, calculating at a much faster, much more irritated rate, than GenAK.

TECH-chick has been side-staring at GenAK for some time. A light illuminates her eyes like she's just put something together. She stands in front of GenAK with a finger at his chest. "Oh, wait. You're that guy." She doesn't back away. "The hero, right?"

GenAK's jaw rolls to one side in a tight attempt to appear like he's unaware what she's talking about. In addition to that being a lie, he's not handling how she's invading his space. He breathes more rapidly by the second.

"Yeah. The one who got himself blown up for trusting a kid." TECH-chick points toward the kid, opening herself up with both hands engaged and nothing covering her torso. "Because nothing bad ever happens when kids are around, right? We can trust kids." She steps so close I can't cut between them if I want to. Which I don't.

"He's not a murderer," I say. "He's a kid." I point to the kid, like they might have forgotten who I'm referring to. His greasy hair and hairless face advertise innocence better than anything I can say.

The golden points which come with him balance themselves, centered on the group whole. ED shuffles his position three times, certifying the numbers are tethered to him as well. His points. His calculating stare makes me miss the child he feared. I much prefer the chubby cheeked version of ED.

TECH-chick points to the number in the sky. "That's a death toll."

I stare upwards. The goal on this level is to collect opposing players' deaths.

"Think of it as eliminating the competition," ED says.

"He's right. There aren't limitless AI housing opportunities for Intelligence donors," TECH-chick says. "That's the whole point of all this."

"I thought it was to eliminate intellectual threats from technological advancement," GenAK says.

The kid's head turns like the jerk of a second hand on a grandfather clock, following the conversation around him with experienced observance.

I side with GenAK, even though my instincts line with GenED.

ED crosses his arms and catches my eyes. "Military source would assume that." He then turns to GenAK. "You know AKs get eliminated faster than TECHs get infected."

I point a finger at GenAK. "My wiped face—on that level… It's not just a nightmare."

ED stiffens. "Fear doesn't cross levels." He rubs the tips of his fingers over the stubble on his chin, swallowing as if fear alone follows us through each level.

If there's truly a virus in the game, and it means I'm going to lose my face… I don't want to know anything more about it. I recall being blank like it's a whisper under my skin. Like I'm already a carrier.

8

M inutes pass before we again focus on the sounds of tires burning against pavement, brakes hugging highway. Vehicles ram each other before we think to move. "We need to find cover and regroup," ED yells over metal crashing against glass. "Come up with a strategy."

"We don't have time to plan," GenAK says. "We need to get in the largest machine we can find and take out the competition." Suddenly GenAK is all about winning. He and ED square off, neither one willing to give ground for the other to pass. They both puff like seals ready to bump chests in some territorial display of stupidity.

"I propose we find a tank," ED says.

"Where are you going to find a tank?" GenAK stretches up to his toes, now face to face with ED.

"Maybe there." TECH-chick points to the other side of the overpass, across the entire five lanes for both directions of traffic. We're talking ten lanes of murderous drivers. A military armory, complete with Humvees, choppers, tanks, and even drones. "Can you pilot the chopper, AK?"

"It's GenAK. Don't nickname him." How dare she? Her nickname feels like staking a claim on him and I hate it.

"I don't know. Maybe I can fly it. It's not really my area," he says.

ED turns to the kid. "What's your source code? What can you offer the group?"

TECH-chick looks skyward, raises her eyebrows, then gives ED a look like, *we already took his score and almost didn't let him live, and now you're pressing the dude?*

"GenCiv," the kid says with no indication of attachment to his ID, like a peace offering. "I know you have to get keys to drive anything and those aren't easy to come by." His eyes dart to me. Am I the only person who sees how he sidestepped the question? "GenE has a key."

TECH-chick looks up so abruptly, her eyes scan all visible surfaces on me. I anticipate her pointy hair to be whiplashed off her scalp. Thankfully, she doesn't appear to have x-ray vision, or she'd no doubt tackle me for the useless item. In a level filled with cars, I have no way of knowing which one the key belongs to. Thus making it pointless to bicker over. Still, I don't want to give it to *her.*

ED grips my bicep and walks me to the edge of the highway, as if I'm about to get lectured regarding key possession. My other hand moves to my belt in search of... something that's still not there.

TECH-chick jumps to ED's side, practically pushing me into

the road. "Let's see how lucky you really are. It's not like an Es ever accomplished anything intentionally."

Our team already has a girl—me. *Please let a car miss me and sideswipe TECH-chick.* Whatever I expect to find on my belt, ED's lucky it's absent. I'm sure it would change his game if I were armed right now. I'm not opposed to violence, apparently. With his hand around my arm, I am currently violently opposed to ED.

"Where do you get off?" GenAK steps in front of ED. Once again GenAK changes his tune. His goal: bloodshed. Except when he remembers ED proposes the same game plan. Then he switches to some moral code.

"Your plan is to blow people up? For points?" I ask. Everyone looks at me.

"You have a better idea?" TECH-chick asks. "How do you expect to win?"

"I thought we were going to see if we could get groups to join us, pool points."

A fast-moving van crests a hill in the distance. Swerving out of the way of debris in the lanes, the car spots us and accelerates an already difficult to manage high speed.

"You want to wait and see if they'll stop to talk?" ED asks, shaking my arm. "Maybe offer them a lollipop and see if they want to join our team?" I know he's mocking the fact we're responsible for the boy on our team, thanks to my ill thought-through strategy.

The kid mouths 'lollipop'? I can't tell if he's offended, or wants to know why he doesn't have one yet. I also can't tell which option would make him less threatening. He's a bloody mess and hasn't slowed. Something's off about the kid.

"We need to arm ourselves," ED continues his 'we're assassins' agenda.

A median doesn't slow the van's progress. It does, however, burst one tire and send the back of the vehicle sideways, sliding toward the front. The spin gives us time to run for cover.

"You can never split the points with more than six people," the kid says. The kid waves us toward a parking structure, several steps ahead of us and not at all hindered by his injuries. Everyone runs for cover.

"How many people do we have? Five?" I ask. I know it perpetuates the notion I'm not smart, being an 'E' and all, but it's been difficult to keep track of players with all the chaos and digital loss.

I can't quite call it death because we're already body vegetables laying on a slab somewhere, right? With only our minds functioning, harvests for our human way of thinking, and uploaded into a metal body on the condition of a win. Whatever 'win' means.

Watching people drown, getting hit by cars, and burning… this game promises dying all over again. Here it's real, and scary, and way too close. The rim of the van's tires spark against a cement curb, discarding hubcaps which roll toward my hiding place.

I count it up, lifting a finger for each person in our group. Me, GenAK, ED, TECH-chick, and the kid. I nod. "Yeah. We're five."

"Can we get a better Gen than E? I mean, if we're limited to six, we can do better, right?" TECH-chick says. She keeps hammering my fake Gen, pushing me to the point of almost admitting I'm not an E—I'm nothing. Except, nothing is sure to be worse.

ED contemplates the proposition. To get my points, he has to kill me.

My own group wants to kill me for points? "Let's survive the murder van before we do anything else," I say.

ED's keeping too close tabs on my every move for comfort. I run toward GenAK. He's crouched behind a thick pillar. He didn't come to my defense regarding TECH-chick wanting to off me. The kid scrambles from where he's hiding with TECH-chick and slides in next to me. His blood from the previous car accident streaks on the cement like a directional target: *this is where we're hiding, come steal all our points by murdering the crap out of us.* Idiot kid.

"How can you run?" GenAK asks the kid. "Aren't you in pain?"

"I had a life pack. I used it when the car hit. Probably why I didn't die."

GenAK stiffens so minutely, I'm certain no one else notices. He doesn't look at me, so I have no clue if he's aware I catch his reaction. Not sure it matters. I can't read his body language. He's all 'I'm rigid' all the time.

"Where did you find a health pack?" ED appears at our side, one hand around the kid's back.

"But you're bleeding," I say, cutting off ED's need to locate more 'health packs'.

ED steps back as if giving the kid room to respond. The kid

tugs at his shirt. "The blood is in my clothes. Can't make it disappear, but my body is healed okay."

"So the life pack?" ED asks, weaseling the conversation back to his interest.

"It was on someone else." The kid turns to GenAK, dismissing ED, who doesn't back off. Instead, ED watches the kid talk to GenAK like it's the final match of some tennis tournament. "How many levels is this place?"

"No idea." GenAK keeps his answers short and his attention elsewhere.

"This is my first, but if they get much harder, I'm in trouble. All my gaming experience comes from RPG and SIMS stuff. I have no idea about car-jacking or war strategies. I didn't anticipate those skills being needed for an AI donor," the kid says.

"You knew you'd be a donor?" I ask.

The kid points to his head. "Cancer. Couldn't be cured." He mimes using game controllers. "All I did was practice when I wasn't asleep or having treatments." He pauses as if remembering the good old days inside a game but not inside-inside, before being an official donor. "And one of the early levels is beyond my skill set. Can't help but feel like I'm letting my mom down. She wanted me to live, you know."

I look around. The only one in our group in their element is GenAK. Everything has been under his skill set, as far as I can tell. Whereas, I haven't been ready for anything. I barely survive running scared.

The van slams into the parking garage, ending our impromptu get-to-know-you session. Cement crumbles against the rebar supporting the pillar the van now wraps around. As if taking a cue from the falling concrete, darkness bulldozes daylight out of the sky.

"You've got to be kidding me." ED points to the evening sky. Stars twinkle too perfectly to believe. He turns to the burning wreckage extending his hands 'and now this?' style, like the entire level is too amped to take seriously. "They keep knocking themselves out before we get a chance."

"They're kids." I stare through the windshield. A group of four girls, all of whom look younger than the kid but not by much, recover from the impact without airbags.

"In my experience, those are moms who think they're the same age as their teen daughters." TECH-chick grabs a crowbar and drags it toward the van. Someone has mommy issues.

My eyes stay with GenAK. No one tries to stop TECH-chick.

"No," I say. GenAK lets air out of his lungs. He could have been the one to say no, why wait on me? "You can't go whack a bunch of teenster-moms."

"They can't join us, it's too many. And we still have to reach our objective. It's not easy to get over a million points," the kid says, his voice cracking like he's still undergoing puberty.

"A million?" I turn to GenAK who we entrusted with the objective from the booth. He failed to share that detail. I get now why he doesn't stop TECH-chick. Someone has to get our team points if we're going to level up. He can't bring himself to stop her. "There has to be a different way to go about it."

"So far the only points we've gotten are from people bent on killing us." ED holds a sharp object in his hand. "We could set a trap. Anyone who tries to steal our numbers gives us theirs instead."

"A trap? That's the best we can come up with?" I ask.

ED drops his weapon and steps so close to me, I can smell 'college degree' in his hair and on his clothes. He smells like late nights with stale pizza and cheat sheets. His razor sharp gaze traps me on the edge of his words. "Tell me. What do you suggest?"

While he's close I whisper, "How long were you trapped in the previous level before we came by?"

A long pause follows until the teenster-moms kick the doors out from their vehicle, drawing the attention of our group. I look away from ED. Then, with my eyes averted, he leans in so his breath warms the strands of hair against my ear. "It's like it's still with me, hidden below the surface. Felt like years, probably more like days."

"Were you with anyone? I mean in a group, before you met us?"

"Yeah."

"Did you all level up at the same time?" My whispering grows louder. GenAK stills. I know he's listening.

"I've never leveled up with anyone." The way ED says he's never leveled up with anyone has the tone of design where coincidence should be. "We got separated."

I need to watch my back around ED.

There's no more time for Personal History 101. I nod as the teenster-moms fall to the pavement. One of them pulls a gun from a handbag. "Holy—hit the deck!"

Shots ring out in the darkness.

9

Bullets burst against the cement floor, peppering layers of vehicle interior, and graze the pylon next to ED.

"They have guns!" TECH-chick screams.

"I told you we needed to arm ourselves." ED crouches, completely obscured behind the half-sized pillar, thanks to his lean frame. Good thing too, because the teenster-moms are out for blood, any blood they can get. Lucky for us, they're terrible shots.

"I have an idea," ED shouts. He pushes up from his cover and runs the long way around vehicles toward the back of the van wreck.

One of the firing teenster-moms keeps both hands on her gun's grip and tracks his escape with one eye shut. Her finger pulls against the trigger several times, seconds behind ED's progress. He crosses behind the pack of female gamers. The firing teenster-mom is so intent on ED in the background, she doesn't even check her foreground. She fires and strikes one of the girls in her posse.

The struck teen drops to the ground, head lolling backward. It's an overly dramatic death scene, but in her defense, she did survive a head on collision with a stationary object. The shooter curses and lowers her gun. ED continues to circle around. None of the rest of us leaves our cover. No one so much as high fives ED's accomplishment.

"Now there're three," he yells.

Tipping my head, I sneak a glance at the attacking group. The teenster-mom on the ground flickers green. Strands of familiar black and green code fly into the air, circle around on themselves and re-materialize as coins popping in the sky, adding to *our* number.

"Nice job, ED," TECH-chick says.

I have to hand it to him. He wasn't the one who fired, and he still managed to get us points. Maybe that's messed up of me, but them killing themselves instead of killing us feels morally acceptable. I might return to favoring ED, if it weren't for the smug expression on his face.

"How many points do they have left?" the kid asks.

"Hard to tell, their score's above the second story of the parking garage," TECH-chick says.

"Why is ours hovering so low?" ED asks.

"Maybe higher scores float higher?" TECH-chick says.

"That would mean they have a high score." ED whips a lead pipe through the air, ready to strike.

"Those gals?" GenAK joins the conversation. "They can

barely hold a weapon, and they drove into a column trying to flatten us. There's no way they have a high score."

"The lower the score, the higher it floats?" TECH-chick puts out there.

"Doesn't matter. They're regrouping. Move, move, move!" GenAK jumps over the hood of a car, not waiting for anyone else.

For someone who pointed out the teenster-moms' unlikelihood of having a high score, he's sure leaving in a hurry. Then I hear the 'beep, beep, beep, beep' of a javelin rocket launcher locking on target, and race after GenAK. Away from the well-armed, yet crappy drivers, trying to murder us.

"Where are they getting so many weapons?" I scream.

ED catches up to me, grabs my arm, and pulls me to the ground before I reach GenAK. My free arm instinctively covers my head and we both tuck into balls as a whooshing sound passes overhead. It clears us. Relief. I jump up to note where the missile lodges at exactly the time it connects with a cement wall. Heat blows me back against the car door behind me before I hear the deafening boom of impact.

An indent the size of my behind remains in the driver's side door. GenAK comes out of nowhere to drag me up a ramp and away from the heat of the explosion.

"What were you thinking?" he snaps.

Still reeling, I can't respond.

ED scrambles from the opposite side of the car I hit, toward GenAK and me. "GenE, you okay?" He grabs my head and forces one of my eyes open, then the other. I don't know what he's looking for, the scared little boy inside him again. It's a warmth missing whenever ED remembers GenAK is present.

"She's fine." My arms are practically ripped from my sockets as GenAK pulls me out of ED's hands. "Why'd you let her stand up back there?"

"Let her? She jumped ahead of me. There was nothing I could do." ED steps closer to GenAK. "What about you? Running off, ditching us all?"

"That girl sighted me in. Weren't you watching? You could have all stayed put and been out of the line of fire."

"Why would she sight you? They're after our points, all of us."

"In case you haven't noticed, our group pivots around GenE. Our tally stays primarily over her and barely balances between the rest of us when we spread out. I happened to be next to her. They must have thought since I'm a big guy and all that I'm the team leader. They wanted whoever was going to give them the biggest boost."

"Team leader?" TECH-chick arrives to the yelling match. "No way is Failed-Ads-Barbie our team leader."

"I'm with her, that's all I know," the kid says.

All eyes fall on him. "You're with *her?*" TECH-chick says, the tone of her voice rich with disgust.

"Hey, you were coming to kill me, remember?"

I can't help but feel a little morally superior to the rest of the group right now. Or at least relief they might not kill me.

Wait. If I'm the team leader and they kill me, they get all the points associated with the leader? Am I a bigger target or a lesser target?

"So you give her control over all your points? You earned that number, not her," TECH-chick says, one hand in the air toward our group tally.

"She could have killed me," the kid says. "But she didn't."

ED kicks the cement. Then curses. "I didn't know they targeted you. You could have said something like 'drop, I've got this'," he says to GenAK.

"So we're all okay with this weak-ass GenE being our team leader? Like, if she goes, we lose everything? How is that cool?" TECH-chick asks. "I could take her out with my pinkie. We're putting all our stock in her?"

GenAK stands between me and TECH-chick. I'm only able to crouch and though I can hear the exchange that's been taking place, my voice fails when I try to speak.

"Yes. I'm sticking with her." GenAK nods down the ramp from where we've all gathered. "But if you want to switch teams, I'm confident there's an opening down there."

TECH-chick licks her lips. Apparently the offer is still worth considering. What do I care? I don't want her on my team anyway. TECH-chick runs to the ramp, screaming toward the teenster-moms. "What level are you on? How many have you passed?"

Everyone entering the donor game at different levels makes it impossible to judge skill sets from one challenge to the next. It also explains how everyone in the previous levels, who weren't in physical contact with me, doesn't materialize where I have.

"Still working to pass our first, but we almost have it in the bag."

TECH-chick falls backward on her butt, then turns to her

knees and can't keep her feet under herself as she tries to run back up to us. "Heavy weapons!" She can't get back to us fast enough, I'm sure of it.

"Climb!" My voice returns. "Head up, not over."

Everyone looks around for something to clamber skyward. I have no idea what I'm even talking about. I can't believe they're listening to me. Trying to get to my feet, I slam back to the vehicle ramp. My left leg isn't responding at all.

"Pretty sure my leg broke." Maybe it's worse than broken, like gone.

I'm in GenAK's arms, dangling like a ragdoll, before I can mention the fact half my body tingles numb. I might snap from his jarring sprint when he reaches the ramp's upper curve. Somehow he manages to get us both to the higher level. His hand reaches back down where I can't see. When he lifts his arm the kid clings to him.

A click echoes through the structure, followed by a whizzing and a crash. Layer after layer of parking structure collapses directly above the teenster-mom's heads.

"She shot straight up?" ED laughs.

We don't have time to laugh at the wasted missile. "Keep moving," I scream. "Toward the exit. Jump for it." It's more like directing GenAK where to go. My lame side rests against him as he runs, jostling me with every step. Footings get trickier as more rebar is exposed with every ripple of explosion.

The building shakes. Chunks of ground fall beneath us. Too many holes open in the building, no sure footings left. We reach the ledge. Three garage floors down, asphalt and yellow barriers look ready to impale anyone insane enough to jump. This gamescape makes no sense, structurally speaking.

"Jump," GenAK hollers.

The building crumbles from below us. I hang on as GenAK holds my head against his chest with his other hand to make sure I don't hit weird or jerk around as we fall. The kid follows immediately after us.

"They're going to get our points because you're all morons," ED says. He leaps from the parking structure though. He falls after me.

The ground refuses to give when GenAK's knees connect. His knees, however, give.

"Something broke," he says.

TECH-chick hangs from her hands before dropping, lessening the distance of her fall. She rolls on impact and manages to stand where the rest of us are gripping body parts and moaning.

"The whole thing's coming down," she says.

"What about getting those points?" ED asks.

"You want them so bad, go in and get them," GenAK challenges.

ED's eyes narrow. "What'll you say when it's time to level up? At least we didn't murder anyone?"

"You haven't taken as many lives as I have, so don't talk to me about 'the right thing to do.'" GenAK addresses the rest of the group. "We need a heavy duty vehicle."

"Why?" TECH-chick asks.

"He wants to complete half the challenge," ED tells all of us. "We have to travel over two hundred miles in order to complete our mission."

"What? To where?" I ask. GenAK's leg doesn't look capable of depressing an accelerator.

"Doesn't matter. Two hundred miles total. To anywhere."

"We need a fast car, not something heavy duty," TECH-chick says.

"That's fine, but we need to move before some other team completes the mileage task and comes after us to take our points in order to finish their goal," ED reminds us.

The parking garage continues to topple inward. The hole from the upward fired missile eats away the layers around it. "So much for all those cars."

"You think they lived?" TECH-chick asks.

"No idea."

"We're not up points," she says pointing to our hovering tally.

"Guess they lived then," I say.

"You don't get points of accidental death in your vicinity," the kid says. "I'd be leveled up days ago if that were the case. Lots of people blow themselves up when they pick up a rocket launcher and fire it wrong or load it wrong. It happens."

"We got your points," TECH-chick reminds the kid.

"I joined your team. If I'd died, you'd have nothing."

"We'd have a tally in the sky with your blood on it." ED points up.

"One point," the kid says. "You wouldn't get everything we'd accumulated as a team before I joined you. I know. I've been on this level longer than you have."

GenAK faces me. "Can you walk?"

"Can you?" I ask.

"Not what I asked," he says.

My entire left side sleeps, unresponsive from my shoulder down. "Just find a fast car. Let's finish this thing."

He nods, pulls against a yellow barrier to stand, and limps away.

"Whoa, we're separating?" ED stands between where I sit and where GenAK hobbles away. "If you die while you're away from the group, what happens to your points?"

No one knows so no one answers.

"I'm staying with GenE," ED folds his arms across his chest. "She's our leader."

"She's the point anchor. That's the only reason you want to stay," GenAK turns to argue with ED. "If you could scavenge a car without me, you'd be gone, but you know you'll fail."

"Is that what you think?" ED stomps toward the highway. "I'll find us a car. The best car."

"Don't stand by the highway. We've had enough high-speed rammings for one day," I say.

"Come on, ED." GenAK's eyes roll even from a distance. "I could use your help."

The parking building crashes some more. Large chunks dangle and scrape before coming loose and tumbling to the floor below, causing new levels of crumbling, dangling, ear-splitting noise.

"You should offer the survivors a place in the group," the kid says.

"They didn't seem interested earlier," I say.

A golden number drops from the clouds above. The number lessens with every inch of altitude lost. Everyone in our group looks around for where the points are going. Our tethered score hasn't gone up.

"Who gets those points?" TECH-chick asks, her eyes intent on the altitude and zeroes evaporating.

"Why don't you run in there and find out," I say, so it shouldn't surprise me as the pipe she's still holding connects with my ribcage. My good side can feel it. I double over and brace for a second impact. I can hear the inhale of TECH-chick lifting her arm for a second blow. Her motion clears a visual path to a box with a big red 'X' on it, or maybe it's a plus sign. A health pack.

"What're you doing?" GenAK's palm stops the pipe from slamming into me a second time.

It gives me the distraction I need to fall forward on top of the box. I click it open while they continue talking.

"If I take her out, do I get the score to myself?" TECH-chick yanks to free her pipe and strike me again. Honestly, I'm surprised it took her this long. Inside the box nestles a syringe filled with green liquid. I lift it, slide the plastic from around the needle, and plunge it into my left thigh while everyone argues. There are four more plastic wrapped syringes in the box. I shove them down my shirt. I could really go for some pockets.

"We can't turn on each other," ED says, but his eyes aren't invested in his words.

At the far side of the parking garage a new golden score counts up, rising at the same rate the teenster-mom's number drops.

"Competition," TECH-chick points out, dropping the pipe.

GenAK releases her wrist. "We need to move," he says.

"We all know that." ED rushes to lead out before GenAK. "Stating the obvious makes you look like a commoner."

"Yeah, *I* look like a moron," GenAK says under his breath.

Wreckage spreads out before us, turning ramps, roads, medians, and grass areas into a parking lot for four-year-olds with driver's licenses. Vehicles turned on their sides, upside down, half on top of other cars, or torn in pieces, litter the ground for a quarter mile.

"How does that even happen?" I point to the vehicle parts separated by large spans of distance.

"I don't want to know," GenAK answers. "Let's find something working."

"Can anyone hotwire?" the kid asks, causing all of us to turn around as if we forgot he was there. "That's how we got the last one." He shrugs off the four of us staring at him with a confidence beyond his peach-fuzz face. I assume he's referring to the car his former group tried to kill us with.

"TECH isn't just a source, it's a skill," TECH-chick answers the kid while picking at her black polished fingernails. Everything from the tilt of her head to the jut of her hip screams she's pretending to play down awesome hacking skills. Like she's the absolute godsend to computer programming.

Can she be more full of herself?

The kid runs ahead of the group, peering through windows and kicking tires. He's experienced at this aspect of the game—scavenging. "You have the key from earlier?" he asks me.

"You mean like the health boost rations stashed down your shirt?" ED asks, giving me a sideways glance.

My hand goes to the narrow space between my B-cups.

"Found something," TECH-chick calls back to those of us lagging behind.

GenAK rushes to her side first. A beige sedan with so many dents, it's impossible to open the four doors to their full capacity. It has enough seating for five, but not if it includes the five of us. No one seeks close proximity with anyone else in our group. "It'll work, but this isn't a fast option."

Sticking her hand through the busted driver-side window, TECH-chick dangles a set of keys in her fingers. Real keys. Not like the one I have stashed away. "But it is an option."

Without more debate, the rest of us yank door handles and claim seats. The kid buckles instinctively. ED and I sit next to each other in the back with the kid on my other side. In the front, GenAK rides shotgun with TECH-chick behind the wheel. He reaches across her, pulling her belt tight and clicking it securely in its place. Looking for my own safety latch I find nothing. Whoever sat in my seat previously either cut their way out or didn't make it. My hope of surviving crushes by the second.

The key turns in the ignition and... nothing. TECH-chick bends it so hard toward the dashboard it might break off in her hand. No groan of power. The car won't turn over.

"You didn't test it before we buckled in?" I say none too quietly. "We're sitting ducks now."

"No one told you to get in," she shouts back.

"She has a point," the kid says.

"No one asked Tag-Along Kid Brother and Bra-Stasher Barbie," TECH-chick says, her eyes on me in the rear-view mirror, waiting for my reaction. I remain stoic to spite her while imagining ripping her rainbow-spiked hair from her scalp.

"The chick has a point," GenAK says. "The kid doesn't have a say."

The kid squints one eye in GenAK's direction, clearly not in agreement with the balance of power.

A cough of power connects with the engine. It turns over. Collectively, our shoulders drop in relief. TECH-chick pulls the gear shaft between her and GenAK. She grinds into second, bypassing first gear altogether, and maneuvers through the vehicle graveyard, which no longer works to camouflage us, toward the highway.

"We've got company," TECH-chick says.

10

I twist in my seat, unobstructed by a seatbelt like everyone else. Three vehicles pick their way through the car cemetery from far corners of the wasteland, alerted to our escape by the sound of our engine. They're all closing toward us as if they're coordinated. Hope they'll get distracted by each other isn't anything to bank on.

"Step on it," GenAk, says grabbing the gear over the top of TECH-chick's hand, forcing the car into third.

I shift forward so I'm more between GenAK and TECH-chick than on my designated seat. "Faster."

"I'm going as fast as I can," she says. Her shoulder slams back, connecting with where my hand grips her seat. How am I bothering her more than GenAK manhandling the stick?

"Some of us are moving faster than others." I practically climb the seat, getting as distant from the approaching cars as I can, even though it really makes no difference. We're all in the same car. The all too familiar sound of smashing metal gets closer. "Isn't there something you can do?"

"I'm doing it," she yells. Her long legs depress the accelerator to the floor. For good measure she slams her foot once against the pedal. I still think she could push harder.

"You're in third gear." GenAK and TECH-chick swat hands trying to claim control of the gear shaft.

Two vehicles crash into each other behind us. "Two down," ED hollers over the sound of the engine and our scream-conversation about how to drive a standard.

GenAK forces the vehicle into fourth, while TECH-chick then fights to jam it into fifth. The transmission screams refusal to save us.

"I take it back. Only one of the vehicles chasing us fell behind," ED says. He's turned completely around, his knuckles white against the headrest. His eyes widen as the much larger, much faster vehicles close the gap.

"Hurry, get to the highway," the kid says, shouldering me aside in order to be the voice of navigation. He points where he wants the vehicle to go. "And hope it's crowded."

"Why would we want that?" I turn toward him. "We're outnumbered as it is."

"So they go after bigger numbers," he says, not looking behind at what we're running from. The kid's probably seen it before, having been on this level longer than any of us.

TECH-chick turns onto a two-lane road with no cars. "Which way to the highway?"

"How should I know?" the kid says, sitting back.

ED almost coughs on himself. "It was your idea." His hands

stammer in gestures that somewhat approximate the hand signals the kid used to guide us moments before. "You pointed!"

"I'm not the one driving," he says.

"We're not going to last long." ED presses his back against the back of the driver's seat as if the six inches he put between him and the approaching cars will save his life. "Give me one of those." He points to my chest, at the same time GenAK happens to look in the rearview mirror.

"What?" GenAK lets go of the stick and stares at ED, invisible daggers aimed at him. "What does she have?"

I can't tell if he's upset at me for having some tool he doesn't know about, or ED for being a selfish prick. If he'd been paying any attention to me at all, he wouldn't have to ask. "Like you'd notice," I say, twisting my attention back to GenAK's hands over the top of TECH-chick's grip on the gear.

"GenE has health boosters." ED holds out an expectant hand.

The kid puts his lanky arms up interlocking his fingers behind his head to better enjoy the chaos.

"You do?" TECH-chick asks. "That's what you stashed down your shirt?"

"Is that even safe?" GenAK asks, patting his pecks as if he's imagining being stabbed with a needle there. He's obviously clueless as to the many storage options a bra has to offer. The shots aren't needling into anything, safely tucked at the base elastic.

"Saving them." I glare at ED. "For when we need them."

"I want to be in charge of mine," TECH-chick announces despite the fact I didn't say there was enough for everyone.

I'm saving whatever I have for whoever needs one. Meaning, I take priority, no matter how many times I need it.

We swerve up an onramp. Highway bound.

"They aren't *yours*," I say with a hand over my heart. "I found them. We'll use them when I say."

"What happens if you're wiped out with those on you?" she asks.

"They green code too," the kid says casually.

Suddenly everyone has a hand out. "Give me one now," TECH-chick demands.

"I'll exchange one shot with the person who took my key. That's it." I don't actually know if anyone has my key, but it's worth putting out there.

ED punches the seat. He happens to be seated behind TECH-chick.

"Ow, hey!" TECH-chick complains. "Watch it." She avoids tire tread, lost bumpers, and stray hub caps along the highway while pressing the pedal to the floorboard.

Everyone notices there's no traffic at the same time.

The kid stares wide-eyed out the side window. His lack of interest in the open freeway ahead grabs my attention. I'm immediately sorry I follow his gaze. A huge semi-truck races up a nearby ramp, on a collision path with us. His hand brushes against my leg, fist closed around a key. My key.

I clench my jaw and place my palm under his hand. He drops the key into it. My fingers tighten over the metal. Keeping my teeth together, I grunt out the words, "You took it?" The kid? I trusted him over the rest of these losers.

"You got my score, right?" he says, like it's some sort of tit-for-tat. "Give me the shot." He doesn't hold out his hand. His gangly form is as tense as his meager muscles can manage.

By this time everyone in the car waits to see if I'll follow through on my promise. No one gives the kid the look of disappointment he deserves for being dishonorable in the first place. I plunge a hand down the front of my shirt.

The mega-sized semi gains elevation from the angle of the onramp. It's at our side now, with huge diesel exhaust pipes spewing black smoke close enough that we breathe in the gaseous odor.

"Use the brake." GenAK mimes slamming the brake with his foot, like that'll slow us before we lose this game of side swipe chicken.

I pull one syringe and slap it into the kid's open palm. He licks his lips and smiles with a head turn.

"Nice knowing you all." His right hand pulls the door handle.

"What the hell?" ED screams, grabbing for the little handle attached to the roof material over his door. He slides his toes under the seat in front of him, wedging himself in place.

A beep accompanies the rushing air of the kid's open door. It doesn't remain wide open long. As soon as he leaps, the force of our speed slams the kid to the asphalt and flaps the door back into latch position. It's not sealed tight, but the kid is definitely gone.

"No!" I scream. My hands fumble for the kid so long after he's gone, it's insane. Like I can retroactively prevent him from being highway hamburger. My reflexes suck. The kid's body bounces against the pavement behind us.

"I see how he had such a high score to begin with," ED says, still edged in place. "Smart kid."

"He jumped," I say in total confusion. Smart people don't voluntarily leap from speeding vehicles in a death game.

"He joins teams, gains their trust, finds health packs, and lets them die," ED explains like I'm a moron, which I totally feel like anyway without the addition of his condescending tone. "He's tethered to our score. When we go, it's all his."

"If he survives." I say.

"Probably why he picked GenBarbie to be the anchor," TECH-chick adds. "Easy out."

The two guys nod. How dare they agree with *her*.

"He didn't pick me," I say.

"He totally pegged you for a sucker," TECH-chick says, exhausting my last ounce of restraint.

I reach an arm around her seat. I'm in the center making my attack angle weird, catching her chin above my elbow and hug myself against ED, who won't let go of the back of her chair. "Brake or I'll freaking kill you myself." It's like she wants us to get hit. She can't possibly believe our little vehicle would win in a side-swipe-smash battle against a semi, can she?

Her foot taps the brake. Our car loses control. ED's hand slides down my shirt. I let go of TECH-chick's throat to slap him away. He slips a syringe out in his fist.

"Worth it," he says, seconds before our car hits the rumble strip separating our lane from the oncoming traffic lanes.

TECH-chick throws the steering wheel into a spin. The car obeys the motion with a grind, and smoke escapes the engine.

"Don't die, don't die, don't die," she chants, patting the dashboard.

I'm internally chanting the same thing about more than the dang car.

The semi-truck cranks into a loud terror-inducing gear, barely avoiding jackknifing in pursuit of our little car.

Our spin becomes an out of control U-turn, reminding us of the danger at our backs. Two cars are coming fast.

ED puts a hand on the door.

"Are you kidding me?" I say.

"I'm not letting a kid beat me." ED's words get GenAK's attention. From the cut of his grimace, he takes it as a personal attack. He launches himself sidelong across the opening between the two front seats, smacking my chin in the process. Hitting me accidentally slows GenAK from reaching ED before he pulls the handle.

I reach out to grab ED, too. He leaps from the car and I miss him. His shoulder hits first. There's little chance he can use his arm now unless he can relocate it back into its damaged socket. The rest of him rolls toward the center lane. The semi-truck drives for him.

I turn my face forward, unable to witness whatever happens next.

Both GenAK and I look at each other for a second.

None of us says anything.

Our car veers and jolts, demanding our attention forward again. "We don't need him," TECH-chick hollers as she shifts gears. We barely avoid a rear-approaching vehicle, which guns too early, zipping harmlessly past us. It hits the side of the semi, sending sparks as it scrapes along the crates being towed by the beast vehicle. Engine brakes roar over every other sound, until a boom of fuel and fire override the cranking brakes.

"Shit!" TECH-chick cranks the wheel away from the exploding lane. We're seconds away from another head-on collision with the car cemetery crowd.

GenAK grabs the wheel and yanks it hard to the right, sending us careening over a guard rail and down an embankment. "Off-road it." He speaks like it's a command.

"No!" TECH-chick lets go of the wheel to cover her face. All her apparent coolness falls away when she takes cover. She's just like me—a coward.

Disbelief at her answer causes me to hesitate in what reaction I should take next. I dive for a belt since I'm the only one not buckled. Smoke from the burning rubber fills my lungs. No matter how fierce TECH-chick presses the brake, she can't stop us from gaining speed. *Please let me be cooler than her.*

Above us, on the highway, the crashing of a truck and car booms. Still fumbling with the belt, I look out the rear window as a cargo trailer bounces over the rail. The cab of the semi, still attached, drags toward us.

"You've got to be kidding me." The sliced belt offers no safety. I drop it and curl into a ball on the seat, arms covering the back of my head. I consider the floor, but figure we're flat when the beastly semi overtakes us. The cushion probably won't help, but my head says it might.

"I didn't see a code on your arm," TECH-chick yells over the exploding sound of the semi-truck. "You know, when you tried to strangle me."

"Is this the best time?" GenAK shouts.

Looking up from my protective crouch to scrutinize GenAK's motives behind his words, I run fingers over the naked skin of my left arm while tugging my sleeve low again. How do I keep letting it slip? She tries to steer our car away from the semi's path. Our chances of evading being crushed make her effort pointless, but no way would I tell her to give up trying.

"You're a plant." TECH-chick shouts. "You're not helping us at all."

"A plant? Like a shrubbery?" Humor isn't likely to get me out of this, but maybe it will piss TECH-chick off enough to derail the confrontation.

"Sabotage," she shouts.

"What? No." I look to GenAK hoping he'll have my back again.

GenAK says nothing. A lot of help he is.

"It's..." I don't know what to say. I have no idea why I'm missing my arm code. "Damaged in the game. I used the health shot. I guess it didn't regenerate my code... yet."

TECH-chick *pffts* me.

"Wait. It's reappearing slowly. Like a reverse fade." I smear my hand against car grease from who knows how many mangled crashes this vehicle has been through and hope it looks some-what like numbers materializing. I don't have time to force my forearm into her view, though. A front tire catches on uneven earth, sending our car into a roll. ED's door never fully latched after he bailed. It snaps off. I slide toward the open hole. My hands slap the seat in search of something to hold to keep me in the car. I get nothing. My fingernails can't dig into the fake leather interior to stop my slide.

A strong arm reaches through the gap in the front seats. GenAK slaps my forearm down and pulls me back. "Hold on."

The grease I smeared on my arm makes the gesture of gripping me near impossible.

The car rolls again, sliding me away from the open hole. The roof slams into my back, knocking the wind out of me. GenAK lets go. When the car rolls a full circle, I slide toward the doorless hole again. This time, the dirt grabs me. The only thing I'm left holding is weeds. Mud cakes my mouth. Or maybe it's blood.

11

There's no time to yell to the others as the car ricochets off rock and reed down the slope. The semi storms toward the spot where the dirt holds me fast. There's no time to move and no energy even if I had the time. Any healing I accomplished earlier is shot to hell when something snaps to the left of my collar bone.

Pulling a syringe from my bra, I rip the plastic with my teeth. Having use of only one hand makes it difficult to slam the needle into my chest. I don't know how the serum works, but can't risk healing any other part of me than my beating heart. I guess I could have shoved it into my spinal cord to keep my brain whirring, but it's too late now. The plunger depresses and cold liquid bleeds inside me. The cool sensation spreads, pumping out with whatever powers me.

Weight from the semi forces me into the dirt. My chin presses deep into soft brush, leaving the rest of me at an odd angle. My back snaps. I can hear it, even though I can't feel anything.

Blackness covers my eyes. My ears are buried in the earth along with my mouth and nose. The health serum won't revive me from extended suffocation, will it?

My heart races so fast, I might have killed myself on accident. A self-induced heart attack. I've overdosed on life juice in an attempt to cheat digital death.

I'm blinded by bright blue sky. My hands flail with no ground beneath me.

"Are you insane?" ED asks. "I wasn't sure that would work. Why would you do the same thing seconds before the semi rolls right in your path?"

ED's pontificate voice is the last sound I want to hear. Does everyone sound like him now? Because that's the only explanation for him surviving the wreckage. Ed flung himself into the crash. I never saw him stick himself with the booster before he jumped.

"What happened?" My heart still feels ready to burst out of my chest—racing, bounding, pounding. "Where am I? GenAK?" I look around for the person who has been with me the longest, the only person I remotely trust as long as a short-skirt wearing TECII floozy isn't nearby.

"Unless you left them a health boost, I don't think they're going to make it." ED nods down the hill where the truck rolls over the car I was thrown from. The semi rolls over once more, landing on its side, wheels spinning. "That's sure to blow," he says, regarding the wreck. "Classic game MO. Car rolls and explodes for absolutely no reason."

"But our team is down there." Breaking ED's grip on my sleeve, I run down the hill. What have I done? There's only one shot left. If both TECH-chick and GenAK are still alive, will he let me shoot him over her? I won't give him a choice.

"Seriously? You're still going after that guy?" ED hollers, not at all trying to stop me from running into the explosion.

That guy? GenAK is not *that guy,* he's *the* guy who... who... The guy who freaking dies if I don't get to him in time. I run faster. Motor oil and gasoline dominate the air. No amount of waving my arm through the haze lessens the throat burn.

On top of rivers of gasoline, the truck engine roars. ED's right. The whole area's ready to blow. I roll my eyes. Freaking accurate ED predictions.

"GenAK," I call before I'm close enough to look into the car. No answer.

I fall onto the undercarriage, now the topside undercarriage. "AK!" I use TECH-chick's nickname for him, trying it out for how familiar and intimate it feels to speak it. Crouching low, I peer into the battered vehicle. TECH-chick moans and reaches out for help. *Move. Out of my way.*

Her hands pull my hair, not much strength left in her. It barely deters me. I push the release on her belt to get her out of my way. I grab a syringe from its secure location, in order to prep it for getting to GenAK. "AK?"

He dangles upside down, his head lolls to one side, suspended. TECH-chick lies where she falls, right in my way. I have to get to GenAK. I roll her toward me to move her so I can crawl inside.

She moans. "I need a shot." She pulls at my arm holding the vial.

"I'll shoot you with a bullet before I use the last needle on you."

Once she's free of the wreckage, I crawl inside. The upside down roof wobbles under the weight of my knees on it. Dangling belt straps are too much for me to handle. Swatting them back, I want to rip the belt out of the seat. No. I want to rip the seat out of the car, to get it out of my way. I need to get to him. Everything blocks me.

The syringe breaks while I hold it in my hand navigating uneven ground. I must have put too much pressure on one end of the tube. Liquid pools inside the plastic covering. "No," I say in disbelief. "No, no, no." I almost throw it at the dash above my head, but change my mind. Maybe it works differently depending how it's applied, what if I force him to swallow it shards and all?

Glass mingles with the juices inside the plastic seal. That's some heavy-duty plastic. Tipping the contents of the syringe so one side stays dry, I puncture the plastic by biting it, trying to create the smallest hole possible. GenAK bleeding out internally from swallowing glass won't help me.

Taking a breath, I tip the liquid so it drops into the roof of GenAK's mouth. He's still hanging upside down. He coughs and snorts. It must have gone up his sinuses. I don't stop pouring.

"You're wasting it," TECH-chick moans. She has no ability to stop me and I know it.

GenAK doesn't jump into action like I hope he will. Maybe I am wasting the serum. Or maybe it hasn't hit his bloodstream yet. I unfasten his belt and dive aside when his body crashes against the roof of the car. There's no way I can drag him out. He weighs twice as much as I do, maybe more.

My back brushes against the headrests above me. There's no room for pulling someone out of this upside down crunched mess.

"Move." ED's behind me. I haven't figured out what benefit he gains by coming to our aid, but I'm certain it plays into a plan benefiting ED alone.

There's no time to refuse assistance. "What if I push?" I scuttle backwards out from the car and rush to the gas-soaked ground on the passenger side. The window shatters, making it possible for me to push against GenAK without fighting the still intact, though horribly mangled, door.

ED pulls from the driver side and I push. GenAK slides along the ceiling of the car. Once beyond the frame, I run back to the side ED's on and join in pulling GenAK free from the pending vehicle bomb. ED takes a beat to look me in the eyes. Behind his pupils hides the little kid without a hand to hold. ED, the one everyone sees, puts on a show of superiority, but that's not his insides. Selfish sure. No denying that. Also fiercely dependent and terrified anyone might find out. Probably why he didn't get far after he jumped from the car.

"It hasn't blown yet," I point out.

With my words damning us, everything becomes a blaze of orange and yellow. Oxygen-sucking air punches us back from the wreck. ED and I slam to the ground. I roll, afraid my legs will catch fire from wading through the gasoline mud. My heart races from the health shot I took like an adrenaline boost. Surprisingly, the health serum still works. Even though I have burn marks, my legs smooth over almost instantly.

GenAK doesn't respond to the liquid dripped into his mouth.

He's not moving and his burning skin puckers into tight white scars.

TECH-chick lays flat on her back like she's prepping to make a snow angel in the mud. Her face bloody and arms battered. "How many miles did we get?" She has a few burns, but nothing like GenAK.

"Car's doing a napalm thing. *You* can check the odometer if you want," I say.

"I'd guess less than five miles," ED answers like he's the keeper of all unwanted facts.

"We're never going to get the mileage under our belt," TECH-chick says. "We can't win."

No one argues.

A moan comes from GenAK.

"He's alive," I shriek, then cough to cover my excitement. ED is looking at me when I finish my forced coughing fit. "I mean, he's moving."

"We need to get out of the open. If anyone sees our score up there—" ED points up. Our score has grown by thousands, and risen higher in the sky where more people can spot it from farther away. Apparently we benefit tally-wise from the horror shows we survive.

"GenAK can't run," I say. "We need a car."

"Yeah, cuz that's worked out so well for us." TECH-chick moves so she's propped up by one elbow. "We need military grade vehicles." She points to moaning GenAK. "Make him tell us where they keep the heavy-duty supplies."

"How would he know? He didn't design this world." I stand over GenAK, ready to slap the pretty off TECH-chick's face.

"He's AK, of course he designed it. It's hidden in his head somewhere," TECH-chick says. Though I suspect the TECH gen are more likely to be the architects of a digital world.

"That's not how it works," I defend him without having a clue if I'm right.

"It might be. Makes sense," ED says.

"No one asked you," I say.

"I helped. I didn't have to," he says. "I could have left you all to die." Except we both know he couldn't leave us. ED self-preserves, after all.

"But you can't leave because I have the health boosters and our score tethers to me so you'd be farther behind than ever," I say hoping no one realizes I, in fact, don't have any more boosters. "Don't pretend to be something you're not."

ED doesn't say anything more.

"So the kid underestimated us?" TECH-chick laughs. "We screwed him."

It's the funniest thing I've ever heard. I can't help laughing. ED joins too. GenAK doesn't join in our joyful hysteria of survival.

"He does have a health booster," ED says, wiping his eyes.

The laughter stops.

ED and I help TECH-chick to her feet. We fashion a crude three-point carry with ED and I under each of GenAK's shoulders and TECH-chick holding his feet. It's our only method to drag him with us. All of GenAK's weight packs in his upper body, so TECH-chick has it pretty easy. Doesn't stop her from whining up a storm.

On the other side of the wreckage lies a helipad. A chopper

rests off the concrete square, like someone missed the mark when landing it.

"You think it's sky-worthy?" ED grunts under the dead weight of a barely alert GenAK.

"Find out," GenAK orders through gritted teeth.

My insides shake with the possibility of flying out of here. "Can you pilot?" I ask GenAK.

"My feet," he says.

"What?"

"Let go."

TECH-chick drops his feet, not too gently. "No problem."

"You can fly that thing?" ED lets go of GenAK's shoulder. Too much weight falls to me and my knees buckle before ED realizes GenAK can't hold all his own weight. "Whoa, sorry." ED can shine all shades of nice when he requires help. He grabs GenAK's arm and wraps it around his neck, pulling him off me, greedy survival in his smile.

"No idea," GenAK grunts. He leans in the direction of the chopper. We shuffle the rest of the way to the helipad, none of us sure what sorts of traps or tricks await us.

12

The three of us strain to lift GenAK into the back section of the helicopter. TECH-chick eyes the cockpit while ED and I heave all of GenAK's weight.

"I've got this," TECH-chick says. "It's mechanics, right?" She climbs into the pilot's chair. "That's all."

Mechanics I know nothing about. And as to whether or not 'that's all,' I can't say. Though I suspect TECH-chick of showing off. Her rainbow hair browns at the tips from being tousled by heatbursts. I check the edges of my hair. It's singed with curled black tips, not the bouncing gold of earlier. I can't one-up a dang thing over TECH-chick.

I slide in next to GenAK. ED crawls over both of us, elbows, hands, knees, and feet wherever he needs to put them to get to the other front chair. One of his feet manages to step on GenAK's thigh or maybe higher. GenAK yells out and folds into a ball, rolling onto his side protectively, too late to actually protect anything.

"Sorry, man," ED smirks before settling in next to TECH-chick. "Are those feet controls?" He points to two pedal looking bars in front of the pilot chair.

The pink tinge to TECH-chick's skin fades. She's completely white. "There's like four controls," she says, staring wide eyed at the machinery in front of her. "This is stupid, I can't do this." She stammers and stands to exit the chopper.

For once, I'm more irritated that she isn't aces at something than the fact she admits she sucks just a little. "No." My hand on her shoulder makes her pause, but I know I can't hold her in the chair. I force encouraging words through every clenched muscle in their way. "Try. Just try." The reality is we have no other option. We either die trying to fly out of this part of the gamescape or die when the next wave of crash-maniacs crests the hill. "Or would you rather I sat in front?" ED's head shakes side to side, slowly but firmly negating my offer to fly us out of here.

The snarky edge matching TECH-chick's spiked hair limps. Everything about her flattens. Even her hair loses sharpness as her confidence dips. "We're going to die," she shakes.

"Probably," I say. "Push something." I reach between ED and her, flipping silver switches and pushing green knobs. Something has to engage the engine. When a turbine sounds I know I've activated something.

ED puts a hand up at an angle. "Don't... Don't touch." The blades overhead spin at a slow rate, then increase too fast.

The roar of broken mufflers, sparking bumpers scraping pavement at too high of speed, and the odd sound of no one engaging brakes rises in the distance. I turn to TECH-chick. "You're the pilot. Figure the rest out." I push myself back from the piloting space. Finding some straps, I lock GenAK into place before securing my own buckles. Thank goodness I have buckles this time. There's no door over the opening at my side.

"Strap in," TECH-chick says over the whipping blades overhead and highway cacophony getting closer.

I want to snap back about how I'm not stupid and I'm already 'on it', but resist.

"Scores, up ahead," ED points out the front window. "Getting closer."

"Don't pressure me," TECH-chick screams. "I'm moving as fast as I can."

"Move faster," I say.

"Back-seaters don't get a say." TECH-chick flips more switches. The engine rotating the blades stops.

"Hey!" I scream.

"Wrong switch." ED reaches over and re-flips the same control. The blades rotate again.

"Get out of my space," TECH-chick yells.

"Do it right. Pay attention," he says.

"You want this job?" she asks.

"Maybe I do. I would've corrected my mistake in a second, I know that." ED's hands are still at the switches he can reach.

"I've got this." TECH-chick swats his hand away from the switch controlling the blades. "Back off."

"Do you?" ED challenges. "Even E-Barbie back there sounds more confident."

My glare shifts to the back of ED's head. "Hey."

TECH-chick moves her shaking hand over the controls at her seat. "I've got it."

The chopper rises off the ground. My hands fly out, unprepared for the shift in gravity. I grab a handhold over my head and hold on tight. I doubt it makes any difference in whether or not we die, but holding it feels safer. We rise several feet in the air then crash back to the grass and bite into the chopper pad.

"Whoa!" I yell.

"It's good, it's good. Keep trying." ED encourages.

I'm ready to tell TECH-chick to forget it. Any higher with a drop like that and I doubt we'll need to fear the approaching golden numbers coming to steal our high score.

"Shut up!" TECH-chick shouts in ED's face. Praise and stress make a poor cocktail. "Everybody."

We raise several more feet and center above the helipad.

"Higher," ED says.

"What do you think I'm doing?"

"Other than scaring the crap out of us?" ED says.

The chopper lifts even higher. We're sure to die a horrible death if we lose altitude fast now.

ED's head drops between his knees. His breath rattles as loudly as the machine we're strapped to. "This was a bad idea."

Golden numbers grow in size on the horizon. Some of them are massive, way over the goal or objective number according to what GenAK and ED have told us.

"Those numbers are huge. Long." Everything I say sounds stupid compared to anyone else in our group. I'm the Barbie who failed ads, according to them, and I'm starting to feel like it's true, even though I made it up.

My right hand brushes over my left sleeve. I'm not an E. I'm a blank slate. I can be whatever I want to be, whomever I'm willing to replace. Right now, I want to be the person who wins. I want to win. Not die in an ill-flown chopper.

"Stop moving your feet," GenAK says.

"I'm trying to go higher, not land," TECH-chick says. "Let me do this."

"You're going to put us in a spin if you don't stop moving your feet." GenAK grabs ED's seatback and pulls himself closer to TECH-chick.

"Please don't spin." ED covers his mouth.

Instead of alternating her footings, as she'd been doing, TECH-chick shoves the stick in her right hand forward and we're all thrown forward.

"Not that one!" GenAK's belt slacks unsecured. He flops against the seat in front of him. "Use your left hand. Push forward to go up. The right is back and forth."

The helicopter levels.

"Your feet move us side to side, or, I don't know how to say it, we point or turn. Like a pivot," GenAK says.

"Okay, okay. I got it." TECH-chick's hands both push forward at different rates. We go up and move closer to the gold in the sky.

"What are you doing?" I lean out the window to look behind us, where the sky clears. "We have to get out of here."

"AK, can you handle guns? Like machine guns?" TECH-chick yells over the roaring blades holding us in the air. "In your current state?"

His brow falls, offended by the mere suggestion he might not be able to handle a loaded weapon. "Of course."

"I think I saw some kind of gun assembly back there. Aim it

out the door. We'll take those suckers out before they know what hit them."

"We can't be the first people to find aircraft," I yell. It's so loud in the cab of the helicopter I can't decide if the rest of the team ignores me or can't hear me. "We barely know how to fly. There's no chance to outmaneuver other aircraft."

GenAK assembles items from a case he finds. It looks like a barrel and bullet-feeding belt.

"You can't be serious." We're likely to explode ourselves before causing damage to anything else.

ED's head dips below his knees again. He tries to say something. But he can't between the gagging and belching noises escaping his throat.

"Those are impressive scores. People who know what they're doing. We don't stand a chance," I say.

No one stops their current task.

The gun assembly almost complete at my side, GenAK angles the barrel out the door and points it forward and down. His legs twitch, the serum I dumped in his mouth finally demonstrating some recovery.

"What we need are miles," I scream as loud as I can over the howl of the engine and rotating blades above. "*Miles*. Like turn and run."

A bullet erupts at my side, hitting the dirt below. GenAK tests another shot against the pavement below. "It's a little sticky. Not a smooth release, but better than no defense."

"This is not our best idea." I'm not giving up on the turn and run plan.

"She's right," ED finally manages to add to the conversation, and yes, he's on my side.

GenAK squints in the direction of ED. He contemplates the gun, as if he wills it slipping and nailing ED instead of the road below. He flinches, catches my eyes on him, and smoothes out the crinkled squint. "It's a game," he shouts. "There's only one winner."

"Is there?" The screaming takes a toll. My voice turns to gravel. I'd never survive life as a rock band roadie. "What if everyone could win?"

GenAK doesn't look at me anymore. His attention aims out the window, forward, gun aimed low, finger on the trigger. I lose his attention long before he has something to aim a gun at.

"Maybe that's what they want you to think," I shout.

"We're going to take out the other teams..." GenAK's sentence hangs heavy. Up to now, the military man has seemed less violent than the others. Something changes. "We haven't covered anywhere near the distance we need. I'm not sure this method of spinning circles is going to get us leveled up."

What happens after the other teams are gone? Do we strangle each other at some point to eliminate each other as competition? How badly do I want to live forever?

13

The chopper gains altitude. Nosing left and right like a confused feline, ED returns his head to his protective knees. Like that'll help.

The landscape flashes past so quickly, despite the swishing motions of TECH-chick's terrible piloting, I can't make out the parking garage we escaped from except for the smoke clogging the sky. We zip forward and sideways at the same time, crossing over highways and distancing ourselves from our mess, acting like a homing beacon to anyone looking for an easy pick.

GenAK keeps his eye and gun sighted on the ground ahead of us with unwavering concentration. Nothing can escape his aim. Except maybe a faster flying machine zipping overhead with double barrel firepower and missile launchers. The aircraft banks side to side, like the pilot hasn't mastered firing while flying yet and can't sight us in.

GenAK lifts his head and unsquints one eye. "It's an A-10." He slams his back against the seat.

"What's an A-10?" ED says from between his knees, his voice bounces at us from the floor, losing all volume.

"I thought you knew everything," GenAK mocks. "Ground assault jet." He surveys the chopper like it's a tin tomb. "That thing can take out a tank."

"Now what?" I shout, hoping the fact we're not in a tank helps a little. TECH-chick wobbles on the controls shifting all of us to her side of the chopper. We continue to race through the air, but it's not like a chopper can slice through the sky to escape an aerodynamic jet.

"Pretty sure we get blown out of the sky," GenAK says, his voice only making it as far as my seat. No one in the front of the chopper hears him. The fighter jet dips several hundred feet then rises rapidly, like the pilot doesn't have control. GenAK sits up again. "Hold up."

"What do I do?" TECH-chick shouts.

"What if whoever's in the jet doesn't know how to operate the guns?" I base hope on the sporadic flight pattern of the death machine.

"No way." GenAK repositions himself behind the gun and stares through his sights. "If someone knows how to get in the air, they know how to fire."

"Shouldn't we be going away from it then?" TECH-chick shifts her feet, sending our flight into an almost spin before she counters. ED dry heaves between his legs. High scores anchored to passing vehicles pass through our chopper at the same altitude and continue safely away from us.

"No!" GenAK looks ready to strangle TECH-chick for her

flying inability. "They might have sustained damage. Get me closer."

"Closer?" Both TECH-chick and I say together.

"To that thing?" I point to the airship bullet, ready to shred us.

"Closer?" ED lags a few seconds behind.

"I know where to shoot, but I have to be closer." GenAK winces with a hand at his side. He's not doing as well as he's been letting on.

"Bad idea," ED says, again agreeing with me.

"There are no good ideas." TECH-chick presses a pedal directing us to the A-10 and thrusts the forward gear.

"Side me up." GenAK waves a hand in a tight circle.

TECH-chick manipulates the floor pedals so GenAK's door and machine gun are directly facing the aircraft, which battles for level ground in the sky.

"One minute," he says with a hand on the trigger and one eye closed. "Just one minute."

"I can't hold this position all day. Shoot." I'm surprised she can hold it at all, considering none of us passed flight training to get here. TECH-chick dips the chopper then raises it again.

Lifting his head, GenAK hollers, "You can hold it one minute!"

The chopper steadies. GenAK returns his eye to the sights and squeezes the trigger. The bullets whir, invisible. We wait for some reaction from the not too distant jet, but nothing happens.

"Did you hit it?" TECH-chick looks over her shoulder to get a better view. The aircraft leans with her movement.

"Stop talking," he shouts, more toward his own armpit than anyone in particular.

The sky electrifies our tension. It binds us like a static charge. GenAK refocuses once more, peering with one eye, all concentration pointed at the jet. From where I sit, he targets the cockpit.

"It's the kid," GenAK shouts. "That prick's still after us."

"Shouldn't have agreed to anchor his score to Fails-A-Lot-Barbie," TECH-chick says.

"Would you two knock it off?" ED gags as if contents are trapped in his digital stomach.

"What did I do?" I say.

"The kid's more experienced than he let on if he can fly an A-10," GenAK says.

ED dry heaves when he opens his mouth to banter.

TECH-chick accidentally pushes the throttle forward while arguing. "Maybe he's just lucky."

"Steady!" GenAK shouts.

"Sorry," she yells over the constant gale of noise.

More ground vehicles are headed our way. On the horizon, golden scores race toward our blades. I press my eyes closed. Numbers might interfere with our flight, but they pass through with more still coming. One jeep has a rocket launcher mounted to the roof. *A rocket launcher.*

"Incoming," TECH-chick shouts. "You've got air *and* ground to worry about now."

"Can we use it? Like with the teenster-moms?" I ask.

"The who?" Everyone asks at once. No one else nicknamed the dead-group of chicks. And apparently none of them listen to a thing I say, since I've already thrown this term out there.

"She means draw fire in order to take out another target," ED says, his head still between his knees.

"Line us up between the jeep and the jet," GenAK says.

"On it." The chopper thrusts right, throwing me into GenAK despite the belt holding me in my seat. TECH-chick pushes the thing making us rise.

Strong arms wrap around me, holding me tight while the chopper tips my way. I don't resist or remind GenAK I actually have a functioning belt strap this time. I stare out the opening toward the ground below. It looks both too far and oddly close, what falling might feel like. My feet plant against the rubber mat on the floor. I push deeper into GenAK's hold.

Everything tips back to level. The warmth wrapped around me lifts, leaving extra cold where GenAK's arms had been, like a freezing imprint of the protection I'm now missing. Maybe he had hold of me to use me as a cushion to break his own fall if we hit.

"Tip us again. A little higher," GenAK says.

His hands are on his weapon, aimed toward the jet with the kid behind the controls. Bullets peck at the hull of our chopper.

"We're hit!" TECH-chick shrieks. The panic in her voice makes not just my skin feel cold, but my blood and brain too. "We're going down."

Everything freezes, even time. GenAK's finger moves slowest of all. *Load the dang gun.* Orange-blue flare of the bullets fire in the chamber, skimming through the air, and connect with the kid's covering. They have no impact on the kid. He's completely unharmed. His jet bounds and skips like little laughter ripples in the sky while we lose altitude.

It's only been seconds from the moment TECH-chick declares our doom, but it feels like we've been trapped in a time warp of bullet death and freefall for years. Heat whooshes so close to our crash landing, it pushes us sideways.

"What was that?" ED screams, lifting his head from between his knees.

Too close for comfort, the A-10 bursts into a shrapnel bomb at our side. The exposed openings can't protect us from the heat and fragments riding the deadly impact that's now pushing away from its accidental target. ED's hands cover his head without need. He's not in the open like those of us in the back. GenAK twists, covering me against his stomach, his back to the metal shards slicing toward us.

"It's alright," I say.

"Like hell it is," TECH-chick says. "If we survive landing, we've only narrowed the gap between us and those other vehicles, namely that jeep." She points to the horizon where a jeep speeds along the highway. I can see the driver inside. "And we've only managed a little over a hundred miles."

I'm relieved we gained any miles. The time wasted in figuring out how to handle the chopper felt like a progressless horror show. Trying to calculate miles in my head, it doesn't add up over perceived time lost. I'm sure the odometer, or whatever reads distance in a friggin' chopper, is reliable. Can we gain mileage from all the shaking and altitude gains and losses caused by TECH-chick's crap flying skills?

TECH-chick regains control of the chopper before we're road-smear, moving us ahead of the jeep. We're aligned above the driver, so we can't be shot if he gets such an idea.

"What if we climb up?" ED covers his face with his arms, and folds in half. His words sound like. "Wufu kaim."

"Go up, just go up," GenAK shouts in my ear. He has me completely engulfed in the cover of his body.

"We're damaged," TECH-chick says.

"Just do it!" I shout, despite the fact that I'm completely in the dark about this strategy. I figure if ED and GenAK are agreeing, it's probably our best option.

"Your funeral," TECH-chick says.

But, she's wrong. It's *our* funeral. We're all going to die here. The air burns hot where the jet once flew. Knowing the traitorous kid toasts in the fancy jet rubble comforts me. We pass through a cloud of waving heat and stench of burnt wires, gasoline, and fried everything. I cover my nose.

"There's no smell here," GenAK whispers in my ear. "Don't let anyone else see you do that."

My brow furrows. What's wrong with him? How can he not smell it?

"Now gun it forward, as fast as you can. We're going to get as far as we can until we fall out of the sky," GenAK orders TECH-chick.

She pushes the throttle forward so hard we're all thrown back, straining our necks to see what horrors are headed our way. Or we're headed for. "This'll never work."

No one argues. We all know she's right.

14

The engine sputters. "One of those bullets must have hit a gas tank," TECH-chick says.

"Lucky it didn't blow the whole rig." GenAK's back has small metal fragments sticking out, which I try to pull free without getting cut on the pieces myself. It's a total mess.

"That's only in movies, in real life the variables have to line up—"

ED is cut off by GenAK who screams so hard the veins in his forehead look near bursting. "This is not real life!"

ED lifts a hand to demand vocal space to argue.

"You're already dead." GenAK turns, stopping me from removing the shrapnel in his back. "We're all dead. Don't you get it?"

I get it. I feel it. Like parts of me don't belong together. Probably my thoughts, since that's the only part of any of us that's carried over from our previous lives. On the inside, I feel like I was one of those indoor recluses, the kind of person who never had a life.

"I don't know about you, but I want this second chance to go somewhere." TECH-chick battles the levers, pedals, and throttles with a tremble that starts in her slender thighs and continues to grow until it's a full-blown shake at her feet. She resorts to flipping switches, which we all know could turn off the rotating blades keeping us in the air.

"Don't do that!" I yell.

TECH-chick gives me a look of murder. "We're all about to experience permanent death. If you're not on board with that, jump the hell out. Now."

GenAK stares at TECH-chick in a way that burns my face for witnessing it, and I feel like I got stabbed with the piece of jet I pulled out of him. What does he see in her? I don't get it. She's not endearing. More like loud and biting with sharp pieces sticking out like barbed wire if anyone gets close. Sure, she's technically perfect physically. I stare at ED in an effort to get back at GenAK for staring at TECH-chick. *Stupid.* I want GenAK to look at me. *Look at me, Stupid. Not her.*

ED catches my stare and I break away. "We're all going to die," he says like it's a fact he read out of a history book. Not what my longing stare was hoping ED would reciprocate. Effort wasted.

I reel back, my spine against the rear seat. I quickly check to see if GenAK has a reaction. Other than leaning away from ED, nothing.

ED laughs and returns his head to between his knees, dry heaving.

"Sometimes I think you're not all that smart," I say holding out a bag in case he loses it.

"I'm highly educated," ED coughs.

"Not the same thing," GenAK shouts directly into ED's ear, causing ED to put a hand over the entire side of his face.

The chopper loses altitude like a rock dropped from the sky. The blades aren't doing a thing to hold us up. "We're losing her!" TECH-chick says.

"We're losing," ED clarifies.

"Shut up, ED!" GenAK yells.

"Can you crash on top of the jeep?" I say. The jeep races out of reach, then donut-style U-turns our direction for a second attempt. "You know, so they can't shoot us if we survive the crash?" The fact that I try to say all those words in a noisy, crashing, hormone-filled helicopter in the middle of a firestorm reigning outside means no one really hears or answers me.

Turbulence slams me into the back of TECH-chick's seat. My face slides, cheek streaking against the upholstery. Headphones stare at me from a box slid under the pilot's seat on the floor. "These were here the whole time?" I lift a pair.

Everyone stares at the earphones that could have saved us from yelling our throats raw. Then we hit.

No logic explains how we survive. I know this for a fact because ED explains to us in several ways and in diverse means. We're all lucky SOBs who should have coded the second our helicopter slams into the roof of the jeep.

Even luckier, everyone in or hanging on the jeep jumps from the vehicle.

"Quick. Everyone in the jeep before it veers off road," TECH-chick yells.

GenAK and Tech chick manage to unbuckle and swing down inside the jeep through the opened side doors like it's basic level parkour.

I'm still fumbling with my straps when ED scrambles in the back and stares out the opening. "How did they do that?"

"I don't know. They're perfect for each other." My throat's raw from all the screaming over loudness, and the words come out in ripples.

Emotions aren't in short demand in this computer world. What we lack in maturity we make up for with drama. What if I'm a pre-teen in real life? And I'm crushing on a thirty-year-old in his previous existence? How gross is that? *Please don't let me be a naïve pre-teen liking on a perve.* Worse, maybe I'm the old one! *Don't be a teenster-mom cougar!*

ED doesn't notice. Or maybe doesn't care. He dangles his feet even though we're still traveling high speeds for attempting to switch vehicles. I have little hope the chopper is going to remain lodged atop the jeep. The rocket launching device holds everything in a mangled metal catch for now. It can't last. The vehicle continues driving, mostly because we're all afraid to stop and wait for whatever comes next.

"Use the landing bar as a step down and slide through the windows. They're all open," ED hollers, instructing me how to transition.

I nod. My straps release. ED disappears into the jeep below. The chopper tilts to my side when I move. Every shift of my weight brings the wind-thrashed, temporarily-lodged helicopter much closer to toppling onto the racing highway below. Maybe if I try the side ED exited from. It's less wobbly.

Sucking in a deep breath I slide to the landing bar, then slip inside the window with the help of some strong hands. Secretly hoping it's GenAK, I'm disappointed when ED guides me through the window.

"You made it." ED sounds surprised.

TECH-chick sits behind the wheel, as usual. GenAK, at her side, alerts her to obstructions in the road and turns knobs on the dash. The longer they're together, the better they work. And it really pisses me off. I saw him first. Maybe I didn't like him right away, but I saw him, and it still counts for something.

Our vehicle tips to the driver's side. The chopper still lodged to the roof pulls the entire rig off its tires. I can't take any more crashing. Popping bolts spring from the roof and the launch device rips free. Our right side slams back to the road at the same time rotary blades spark and slash at the jeep. I cover my head. Within seconds of being sure we're heap bound, the chopper breaks loose, exploding behind us.

GenAK points to something off the highway. "What is that?"

"Where? I don't see anything," TECH-chick strains her neck, peering through smoke and flames toward what GenAK points at.

A lone gangly figure with short stature walks from the jet wreckage.

"You've got to be kidding me," GenAK says. "It's the kid."

ED and I bonk heads trying to fit through the gap between the seats to verify GenAK's statement. "No way," he says.

"How is that possible?" I ask. It's difficult not to yell every word after riding in the chopper. Everyone flinches at the loudness of each other's words in the relative quiet thrum of the jeep.

"What about cheat codes?" ED says. "TECH? You ever heard of that?"

"Sure, but, he's not TECH, is he? I can't see a GenCiv even knowing about cheat codes, much less hacking them."

"You can hack the game?" I ask. In the front seat GenAK stiffens. He immediately over-exaggerates a more relaxed pose to cover his reaction. "Can you hack levels, like level up without reaching your objective?"

"They have fail-safes for stuff like that." TECH-chick puts a hand on GenAK's knee. On his knee! Right in front of me. Like he needs a supporting squeeze. TECH-chick takes her eyes off the road to look at me out of the corner of her eye. When she returns her stare to the road she flinches. "He's running."

Everyone looks out the front window. He's indeed running—toward us. As we're driving toward him. When the rules of chicken were being explained, the kid must have been in the bathroom, because he can't win a head-on collision with a jeep.

A siren blares over the sound of tires against highway seams. "What's our mileage?" I ask.

"Not enough," TECH-chick says. "There's no way we're even close to two hundred miles."

"But, the kid was in a jet…" I look at each of them in the car in turn, then reach in front of TECH-chick and force the wheel to head straight for the kid.

"What are you doing?" she yells.

"He's still on our team, in our group. Pool the miles." Move faster, jeep. We're out of time. "He was in a freaking jet for twenty minutes or more before TECH here learned to fly the chopper straight."

"I saved your—"

"He tried to kill us," ED shouts, trying to pull me away from the wheel.

The leaderboard gleams on every billboard within sight. Codes one through ten of the players to beat. GenAK isn't listed at all this time. None of us are. Not a great motivator this round. Keeping my eyes off the screen, the movement of which I've come to refer to as a 'motivational scene' consisting of family, friends, media, and corporations. All wait to celebrate the winner of eternal life, wearing their metal, robotic body. Right now I need to pass this level, not fantasize about what's on the other side of this murder-fest.

"We need him. He's not a cheat code. He doesn't want to die. He managed the miles on his own." I point to the greasy hair and flailing limbs running pell-mell toward us. "Why else would he do that?"

GenAK lifts ED's hands from my arms. "She's right. We have to pick up the kid. He's with us."

TECH-chick slaps my hands away. "Let me do it." She presses the gas harder in the direction of the kid. The blaring siren gets louder and faster.

"What about anyone who isn't leveled up? Do they keep existing here? In this hell hole?" ED asks. "Until they die or something?"

"I don't think so," GenAK says. "See those clouds rolling in?"

Far in the distance a greenish yellow haze boils in the sky. "Those are clouds?" ED stammers. "Looks like poisoned gas."

"Same thing," GenAK says.

ED slaps his forehead. "Nothing's the same thing. Be specific about the danger pressing upon you and you might find a solution in the distinction, wherein if it all blurs together there are too many variables to solve."

He has a point. Level-up methods vary from gamescape to gamescape, making it impossible to anticipate a win. Specifics are exactly what I want. And assurances. At least one thing I can count on.

"Shut up, smartass," TECH-chick shouts, providing that one thing I can count on. "We don't have to figure it out. We're picking up the kid."

In the near distance, the kid turns and runs away. Probably sure we're coming to run him down and why not?

"If we run him over do we get his miles?" TECH-chick asks. Her fingers twist around the wheel in eagerness to splatter the kid across the grill.

"Can't risk it," GenAK says before I have the chance.

"I don't think we can risk taking him with us to the next level," ED says.

"You figure that one out yourself. I'm leveling up," GenAK says.

I have to agree with him. With such a simple solution in front of us, even though he's a total traitor, it's not worth the uncertainty of not taking the kid with us. For now.

"Hurry. That siren isn't getting any slower."

The clouds are coming fast as well. The jeep makes a sharp turn seconds before plowing into the back of the kid. "Go AK," TECH-chick shouts. She slams the brakes as GenAK leaps from his seat. He runs after the kid. The siren bleats a single constant howl.

"If we're doing it this way, we better all run for it," ED says.

"He's right." The driver's door opens and TECH-chick runs after GenAK.

"Are you kidding me?" ED complains before jumping out and running after the rest of our group.

I'm a second behind. My knees buckle when I hit the ground, but I steady myself and push through the blaring siren and fatigue. I have to level up.

GenAK jumps at the kid, tackling him to the turf. The yellow cloud rolls closer. TECH-chick falls on top of GenAK followed by ED in true dog-pile fashion. Can I make the pile before the cloud covers them?

"GenE is our anchor!" ED screams. "We have to have her." He reaches a hand back for me.

The cloud touches TECH-chick's calves where she lands at an odd angle. Her screams trip my progress. Her voice rises above even the constant bleating siren. "Ruuuuun!" Her hand reaches out to me. She doesn't like me. It's all over her face. She'd rather leave me behind, only she can't. I leap for their hands.

The pit of my stomach sucks through the earth in the same moment I reach the group.

15

A digital screeching follows me like a breadcrumb trail. Green and black are the only colors I can see. Coding. Everything hurts. It must mean failure. Then I realize I have my eyes closed. Opening them doesn't improve the landscape. I have no idea where I am. Bodies lay everywhere around me, next to me, on top of me.

These bodies haven't coded, or disappeared, which relieves and concerns me. I'm happy to know I won't simply disappear out of this level, but being a rotting-ambiance-carcass for eternity doesn't sound a lot better.

Through a gap of lifeless limbs, I survey the scene around me. Blood pools in thick puddles, streaming from stacks of twisted limbs and slack jaws attached to clouded-over eyes. Steam rises from the red rivulets joining small rivers and pools of copper-scented liquid. The air tastes like steel wool set aflame with battery acid.

"It gets worse every time," ED says somewhere out of view.

"ED!" I push against the weight pinning me under corpses. "Where are you?"

The load above me lightens. "Oh, sorry. You're under there?" Standing over me, he wipes blood from the front of his green uniform. He's dressed for war.

"Where's everyone else?"

"I don't know." He rolls a man-corpse off my body.

"Why aren't these people coding?" I ask. "They're still lying here. Dead." A worse thought crosses my mind. "They're dead, right?" I cannot handle these things suddenly animating and attacking me. Zombies are not cool.

He pushes his hair out of his face. It's grown since the last level. The blood from his uniform, now on his hands, leaves thin streaks across his forehead and greases his hair with the red mess of ended players.

"GenE!"

ED and I spin. The sound of my name comes from between two buildings not so far off. Across a courtyard of blackened craters, cobbles from the street pile aside like drifted snow. And bodies. Everywhere there are whole and partial bodies, charred and gashed, bleeding into the cracks left from whatever caused the awful scene.

"Where are we?" I ask ED as we both visually scan dark doorways for the source of the voice.

A hand reaches up from the side of my feet. "Don't leave me." It clings to my ankle. Instinct triggers a shake-it-off response. Everything here horrifies me. I have no desire to look on the face belonging to the hand. I expect a mangled, bloody face of death. Yet I force myself to check, to be sure.

"Kid." So, he made it, along with whoever remains in the shadows between the building. I hope it's GenAK. If there's only one more person from our group, let it be him.

"Hurry," the person between the buildings says again.

"Grab his arms. We can't leave him here," I say.

ED grumbles, but finds the kid's other arm. We drag him like a soggy noodle over the body field to the gap in the buildings. TECH-chick and GenAK are there. But it's not all good news.

"What're you wearing?" ED asks GenAK, who is clearly in a different type of uniform than the rest of us. TECH-chick wears the same colors as GenAK.

I point to the different uniforms. "What does it mean?"

"We're on opposing teams," GenAK says.

The smirk on TECH-chick's face slaps me back to immaturity. I'm pretty sure, if she was armed at this moment, she'd shoot me in the forehead, too.

"You're with her?" I scoff like he gets to choose how he spawns.

The kid wheezes from the ground. "What? We supposed to kill each other now?" He obviously has some sort of disadvantage. Maybe because he's a freaking traitor and this war zone level has it out for traitors. "And everyone is okay with it because that's the game here? Different teams, different rules?" He coughs blood after he speaks.

We all stare at his bloody hand.

"No one's killing anyone," ED says, ever the diplomat. "Not yet. We have to figure out what's going on. Our objectives."

"The bodies aren't coding. What does that mean?" I say.

"Maybe the first levels were like do-overs," the kid says.

131

"You know, if you fail there you can start again on one of those levels."

"Why would you say that?" GenAK looks at him skeptically. No love lost between them.

"Because I am way too good at flying a fighter jet for someone who's never done it before," he says. What I hear is 'memory loss', a shared trait to some extent.

"Kid has a point," ED agrees.

"So we were fine? We would have been fine?" TECH-chick asks. "We didn't need to go balls-to-wall insane to try to win a level? We could have had a do-over? Gotten more skills? Been way more awesome at it?" Her voice rises.

"The point is we made it. We leveled up and we can do it again," GenAK says.

"Can we?" I ask. "Look at this place. It's worse than anything we've seen." Smolder pockets litter the air. Blood spatter and char mar all surfaces. Bone fragments and other non-identifiable shrapnel embed in walls and ground near what appears to be the strike zones. Craters of ash and bone with crispy muscle matter turning to blackened flesh and singed cloth the further you radiate from the center of each strike area.

"I don't know. I see bombed city center." ED nods to the charred holes in the cobblestoned street and the fountain in pieces. Not to mention the rivers of blood. "We should be safe here until we figure out how to level up again."

"How're we going to find that out? We're on opposing teams!" I say. "That can't be good."

In response, GenAK bites his lip. I have no idea how to take that. Everyone takes a moment to contemplate their place in this new gamescape and where we all stand.

TECH-chick rubs the space between her shoulder and neck. ED looks down and the kid smiles despite the fact he coughed up blood. *Punk.* "We travel together until we meet someone who can tell us what to do. Whoever isn't wearing the same color uniform as the person we find hides," ED suggests.

"Because that'll work." GenAK bends down to rifle through the coat pockets, pants, and satchel of a deceased soldier.

"What're you doing?" ED asks as though GenAK is somehow violating the memory of complete strangers.

"Looking for a radio, transmission, notes, orders, clues, hints. Anything." He holds up a two-way radio. "I'm not going to wait around to be shot as a traitor for being seen with the enemy."

"Whoa." I stand in front of GenAK, blocking him from taking off without me. "You're going to leave? How will we know if you're alright, if you level up?"

ED appears fine with the new plan. Eager even. He helps GenAK gather more supplies from bodies wearing blue uniforms.

The kid scans the bodies on the ground, grabs his green vest, then punches the closest blue clad corpse in the shoulder. "No dead green."

"They're in the courtyard, idiot," TECH-chick says.

"We're not trained for this," I say, blocking GenAK's path. He tries to sidestep away from me. I match him. "You can't expect us to survive without you."

"Yes, I can." He speaks so matter-of-factly, I almost believe I can survive this level.

"How will I find you?" I know I sound desperate, afraid, and a fool. I can't help it. I win nothing without him. He's been with me from the start. What if he's the only reason I'm still alive?

"You've got the kid." GenAK nods toward the person I trust the least. "He's handy and seems to have an endless supply of health packs."

ED points to his own chest like, 'aren't you forgetting the most valuable resource'.

"Your team blew our team to smithereens?" The kid stands at the maw of the buildings, taking in the death toll.

"We all arrived at the same time, remember?" ED risks a hand on the kid's shoulder, pulling the kid back while stepping forward himself. The kid moves so the gesture doesn't connect. ED steps forward anyway. "We weren't on either team when that happened. We're not enemies yet."

"We will be. It'll be us, and it'll be them." The kid turns his stare on TECH-chick and GenAK. She is all too quick to return the war-stare. They look ready to seek vengeance on deaths they've had no part in up until the last three minutes.

He's right. The team whose uniform we're wearing definitely lost this battle. The opposing team lost a few men stationed in alleyways—the point men, the ones painting the target maybe. But their side won.

"Give me the radio," the kid demands of GenAK.

"No."

ED swipes the air in front of GenAK for the device, a good three inches shy of coming close to grabbing it. Obviously not skilled athletically, which isn't comforting knowing he's now a big part of my survival on this level.

"Give it to me." The kid stamps a foot.

"How will it help you?" GenAK says holding the radio over his head, out of reach from the two idiots wearing the same green I do. "It's not from your side."

"Exactly." The kid steps toward GenAK with taunting surety he can obtain the radio. We all calculate his error by the size difference between them. GenAK broadens beastly and the kid... well, someone who is referred to as 'the kid' generally portrays small, weak, needy traits. "I can use the radio to infiltrate your blood-lusting unit and give them a taste of their own medicine."

"You're not going to do that," I say more to win points with GenAK and possibly encourage him helping us. I actually think the kid has a valid point with the whole 'use the radio against them' tactic, but can't figure out where to throw my chips in this game. I want to not die. "We don't even know whose side we're on. Who we're supposed to be fighting for." Based on this whole experience so far, I'm convinced we're all fighting for ourselves.

ED and the kid both gesture at their uniforms, like it's obvious whose side we're on, and they're right. I know it, but I don't want to fight GenAK. It negates the fact I saved his life.

TECH-chick tugs on GenAK's arm, trying to get him to draw back out of the alley and leave us with the dead. She catches one boot in the strap of one of her former team's packs and almost trips. GenAK, the gentleman he is, reaches for her, catching her before she falls. I look at the ground. Who wants to see that?

I notice a health pack, or the corner of one, and flinch. The kid notices my movement and follows my gaze to what I'm staring at. He sees it too. It's how he keeps surviving. Hit your-self with a health shot before certain doom and you can survive anything. He survived an A-10 jet falling out of the sky and exploding on the ground, so I'm pretty sure it makes you invincible, at least for a while.

"I don't trust the kid," I shout before GenAK runs out of the alley. He stops and turns to face me.

"Ouch," the kid says. "Thanks for the confidence boost."

"They have failsafes, background checks," ED says. "Criminals, mentally disturbed people, anyone with anger problems or control issues, power seekers, or abusers. They could never make the donor program based on personal history alone."

I stare at ED, wondering if he's genuinely that naïve, or simply has a need to regurgitate things he's read in articles. Movement out of the corner of my eye distracts me from gaping at ED's defense of the kid. GenAK leaves before I plead my full case.

"Not every criminal is convicted," I shout. My eyes shift the slightest from GenAK to TECH-chick. I pray he sees it, notices the warning. She's next in line on my 'do not trust' list.

Echoes rise up the sides of both buildings. Dust and brick fragments fall down on our heads.

"Feeling loved," the kid says, rich with sarcasm. His eyes are tractor beams on the health pack.

Neither of us goes for it yet. We're waiting, but I'm not yet sure what we're waiting for.

16

"**N**ot all criminals are identified? Really? That's what you think of me?" the kid asks.

TECH-chick runs deeper into the shadows of the buildings, away from the burnt-out center. GenAK follows behind with his radio in hand. I'm certain they'll make contact within minutes with whoever listens on the other end of the signal. Knowing TECH-chick, she'll report enemy survivors before we're ready to defend ourselves.

"ED, you're in charge of the health pack," I say, keeping my gaze locked in on the kid.

"Is that because of my undiagnosed criminal intent?" the kid asks.

"What health pack?" ED looks confused. For a scholar he's an idiot sometimes. I point to the white corner where a triangle of red peeks below the canvas flap. "How'd AK miss that?"

"My guess?" I look back at the long vacant alley. "He didn't. He knows we're going to need it."

The kid steps against the wall, his face in my face. "Am I unfit for duty, General? Based on my personal history and tendency toward violence? Because I'm pretty sure that rules you out, too." The kid grabs my arm.

"Don't touch me." I pull away so sharply it draws him off balance. "What I said was a message. I only hope it was received."

"Great. Already speaking code and we don't even know who we're actually fighting." The kid crosses his arms and kicks a dead body's stray hand, which thuds back to the earth without resistance. He then stomps ahead of us, entering the wreckage of the center without being phased by the carnage.

ED grabs the white and red pack and catches up with me. "I think I could be good at code," he says.

"I'm counting on it," I say.

"Where to?" The kid stops at the opening of the courtyard.

"From the direction the bodies are laying, I'd guess they were trying to get…" I turn to match the general flow of the massacre. "There. Then they were hit without warning." I point toward stone pillars appearing to open to a passageway between tight buildings before reaching open fields. My hope is there are some foxholes in those fields and they were headed for cover, because otherwise we're on the losing side with no hope of winning.

"We're crossing back through there?" ED asks.

"Is it the smell that bothers you or the overall deathness?" I ask.

"Smell? What smell?" ED asks. GenAK wasn't lying. No one's nose functions?

The kid turns toward me, but catches himself. I know I've messed up. "Testing you," I say. I flourish a little too much, trying to sell the lie. "Everyone passes." I catch the kid sneaking an evaluative glance at me before turning away. "Hand out those boost shots."

ED clicks open the case. Five shots. Like last time.

"One each, save the spares for in case we find trouble," I say.

"How soon till they call us in, you think?" the kid asks, nodding back toward where TECH-chick and GenAK retreat.

"Stop wasting time." I rip the plastic from my needle. "Shoot up and run for the far pillar. Find your own path." I thrust the metal pick into my thigh. I have no idea the best location to stab, but do know my heart could burst if I try shooting myself in the chest again.

ED cradles the health pack in his arms after jamming his needle into his thigh. The kid takes it in the arm. I maybe should have waited to see what he does before deciding on where to stab myself. He has more experience than I do.

A green light on each of our vests lights up. A low buzzing sound accompanies the light. "What's this?"

"Can't be good." The kid runs, side-stepping torsos, limbs, and rock mounds.

"He's right." ED tries to pick his way along the same path as the kid. "These craters look like where mines were buried to you?" His tone implies that's exactly what he thinks they are.

"Now they do." I stop running the path I've chosen, which is relatively clear of debris. "Dangit, ED. Are there mines here?"

"I don't know, but it's something to consider."

"Consider? We're in a war zone. There's no stopping to think."

The kid reaches the far side of the body field. No mines or traps have been set off in his path. "My light's flashing," he hollers back.

Both ED and I look at our vests. Sure enough, they're flashing. Static crackling nearby catches my ear. Sucking in all my bravery, I run for the sound of a radio transmission. I backtrack as close as possible to craters and debris piles, making sure to avoid any untouched spaces for fear they harbor triggers.

"Likelihood for buried mines is slim," the kid says.

"I didn't see you stepping on open roadway," I remind him.

"I'm not an idiot."

The static sound continues from a greenshirt radio. It's transmitting a signal. Twisting a knob on the top of it doesn't clean up the sound.

"Bring it," ED says. He's already at the kid's side.

The flashing green light in our vests turns solid. The buzz becomes a constant hum. Looking skyward for any indication of attack, or explanation for the vest light, I reach for a door by one of the pillars.

The kid taps his light, presses against the circular glow, flicks it.

"And?" ED's eyebrows are high on his head in full 'I judge you to be foolish' mode.

"We haven't blown up and no sky torpedoes have struck," he says.

"Sky torpedoes? Really?" I say.

"Us crim-in-als," the kid speaks with a slack-jawed yokel accent. "Don't know no dif-fer-ence, tween a water rocket and sky ter-pee-doh."

"Knock it off you two." ED grabs the transmitter from my hands.

There's no way I'm as immature as the kid. How dare ED lump me in with him like that? "I've got the radio," I insist, whiffing air inches from ED's control over my find.

ED moves it out of my reach and slaps my hand down.

"Hey!"

"Hold on, I've got something." Adjusting the knob in minuscule increments, ED stumbles on a transmission.

Your objective is to find and destroy the enemy. In order to proceed in this game, you must be the only color standing when the siren alarms. It is possible to have a total loss of level. In such a case, the level is wiped and we start over with fresh recruits willing to do what it takes to get the job done.

"What does that mean?" The kid pushes between us, crouching down like he's the one man out of the huddle.

"It means we have to get out of here." ED shoulders a military pack, one he wasn't wearing earlier. When he turns around there's charred, burned skin still clinging to the pack's side. He pulled it off a body. Literally.

"Total loss of level?" I point to the open courtyard. "There's the opposite suits in the alleyway. You think we're fresh recruits?"

"Status upon our arrival doesn't really matter. The point is, we have to get out of here before Captain General"—he means

AK—"and his SteampunkAss girlfriend"—TECH-chick—"come back to finish us off," ED says.

"His girlfriend?" I cross my arms and stare at the alley where GenAK and TECH-chick disappear. "No way."

"He's right. Those two have combined combat, hotwiring, tech-hijacking skills and what do we have? A flunkie, the guy from Lit, and a parolee," the kids says.

"So you admit you're a con-artist?" I turn toward the kid.

"I'm not the con." The look he gives me leaves me bare and exposed. I fold my arms over my chest hoping to appear bolder than I am in the moment. It also conceals my forearm. He smiles at my subtle reaction, which makes me even more upset with him. "I'm saying we don't compare to them on this level. It doesn't play to our skills."

"Exactly." ED surprises us both. Neither the kid nor I ever expect ED on board with the fact we're totally screwed. "We need to play the level to our skills."

"I think what the kid said was opposite of what you said, in a, 'that makes no sense, you're high on motor fuel' kind of way."

"What are we good at?" ED says. "I can work patterns, codes, and probabilities." He waits, like we're supposed to morph into assets for a combat situation. "Kid?" ED prods.

"I don't know... maybe find an enemy uniform and play them."

"Like you played us last world?" ED's hand on my shoulder stops me from getting in the kid's space. Nine-year-old me wants to beat the crap out of the punk kid.

"I'm good at it," he shrugs.

"He's right." ED takes the leadership role, which makes me

uncomfortable. I don't like anyone in control of my future other than me. On the flip side, it's nice not telling the kid what to do and ED seems to have himself under control for the time being. "You need an enemy uniform." ED stares out across the body-filled courtyard to the alleyway we ran from. "There were a couple less damaged suits in there."

"You want me to go back there? Alone?" the kids asks.

"Yes. Quickly," I say.

"Are you kidding me? We just ran from there." He points at his vest with the solid green light. In all honesty, since it isn't beeping, I forgot about the fact we're lit up.

"I'm not kidding. Move." ED stands up, suddenly looking the image of authority.

"You'll ditch me. Leave me behind for the others to come back for."

"How would that benefit us?" ED asks.

The kid's eyes search the cobblestone steps in front of the pillar. His breathing gets faster, more ragged. Then he nods his head, psyching himself up. "Okay, you're right. I'll do it. Wait for me." He runs across the debris of expended life. Like before, the kid is careful to not step on any ground that's not broken or charred already. No point in risking it.

"I actually *was* going to ditch him," ED confesses once the kid moves out of earshot. "But it's also true that it won't help us. I'm not sure how traitors factor into this game, but I wouldn't put it past him to turn us in if we did ditch him."

"Good to know," I say. There's no guarantee he won't turn on us either way. The kid is nothing if not a survivalist, willing to do what it takes to preserve himself.

"So, your strength?" ED asks. Lack of confidence in my assets penetrates every syllable he speaks.

I throw my arms up in surrender. "I have absolutely no strength, no purpose, no point in all this." And I have absolutely no idea what I am, but I'm not an E.

"You've got to have something," he says. "You made it this far."

There's no reading ED. I suspect he distrusts me by the way he says 'you made it this far'. None of us trust each other, yet we're stuck together by choice. It's the weirdest sense of dependence we have upon one another. "I'm still scratching my head at that fact."

"I can't have a member of my team who has nothing to offer," ED says. His tone assumes I'm hiding something, like I have some secret skill I haven't confided. Also, I'm not a member of *his* team? If anything, he's a member of mine. And as far as stuff to offer, why does he deserve anything I have to offer? The nerve.

"For now, see if you can salvage some working weapons," ED commands me. "Keep thinking on your strength. Or anything you bring to this team." Without GenAK to keep ED's ego in check, he's a total ass.

I don't have to justify myself to these guys. I don't have to prove my value. Still, I wade out in the blood and gore to find any non-totally-destroyed weapons. There's not anything functional I can see. Everything's been charred, melted, bubbled, or burned. There are a lot of bubbly-burn marks, not just on the bodies. The weapons have that mark, too. Like something was dropped on them and ate through the top layer of clothing and skin, leaving whatever was left to puddle and pool. I find one pistol underneath a body, super gross to move.

The kid barrels back toward the pillar, running much faster than when he left. "They're coming back," he explains in an exhaled breath as he passes me. He turns and looks behind himself, at me, when I don't follow right after him. "A lot—all with green lights like ours."

I look at the light on my vest. Centered. Right over my heart. "It's a target," I say.

"What happens when you get shot?" the kid asks.

I raise the gun, aim it at his chest. His eyes go wide. I want to laugh at how ridiculous he looks all scared, instead I pull the trigger.

"What the...?" ED races down the steps to where the kid knocks his head against the stairs. "What did you do?"

"Testing a theory."

"You shot our own guy," ED says. "I did not tell you to do that." He reaches the kid and bends down to try to revive him.

Tell me to do that? If ED isn't careful, I'll shoot him too. TECH-chick's less stable than me. What kind of danger is GenAK in? Can he trust her? Of course not. If she shoots him to test a theory, I'll kill her twice.

The kid shakes in ED's hands. "You really shot him!"

"Yeah." I nod. "I did."

The green light on his chest flashes, flicks.

"His light," ED says.

"Now we find out if it never comes back on or if we have second chances here."

"Don't you think we could have tested that out on the enemy?" ED shouts at me.

I look around, nervous anyone could have heard him. And remember the kid told me the enemy is coming. They're coming back. And I've wasted our escape time on a stupid revenge-fueled theory. "Probably could have, yeah," I say.

The kid convulses, his eyes solidly searching my face. "I had to know if you were the enemy," I explain to his pleading, hurt-filled eyes. Or maybe it's vengeance leaking through his overly wide pupils. "It's hard to tell with you."

His brow wrinkles with things he can't manage to say. His vest-light blinks off.

"What did you do?" ED asks again, standing so the kid's motionless body joins the rubble of the dead.

"We've been over this," I say. "I needed to know something, and this was the best way to find out."

ED runs his fingers over his tight crop, stretching his fore-head up. "No. It's not."

"Do you trust him?" I point to the kid.

"I sure as hell don't trust you right now."

"We have to go," I say.

"Now?" ED lifts the limp body of the kid like he expects us to drag it with us.

"Yeah. The opposing team is coming." ED looks at me like I'm making a joke. "The real enemy." The kid's body crumbles to sand. Black and green numbers fall to the cobblestone and red murks at our feet. I stand from my crouch. "And now we know."

"Know what?" ED backs away from the code strings as they gather and fly into the air reforming in front of the alley where we first congregated on this level. "That, thanks to you, the kid will never fully trust us, so we can't trust him?"

"If that's what you prefer to take from this. Sure." I indicate the swirling pattern materializing into kid shape. "Or that, thanks to our boosters, we can come back." All three of us boosted. How long do they last? Maybe I'll get a chance to test that theory later.

"Do we wait for him to reform into something?" ED asks. "Where's the code going?"

"How should I know?"

The strands of green and black arc and dive for the ground nearest the alleyway. They pile into feet, which form legs, and a torso fully clothed in a uniform of blue.

"Was he wearing the enemy uniform when he ran back?" ED asks. The kid had been looking for enemy colors to put on in an effort to trick the opposing side. I can't recall if he was wearing anything he'd found, and what he's wearing now materializes as if pressed and steamed.

"I don't think so…"

"He came back as the enemy!" ED grabs my shoulder and pulls me higher on the platform, away from the courtyard and out of the open. "Do you suppose he remembers anything?"

"Does it matter? We can win this thing," I say.

"How?" ED asks.

"We can shoot the other team. Guilt-free."

ED drops his head between his shoulders, not hiding the fact he presumes I'm an idiot. "That's been the point from the beginning."

"No." I lift his head in my hands. "We can shoot them and

not kill them," I say. "They regenerate, if they've had a shot, and switch sides. We're not murderers." More importantly, if TECH-chick tries to kill GenAK, he'll come back to me.

"You're right."

"GenAK, TECH-chick, and even the kid…"

"Wait. What if they don't have a health shot? For that matter, how many regenerations do we get?" ED peers around the pillar we're tucked behind. "What if it's one and done?"

ED gives me a distrusting glance, probably hoping I don't try any more scientific methods of satisfying my curiosity again anytime soon. At least not on him. "I guess if that's the case, we let ourselves get killed," I say and swallow hard. I don't like that plan. Actually, I hate it.

"But how do we know?" ED looks at the gun still in my hand. "I don't want to get shot to find out."

A non-distinct person in blue appears behind ED from out of nowhere. I panic, raise my weapon and fire, nailing the enemy smack in the center of the forehead. I'm a dang good shot. Where did I learn that skill? ED and I both look at the weapon in my hand. Maybe I have a strength to bring to the fight after all.

"What the hell! I said I don't want to get shot!" Obviously he didn't see the lurker behind him. He must have thought I was aiming for him and missed. *Pfft.* As if I'd miss.

The person drops to its knees then collapses on its face. ED turns, staring at the body, waiting for it to code green and reappear in one of our uniforms. "Why isn't anything happening?"

"The bigger question is where did it come from and are there more?"

"No. The question is definitely why isn't it coding. You killed it. Why hasn't it changed?"

I touch the strap on ED's shoulder. "The health boosters."

ED adjusts his pack, protective, like I'm going to take it. "What about them?"

"What if the boosters were from the other team?" Everything complicates and compounds, I can't keep track of all the variables. "We all shot up, and when I shot the kid, he wasn't invincible." On the previous level, the boosters prevented us from dying at all. But the kid coded for a second, even with the serum in his system. "Maybe the boosters were issued to the blue team. And that's why he regenerated…"

"Can we shoot people or not?" ED pushes his dirty hands back into his hair, tight against his head as if he's trying to smooth out his confusion and press his thoughts into line.

"We have to get shot to figure out if it only goes one way."

"Nope. Not doing it," ED backs away from me, staying low, like threats could come from anywhere. "The risk isn't verified. The kid's already sort of an anomaly. I mean, last level? I'm still not sure he's not a plant."

I consider testing the theory on ED, but I don't want to die to test a theory either. "So now what?" I ask. "We know the enemy's coming from more than one direction, and we still don't know if we can shoot GenAK and TECH-chick without harming them."

"Let's assume, for now, we can't," ED says.

I nod. TECH-chick still has an upper hand over me. She knows it, too.

"We find a place to hide, watch what everyone does, and go from there."

"Like cowards? We're going to hide?" I mumble "We're never going to win that way." My hand paws the gun, which I've holstered in my belt for the time being.

"Climb," ED commands me again and it's all I can do to not turn my weapon on him, too.

17

The outer walls of the courtyard don't have a lot in the way of cover to provide a secure hiding location. It's basically a shell in which our team was dumb enough to get trapped.

ED pushes me up a broken pillar near the outer edge of the walls on the opposite side from the alley. Once I'm halfway up the pillar, I pull myself the rest of the way to the top. Bodies litter the tops of walls and pillars of this circular massacre site. Whatever struck these people wasn't contained to ground level.

I extend an arm down to ED. "Come on."

He struggles for footings with no one below him for leverage. On the roof of the outer wall, we both lay flat on our stomachs and take in the landscape. Smoke billows in the courtyard as well as in the roadways beyond. Low buildings, either linked by stone walls or built so tightly they depend on each other for support, stretch out beyond the smoldering center. Everything has an ancient European appeal. Aside from the char, smoke, and smell of death.

"Total level annihilation," ED whispers.

"Looks that way." I jut my chin toward craters pocked every ten to twenty feet. "What do you think those are?"

"If I had to guess…" He's not guessing at all. ED calculates, fingers wagging in the air like he's tallying dust particles. "Each detonation is spaced as close as possible with minimal overlap and maximum damage."

"But the buildings are barely damaged. It's the roads and people blown to pieces."

ED stares at the buildings in front of us. There are holes where something blasted through at least one wall of each building, but none of them are leveled. On the ground are heaps and mounds of uniforms, both green and blue.

"Is this normal? Like, does the level start like this for everyone?" I ask.

ED's fingers jiggle in his calculating way. "It gives me an idea."

I point. "Does it include the massive swarm of blue uniforms and their glowy green vest lights?" The far side of the courtyard fills with suit after suit, accompanied by none other than the kid.

"You had to shoot him." ED shifts his weight nervously. His fingers wag more severely. I assume he's calculating our odds. I can also conclude our odds suck, because he pauses several times after only three counts and starts over. His finger-pacing makes me nervous. And the waiting. The time it's taking ED to come up with a plan is going to be the bullet in the vest neither of us wants. I pace to match ED.

The next building over stands close enough to jump to its low roof. We have to stand to run, which will give away our position. "What do we do?"

"For now?" His fingers stop moving long enough to look up and see how close the enemy line is.

Duh. I nod.

"We stay here. If we're spotted, we jump to that building and test the whole getting shot thing." He twists to remove his pack without drawing attention from below. ED unlatches the clip on the white and red case, palms both health shots, and hands me one. "Just in case we need more."

I close my fist around the health boost. There's no way out of this. Searching the roofline we're on, I notice weapons nearby, clutched in dead hands. The persons stationed on the roof prior to us didn't survive. Confidence drains from me.

ED tucks and rolls in the direction of the nearest body.

"What are you doing?" I whisper scream.

"Getting backup." He puts a hand on a machine gun. "We have an objective, too."

"You're never going to take them all out. And what if you hit one of ours?" Mostly my concern belongs to GenAK. Not so much TECH-chick or the kid.

"They aren't 'ours' anymore," he says, rolling onto his stomach and sighting-in the ever increasing crowd below. "This gun works weird, the laser shines, but the trigger—" He squeezes three times on the trigger.

"You can't do that," I almost yell above the sound of a whisper. "If that had fired we'd be dead already. Think!"

"Yeah, but why won't it work? We're defenseless up here."

"Shhh. Keep your voice down." I peer over the ledge of the

wall, hoping no one can hear us over the thunder of their ranks filing in. No, wait. The thrum is different. It's aerial.

I look up.

ED takes his finger off the trigger again. The thrum remains.

"It's a target painter," I say. "Aim it down there and keep pulling that trigger."

"I figured that out, but thanks for the redundancy." ED hoists the thing on his shoulder. It looks like he thinks he looks cool, but in real life, he's just a stretched man whose worth is dependent on a degree, holding a weapon he has no knowledge about.

I could punch him in the ear right now. He doesn't need to prove he thought of it first. *Target the dang enemy before we paint ourselves as a target on accident.*

"Are we too close to the kill zone?" I ask.

BOOM!

Our wall disintegrates, exploding out from under us. We blast back against the nearest building. I hit a window, which bashes my shoulder as the rest of me breaks through the already damaged wooden frame. "ED?" I scream. "You, idiot!"

The buzzing in my head isn't as bad as the silence outside of it. I crawl to the opening in the wall and stare skyward. Blue and nothing else. No sign of aircraft.

Where's ED? The ground spills with new carnage with bright fresh red among the pomegranate jellied mess from before. GenAK might have been in that group. The window I've blasted through is seven feet from the cobbled street. I drop to ground level. Stabbing ice attacks my heels, races through my shins and pools in my knees. It stings. But I'm alive so I grit my teeth and bear the pain of landing solidly on my feet.

None of the blue suits are coding. No strings of black and green race each other for a new spawning location. "No one's coding…" ED. Where is he? "No one's coding!" What if ED already changed over to the blue uniforms? That could happen. Right? "ED!"

I still can't hear anything. My ears are broken. The bomb broke my ears. A cloud slowly passes overhead. It's not dark in a bad omen sense, but it's not white or fluffy. A darker shade of death claims the scenery. The courtyard is the same as it was when we spawned here. Limbs and burning flesh.

We caused this damage. ED and me.

Stumbling, I walk toward the open circle. The steps aren't entirely covered over with corpses. I pick my way down the three shallow ledges to the base of it all.

GenAK, TECH-chick, the kid. They're all in there. Somewhere. Or what's left of them.

"This whole thing—it's made up." I turn and face the buildings still standing beyond the courtyard. They're tightly packed and beautiful as they crumble from age like they don't even know a bomb devastated the real estate to the south. "What's the point? I don't want to survive this. I don't want to be here, living in this mess. What kind of a world is this?" I extend my hand over the heaps and blue suits on top of green uniforms, over broken stone. "This? Anyone who survives this… what good are they? This isn't right to keep in your head." The word *this* sounds like nothing. It's a throw away word, but it keeps rolling over and over in my head. *This, this, this…*

I realize I'm no longer holding a gun. I should be. Where's my gun? I'll test the uniform theory myself. Find a gun.

Digging through the mangled bodies proves difficult. It's not as easy as it seemed. This hand goes to this torso. It's much more. These limbs are tangled and the skin melted together. Move one and a domino effect crashes down on the rest. Skin ripping here, cracking, popping there. Crinkle fried clothing disintegrates at my touch.

I pull back. I can't do this.

"Help me." A voice.

"Where? Where are you?"

"Help."

I run to the sound, but lose it. "Say it again. I'm coming." I turn, making noise with each sway of the fabric against my legs. I stop moving so I can hear the voice.

Nothing emits sound. Maybe it's all in my head. My ears ruined by the blast. Did I imagine the cry for help?

At my feet lies a gun. Separated from its shooter, the gun stares up at me with a free trigger and safety off. I reach, then stop. The boost syringe. I remove the plastic with my teeth, not because I have to this time, but because the moment calls for a little drama. I stab my arm and plunge the depressor into the heart of the tube. Liquid forces into my body. I have no idea if I need another shot after being exposed to a death strike, or if I'm some sort of addict at this point.

"Just in case." Will turning myself into a blue uniform make up for the massacre before me? The gun burns my hand. I don't expect that. I want cold metal weightiness. Instead I get insignia branding from the residual heat the metal won't let go of. "One, two..."

"What are you doing?"

I don't actually hear him. I raise my hand with the gun pointed at the side of my head. ED covers the barrel with his palm and twists it easily out of my hand. For a nerd, he has good gun disarming skills.

"ED?" I scream over the terrible emptiness.

"You said we needed a gun, so I started looking." His lips move, but I only catch a few words. "The next thing I know you have this." He raises the pistol. "Aimed at your own head."

"I couldn't find you."

"I answered. I followed your voice."

Following weakens intelligence, the ability to think for oneself. I don't grab for the gun back. I let ED take charge. He shouldn't follow me.

ED's lip shifts. His tongue moves over his teeth, moistening the surface so his lips don't stick to his gums. "I think I drank alcohol once."

Weird segue. Has ED lost his mind? Why talk about drinking in a world where we don't rely on human needs for survival?

"It's just," he goes on, using a distinctly non-ED word. "I've never been a 'drinker'." He uses air quotes. "Nor a drunk."

Unsure where he's going in this 'confession' moment, I roll with his nostalgic tangent. "Okay. And now you want to be?"

"No, not that." He tucks the gun in his belt. "The best minds —the brightest, unadulterated—are the only ones who make the cut for GenED, you know." He stares at the piles in front of us. "Right here. That's us. The best, most talented, brightest minds in human organ donors, battling each other for a shot at living forever." His eyes get dull when he thinks of his life before this game. "Maybe that one drink, that one time… I'm not 'the best,' you know? I'm weak sometimes."

Honestly, I think he's better, stronger, and wiser for admitting he's weak, but I can't tell him that. ED isn't the type to value being valued for weakness. "Do I need to take the gun away from you now?"

ED covers the pistol with his palm. "Don't you see?"

Not really, no. "You don't think you deserve to be here?" I ask.

"Not that," he cuts me off. "We're the best. Better than all those guys and all the ones before them. We pass levels guys at work can't survive. Yet here I am. Beating everyone."

That's when I realize the look on his face isn't disgust at the carnage he's caused. It's awe. He's in awe at the achievement he's made. Maybe I *should* tell him his best quality is weakness. "But ED…"

His illuminated face shines on me, burning deep. "Yeah?"

There's no winning. ED won't win. He can't. I won't let him. Anyone who values death as achievement doesn't deserve to win. Myself included. "You still have your booster shot?" I ask more to cover the fact I'm trying to figure out how to end his game before the bloodlust behind his eyes defines him. It's that way here, ready to kill yourself one second and homicidal-and-ready-to-survive the next.

"Lost it in the explosion," he says.

I don't know if he's lying.

"You?" he asks.

Now what? Tell him I used mine? What if he tries to kill me to see if I switch sides? "Lost, too. Er… I mean, it broke."

"We'll find more." ED adjusts his vest, pulling on the seams so the lines are straight and crisp. Green brings out the arrogance in his eyes.

Movement from the far side of the courtyard draws our attention. It's the alley where we separated from GenAK and TECH-chick. "We have company." I flap my hand for ED to stop preening over his uniform and run.

ED yanks once more on the bottom cuff of his vest and barks a command, like he's been knighted leader between the two of us. "We have to go."

I know he's genius level smart outside this program we're trapped in, but statements like that, practically restating what I said, but dumber... it gets on my nerves.

With the outer wall on the sun-most side gone, which makes me assume it's south based on how the sun moves across the dismal sky, we run for the tight packed buildings. ED lets me go first. I'm not sure if it's his self-preservation skills or some demonstration of trust. I'm also not sure which I would prefer—him out front in a protective role or behind me. I distrust every choice.

18

Dark chases away our escape light, at the same time hiding us from pursuit. Once again, confusing the ever-living program out of me. If something works in my favor, I'm crippled by it at the same time.

"We should keep low. Look for places we can take cover," ED says.

"Won't the enemy assume that's what we'd do?" We have to do the least expected, yet still beneficially advantageous thing. "Turn on your radio."

"Why?"

"The airstrike team never came back," I say. "Maybe they gave instructions."

ED shakes his head. "We weren't meant to survive that. Anyone close enough to paint that particular target would have been in the blast radius, based on the layout of the surrounding buildings. The pilot would have known that. They assume we took one for the team, I'm sure."

"You can't know that."

"That's war. We're at war. They'd assume—"

"This is a game," I say. "Not war."

"Same thing. Moves and counter moves." ED points behind us, toward the smoking wreckage we caused. "And it's a war game, so I'm still right."

"Shut up." I point my finger at him to reiterate my point. As smart as he thinks he is, he doesn't seem to get it. "No one in this game wants to 'take one for the team.' Everyone wants to win for themselves."

He closes the lead he's been letting me have and presses the radio into my hand. "Go ahead." He steps back. "Turn it on. See for yourself."

"I will," I say.

"Do." He spreads his hands wide, like he's giving me the stage.

"I am!"

I'd rather be stuck with the kid right now than know-it-all ED. Still, I look around the narrow street. Everything made of cobbled stone and four story brick buildings. There aren't bodies here like there were in the other part of the town. Here there's evidence of life, but nothing living.

A single boot with a hole out the side as if the person who wore the shoe jumped out so fiercely it burst the seam from the sole.

A satchel. ED makes quick work raiding that.

The occasional threadbare jacket, hat, or belt. Never trousers. No one's ditching those along the path.

I don't turn the radio on.

Whose territory do we occupy? Are we behind enemy lines? Are we walking to the heart of green uniform camp, soon to be welcomed as the heroes who took down a hoard of blue coats?

ED's in the lead while I waste time contemplating things left behind. He puts a hand up. "There's open ground ahead and over the rise." He gestures beyond the buildings.

My mind conjures rolling green hills beyond the houses and cobbled streets, but it's dirt and gray. More depressing and dark than being in the shadow of a crumbling row house. The open space threatens to swallow us whole if we step one foot beyond the pebbled ground.

"I bet there's a regiment out of sight." ED squats with one arm on the closest building, staying low and centered.

"A regiment? You speak army now?"

ED bounces on his haunches once. He pauses so loudly before speaking, I can hear his brain cranking out my possible comebacks before I get a chance to think them up. "Why do you have to make it so hard?"

I squat next to him army-like, pressing my mouth to his ear, then yell directly into the canal. "Because I hate this. All of it. None of it makes sense and it's all terrifying." I wait for him to slap me, react, something. He stays put. I probably blew out his eardrum and he doesn't even flinch? I rest on my haunches, no longer shouting. "Look out there. We have no idea what to expect, and other than the fact we're supposed to—what? Kill anything dressed differently than we are? We know nothing."

ED doesn't turn to face me. We're not having a conversation. I'm talking to the back of his head. "Does it matter?" He asks.

"We signed up for this." We're 'Donors' with a capital 'D'.

"Did we?" He surveys the terrifying open before us at my question. The gray and humid dirt promises threats more than opportunities. "You failed ads, what other choice did you have? Quit?" ED goes quiet. I turn, staying in a squat, sure we've been discovered and ready to defend our little cobbled corner. When I finish my hoppity-surveillance rotation, I catch ED's head flinch away, no longer observing my reaction. "No one would quit. Not on the chance to live forever. Maybe you didn't sign up for games, but you signed on to be a part of this, and your inability as an actress landed you here." He stops talking. His hand hitches on the pistol. The one I had held to my head. He must have realized I seriously thought of quitting.

"Why do you want me to come?" I fold my arms. "You've done everything you can to ditch the group. It's no secret you're playing the 'every man for himself' game."

"Because it's you. Not the rest."

I feel the same about TECH-chick. Anything without her is bliss. Well, not literally. Not here in a land fertilized by blood and body parts.

ED sits next to me. "You shot the kid." He stifles a laugh. "How badass was that?"

I giggle because for some twisted, sick reason it's hilarious. We're expendable, in a program world. And the kid won't freaking die no matter how many times I kill him.

"I probably shouldn't have done that."

"Definitely." He switches to smug scholar before I can adjust. "That was stupid. You need to think before you act here."

Now I want to slap him instead of laugh at his side.

"You ready?" he asks.

I turn on the radio, purposefully ignorant. Static screams our location. Looking around for signs of being found out by the enemy, I skootch against the building. I keep my back to the wall, breathing heavily, twisting the dial until feedback isn't just feedback.

Status quo 349 to 122 GB. Delay in round. Continue as usual. Status quo…

The message loops.

"Continue as usual?" I turn off the radio. "How are we supposed to know what that is?"

TECH-chick appears out of a thin space between two tight buildings. Damn, she's agile. "Simple. You lose."

I have no idea how she manages tucking in so long, listening. A gun in her hand points right at my head. Her finger pulls the trigger against the butt of the gun. It catches with a lifesaving click of failure. And it's not my failure, it's the stupid weapon safety. TECH-chick's finger rages against the stop, but she can't press any further. Her other hand comes up, slaps the gun, pats the butt several times like that'll fix it.

"I'm running for it. You're coming with me." ED backs up one toe-step at a time, bouncing on bent knees, eager to race across the gray land.

We have a gun. I don't know why we don't shoot back. He grabs my arm tight. Bruises form where his fingers hold.

Fumbling, I tuck the radio into a cargo pocket on my vest. Might as well go for it.

We dash over the uneven ground, fighting for balance while

putting distance between us and TECH-chick as she slaps her gun in the narrow street.

It fires.

The echo lasts forever, even though it's only seconds until it reaches our ears. Does she shoot me? ED?

I trip, dragging ED down with me.

19

We've fallen into a semi caved-in trench. It's almost a tunnel. The walls are held up with chicken wire and two-by-fours providing structural support. There's a rot smell different from the city center before. This time it's more like the smell of festering human waste. Except there aren't any other humans.

"Are you hit? Did she shoot you?" I ask ED.

"I don't think so. No." He rolls onto his back. "You?"

"I don't know. I guess not." I lift my head, looking back to where the shot fired from. "She missed?" I can't believe it, but I'm too shocked to laugh about it. "She sucks at guns."

"Move." ED gets to his feet and runs. He doesn't help me to my feet or wait for me. Despite his earlier insistence otherwise, it's everyone for themselves. No one's hiding that fact. Bullets slicing past our heads make us cowards.

I push up to all fours and stand. I'm right behind ED. Okay, I'm lagging by a lot, but I'm coming. The tunnel widens out ahead. The ground crags of hardened mud and tracks from heavy vehicles. Ed takes a sharp corner and stops cold. I plow into his back, pushing ED forward into a line of soldiers.

We're surrounded by an army of blue shirts.

Blue.

We're in green.

Guns lift and point at our heads. I have no idea why they hesitate. No one here knows us. Why not fire? Kill us already.

"Either of you read code?" a blue soldier asks.

I turn to ED. He does the same to me. Both of us weighing an answer. To read code would benefit us. An asset instead of a corpse.

"Yes!" we say together.

"We'll see," the only person whose eyes aren't sallow says to us. He looks strong among the hunched and hungry. Either he's fresh to the game with military savvy, or he gets rations and privileges no one else does. "You're not the first to claim they can read code."

"Follow me," one of the bleary blue-suit masses says to us. It takes me a minute to figure out who I'm supposed to trudge behind. They all look the same.

We walk behind the soldier. He shuffles slow, giving us time to look into the faces we pass. Every face says, 'it's stupid to let them live'. Soldiers play at putting a bullet in my head as I lumber through their ranks. Why are they letting us live? Game objective being: *Kill the enemy. Every. Last. One.* Last I checked, it's green versus blue. They're blue and we're green. They outnumber us. Nothing adds up. Apprehension grows to panic.

It smells of grease and mold like railroad ties. The trench

goes on and on. Blue and gray and caked mud. There are no other colors. There never were. Even the whites in their eyes are gone, leeched from this place and replaced with gray.

Gray. Gray.

"Here," the soldier leading us says.

He points to a structure built into the ground. It has a door and more wire. The walls are wire-held clay with straw drying everything out like kindling. This whole place is crisp, like a fuse ready to light. The only thing missing is a dry match.

Inside the cellar, men stare at blueprints. They stand in line in front of papers, obscuring the writing from our view. A door swings wide. ED and I stumble, pushed inside. A single bulb hangs over the wood table where the printouts lay, barely lighting the room.

"What's this?" another man asks. He must hoard rations to maintain his size.

"Claim they can decipher code."

We wait through exchanged gazes. A weapon jabs at my back against the open sores from falling in the trenches. ED moves forward at a gun-barrel prod.

"Go ahead. Show us what you got." A nameless trenchman goads us, like we're a magic side-show about to cut and paste reality.

The thin paper looks like a printout of computer circuitry. ED and I look at the papers, then at each other. Keeping my head down, I try to take in the layout of the room. Programming language fills the margins and every open space of the page.

There are a lot of persons filling the room. Especially against the wall. Scores of bodies. I squint to size up what I'm up against in this room if I did try to escape. The shuffling forms near the wall have no faces. They're moving, alive. Faceless.

I jump back into the barrel of a gun.

"Not so fast, Codereader." The gun presses hard into my skin. "You said you could read it."

ED notices the people lining the walls now. He almost falls over. His hands slap the table, catching himself. I step back to the edge of the wood surface, placing my hand over the top of ED's. He breathes fast, ragged.

In the dim light, it's difficult to distinguish the color of the faceless soldiers' uniforms, but the pockets are more like the ones on my outer jacket—long with a snap. Green shirts. All of them. Our fate threatens to match theirs. Our reward for helping is being wiped?

A flame glows orange near the door. A cigarette lights, its smoke making the already gray world more gray, but it helps with the smell. The soldier closes fingers over the match flame before it touches anything in the room. His fingers tuck into a snapless pocket on the front of his uniform.

Matches. He has matches.

"They don't have faces." ED bobs his head toward the green shirts with divots in their face where features should go. "What did you do to them? What will you do to us?"

"You can decipher code. Isn't that right?" The large man bends so his metal pins catch the light. I'm sure it's supposed to intimidate us. ED gives the blueprints another glance. His fingers dance at his side, not drawing too much attention, but moving the calculating way he does. He's working out the problem on the page already.

"How long have you been on this level?" I ask.

ED shoots me a sidewise look, urging me not to talk.

"No longer than anyone else on this level," the man says with a craggy edge to his words.

"Not true," I say. The paper in front of me has so many lines of different colors, all of which are easily distinguished under the single light bulb. I stare. My eyes wander to the outer edges of the light's reach where everything takes on the overwhelming grayness. No color reaches beyond the last ring of light. "This code has nothing to do with painting a courtyard for aerial assault or how to target all the greenshirts." I point to the corner. "They're not concerned with single-level objectives. I don't even think this has anything to do with game level codes." No one stops me from talking. I pause because I expect laughter in my direction or higher ranking people talking over me. "This is something else, something bigger. And it took a lot more time than one game cycle to get..." I flip the layers of thin sheets of paper—dozens, "this much code."

While I'm talking, ED's eyes search the lines, the organization and arrangement of each section. He pulls one page off and tilts his head for a fresh perspective on the symbols and dashes covering the page. "She's right."

"Of course she's right." The pages are snatched from us. "Don't get any ideas."

"How are we supposed to help if we can't read the schematics?" ED's boldness sets off a wave of tension in the room. The faceless greenshirts stir and one gets to its feet. "Can they hear?"

ED leans into the darkness. I'm sure he's searching for indication of an ear-hole.

I know from experience they can hear. At least if it has anything to do with what happened to me in the fearscape.

"You remember the ads that made you sign up to be an intelligence donor?" the commander asks.

I wait for a response from ED. I plan to shadow his answers. "Yeah. I thought it was an unparalleled opportunity. The chance of a lifetime," he answers.

"Uh-huh. Me, too." I follow with a nod.

The large man narrows his eyes at me. I pull on my left sleeve until it covers half my fingers. "Why is that?" the commander asks. I hope he's referring to my answer, and not my movement.

"The chance to live forever, to do something more. Live more, I guess. Keep learning. I'm a scholar after all. Learning defines my life." ED pushes his glasses up his nose in a scholarly fashion.

"Does it now?" The commander steps in front of us each in turn, pulling on his sleeves when he passes ED, his attention lit on our reactions. When he passes me, he presses one finger up the bridge of his bare nose.

ED stiffens.

The commander notices the movement and redirects his lean ED's way. "You don't consider learning a threat to AI?"

"No." ED answers matter-of-factly. Of course learning is no threat. Education is the pillar of ED's value. Without academic accolades, ED would cease to be ED. And if that were the case, there would be no GenED at all. I straighten, buoyed with confidence.

"Learning is a vice. An addiction," the man says.

And there goes my confidence. My posture wanes, too.

"These worlds are designed to eliminate vice. Eradicate any and all threats, including individual thought, human emotion, learning… You're never really on one level long enough to offer anything more than a glimpse of your instinct, am I wrong?" He flourishes his arms around the room and the men along the walls raise a murmur in support of his words. "Free thought is a threat. You can't have an immortal who thinks for themselves, now can you? The threat independence poses to governments alone… They want sheep and goats to claim their uploads, not leaders." He jabs his barrel at the stack of papers like the manufactured image can be intimidated. "You know what they had me doing when I entered the game?"

I shake my head no, hoping I can come up with an escape plan before this big-talking idiot runs out of breath.

"Stacking damn blocks. Big ones." His arms stretch wide to illustrate largeness. "Any fool can teambuild. I want to lead the future, not cower under some TECH nerd fail-safe designed to push any yes-man through the system."

"I don't get it," I say. "What's your plan?"

He points to the table where the plans laid before his men snatched them from us. "Hack the system."

"With reams of paper?" ED laughs. "Good plan."

The man near the door, the one with matches in his pocket, steps closer. If only he was a little closer still. I could feign a trip and get those matches. "And how do the greenshirts in the corner come into play in all this? What happened to them?"

"Failed viral code." The obvious Commander—the healthiest, best-fed looking one—says to us. He steps back into shadow near the greenshirts, drawing our eye to their disturbingly void faces.

"Are you building software or deleting hardware?" ED cocks his head, as if he can read plans through the rolled-up sheets.

"You are good," the Commander says.

ED waits for an answer. When the Commander says nothing more, ED goes on. "You need us to write code or rearrange it?"

"Exactly."

For that we get a fat finger pointed at our faces. ED gets most of it. I side step into the ray of the accusingly praise-ish finger jab, not wanting to be left out.

"They need us to survive the code," I say. "Not become infected."

"Infected?" ED's voice rises as though he's horrifyingly familiar with the term.

"The virus erases your personality. I'm guessing it takes more than that, like features." Why do they keep their failures? "What do you do with them?"

"Doesn't matter." The man steps close to ED. He slides the blueprint rolls out of the hand of his soldier and places them in ED's hand. I want to slap the 'honored' expression off ED's face. *He played you, you idiot.* "You need to find the errors."

"Why?" ED challenges. His words come across bolder than the curve in his spine since the mention of infection.

"Because they're going to upload into you," I say. "Me, too."

ED turns to me. "How could they do that?" He slaps his coded arm like he's really a person.

"It's like the health shots." I point toward where I think the courtyard is from where we now stand. It's hard to feel directionally proficient in a hole in the ground. "Not dying is a code, like a cheat."

"Exactly like the health shots, actually," the man says. "That's our program. Had to eliminate my competition. Anyone who uses one of those boosters won't be able to complete the program. Corrupted, I think is what we call it." He grins at us in the dim light. His teeth shadowed by his looming upper lip so they look brown and corroded. "Most gamers come into this world with a preconceived notion about items in white cases with red crosses. Life packs I've heard them called. Health boosts. Plus-one shots. You name it, some idiot will fight for it. I don't even have to hack the ads program in order to train the fool players to inject themselves."

ED and I both look at each other. We're already infected with a failed code. We injected ourselves willingly, hoping to cheat the game by not dying and level up another round.

ED grabs a blueprint tube, strikes his palm with the roll of papers, then the table. If a soundtrack could rise, this would be the moment for a cresting power chord. He spreads out each roll, using his elbows to weigh down the sides. "Errors in the code?" He scours the page. "What do you want it to do? Skip a level? Two levels? Different loading port for final upload? Redirect current winners to lower levels so they start over?" The soldier nods to all of ED's proposals, in an 'already covered that get on with it' laze. "Do you have any idea what's left? What you're up against?"

"We want to win. For all of us." A soldier steps from the darkened wall, joining the commander nodding impatiently under the light. It's GenAK

My mouth falls open and I have to tell myself to close it.

"I knew I didn't like you," ED says. "You set us up?"

"No," is GenAK's response. Like that's an explanation. It's not.

"Yes, you did. You totally set us up. You're a traitor."

"I arrived same as you."

I scrutinize his posture. He's stiff, more so than usual. GenAK is ill-at-ease. ED calls him out on it. "No. You didn't. You've been here before. How?"

"I managed to go back down the levels and bring people I thought could help."

I can count several of his near-deaths. What a dumb plan, if he's confessing truthfully. "Good thing you had a hint on those early levels. That could have ended very differently for you," I say, hoping to remind GenAK he uploaded in a losing position when we first met, in the submerged end of a water trap. Whoever sent him probably didn't intend for GenAK to return successfully.

The Commander stiffens. His shoulders twitch forward and his eyes narrow on mine. It's a classic, 'you called me out, didn't you' posture.

"Here's one problem," ED says. He's oblivious to any tension currently in the room. All his thought is on the rolls. "See this break? Right there." He taps the page at one edge near the top left corner. "That prevents information from recycling or being processed and defragmented. The buildup could lead to overload."

The Commander leans in. "Would that cause code to blank?"

ED nibbles his bottom lip. "Now that…" He scratches his head and pushes the paper away. "I don't know about that. It's a blockage; a break in the flow of information."

"I want you on this right away." A squad of toadies step forward from the shadows in response to the Commander's booming voice. "I need a new serum to test. You." He points to me. "You write the program."

GenAK looks everywhere except toward me. Trying to catch his gaze, he shifts tactics like there's something more he doesn't want me to figure out. His head faces forward, but his eyes cast down.

An alarm sounds outside. It's faint, but sends everyone into panic.

"The raids are getting closer." The Commander walks to the door, surveying through a crack. "I'd say we have five minutes."

"How do you keep staying here?" ED asks. "What happens if green soldiers win a round?"

GenAK laughs, causing ED to bristle.

"Blue only wins here simply because we exist. The other team can't touch us, so they have no chance of eliminating blue soldiers." GenAK rolls his shoulders, regaining military composure. "The only way to live, to win, is to spawn blue."

"Is that why the serum changed the kid to a blue suit?" I ask.

"If you're green and you take the booster, you re-enter the

game, upon elimination, as blue," GenAK says, head bowed. "Blue soldiers stay blue."

"So you knew we were screwed when we arrived?" ED asks.

"You had to be green. Experimental soldiers are always green. You can't risk hurting your own ranks. It counts against you."

ED gives me a look. I shot the kid. Ding on me. However, one thing pings around in my head. TECH-chick spawned blue. If GenAK had any say in who was subject to being a guinea pig, he chose not to put that on her. I hate her.

"Time," someone says.

Blue suited soldiers fall into a routine. I'm unsure what happens other than the alarm might mean leveling up, but they don't seem under the impression they're leaving this place.

The Commander lifts a handle, uncovering a hatch in the dirt floor. "Move."

ED and I go down the hole at barrel-point.

"How is that going to save us?" ED asks.

"Off-grid. Don't count as game when you're not on the battlefield," a nameless soldier says.

The faceless hoard of green shirts doesn't shuffle down with us.

"They don't count," GenAK says.

The Commander follows behind us and GenAK behind him. The room tightens as we pack together, lit by just one light bulb. These people have a thing for dramatically dim spaces, I guess.

Two more soldiers dressed in blue descend the stairs with us. The blueprints are in this small space, too.

The pages shuffle hands, stopping with ED. "Keep working," the Commander orders.

The hatch shuts. It's darker in here than the previous space, but cleaner, too. It's not a room made of dirt. It's like being in a subway with pipes, wires, and cement lining the walls.

"This is a hiding place?" I ask.

"Shhh," the Commander barks. "It's not soundproof."

One man counts down with the fingers on one hand and then clenches his fist. Screaming follows directly above us.

20

Shrieks from above disquiet my insides. I've never stayed on a level to listen to what happens to those left behind, those who don't escape by moving on. My mouth opens like I'm going to vomit. A hand clamps hard over the entire bottom portion of my face. GenAK holds me against him, his hand preventing me from screaming. He borderline cuts off my breathing.

A smell fills the room, acidic and burning. My eyes widen in panic. No one else reacts to the smell. Why is that? Why can no one smell? What's wrong with them? Or me...

What's wrong with me?

Yellow smoke filters between a slight gap at the hatch. Gas. *We're being gassed!* I struggle to free my face to warn everyone. *We're being gassed!*

GenAK tightens his grip, squeezing my arms to my side. The scruff of his chin scrapes against my cheek as he indicates 'no' twice. I can't see ED from where I'm held, but he's probably restrained, too. There's no way he's handling this cooler than me.

Screaming and pounding continue from above. Someone pulls against the hatch door, trying to lift it. I squirm, desperate to reach the door. Someone wants in. Let them in. Why aren't they letting their own in?

Yellowish-green liquid comes through the tiniest crack, joining the trickle of smoke. A single drop falls to the floor. Everyone jumps away from the drop. A second dribble follows the same path. GenAK pulls me back from the dripping, which is now a steady trickle.

The pounding and pulling on the hatch stops, but it doesn't stop the liquid. Then the screaming ends. No one moves in our little bunker. I stare at the dripping liquid, along with everyone else. We're all waiting for the ooze to congeal, I guess.

Eventually the trickle returns to a drip. Then a once-in-a-while splat.

Then nothing.

The Commander steps toward the hatch and knocks. I don't know if he expects anyone to answer. When no sound replies to the knock, he moves aside and signals a lower ranking soldier who twists a knob and disengages a digital code. The door opens. The blue suits go first. GenAK lifts his hand from over my mouth.

Following ED, I climb the ladder back to the bunker room. Empty. No more disturbing faceless greenshirts. Not a sign they were ever in this space. A second hatch door opens in a far corner. The dim light inches out from within, drawing my attention. Several of the blue officers step out. A third, fourth, and fifth door opens from the dirt floor.

"Lots of hatches, then?" ED says, pushing his frames up the bridge of his nose.

"We've been here a while. We started with the one and we've built more as time permitted and our number grew." The Commander walks to the table still standing in the center of the room. He doesn't touch its surface though. "Someone clean this. It still has rain on it."

"We're indoors. The rain got in here?" I ask.

"If donors are anywhere, so is the rain."

One of the blue shirts tears off a section of his shirt and rubs circles over the table.

"Watch it," GenAK says. "Don't get it on you."

The wiping soldier nods, annoyed, then jumps back. He gasps and rubs one hand against his trousers. "No. No, no, no…"

"I said to be careful!"

The soldier walks in the direction of GenAK, desperation on his face. His hand bubbles, and oozes. The same yellowish-brown liquid burbles from his fingers, then his wrist because his fingers and palm aren't there. His arm liquefies, followed by his shoulder and neck. The gurgling is in his throat and pours out his mouth before his head turns to a mess of— I don't even know what. It's awful.

Without realizing it, I've backed against a wall to get away from the soldier as he disintegrates. I look at the floor. It's wet. It's yellowish. The liquid clings on my army regulation shoes. I panic, stomping and smearing the souls of my shoes into the dirt.

"Stop," GenAK warns me. "It only eats the skin code and anything under it."

"What if you've had a health pack booster?" I ask, knowing

it prevents a player from winning, but does it still prevent us from dying even in the face of not leveling up?

"Then you're fine," the Commander answers before GenAK has a chance.

GenAK holds still a millisecond too long before nodding his agreement. I don't feel safe. Still, I plan to keep a booster on me at all times.

The Commander points to ED. "Now, you find the flaws in my design. And you." Finger in my face. "Write it. I'm running out of time here."

"I don't get it. If you can avoid being rained out, you should have limitless time," I say.

"You'd think," he answers.

ED twitches. His breathing quickens. I'm not the only one who notices the change in his demeanor.

"What'd you find there, greenshirt?" GenAK says.

I step in front of GenAK. "It's ED. Call him ED."

The Commander puts a hand on GenAK's shoulder. I'm not sure if he's holding him back, calming him down, or if he wants a better look at the situation and GenAK obstructs his view. "We don't have names here. We have code source and numbers."

"What are you? AK1 or something?" I say.

"AK's aren't like the rest. The higher the number, the more rounds you survived." He shows his arm. All the soldiers push back their sleeve. Black numbers arrange themselves. For a few, they carry into other places on their bodies. Their codes adjust before my eyes, adding to the tally like a living tattoo.

I look at GenAK, knowing his number fills beyond his forearm. Maybe that's why he's often on the leaderboard. *Whatever. Like I care.*

"He saw something, sir. I saw him flinch," GenAK says 'sir' in a way that makes his own size diminish.

"No, I didn't." ED shakes his head nervously, looking guiltier than before. "I did not flinch."

The Commander presses GenAK aside and leans in toward ED. "If you know how to fix our booster... If you know what's wrong with it, and you're not telling me..."

"There's nothing wrong with it," ED blurts. His words spill confession like he peed them out. He stands there, staring down where his voice falls upon the pages. We both know if they don't need us, we're going to end up like the other greenshirts. Left for the death-rain when the next siren wails. I can't let that happen.

I lunge for the Commander. He catches me as if I'm falling. I grip the hilt of his gun and pull it free from his hip, turn and point the weapon between ED's wide eyes.

ED stares at me in confusion. He mouths, "No!" but I don't hear it. I've already pulled the trigger. His glasses jolt askew from the impact.

A hole above his left eye spills red liquid while his eyes cross, as if to look at what's been done to him. He drops to his knees like a chopped stump and falls solidly to the side.

My hand goes limp. "He took a booster," I say. "He did. I know it." Didn't he? Or was he telling the truth when he said he lost his? How long would the first one last? What have I done? "How long do they last?" I ask, searching for GenAK's face in the crowd. I can't tell one blue soldier from another.

No one says anything.

"ED said the shots were fine." My voice trembles. "He had one. He must have taken it."

What if he was lying again?

"I didn't want you to turn him into one of those things." I'm fully shaking now, because I've made a terrible error. ED hasn't turned to code. He isn't changing to a blue shirt. "How long do they last? The booster shots." I needed a diversion to prevent ED from saying too much, but I didn't mean to terminate him.

"You have to have one to survive the new cycle as a green-shirt, which you both did." GenAK sounds like he's talking through a tube far away.

"You didn't tell us?" I say. Now I'm the bad guy.

The dim light on ED's vest blinks once then never comes back on.

No one says anything. I'm left with a gun in my hand. I could raise it and shoot them all. I could.

"Someone hand her a shirt," the Commander orders. "She's one of us now."

The soldiers in the room exchange questioning glances with raised brows.

I guess shooting my own guy disqualifies me from their experiment. Why didn't GenAK hand me a change of suit when I put a hole in the kid? "If I shoot one of you? What am I then?" I say, not wanting to give up my green shirt.

"Officially without a team if you do that. Might as well be faceless," GenAK says.

Sounds like a bunch of made-up nonsense to me. Spur of the moment reasons to redirect my actions. Like that'd ever work on me. I see right through it. I lift the gun with my finger testing the trigger's tension.

The Commander doesn't look at me at all when he says, "No one will stop you, if you try. But know we always boost every new cycle. We will code and come back blue, stronger than ever." He slides a vial from his vest pocket. I look around at his soldiers. They were given their shots by someone else. Yet, no one questions the Commander's personal stash. "We always do." He points to the now empty corner where the faceless people had been. "There's always some that have to try, even when warned."

I know a threat when I hear one. "What about me, soldier boy?" I ask.

The Commander bristles. "What about you?"

"Do I get a reserve shot? A health boost. You know, just in case?"

He nods for two men to lift ED and haul him out of the room. Into the trenches they go. "Refer to me as Commander... And no. You're no good to us now."

I don't know what they need with the enemy if their serum is fine. "Why did you bring us here? I know where your bunkers are to survive the next raid."

"So did the guy who dripped on my rung." He refers to the person who pounded on the hatch but wasn't permitted inside.

"We can't make the serum ourselves," GenAK says.

"That makes no sense. Why?"

"We don't know. That's what we wanted ED to figure out. What the flaw is."

"You can't save yourself," I say. "That's the flaw. ED saw it, too. The game has failsafe after failsafe. You try to manipulate it and you lose." My words have an impact on everyone within earshot. I have no idea if I'm right, but they all seem upset by the idea.

The Commander stays in shadow while his goons drag me out. He's still talking.

"It's the whole point of all of this. We aren't in control. We can't save ourselves. We're dependent on the rules, the system, the game, the gamers…" The door shuts. I'm on the outside, they're on the inside. I stop yelling and speak at a low register. "It's just another failsafe," I say simply because I know they didn't like it when I said it the first time. "You can never save yourself."

I'm thrown in a pile of human waste out in the open trench.

"What am I supposed to do now?" I ask.

Some random passing soldier answers my rhetorical question. "Hope blue wins this round."

"But wearing a blue shirt doesn't make me blue, does it? I mean, I never coded."

"We're all blue." He mimes shooting himself with two fingers.

21

When I move to push myself up, there's ED. Mud and straw from the walls cover him on one side so I didn't recognize him as anything more than a mound of guck before now. He's been tossed here, too. We've both been dumped in the compost pile. I pat the muck surrounding me until I land on a plastic stem. Carefully, I fold ED's spectacles and slide them in my pocket. I'm not sure why I keep them. We weren't exactly confidants.

"ED?" I crawl over to him, lift his head. This all feels so real. Not like a game, a contest, or competition. I hold him against me like I can hug life back into him. "I'm so sorry." A key falls out of his vest pocket, into the dirt.

I stare at it.

My key.

The one I found on the second level, which I used to fray the kid out of his seat belt.

"You stole my key?" I ask. "When? Why?" I pick it out of the mud and brush away the straw where it sticks. I still have pockets in my new blue uniform. I shove the key to the bottom of the deepest vest pocket. I feel betrayed, lied to, angry.

The angry wound in ED's head turns those feelings back on myself.

"I forgive you," I say. But really I'm asking if he can ever forgive me, not that I'll ever know his answer. ED's one chance at immortality, the artificial life version, is over.

"Kill me!" I scream when a soldier walks past me.

Worse than a gun to my head, he pities me. He turns away like he can't stand the sight of me and walks on, twisting his entire body to avoid me at every turn.

I let go of ED. This trench has to have an exit. It has to. It's a labyrinth of turns and bunkers. Dead ends are piled with lifeless bodies. The landscape comes pre-stocked with hopelessness. It seeps into me.

I trip backwards and search for a path that doesn't come to a dead end packed with dead players. I find the bunker after a series of right turns. The Commander pulls the door closed in my face. Not privy to the inner circle.

I keep walking and stumble upon a section of monitors strung together with soldiers manning computer stations. All the technology looks like it came out of the 1980's. Ancient. Code taps out in long strings before 'enter' sends the commands shooting into action. Rockets lift from hydraulics below ground.

"Get a weapon and shoot anything in green you see over the ledge. Or you can man a missile launcher." A soldier taps monitors with green and blue lights dotting every inch. "Aim for green populated areas." A soldier says. He's manning a computer station in a wide section of the trench with camouflage netting strung over the top. Rotating dishes correspond to blips on screens he's monitoring.

I sit down next to him. There isn't a location on his overhead city map readout not riddled with blue and green dots, interspersed. "But you'll hit blue. Won't that make you a traitor?"

"Not if the majority targets are green. Look here." He points to a more concentrated green dot area. Blue shines from within the glow. "As long as the majority hit are green targets, it counts as a blue victory. The collateral damage isn't any worse than civilian losses in real war and this is a game."

"But we're playing with people's real lives."

"No. It's their second life. They've already lost the one that counts. My guess is the donor program's been running five years, maybe more."

My knees go weak. One arm reaches out for the chicken wire wall to steady me. All the players, the donors plugged into cables and wires, could already be flatlined by now. So who or what plays the game now? The soldier in front of the screen pushes the stool he's sitting on away from me. He practically trips over himself to increase his distance from me.

"You're infected, aren't you?"

"What? No," I say.

"Yes, you are." His finger shakes accusingly in my direction.

I pat my face, poke my eye. All my features are present. I've seen the infected. Those faceless soldiers in green. Please, don't let that happen to me. "No. I'm not. I swear."

The soldier runs into the depth of the trench maze, leaving

me alone with his array of black screens with crude cityscapes outlined in yellow and faceless, nameless, pointless dots of blue and green moving around the blackness.

The screen with the most concentration of blue, that's the trenches. I know it. Long rivers of blue. Dots practically piled on top of each other in the narrow trenches. I trace my finger along the path on the screen. Green dots still move in the trench. One goes out, then another. Looking over the screen, green dots vanish at a steadier pace than blue.

I spin in a circle. A gun. I need a weapon! How is there nothing here? The computer screen in front of me comes with a keyboard. I sit where the soldier left.

"Coordinates?" I have no idea what I'm doing. I tap the screen, then a second screen. No numbers intersect to help me narrow down a missile destination. My shoulders rise with the intake of breath and I hold it. I have to do something, make a decision, take action.

I type in several numbers, a comma, and more numbers. *The screens, look at the screens.* I can't tell. There's no red target circle to indicate I've singled anything out. This is useless! I slap a monitor. It leans back and then rocks forward. I tip it ever so gently back the direction I originally slapped it.

It doesn't work. The screen falls off the wooden slat it's resting on. When the monitor hits the dirt, the boxy machine sparks, crackles, and a hole erupts from the top right corner. Smoke billows out.

I stand from the stool, looking in every direction. Who saw that? Anyone? It's not sabotage, I swear. With no idea what I've targeted, I press enter on the keyboard. From somewhere behind me, two lifts separate, doors slide away to reveal a cavern, and a missile is lifted from underground.

"Seriously, that's not realistic." I look to my sides for someone to validate my observation. No one so much as blinks my direction. "How long would it take to assemble that kind of thing in a trench?" Still no head nods, no smug hidden smiles confirming that 'yeah this is total bullshit'. I'm talking to myself.

"Well you're all dead anyway, so what does it matter, right?" That line earns a shifty glance or two. The missile ignites yards from computer operators. Heat waves rustle loose-fitting clothing and push hair back to reveal receding digital hairlines. It flies, all six feet of bomb, at a steep angle, barely clearing the trench wall like it's too heavy to pull itself into the air. I bite my cheek, unsure what I've triggered exactly. "That can't be good."

"What're you doing?" GenAK appears out of nowhere.

"Go away."

He looks at the now descending launching device. "What did you target?"

I shrug.

"The odds you correctly guessed an ideal target are slim to none." He sits at the stool and types, glaring at one screen. He notices the one I broke and shifts to another. His back rigid, GenAK continues to click like he can recall the strike I deployed. "Where is it? Why hasn't it struck?"

Clicking taps at my nerves like Morse code with my internal organs. My neck twitches. Then my elbow, my knee, my feet are on fire with twitching. I have to get out of here, away from GenAK and his useless typing.

I want out of the trench. The walls are so high. Why did they dig in so deep? More than anything, I desire to get out, not give up. I run back to where GenAK is clicking away and search the screens. In the river of blue, where are the dead ends? I need a dark one, or one with faint green. Where there are a lot of bodies piled.

One. A dark corner. My finger reaches up and pushes on the black screen. GenAK's hand is on me at the same moment. He clasps his palm around my index finger, not holding me, but stopping me long enough to look in his eyes.

They're blue, like the color of his shirt. Were they always blue? I shake my head. I don't care what color his dumb eyes are.

I back out of the coordinate area and focus all my attention on orienting to the trench, and how the screen is set up in relation to where I am now. My dark corner, the one I must find to get out of here, it's to my right.

"What did you target?" GenAK asks again. "Why hasn't it shown on the screen?"

I don't stop. I need to find a way out of here.

"It would have reached its target on our board by now." GenAK keeps muttering while I progress to the dark corner where I hope to climb to the top.

I turn left, muffling his voice behind me. Next is a right turn, steady on for this part of the trench. I can smell the rot. Code rotting isn't like animal rot or my memory of food spoiling in a fridge. It's plastic and electric melted together in a stagnant pool of battery acid. That's the smell of death in this place. It's every-where. Refuse and forgotten-ness. Death, death, death.

It's coming for each of us.

Why can't anyone smell it? It's so strong I retch.

One last turn and the pile of bodies is all I see. A mound of green shirts and a few blue. Fingers stick out from the pile at odd angles. They're gray, not the color of life.

I run to edge of the mound and try to lift a silent form. I have to carry it to the wall in order to pile the bodies so I can climb out. It weighs more than the chopper from the other level.

"What are you? Descended from anvils?" Heaving the body on its side I only manage to flip it face up. Faceless.

"Agh!" I jump back. I know there's no reason to fear a dead, faceless greenshirt, but it still rattles me. The no face thing… "This isn't going to work."

"What did you enter? Where did you send that missile?" GenAK appears behind me, apparently having followed me. He doesn't even gasp for breath. Not even a courtesy hand on knee to feign fatigue after chasing me through the trenches.

"I don't know."

His brows knit together. "How can you not know?"

"I pushed numbers, whatever came to mind, then hit enter."

"You could've targeted anything," he reprimands me like he's my parent. Fat lotta good he is.

"Help me with this." I lift the feet of the faceless man, letting GenAK deal with the arms that are so close to the featureless face.

"Not until you tell me why you'd take that risk." Whatever risk he's so worked up about, I have no idea.

"I had to do something." I drop the green person's feet. "Are you going to help me?" The smell of dead code hasn't lessened, but my nose blinds to it. Thank heavens. "I'll go. You'll never have to see me again. But I need help right now."

With a deep exhale of breath, I lift the legs again. GenAK moves toward me. I stiffen, unsure if he's helping or about to snap my neck while my arms are too busy to defend myself.

"Grab the hands. Pile them so I can climb out."

He slides something in my front vest pocket.

I refuse to be distracted by such antics. "Come on, move."

He nods once and walks to the head of the corpse. We swing the body together. It still weighs a ridiculous amount, even with two people moving it. When we let go, the body sails a sad, meager distance and lands slightly higher on the pile.

"This is going to take forever," I say.

"I'll boost you," GenAK says.

With that word, my mind goes to viruses, faceless men, coding, not coding. My eyes glaze over and my mouth goes dry. "No, I..."

"I don't mean like that." He rolls his eyes and interlocks his fingers. "I mean give you a boost." He points to the wall. "Out of the trench."

I feel stupid. "Oh."

"I'll lift you out."

A sheepish nod signals agreement with this low brow method of escape.

"Take this." He places a handgun in my palm, lifts it for a split second after it touches my skin, and returns it to my hand. "It's automatic."

My level of firearm awareness doesn't cover much. The

weapon comforts me, but the fact it's automatic means little. I mean, it shoots, right? That's pretty much all I need to know.

GenAK lifts a satchel from across his chest. "There are spare magazines in here, pre-loaded. Switch them out and keep firing." He mimes what must be changing out a magazine.

What does he think I'm going to encounter? A one-person showdown in the center of Greenville? I don't reject the bag. Placing the satchel over my head, I let the weight of the bullets inside dig into my skin.

GenAK climbs to the top of the body pile, still depressingly far from the lip of the wall, and laces his fingers once again. Raising his eyebrows, he motions me over with his head.

Somewhere deeper in the maze of trench, commotion builds. The sound is contagious. It grows and echoes down the lines.

"Hurry. My guess is that has something to do with you," he says.

I wedge the gun in my waistband. It's cold against my skin, refreshing in the mug of grease-burned bodies. I raise both hands above me as I shove off the person we're both standing on. I manage some leverage and bounce.

GenAK thrusts me into the air to increase my lift.

I extend my fingers toward the trench lip—scratching, grasping, clutching—but they pass the mark. My elbows slam against the chicken-wire supported dirt on my way back down. I catch myself. The soft flesh under my biceps scrapes against the wire, but I don't care.

"Push me up," I yell down to GenAK.

He lifts my weight while I slap the open sores on my arms against the uneven ground, pulling myself, army-crawl style, away from the trench. Which side of the trench am I on? The same side I came from, or have I crossed toward a different city?

A hand slaps my wrist, tightly pressing fingers against my skin, bruising me to the bone. I look up as someone forces me up to my feet by forcing my wrist to bend back.

I'm face-to-face with the kid. Who is surprisingly strong for his size.

22

A hoard of ragged-looking blue uniforms stands in a line behind him. Like his own deprived little army. He has a gun pointed at me already, but pauses from pulling the trigger when he notices my blue shirt. Uncertainty flashes behind his eyes. If he looks too close, he'll notice my pants aren't just dirt coated, but original green from spawning here. My only chance at not getting a bullet in the head is if the kid thinks I regenerated to the blue team, just like him.

"Turncoat," the kid says. He releases his grip on my wrist. I half twist, so I can mouth 'ow' and shake out the cramp in my hand. Also, let out a little relief that the kid might not kill me right this second.

Ice fills my digital veins as I pat my pockets. Like this action can hide the syringe in the satchel GenAK gave me amid the mags. Not willing to risk my rank in the game on how long the kid can monologue, I quickly slide the vial from its plastic and pierce my forearm inside the bag, depressing the plunger.

I want to ask how the kid survived the siren raid. Though, I'm more concerned with how the kid will react, knowing I shot him.

"How are you still here?" comes out of my mouth before I can stop myself. I rub the ache out of my wrist.

"I could ask you the same." He nods to my blue clothes.

"They have hidden bunkers in the trenches. Soldiers can wait out those siren raid things."

It's obvious the kid figured out how to survive the switchover, but the group he's leading has no experience. "Don't trust her. She lies." He looks at me like he's been bitten by a dog and has a chance to put it down. I'm going down.

He taps the trigger of his gun, like he's tapping out my fate to 'eeny meeny minee moe'.

Where's my gun? I dropped it crawling out of the trench. "Don't do it," I say.

His head cocks to one side. A sneer curls his lip over his white teeth, revealing red gums to match his bloodshot eyes.

"You don't understand what it'll do to you."

He puts a hand up. I hear the click of the bullet falling into its chamber.

"Listen, listen, listen..." My words come in triplicate. My body zings like I'm overly caffeinated. The health shot races through me as if memorizing my source code, anticipating the need to put me back together. It surges into my fingers, shaking my thighs, quivering my brain, pulsing, raging, falling in on itself. I don't even feel bad about the fact I've taken someone else's spare dose. "*Listen.* It'll change you. You don't want what will happen. I swear, I swear…" My only hope is that, since I have experience shooting someone on my own team, he'll believe me. Or at least hesitate long enough for me to figure another way out of this.

"We were the same team when you shot me," he says. "That's how I know you're lying."

I glance down at my blue shirt. It's a shirt. Nothing more than thin, sweat stained fabric. Not even my sweat. It belonged to someone else, someone who died probably. "This isn't my shirt," I say.

"Exactly."

Metal gleams under a layer of shifting dirt so dry it could pass as sand. The gun. When I twist to acquire my weapon, the kid depresses his own trigger. I don't hear the click of a gun. My eardrum pops under pressure. Everything silences around me. *Is this what a gunshot feels like?* Pressure builds behind my eyes and ears. Then…

BOOM.

Failure has a flavor. It's like burning my tongue on a too hot drink. It sears off every receptor and all that's left is numb cooked flesh. All my senses burn away from the inside and extend outwards.

Next comes bleeding, gasping, dying…

Copper blood and head on fire… But I don't have a head. How silly to think it's on fire.

My ears fill with a mechanical whir, like machine fans cooling critical components. It's so loud. So loud! More than the rush of fans cooling vital circuits. The sky buzzes all around me, zipping to me like a self-destruct hound returning to its master.

Then there's nothing but white heat and a sonic boom, and the microwave ash of bodies all around me.

My missile...

I targeted myself?

Idiot.

But it saved me from the kid and his posse.

Genius.

The whole thing happens while green and black strings of information spiral to a new spawning location. I'm brand new and safely distant before the dust settles. Only this time, I'm blue. I swear allegiance with the Commander all the way to my toes. I want him to survive at all cost. This must be what blue feels like.

The green coats landed unlucky. Not my fault. Not theirs either, but they'll die for it, at my hand if that's what it takes to survive. We must keep the plan moving forward.

"What is the plan?" I ask out loud, surprised by my own thoughts. I slap one hand over my mouth. Everything programs through me, like a reboot, with my new blue team color. I have purpose, but I don't know what it is. Lotta good that does.

Still, it helps me understand GenAK a little better. He feels he has a purpose, something more important than other players. More important than me. Now I think about it, the blue soldier's purpose matters more than GenAK's player status. I need to get him off the leader board, too.

"You targeted yourself? Are you crazy?" Out of nowhere GenAK rams me in the stomach. "Get down before you're seen."

"Where am I?"

"Everyone spawns within one hundred yards of their departure. It's the only way to keep things fair. If the other team knows where the base spawn zone was, they could post snipers and take out everyone as they arrive." GenAK speaks as if he designed the whole program.

The land before me ripples with craters.

"Do you have any idea what you've done?"

I survive. That's what I do.

"The kid…" GenAK says. The kid's back is to us but his small size and huge-ego posture give him away. GenAK takes my hand and pulls me down. "He's Mord now."

"What?" I say. *More something.* I don't even know what that is. "I'm sure it's one of his tricks." Which reminds me. "You lied to me!"

"Shh!"

"Don't shush me." I was never on blue team before the most recent explosion, even after I shot ED in the head. I wouldn't have leveled up to the next round if I hadn't stuck a needle in my arm and blew myself up before the round ended.

He pivots, looking behind us. In the distance a billboard displays the top ten list once again. A scene of idealic recognition of select players' greatness plays out. GenAK is number two, only behind the Commander's long string of code, which I recognize thanks to my internal blue-upgrade. The actors portray a medal ceremony for whoever makes it out of this game.

"It changed." GenAK squints though debris on the wind toward the billboard's winner's ad in the distance. A tiny medallion placed on the shoulder of… rubble and dust obscure it completely from our view.

"What changed?" Everything looks the same to me. Gray, drab, warzone… promise of failure and death. Same.

He shakes his head as if he changed his mind on what he was thinking, shifting tack. "There's no trench."

I look. He's right. No trench. "Buried with the rocket blast?"

"Missile," he corrects me. "And no. I'm certain you didn't manage that."

Glory hound, yes I did. "I totally did this. I'm such a bad a—"

"Stop talking." He clamps his huge hand over my face, covering the entire lower half of my head like before.

The kid stands with his back to us. He drags one leg like he's injured, walking in a half circle, almost showing his face to us, but stops.

Drama much? We've already identified him. He doesn't need to keep up the ruse. Two more forms rise from the ground. I mistake them for disassembled body parts before, but now they're… Something's not right about them.

The kid's head twists in our direction. Only it's not his head. The eyes are missing, but unlike the faceless people of before, the kid has a mouth. A sharp toothed, bloody, snapping mouth, from which he's both smelling and biting at the air.

"He can smell us," GenAK says, gripping my wrist so hard I'm sure it will snap off. "Like I told you, only the infected can smell."

"That's not what the other people look like." Blank-faced goons who shuffle in place in the Commander's bunker. "I can smell, too." I open my mouth. No snapping maniac sounds escape.

The approaching kidlike figure drags one lame leg in our direction, red tinged saliva falling from his mouth without him making the slightest effort to wipe it away.

"It's not the kid, it can't be," I say. Yet, I know it's him. I know it. He has no eyes, but it's him.

GenAK's head falls forward. Every movement heavy with fatigue, but he pushes himself harder, unable to relax. I'm pretty sure it's written into his code. "We leveled up," he says, thick, like sand clogs his throat.

23

The landscape looks like a bombed-out countryside with an ads billboard oddly undamaged in the distance. Smoldering rubble and sun-worn fields spread in all directions. My ears ring from the recent explosion.

"There was no alarm, no siren," I say. For good measure I wipe dust away from under me, demonstrating a lack of level up pad. We weren't on one when we reached the top of the trench and we're not on a pad now. "We can't have leveled up."

"You triggered it somehow," GenAK accuses me like I did this on purpose.

"How could I?"

He shakes his head. "You did. I know it. It had to be you. Every time something happens, you're there. Every time."

For every second he wastes trying to get a grip on the situation, the kid stumbles closer, his teeth gnashing. His head pulls and rips the air sideways, teeth bared, as if he can already feel our skin between his canines.

The kid, however, takes second stage on my list of concerns. "I have to help the Commander," I say without knowing what I'm talking about.

"I was about to say the same thing." GenAK puts a hand on my shoulder. "You boosted, didn't you? Before we leveled?"

"When I saw the kid…" GenAK doesn't know I shot the kid in the city center first. It's probably my fault the kid turned into what he is now. "I just—I boosted in case."

"He changed the formula. We've been upgraded." By 'he' GenAK means the Commander. I understand without requiring explanation.

"Upgraded? Like a software thing?"

"We're programmed to defend him. Genuine worker ants." GenAK stretched his jaw like popping his ears will get the new orders out of his head.

The kid closes in.

"Let's go." GenAK takes my arm by the bicep, pulling me away from the slow advance of the mouth-faced people. With my free arm, I push my sleeve up past my elbow. Clean, blank flesh. No numbers, letters, tattoo symbols of any kind. The pressure to follow orders lessens. Like there's nothing under my skin for the orders to work with.

I let out a breath. I'm me. No code and no memory. Remembering my lack of belonging drives the new programming out of me.

I can't be controlled. I fight it because my arm is bare. I'm not like the rest of the donors.

My head clicks into gear. Commander loyal. I have to reprogram my thinking, and fast before the new string of thought finds a permanent place on my mental shelves. The Commander doesn't get to populate my motivations or personality.

GenAK pulls harder, urging me to keep pace with him. He checks behind us, seeing my arm. Quickly, I pull my sleeve down, covering unmarked skin. I wait for him to say something like 'that should be restored once you're upgraded.' I mean, he has a code still. My lack of 'Gencode' is no longer secret.

Instead of mentioning it, he looks away, dragging me behind as if nothing's changed between us since the dome. In a way confirming that he's known for a while, but he either feels sorry for me, or is afraid of how I'll react if he brings it up.

Fine. I don't want to talk about it either.

I'm occupied with purging the Commander's stamp from my thoughts. *He's here—gone. Here—flush. Oh, there he is, hiding in a corner. Do what, you say? Sabotage the what now? Too late. Thought's gone.*

I need to be me again. Whoever I am.

The gnashing sound fades. There's enough distance between us and the eyeless posse, I wager to test their abilities. "What's wrong with you?" I shout back to the kid. GenAK yanks me back to face forward. "I want to know if he can speak."

"He can't."

"Oh, because you know soooo much." I slap his hand over my arm. "You know everything, don't you? Traveling between levels… I bet you don't even *have* to level up, do you?"

He doesn't respond.

"You don't?" I didn't want to win this fight. "I knew it! I mean, I had no idea, but I *knew it*. You're a plant!" Everyone seems to accuse everyone of being 'a plant'. I have no idea what the accusation really means, only that no one wants to be it.

"I'm not a plant."

"He's infected?" I ask, pointing back to the kid. My steps are less sure. I cross one foot in front of the other and almost lose my balance.

"I don't know, maybe."

"Maybe?" *Pfffft*. Infected is probably a made-up term to scare people into submission. Like fairy tales are used to scare kids into good behavior.

"We made him."

He has my attention. "We?"

"The Commander." GenAK walks several more steps without saying more. I put on the brakes, wanting more information.

"Wait." I shrug my arm free with less resistance on GenAK's part. "You're telling me, if a virus exists, *you* are responsible for creating it? Like that psycho Commander wouldn't have been able to do this without you?" I point to us both, because when I say 'all this' I mean the whole '*Yes, Commander. Anything you say, Commander. I would never defy you, Commander. I am your slave, Commander*' thing going on in my head.

"No…" He rubs his chin like the stubble can actually grow in this stagnant-fake existence. "Maybe."

I walk ahead of him alone. I can handle this myself. I don't need him to survive. I'm better off without him. I stop, turn, raise an arm back to the monsters slow on our trail. "I thought that was my fault."

GenAK stops walking and folds his arms like he's waiting for a child to finish a tantrum. GenAK hesitates in real life. That's probably how he died a hero.

"You murdered the kid. Not me," I say.

"We don't have time to feel sorry for ourselves," GenAK says.

"Yes, we do. Look at them." The kid and the mob behind him track us at such a slow rate, even walking we dust them. "They're no threat."

"They get faster. We need shelter. Tomorrow we'll fight the Mord."

"Another thing." I don't even care if I reveal too much about what I don't know and everyone else naturally seems clued in on. "Explain Mord."

"The dead," he says.

Okay, that didn't help at all. We're all donors because we're dead or dying. "That's exactly what we are," I say. "We're already dead, right?" I stumble tipsy, like my brain is shorting, or rebooting wrong.

GenAK supports my weight over his back, carrying me like a limp branch across his shoulders.

"I'm not an E." I say with a slur, as if he hasn't already seen my codeless arm.

"I know."

"Shh," I say. "TECH-chick is gonna be pissed."

"What did the Commander give you?" he says. "You sound drugged."

I slur laugh with a hand up to let him know to stay 'shush' about me. "No, it's the opposite. I'm working the code out, overriding it. Can't program me... I always say."

He drops me. "You're what? When did you say that?"

"Ow." I try to sit after being dropped, but it's hard to do anything while rewriting viral code. I start to wonder if I can code my own immunity in these stupid games, but lose focus and feel slurred in thought and action. I brush my side free of dirt while my brain tries to work on the most pressing issue, getting the Commander out of my head. "That really hurt. Warn a person."

"You're overriding your code?" He stops and moves his fingers like he's writing something in the air. "No. I don't think it's possible. It's not in the software."

"No. Jeez, don't be so mel-low-dra-dram..." My speech sticks, glitching. I am totally reprogramming. Why else would I sound like this? "Don't be lame." Everything is spinning. *Wheeee.* The kid and his Mord crew get closer and closer. They *are* getting faster.

"Curse it. I didn't plan for this." GenAK lifts me once more, over his shoulders, and runs like there is a hoard of bloodthirsty speed demons after us.

Because there is.

The kid has gone from lumbering oaf with gnashing teeth, to mouth-breathing, scent-honing, speed-walker. He still drags his feet, leaving ski-like tracks where he pushes forward. His thin arms stretch forward swiping the air in front of him, like clearing invisible cobwebs before he runs through.

He's coming for us.

Electronic messages fire in my head, turning gears and changing pictures in front of me. A landscape of fears. Crashing vehicles into soldiers all in a row.

And I find it all ridiculously hilarious.

"Why are you laughing?" GenAK runs, jostling me across his shoulders.

"I don't know. I can't help it." Memories spin out of order and crash together, erasing here and freeing space there, compacting so all the open places stay together and the vital data gets neatly compartmentalized. *...it's so funny!* Something new surfaces, not new. It's always been in my head, but I haven't noticed, like a hidden message. Subliminal, if there is such a thing in programming.

...Objective... it's like the little curser blinks on the page, waiting for me to hit enter and see the rest of the message.

"If you can laugh, you can run."

A switch flips and I can't remember what was so funny. Behind us, snarling twigs point their chins in the air, like hound dogs on our trail. The kid races toward us.

Sweat crackles, electrically pulsing over my skin as though it doesn't belong with the rest of my programming. Something's wrong with me. I'm shorting out.

GenAK outpaces me by a lot. I sprint to catch up. He doesn't wait for me.

"We can't outrun them," I shout ahead.

"Maybe you can't." GenAK says.

"Shoot him in the head." I have loads of experience with this. It's fairly effective.

The barrel of a pistol appears ahead of me so quickly, I almost ram it eye first. Reflex kicks in and I slide to my knees. I can't avoid hitting GenAK in the leg, but it doesn't ruin his shot.

Red sparks pass over my head. Powder-scent burns inside the barrel, smoke rises as I cover my ears and turn to see the result.

The kid twitches backward and falters. There's a hole in his head where one of his eyes should be. Blood trickles down into his gaping mouth. The mob of his kind stops where he stands. The kid doesn't fall down dead. That's concerning. I genuinely anticipated a headshot would terminate him.

"Keep moving." GenAK drops the gun.

24

A voice calls out in a whispered urgency. "In here."

I stop. No idea who said that.

"*Psssst.*"

A crack in the earth lifts and lowers like a spider trap off to the side of where we stand, but large enough for a human.

Bunkers. Underground passages, like the soldiers had worked out in the previous level. I drop to the ground before throwing myself into the gaping maw of the bunker.

"Hurry, get in here," a voice calls from the blackness beyond the rift in the earth. "Underground confuses them unless they can smell you. Then you're in trouble."

I roll inside, not considering there's probably a drop. I fall several feet onto a wooden landing, then crash down splintering steps until I reach the dirt floor.

The trap cover falls back in place after GenAK makes a more graceful transition into the dark. Dirt and roots spill around us. The sound of feet rushing over the top of the thatch and wood door causes my chest to tighten. What're the chances those things fall right through? I stare at a thin line of daylight. It's broken in places by weeds and clumps of dirt. After several seconds of it not opening, I relax.

"What're you doing in the wastelands?" Several people shuffle around us. They smell earthy like mushrooms before they're cooked. Only one person speaks to us.

"Running," GenAK says out of breath. "You?"

It's difficult to make out the faces of those in here with us, or even determine how large of a space we're in. The dark is weighted with humidity and a sweet flavor on the air I can't place. It's like the dew's been sugared. We're not the only ones out of breath. Our rescuers take a moment before speaking again. When they do, it's metered, like they don't want to give too much away. Them not trusting us and still saving us means they're likely using us.

"Someone spotted you from a city tower and sent a relay group to get you before the Mord. Doesn't take long before they learn to move fast," the same voice says. There's enough pause to gauge whether or not GenAK and I know more than we're telling. For the record, I don't.

I brush more dirt off my pants and shirt—developing a complex about how impossible it is to keep crud off my clothes. From the feel of it, I'm still in my blue soldier's uniform.

"Those sightless sons of bitches. Always ready to bite your arm off," a less calculating voice adds.

"Can you kill them?" I can't hide my eagerness, though I doubt any of them register me bouncing on my toes in this darkness, giddy with the chance to kill something *not* on my team or in my group.

"It's difficult because of the arm thing."

GenAK stays quiet. Also holding back information.

"You have to sever both their arms before shooting them in the head," the metered speaker says.

"It's the only way to kill them," someone else answers, making me jump. *How many people are down here?* "Even if you get the left arm, they can find another source code and attach it before they run out of juice. They need to plug into a code to keep going."

"They use other people's source code? Like batteries?" I ask.

"Some of the smarter ones—the ones who've been around a while. They even store arms, just in case. That's why you have to cut them all off, then aim for the head."

"Not a spawning ground." A voice calls from deeper in the darkness. "We'll have to recalculate and start the hunt over again." A barrage of '*shh*' waves through our rescuers group.

"Hey, we're clear. Flip the switch. Let's see who we picked up," a different voice says.

A light flickers to life, revealing a much larger room than my visually restricted mind thought up. We're underground in a massive parking garage with a dirt floor and no cars. Cement supports hold the weight of earth above us. The open space goes on forever under here. The hole we fell through is accessed through a crudely constructed wood platform, but everything else is cement.

The three people with us are of the non-distinct variety. I can't determine their gender. I never know how I'm supposed to refer to them. Everyone's wearing the same standard issue blue soldier vest.

GenAK appears unfazed by their ambiguity. "Lead the way."

The lights go out. "Whoa, hey!" I stumble forward, feeling more blind than before.

"Generators are spotty. Light doesn't last long below ground. It's better up top in the city," someone says.

"Be careful in the dark. We're blind. But if the Mord find their way down, they're never blind," a second voice adds.

"Comforting… thanks," I say. "But didn't you tell us they can't track underground?"

"No. It confuses them is all. It's safest to be in a group," answers another member I've yet to be introduced to. "As long as you're not bringing up the rear."

"Stay close," GenAK says in a whisper. "I know how to handle these things."

I whisper back. "Running across a barren wasteland was working great. Nice to know I'm in such resourceful and skilled company."

His hand presses my shoulder, slowing me. He leans so close his breath leaves a fog on my cheek. "Who says I'm talking about the Mord?"

I've already had the 'trust no one' lecture from him. I get it.

"Keep moving," one of the persons says.

I keep moving. We move deeper into the belly of the city. After several silent strides I notice a rasping sound echoing in the distance. I can't tell how distant or how near. Whether it's coming from the side, ahead, or behind us, I have no idea. The rattling breath bounces off beams and the ceiling, but is absorbed into silence once it touches the dirt floor.

I mark its closeness by where I lose the echo. To my left. I step to the right, while moving forward diagonally. The breathing bites at a pillar behind me, then it's gone. I move quicker.

"You're doing it wrong," GenAK says.

"Huh?" Doing what wrong? Being afraid? Is there a wrong way to be scared to death?

"The last place you hear them is the opposite of where it's coming from. It's bouncing sound."

"Echolocation?"

"They're tracking us."

My nerves grow nerves. I'm ready to spring if I have to. Or if anyone touches me without warning. My eyes strain into the darkness, seeing nothing, hearing nothing. I can't navigate like the Mord. Too much feedback makes me ear blind.

"Calm down. It won't help anything if you panic," GenAK whispers.

"Panic?" I take fast small steps as if by telling me not to panic, GenAK plants the idea in my reflexes. I talk in the smallest voice I can squeak out, but it sounds loud in this space. So much open darkness. We're all exposed. What kind of sanctuary is this? It's a trap, I know it. We're trapped. "Why would I need to panic? Should I? Is something happening? Do I need to panic?"

"*Shh.*"

"You *shh*," I say in a hoarse whisper.

Then I hear it. A rush of feet slide along the ground ahead of us, not lifting and falling the way sighted people walk. The sound closes around us fast.

"You armed?" one of the receiving company asks us.

"Not anymore," I say.

"Here."

A hand grips mine, twists my fingers up, and places the hilt of a heavy object in the cradle of my palm. Not a gun, it's weighted oddly. With my free hand I slide fingers from the base of the weapon out. It bites, slicing my fingers. It's a knife, or a short sword. Something sharp.

"You could have warned me." I stick my finger in my mouth and hold the blade low so I don't accidentally stab one of our party in the back. The darkness suffocates aim. "How much farther do we have to go?"

"Stop," GenAK says at my side.

Startled, I jab the knife in my hand forward. Luckily, no sees me shaking.

"Wait. Listen."

The rattling breath and dragging earth closes in. Closer, louder, more singular in its location.

"Let them handle it," GenAK says. "Learn what to do."

"How? I can't see a thing."

"There's nine," someone yells. "Nine Mord!"

"Nine?" I can't distinguish a number. I turn, knife out, straining to hear where they are. Resistance pushes against my blade.

"Ah!" a familiar voice screams out in front of me. So near. At the point of my weapon. One of the persons leading us. I skewered them accidently. Stabbed them.

"No. Oh, no," I gasp and drop the handle. Who saw me? How bad is it? Do they know it was me?

The sound of sniffing through open mouths fills the quiet places of the dark. A gurgling awfulness. Then ripping, crunching, sloshing of liquid and a horrid swallowing sound accompanied by an ever present sustained screaming. The cries come from the same voice of our group pierced by the knife in my hand.

"Thirty-Six-Two-Four is down. Run!"

"Run?" I stumble backward. Nothing behind me. I fall without GenAK there to catch me. "Just leave them?"

"Yes!" The voice reaches my ears from far ahead of me. I've been left behind, too.

All I can hear is the sound of dogs battling over a meal, growling, snapping, crunching bone. I push off the ground and stumble forward in the dark. I run toward the sound of lifting, falling feet and away from the dragging sludge of blood-soaked limbs being pulled solidly across the dirt. They're moving again, coming for us. And I'm the next closest target.

25

A far-off light needles at my pupils. My hands won't stop shaking. It's not like the anonymous underground player is the first player I'm responsible for putting out of the game. Why care now?

Ahead of me, three silhouettes take shape in the pinprick light. None of the rest of the group from underground makes it out. GenAK's shadow is broad, moving at twice the speed of the rest. His outline thickens and lengthens the closer he gets to the source of light, where the other two stretch thinner and thinner.

Colors distinguish themselves as light claims more ground. Distances make sense again. It shines so bright into the pillared underworld, I expect to burn the second I run beyond the roofline.

Once I'm outside, it isn't even sunshiny. Contrast from the total darkness fades as my eyes adjust. Tall angling buildings block most direct light, casting shadows crossing over each other, making deeper shadows. What the hell? It's a brighter shade of gloom out here.

"A knife in the dark?" GenAK asks me. "Whose bright idea was that?"

The remaining two rescuers exchange innocent looks. Like a chorus line, we turn toward the maw of underground. "That guy's, I guess," I say, referring to the one who didn't make it out.

"A mistake," GenAK says. His words are a warning for the other two more than excusing the fact I sliced one of the group. I hear 'Don't trust her' in his words.

We're waved forward by the person who opened the trap door in the wastelands. "We have to get to a safe zone."

"There are safe zones?" I ask. I fully intend to find one and never leave.

An ad catches my attention. On the screen in front of me is GenE247—the *real* GenE. Purple streaks her dark hair, bouncing back to reveal the striking features of her face and purple lips. She has smiling eyes. She made it. She's an ad star. Which campaign does she work with? Maybe she does the 'you've won leaderboard ruler' skits now. What possibly needs to be advertised to the donor players?

I look closer. Her mouth isn't smiling like her eyes. No wait. I had it wrong before. Her eyes aren't smiling, they're open wide, with moisture at the corners. Is she crying? What a strange ad. But man, can she act. A tear rolls down her cheek. The camera pans down revealing a Miss America style banner across GenE's chest. It reads: *Dis-loyalist.* The Commander's code stretches the length of the base of the screen.

"We can't stay here," one of the remaining non-genders says. "It's not safe."

"Wait." What's going on with GenE's ad? It's so strange. I don't know what I expected. Aren't ads something like *Shampoo for digital hair issues? How to maintain your code? Upgrades and how to reboot them?* This image isn't like that.

On the large screen billboard, GenE extends her arm. Her source code fills the screen. At my side, GenAK stares, unblinking, toward the screen. GenE247.

While I'm keeping eyes on GenAK, something happens in the ad overhead. Red pinkens the grey world around me, reflecting off the building windows and the heavy clouds. I know what it is before I look up. In the ad, GenE's arm—the one with the code on it—is sliced, separated from the rest of her with a sharp sword. Her eyes turn green, then black. All black. Her mouth pulls into a tight O, as her entire body falls to the right, away from her severed arm.

My feet forget how to stand upright, or the ground is rolling. Or I am magnetically the polar opposite of that ad and I'm being forced back from it. What happens? It's not real. It's an ad. She's acting.

Print crawls along the bottom of the screen following the Commander's code. *Consider all GenE disloyal separatists. Do not trust them. Turn them in if you can. Sever their code if you must.*

"What source code were you?" one of those walking with us asks me.

"An S. She's subservient, work class." GenAK speaks before

I can come up with a lie. Why cover for me? I can tell he doesn't trust me. "Not good for much more than cooking."

"We don't eat," the person says.

"So, not good for much." GenAK lets out a nervous laugh.

The screen resets and GenE's eyes once again lie a smile. It takes only seconds for the terror to reveal itself all over again.

"Had to ask," the guide raises a hand to the screen. "You know GenE's are wanted. Bad code. Some kind of upgrade malfunction affected all of them. The Commander must be protected—"

"At all cost," the group says in unison, including GenAK.

"...all cost." I catch on a little too late, trailing a millisecond behind the brainwashed blue-uniform wearing crowd. With all eyes on me and my late-to-the-party chant, I turn toward the looping ad with a hand raised to draw their attention back to destroying the pretty, dark haired-chick. "Is that common?"

"Never heard of it before now. The TECHs are taking care of it," someone explains from the crowd.

I've never been happier to be free of TECH-chick. I bet she'd 'take care of it' real good if she were here right now. Bullet in the head kind of good.

Or wait... the arm, I guess?

"Why the TECHs? Why not the AKs?" GenAK asks. I put an additional half step between us, ready to bolt if he decides to 'handle' it.

"It's code. TECHs know code," the someone says.

"They're also most likely to be corrupted by virus," I regurgitate things I've heard not knowing if it's true. Hoping I sound under the Commander's program, like everyone else.

"You mean the hacking issue?" one of the other members of the group says. "TECHs love to hack into systems and change sky programs, alter gravity, set fires, mess with physics laws because nothing has to 'apply' in a gameworld..."

"Yeah. That issue," I say. GenAK exhales low, annoyance thick in his breath.

"That was taken care of spawns ago."

I'm certain the Commander had something to do with it being resolved. Can't trust TECHs. "TECHs, am I right?" I say like I expect us to all fist bump right there on the street. No one extends a fist to bump.

"They've been cleared, I guess. It's the GenEs that're the problem now."

I'm all high alert. Not just my muscles, my brain pulls all its parts together like circuitry I'm trying to keep close at hand. I can feel it, smell it even. Something inside me is configuring again. I don't want to be a drone like the rest of the players I've met on this level. I adjust for efficiency in the need of independence. The scent of myelinated plastic and copper escapes my pores while I fight programming. Can the others not smell that? My insides boil to alertness with all this talk of virus and disloyalists.

GenAK turns stiffly away from me, like the digital robot he is. He's machinery and imagery playing tricks on my emotions. His back to me, he continues walking in the footsteps of the two remaining guides.

"How far to the safe zone?" I ask.

"Three blocks down and one over," someone announces over their shoulder from further up.

The pace of GenAK's walking increases. It's something miniscule to the eye, but the vibration in the earth comes at me with more force and trembling than before. I don't match his new speed. I assess the situation with as much reasoning as I can muster, feeling more and more removed from the idea of *human.* It's a difficult thing when every nerve inside screams with murderous rage.

What is wrong with me?

I bite my bottom lip. Not too hard. My jaw swirls the computer-generated copper flavor of my boiling brain around like the taste of blood on my tongue. I can't take my eyes off GenAK. If he turns around now and sees my face, I'm certain he'll scream like a little girl.

Ha. That's funny. I sort of want to witness that.

No.

Stop it.

Pull yourself together.

Clenching my jaw works much better. Yes. A lot less sinister, I'm sure. It's not like I intended to kill the kid. Or call the air strike. Or leave TECH-chick to die. Or ED. Or the kid—again. Or dude in the garage back there...

Whoa, I've done a lot of damage.

There's a taste of bronzy metal again.

The block stretches between our ragtag group with GenAK passing the other two, taking the lead like he knows where he's going. I saunter at the rear. The fear of Mord is still present, but GenAK's apparent lack of trust toward me feels more pressing, like it's something I have to deal with. I don't know why it matters, but it definitely matters.

The GenE ad has its place on my list of concerns as well. I don't want anyone bringing a machete down on my left arm anytime soon, despite the fact there're no letters there. GenAK covered for me... yet he's keeping his distance. He doesn't trust me. I don't know what to make of it.

So I saunter, or swagger, to buy time. If a Mord appears, I'll run. I'm not an idiot. Actually, lopping off one of the guides worked out well last time. I'd consider dismembering someone to save myself again.

No! Seriously, what is wrong with me?

Sacrificing one of the people who recently saved us? Not an option.

We pass a second screen playing GenE's ad. It's sad she's immortalized in her death. What a thing to play over and over. The more I stare at it, the more beautiful the red, and how it plays pink off the gray gloom around us.

See, that's a nice thing. Adding a happy color to the cold, dark world.

Stop it.

I stare at the footprints in the slush ahead of me. One at a time, I slide my feet in to match. Maybe GenAK was right all those levels back. I am infected. What if I'm turning into Mord? Sliding steps, so they don't trip from blindness. Thinking the way they do. Do they think?

One foot into a print. The next. Match and lift my other foot. I continue this way until there are no footsteps in front of me. I look up. A high rise building before me. The door, yards away, opens. Blackness sucks any hint of what lies inside into a pit of curiosity.

My head tilts for a better viewing angle beyond the open black barrier, uninviting building. Feeling exposed, as I am in the center of an abandoned street, I check my side.

Sure enough, GenAK stares at me from the side block. His arms remain at his sides, like the soldier he is. Folding them across his chest would demonstrate insecurity. He's nothing if not secure.

Our two guides wave him into a building. They appear impatient. How long has GenAK been ignoring them? His attention tuned to me?

I move beyond the building with its mysterious open door and turn toward GenAK. He doesn't wait for me after that. Blinking several times, he bends his head too low for me to read his expression, and enters where the guides motion.

They continue to wave me along. Funny. I sort of figured they'd shut me out once GenAK passed through.

"Haven't seen Mord for a while," I say when I catch up with the group.

"Change is coming," one of them says.

And he's right. That's what it is. Change. It's pink like the color of reflected blood, feeling like a tattoo whose needle pricks too deep for ink to show on the surface. It has the sound of ragged breath and tastes like burning metal.

"They always switch shifts at this hour. It makes it safer to travel. We'd never have found you otherwise," the other one says.

Oh. By change they simply meant the Mord shift change. The fact the Mord have something like job shifts adds to their creepiness.

What concerns me is how the serum the Commander shot me with is uploading into my brain. Does GenAK fight the same murder urges I am? Is there any way to shut off the creeper-stream taking over my brain? It's starting to freak me out a little. "I had a booster go bad. Anything for that?" I say. "My reboot has been a little jittery."

"That explains it." One of our guides lets out a breath along with the admission of relief.

"Explains what?" I ask.

"For a second," the person looks around to ensure no one else listens in, "we thought you might be GenE source code. You know, acting 'off,' a little wild-eyed."

"What?" I say, unable to conceal nervous laughter.

"I must have heard it wrong when we rescued you guys from the first group of Mord. Did you know any Mord from the previous level? They often follow from there." The other guide's shoulders relax, revealing a long sharp blade sticking out from behind the guide's leg, clenched in one hand. Were they planning to dismember me if I got close enough? "GenE... I thought someone said that..."

Reminder, keep my distance from that player.

GenAK standing at my side quiets the person speaking. "We haven't slept. Need to finish upgrades and reboots. We're not ready for multi-level mission status."

Multi-level missions? What kind of holding zone are we in? And who needs sleep? We're already dead.

"Sure. Seventh floor for charging ports."

Or maybe it wasn't the worst cover. They bought it, after all.

26

The narrow walls in the elevator force me to stand closer to GenAK than I intend.

I'm not so much on edge now. He pushes seven. I cross my arms in front of me like I'm tough, though I feel like a balloon has been deflated in my guts. The darkness and hum of the elevator gears fill everything in between us.

"We're really going to the seventh floor?"

"The elevator is."

"And we're…?" I don't know what to fill in.

"Move back." He lifts the service hatch on the elevator.

"They have video monitoring?" I assume. The Commander seems to be five steps ahead of everything. How else is that done unless there's surveillance?

"Maybe whoever's monitoring won't mention anything." GenAK lets go of the panel and grips my left wrist. With his other hand he forces my sleeve high up my arm. He pulls so my unmarked skin passes under every ceiling panel, the most likely place to harbor a hidden security camera.

"Hey! Stop it." I attempt to pull my arm away, smacking myself in the chest when he lets go.

I recover my arm, despite the obvious fact he and anyone watching know my arm lacks code. "So... how long have you known?" He didn't react to my exposed, flawless skin while running from the Mord kid, so he had to know before that.

GenAK doesn't pause to contemplate. My facade shatters before my eyes, and he can't so much as shrug to satisfy how exposed I feel. "About your code?"

I nod.

"I've always known." He scratches his own marked skin, confident in his branding. Lines from where his nails rake over his code redden the skin, but has no effect on the numbers stacked in a neat row along the length of his arm.

I want to bite the center numbers out from their line.

Like this thing I've been afraid makes me different doesn't matter for him. He's known and not shared. He's let me work at hiding my arm when I didn't need to. He could have assured me he's got my back, at least.

"Maybe we should find someplace to talk," he says. Feeling sorry for myself is replaced with dread. I'd rather go back to pretending, ignoring. Anything but talking. "We shouldn't be here," he says. Not helping the whole 'something's off' thing going on with me. "It's overrun with Mord. The Commander has obviously switched tactics. This is a dumping ground where he reassigns plant-players to other levels. It's not a real game level."

That explains the fact we never reached a game pad to advance like normal, and how things overlapped all weird.

The vent system accessed from the elevator shaft isn't exactly large enough for a person of GenAK's breadth to crawl around inside. He wriggles through the opening to the maintenance space between the floors. It's about two-and-a-half feet of cables, pipes, and tubing. Not comfortable, but I doubt there are cameras here.

"How'd you know?" I ask once we're 'not here' or wherever GenAK didn't want to talk. He's acting like there is no place he wants to talk. I push aside hanging cords and duck under rattling pipes while pressing the subject. "About my arm."

"It was my mistake. When I programmed you, I forgot to include some made-up source code."

I stop following. While I think back on first meeting AK, my body can't move, like in a dream. *Whoa. Hold up. He what?* Paralysis releases my tongue only, while the rest of me is a word blender, trying on the fact that he's always known in the feel of my murderous hands and how that phrase cushioned my coward feet through previous levels. "Explain."

"I'm a military software engineer. I make and break codes. I don't look like this in real life." He motions to the panel reflecting back his broad shoulders and chiseled muscles. "I'm a short wiry nerd who plays with numbers and programs drones. When I met the Commander, he took one look at me—this avatar me." He waves a hand in front of his broad shoulders. "And I was in his circle right away. I saw what he was doing, cheating to reprogram donor loyalty. In his eyes, he's only redirecting sheep, clearing his own path. He used me and other programmers to tamper with booster packs until he learned he can make his own health shots using anyone not in his inner circle."

I gave GenAK some of a booster shot when he was unconscious, unable to make that choice on his own. Does that make me responsible for him being subject to whatever the Commander added to gamer programming?

"Cheating comes at a cost—Mord. Well, one way to Mordout, at least. There's more ways to become Mord. It's sort of an out-of-control computer virus at this point. Pretty soon the whole system will be infected."

"Can't they reboot the system?"

"I assume the people running this little experiment for AI have that in mind. That's what the Commander believes."

"What's wrong with that?"

"I doubt those of us playing this version are still around in fleshville to plug back in when all the bugs are taken care of. This is our one shot."

"Debug means total fail for this donor batch..." I see the dilemma and increased desperation. Time is running out. I'm sure there are investors waiting for results. What happens when they run out of patience?

"I created my own code using Mord parts. I made you."

"Me?"

GenAK doesn't look at me. "You had to upload outside the game for the system to accept you for what I needed. I wasn't sure I did it right. Especially when I ended up in the dome instead of back on the Commander's level where I could monitor your progress. But I knew it was you right away when I met you."

"You didn't say anything? Why? Why would you keep that from me?"

"I noticed immediately I'd messed up. I made two major errors. One, you had no source code tat. It's a dead giveaway you're not a human donor." He curses as though he might still be able to go back in time and fix the error. "I screwed up big time overlooking that. I honestly don't know how you'll reach the last level without a source code."

"We're not on that level, are we?"

"We're in a holding level. Big time not good." He crawls ahead so his voice gets more faint. "And two, I made you to be a killer. When I woke up with your hands on my neck. I thought you were going to end me."

Hearing *killer* relieves the itch in my nerves and satisfies my craving for a weapon. I'm a weapon. I relax, resting my side against the cold tin of the vent before everything rewinds and reverses itself to wherever it is I store my sensibilities. *I'm the bad guy?* "You what? I'm a what?"

He rips a cord out of his way and wipes his face. "Not only that, but I'm pretty sure the Commander figured out what I was doing. I'm not going to get a second chance at hacking his plan." GenAK pauses. He mumbles while contemplating where the vent diverges.

The vent wall's coolness no longer comfortable, I push off the side with my shoulder, making a warbled echo. GenAK cranes to silence me with a glance. When he looks at me, it's not to hush an equal.

Not human.

He turns away and I drop my shoulder back against the vent side so that it warps and strains louder.

Not a player.

His expression the second time is 'the glue on my model car isn't holding'.

Not even well programmed...

I've been *designed.*

"I'm double not real. Awesome." As in anything but awesome.

"You're real."

"No. I'm not. You are. Even the Mord are more actual 'human' than me."

"The concept of real is sort of moot. Don't you agree?"

I press my hands against the sides of our metal pathway, knowing it will make GenAK squirm. He can't control me and it matters what I do. If my actions matter to him, he should under-stand that existing, being able to claim 'human' as what I evolved from, matters to me.

"No. I don't. This whole place is based on ideal human intel-ligence populating artificial life. Whoever thought they needed this place doesn't want a fake." I point my own finger at my chest.

GenAK waves a hand as though I'm being overdramatic. "You're not designed to populate robotic thought." He selects a path and moves on without checking to see if I'm following him.

I scramble to stay near. The man has the power to define me. If he's not nearby, what defines me? "But, you said..."

He cuts me off. "I said you're a weapon. I was clear about that. Why can't that be real?"

He's lucky we're confined to a tight space. If I had room… "This whole time, my goal has been to level-up, to advance. To make it to the end."

Realizing we're not going anywhere until I get the answers I want, GenAK stops crawling away and shifts so that he's almost facing me. He can't turn around completely. "I had to make it so you appeared as normal as possible. You had to have the same exterior motives as everyone else in the game."

I punch the metal. Why is he not getting this? GenAK created me to act and think like I'm a legitimate player. Discovering I'm a tool, or as he clarified 'a real tool,' is pretty damn upsetting. The metal sheets don't fit together as well in this section and instead of a warble, the seam splits. I move forward into the next section of tube, forcing GenAK to move forward with me. He advances into a section filled with cords and cables, so that he has to push them aside and up in order to make his way through.

"I want to win," I say. "For real. I want that. To live." And yes, I realize how stupid I sound right now. Fighting the dangling cords, I have an urge to pull them all down as if they're some kind of life support to the whole program, which I know they aren't.

"Do you even know what 'live' means?" he asks. And I realize I can't answer. Not because I don't have an answer, but because I'm not qualified. No matter what I say, he'll be able to tell me that I don't know what I'm talking about. Because I've never technically 'lived' and can't possibly define the condition.

He gives me so long to respond, I think he's done talking, but he goes on. "You're designed to prevent certain people from winning."

"No. I refuse." I sit in my web of cords and cross my arms.

"It's your programming."

"I've reprogrammed before. I can do it again." I reach up a hand and pull on a cable. It doesn't snap or break, or do anything satisfying.

"Before, you were overridden by some new Commander code and went back to default settings. It's not the same thing."

Like he knows. "Shut up!" I put my hands over my ears.

"I coded your program. I know how you work." He pulls more cables out of his way. "I even made sure you had an anti-virus feature." He laughs to himself like it's the coolest thing. Meanwhile he forgot to give me a source code.

Not bothering to yank on the mess of wires, I slap a cable that swings between us and whip GenAK in the back. "You're as fake as I am."

He pulls the cord I shoved his direction, a zip is followed by a snap before the cable snakes to the ground at one end. "If I'm lucky enough to still be on life-support, I'm a vegetable on a gurney, waiting to download into a robot. Assuming I make it to the final level. You..." The look on his face tells me I'm not even half a thing. I'm scrap numbers gathered inside an already functioning system. I'm Frankenstein's monster of the digital world. "You have no real-world counterpart."

"I get it." Not in the cool kids' club.

A muffled dragging causes me to jump. GenAK shifts his position in the cramped space as well.

"You heard it too?" GenAK asks.

I'm occupied with what I am more than the distant crashing of the building's inner workings.

Spare parts.

That's what I am. A monster. There's no place far enough for me to hide from myself.

GenAK moves away from the noises deeper in the vents. I follow like the dog I am.

I want him to say, *"It was necessary."* Or, *"Sorry, this isn't what I intended."* Or plain, *"Sorry."* He says nothing, letting me skitter like a spider retreating into the darkness where I belong.

The rustling sound in the maintenance space gets louder, accompanied by the gurgling breath of a Mord. It's the one with a hole in his head where an eye should be.

The kid.

And he's blocking our path.

"Back out the way we came," GenAK orders.

"He found us." My not moving prevents GenAK from moving. "Maybe he's fighting it, like me."

"No way am I trusting someone without eyes to get within arm's reach."

I hesitate. "I did this to him. Maybe I can fix it." I have an anti-viral after all. GenAK continues to push against me, desperate to get away. Somehow he backs his rump over me, so that I'm between the kid and GenAK. I reach for the kid who slowly stretches his neck out toward my hand. "He's in there. I know it."

GenAK grabs me from behind and yanks me toward him in time to avoid the kid snapping for my arm. With a swift spin and twist, GenAK extends his foot into the Mord kid's face, knocking him back. The effort leaves GenAK out of breath. "You shot him. Can you blame him?"

"I'm trying to fix it."

The kid growls. He takes several short breaths through his mouth like sniffing the air with his throat. Pressing forward through tubes and wires, he doesn't avoid anything hanging in his way. He stresses it till the obstacle breaks and he can proceed. It's a slow process, giving us time to escape.

"Can't fix that," GenAK says.

I twist to follow him. "You're going to fix me and I'm going to fix him."

"Says the chick who recently stabbed an innocent stranger."

"You programmed me, so that's your fault. You can fix me."

"I don't want to fix you. I just don't want you to go apewall on me before I can get you where you need to be."

"I don't want to be a weapon." My muscles clench, straining my words.

"Too late."

My hands are on his shirt, choking him with his own collar. "Fix me."

GenAK looks back to where the Mord kid makes headway between cables and cords. "No." He coughs.

"Fix me, please." I let go.

GenAK rubs his neck where his shirt dug in. "You're not broken."

Another cable snaps behind us. A pipe gongs against the bottom level, ripped from its housing. The Mord kid is getting close again.

Rattling pipes clank and cords are yanked from the ceiling,

sending up sparks yards from where I'm waiting on my haunches to know what to do next. "Move," I tell GenAK because now is not the time to prove anything. Now is the time to live long enough to have a chance later.

27

At the edge of the elevator shaft we wait. GenAK's arm prevents me from moving. His damn hair in his eyes can't help him much. "Don't let anyone know what we spoke about." Behind me the Mord-kid rips his way toward us.

"I'm not about to broadcast the fact I'm a walking scrap pile." I wish I could go back to not knowing. Talk about a confidence killer. I push against his arm. "Move it."

His arm drops. I push past him, feet dangling into the elevator shaft. The lift above us makes it difficult to coordinate an exit. Extending my arms, all my weight supported by my fingertips, I'm able to kick the elevator door with my toes for the floor below us. When the doors open the slightest crack, I let go of one hand. Swinging wide, I almost lose my grip. GenAK does nothing to catch me. My free hand slaps against the elevator door's rubber stripping. The door strains under my effort to force it open.

"Faster would be nice," GenAK says. The ripping and tearing come closer.

"Don't rush me."

I pry one side of the outer lift doors open. It's going to look suspicious to swing out of the elevator shaft when no elevator box stops at this level. Assuming anyone is watching. I don't know how to get around that. I push out, aiming my legs for the open side of the doors and shoot myself through. Seconds later, GenAK rolls into the hall. He returns to the elevator to reclose the sides of its door.

His finger snaps to his lips, demanding silence. He waves 'move out' wordlessly. Arms folded, I follow GenAK to the stairs. In the sanctuary of the stairwell, I open my mouth.

'Shh.' He puts his hand to my mouth, the immediate gesture again. No sound to accompany it.

I tighten the fold of my arms. GenAK taps his forearm, shows two fingers, then four fingers and a downward hand slicing motion. Two fingers at me, at him, then he's pointing up, and some circle-the-air thing and a head nod.

From all of which, I realize first grade math skills are vital to military communication.

As a reply, I hold up one finger and extend the same arm his direction so he can get the full effect of my chosen middle finger. GenAK slaps my hand away. The sound reverberates off the walls, going both upward and downward.

The return sound echo is not a single slap, but a dragging, gnashing, with hands slapping on railing — the unmistakable sound of Mord. Both above and below us in the stairwell.

"How did so many get inside?" I ask, no longer worrying about being heard. Pretty sure they know we're here.

GenAK's shoulders drop. "Because I told you there are *two*"—he redoes the hand motions to go with his angry explanation—"armless gamers on the landing above us, and *four* below. We are going to have to circle around and find a different exit."

"Oh." I imitate the air circle move with my middle finger still in the air. "That."

Mord trip down the stairs, eager to get to us.

"Now what?"

GenAK pulls a gun from his belt. He throws me a second, smaller gun. I catch it easily like I've trained for it. One side of the grip warms in my palm and the other side is like ice against my fingers.

My insides fight. One part of me shouts *Shoot him. Shoot him now. His fault for making you and for giving you a gun.* And the other part of me pushes back with. *Defend the human, champion their cause... Don't be an idiot, you're a tool. Shoot the military nerd.*

The trigger compresses. It clicks and resists, the first safety measure. It's no time before I squeeze it as far back as it will go. A bullet rips through the air, leaving rivulets of code floating in the space around me. For a split second they're visible before moving together. The rift heals.

A single howl calls out, then a body falls backward against the stairs. I shoot a Mord in the arm, right in the center of his number. He rolls from the upper landing and stops at our feet. "Good shot," GenAK says, not having a clue I missed my target

—him. He rushes the Mord and, with his bare hands, rips off the injured arm.

"Whoa!" I holler. "What are you doing?"

"It's the only way."

"With your hands? You don't have a sword or something?"

GenAK lifts his eyebrows and glances down at his tailored military uniform. "Where am I going to hide a sword?"

Good point. "Still."

He shoots the thing in the head. "Fewer Mord would have made it to the upper levels." GenAK grips the railing, ready to run ahead. "You know what?" His eyes are on the gun in my hand even though he too holds a hefty firearm. "You first."

Back to the wall, gun in both hands held at shoulder height. I sidestep up the stairs, feeling every bit the stealthy bad-A. Looking back to catch the impressed expression on GenAK's face I'm sure to find, I trip. My gun clatters to the stairs, sliding two steps down before coming to a stop at GenAK's feet. Impressed doesn't describe his expression.

Worse, snarling battles from below are headed our way. I've basically sent out a Mord-alert.

"Sorry." I bend to retrieve the gun. "Sorry," I say again once I have it.

"Run." A shove at my back isn't needed, but GenAK pokes his pistol at me anyway.

The stairs aren't steep and, being a fake person in a digital world, it's unfair I get winded. This experience comes complete with depleting health levels. I know boost serum can counter the effects of game wear and tear. I'd rather have my arm sliced off than take another of the Commander's mad-scientist shots.

A Mord on the landing above me snaps its mouth, catching a swatch of my shirt fabric before I notice it there. I take it back. I can tolerate a booster shot right now. They aren't bad, are they? Raising my gun, I aim for the Mord's head.

"Arm, arm. Shoot the arm." GenAK slaps his arm like a phlebotomist searching for a rolled vein.

I re-aim for the Mord's string of code tattooed on its arm and fire. It's not like the creature can see the shot coming. It's merely sniffing us out through mouth breathing. The other problem: stairs. The Mord drags one foot over an unanticipated step one second before I fire, throwing his balance off. And my bullet. I shoot high.

The bullet bursts against the tiled wall, spraying porcelain chips into the air. The sound brings the attention of additional Mord several levels above. Three landings below us, eyeless heads stretch atop pale necks, with up-angled chins and open mouths. They're breathing in our scent, salivating and choking on the anticipation of ripping into our code.

"Shoot again," GenAK shouts, firing several shots at the Mord I missed. He connects with the numbers on its arm. The Mord falls to the stairs, limp. GenAK rushes toward it, puts a hand on its shoulder, and grips the wrist to separate the joint from its shoulder socket.

The Mord plays possum. When GenAK bends down for leverage, it bites him on the neck. "*Aaaahh!*"

I can't get a shot without hitting GenAK. They're both in the way, and the rest of the Mord close in on us fast. I point at random faces, reminding myself to aim for the numbers.

"Shoot them."

The Mord opens its mouth, sucks air fast, quick filling its lungs, then redirects its teeth for GenAK's arm.

Can it smell the code? I thought it was smelling us, the way people smell in real life, but its actions lead me to believe otherwise. The way it sniffs. Body odor for Mord is a metallic leeching of binary programming. My breathing quickens. I stand perfectly still. The stairwell fills with Mord, cutting off our escape.

"GenE, shoot!" GenAK fights off the Mord's mouth from clamping down on his arm. I'm certain when its teeth connect, GenAK will crumple. I want to help, but my feet stay planted. Fear, or something else, prevents me from acting.

A dark furrow crosses GenAK's face. He slams his forehead against the Mord, knocking him back, then curls his lips away from his canines and bites the Mord where its numbers are exposed. He rips the patch of skin bearing code out with his teeth. The way they attack players.

"Nasty," I whisper, then slap a hand over my mouth. Silent as possible. The Mord rushing the landing all look to GenAK. Their mouths open and close. He spits the chunk of Mord-flesh from his teeth and the creatures around him swarm the felled Mord like a pack of wolves attacking a weak or injured animal.

As each Mord passes me, I flinch. But not one turns their sniffing mouth toward me. I'm invisible, as long as I don't draw attention to myself. GenAK runs down the hall to the elevator shaft. I follow wordlessly. Once there, GenAK forces open the sliding doors into the pocket and jumps to the far side of the wall where a rung ladder protrudes ever so minimally. The chances of jumping and getting a grip are practically impossible. But, of course, GenAK catches hold like he's a stunt man.

He doesn't beckon me to jump. Instead, he puts a hand up to silence me, motions for me to move aside, and calls out, "Come get me."

Mord rush the open doors before I have a chance to react. I have nowhere to turn before the opening is overrun, so I take hold of the door and swing wide around so I don't get barreled over. I'm forced into the gaping shaft and there's no grip. No rung ladder on this side. My hand slips. One toe still grips the corner ledge of the floor and my hand holds tight to the open-door pocket. I look down to a gaping chasm. One slip and I fall a hundred feet.

The sightless beasts trip over each other at the chance to rip at GenAK. Not one of them seeks me out. Still, it's difficult to steady my breathing. I panic they'll hear me, or feel the violent vibration of my rising and falling chest with every intake of air. Even hiding like I am, I'm within their reach.

One falls when the floor vanishes beneath its feet. Not one Mord following the first hesitates to repeat the same error. Mord after Mord tumbles through the open elevator doors, into the shaft, and down the long shoot. Seven floors. My palms sweat. My grip slips from the door opening. I manage to stay in position until the last Mord falls through.

Leaning toward the hall, I check how many are left.

Too many.

They keep rising from the stairs. I can't hold on. I'm going to slip. My grip drops inches. I manage to slap my hand higher on the metal. The sound or vibration draws attention of one Mord standing at the open maw before the elevator shaft.

I stop myself from cursing out loud. GenAK kicks and pounds at the wall on his side of the metal tube, drawing the creature's attention. He must really need me, to work so hard to keep me alive. It works. The Mord takes one more step out, falling into the deep. At this point I doubt the Mord are all meeting a sudden death. Enough cushion of bodies piling up at the base means they can slink away after falling and do it all again. Climb stairs, snap teeth, fall into elevator hole, repeat.

"Jump," GenAK says. "You have time. They can't detect you."

My eyes widen. I don't want to speak and draw any more attention. Yet I still need to react. *What are you saying?*

"Walk out there, into the crowd. Get a running start and jump."

No freaking way. My eyes have to convey everything. I turn my head to the mob of feral beasts. I'm not putting myself in front of that.

"Drag your feet like they do. When you get to the edge, jump. I'll catch you."

I'm pretty sure my eyebrows leap from my forehead and fly off to freedom in the land of the living bird-brows with how high they extend on my forehead in disbelief. Catch me? He's going to catch me? And if he misses, I'll fall into the churning masses of Mord teeth below? No, thanks.

"Do it. Now."

My foot slides more fully onto the platform of floor seven. I ease my body away from the inner wall and pick my way through the pressing crowd, trying not to draw attention to the fact I'm going against the current.

Insane.

Five yards from the elevator door I shift direction, again trying to remain unnoticed. It's hard to blend into a slow pressing, murderous crowd without drawing attention to my anxiety given the situation. I inhale slowly to calm myself. It's different, my breathing. One head cocks to the side and slowly angles my direction. My heart speeds up.

Oh, no. Oh, no. Oh, no. I have to run now.

My feet dig and push against the floor, no more dragging. I shove Mord aside, keeping my head down, and scream as I leap from the edge of floor seven into the open elevator hole.

"Too much," GenAK hollers. Both of his hands leave the rung. He's not holding on? His open arms catch me as I plow into him, smashing us both against the far wall momentarily. Then we both angle outward, bouncing off the wall after impact, and fall, down, down, down. Then yank to a stop.

With knees tucked painfully through one rung, GenAK has both of us dangling like trapeze artists over a pit of masticating Mord. I'm sure it would make a dramatic finale in a Cirque du Soleil performance.

"Grab the ladder in front of you," he says.

Letting go of him, I grip the rungs below where his legs have saved us. If GenAK was still in the human world I'd predict he needs both knees replaced in a month's time after a stunt like that. Not to mention his bloody neck from the Mord bite.

"Climb," he says.

"What about not giving away our position?"

"With that many Mord in the building? Who has time to worry about us?"

We rise, passing the maintenance space where a single Mord crouches, sniffing the air. A hole in his forehead, like a single off-sides eye, ticks like a second hand following our upward progress on the opposite side of the elevator opening from where it is.

"AK," I say, pointing to the Mord kid.

"That one worries me." He moves as far to one side of the ladder as possible to give greater distance between himself and the kid.

"Why?" I feel it, too. Like he can see us or he's calculating a plan behind the hole in his head.

"Because he's listening right now."

My heart stops. GenAK speaks truth. The ticking head motion stills, with his head tilted like he's waiting for sound cues. His mouth hangs open, following us based on vibrations from the metal sides of the shaft. I close my mouth and push against GenAK's foot for him to climb faster.

The farther we can get from the Mord kid, the better.

28

T he box above us jerks.

Oh, no.

Electric whirring hums around us. GenAK looks through his feet to meet my eyes. His mind sorts through the problem before I register what the problem is.

"Go back down," he says.

The elevator, several floors still above us, continues to bounce. Persons must be piling in. We have no way to guess which direction it'll travel. With our luck, it's coming down, right for us.

My feet slip, but my hands hold tight. Regaining grip on the rungs, I climb in reverse toward the still growing pile of Mord, now nine floors down. When I pass the number for the eighth floor I hesitate.

"Don't stop. No time."

The elevator box comes straight for us.

But I can't force myself to pass the opening where I can feel Mord kid waiting for us, like he knows we'll come back for him. I left him back in the bombed courtyard a long time ago. Every encounter since then has been me coming back to finish the job. Still, I want to save him. Or maybe I want him to trust me to save him. Can Mord think?

"Move, move, move." GenAK steps one foot over the top of me, landing his toe on the rung between my legs.

"Do you mind?" It's not safe being close to me. I press against him, pushing him back, away from his grip on the rungs, forcing him to fall off. I stop myself, of course. I don't want to be the person I'm programmed to be. GenAK doesn't command me. I am *not* his dog. Of course, if he's dead I'll be free…

"No," I say.

Above us, the elevator box stops. Both of us stare at the cable undercarriage. Now what?

"Mord," GenAK screams.

I look down to see the Mord kid with GenAK's shoe in hand. He dangled too close and the kid grabbed his shoe.

"Go back up?"

He doesn't answer. The silence breaks on the piles of Mord below and the single one waiting out our mistakes and miscalculations.

The elevator stays two floors above us, still stopped.

"Up." GenAK climbs over the top of me.

Following behind, my hands shake when they're not holding tight to a metal bar. The elevator bounces and lifts the slightest degree, emptying its passengers.

"Won't it come down now?" I ask.

"Nah." GenAK grabs the cords underneath, and places one foot at the adjacent maintenance space. Below us, Mord kid turns frantic, like he can tell we're close. "My guess is, there's no one below us. Non-Mord, I mean. The button to call the elevator will summon from above. And Mord don't have the cognitive capacity to stop and direct an elevator."

"I don't trust the gamers on this level," I say.

"Have you trusted them on any level?"

"No."

"Then we agree." He has monkey-climbed across the bottom of the elevator and now hangs by his fingers from the floor's lip. "Get off on nine."

Swallowing hard, I follow his example. The cables and wires under the elevator don't feel secure. My only confidence is they hold GenAK and he's huge compared to me. My hand slips. My eyes drift to the darkness beneath my dangling feet. The Mord kid from the maintenance space stretches out the length of the wall, climbing. Thank goodness the maintenance spaces are every other floor or it would have a ladder of sorts to climb. At the moment, the outstretched hand slaps for a grip, toes bearing its weight on the ledge of the maintenance opening.

With all my strength, I swing my free arm back to the under-side of the elevator. At the same time, the box jerks, shaking my grip. One hand falls again, and my other hand slips. Four finger-tips keep me from gravity's pull. "AK…" Sweat beads down my arm, cold against my flushed skin. "Help."

The elevator bounces once more. GenAK looks at me, down

toward the Mord attempting to climb up, then at the bottom of the elevator. Reaching out, he grabs a handful of cables. His legs swing wildly when he fully abandons the wall. My fingertip grip strains. His feet wrap around my middle. I can't tell if it's a tactic to control his swinging or to prevent me from falling.

The elevator rises.

"Now what?" I say.

"Hold on."

The box continues to lift. We're so far up at this point I don't worry about the Mord killing me if we fall. The distance will do that. Wires dig into the under-knuckle of my fingers, the tips purple.

"I'm slipping."

His legs squeeze against my stomach, his muscles lifting me inches higher. It's enough. My other hand finds a grip, but the effort snaps a cord in GenAK's grasp. He curses. The elevator stops again.

"How high are we?" I wish I could turn off my sweat glands. Beads roll off my nose. Shadows and faint gnashing linger below my dangling feet. It's even too high to know the growling sounds below are Mord, not buzzing electricity.

The doors directly in front of our bodies ding, then slide apart. My legs kick to twist me around to face the opening. The elevator box above us doesn't move, yet these doors miraculously open.

Getting a spin going, my vision turns to reveal our two remaining guides from when we first spawned on this level and three important looking figures in black suits. Not military suits.

More like business attire. The center of the three business persons is a female and the two flanking her are non-gender.

Too much momentum pushes me past the company waiting at the door.

"There's a breach in the building," GenAK addresses our company, as if it's normal to greet people hanging from elevator undercarriages. "Mord are everywhere down there."

One of the guides leans forward, eyes angled down to validate GenAK's claim. "You know your mission yet?"

"Don't die," I say.

The guide leans back. One eye narrows at me, almost as if I'm being winked at, except the sentiment behind the action signals annoyance. "Your objective for this level."

GenAK keeps his gaze forward when I look at him for how to respond. Particularly knowing this entire level serves as some weird backdoor program for the Commander. "Kill Mord?" I respond, unsure if it's a gold-star answer, or one that will get my arm macheted off.

"That's an obstacle. What's your objective?" one of the well-dressed non-genders asks.

"Don't mind the feminists. They take issue with gender kind," says the woman in the center. "Particularly the male version."

"Feminists?" I ask.

"You've come this far into the game and didn't know non-genders are feminists?" She chuckles. It's a delicate sound, causing those at her sides to go tense. "How did you survive this long?"

GenAK takes a turn tensing. His legs still wrap around my waist, holding some of my weight. He drops them and I almost lose my hold on the cables under the elevator box. I'm too fatigued to play this game of words and hidden meanings. Either they tell me my objective, shoot me for being a threat, or let me drop.

"Do you mind?" I say, extending a foot to the platform. I hand-over-hand it, monkey-bar style with cables and cords, until I can balance my weight over my feet on solid ground. I fall to my knees, safe from falling. In seconds, GenAK stands by my side.

After a long moment of breathing, I stand at GenAK's side. He too recovers from way too much time using all our muscle strength to avoid dying.

"Objective?" he says. "Are you going to tell us or do we have to continue guessing?"

The female in the expensive suit looks to her right, then left. They nod in turn and she faces us before nodding herself. "You have to cure someone who can help you."

"Who?" he says.

She pulls a folded pamphlet from an inside pocket. "Here's a map. A tracker beacon indicates the location of your target. You'll have to pick up supplies along the way and figure out how to cure the Mord virus. If you can, rescue this Mord." She taps a blinking green dot.

Not green again. Just like the military vests. I picture the kid's light flash out after I shoot him.

"Once cured, the survivor will know how to reach the plat-form needed in order to level up."

"Is there any way to reach the platform without wasting time on this?" I ask. GenAK already informed me the Mord virus is unstoppable at this point. Why bother curing one at a time? Sounds like a diversion preventing us from figuring out what the Commander's up to. Either that, or he needs players to buy him time on the outside of the game—so whoever's in charge doesn't pull the cord and start over before he can get out. All eyes stare at me, unblinking. "Just asking."

"This is the task," the woman says. "This is the game." She might be trying to sell this whole 'really real not-made-up level' thing a bit too hard.

"What about you?" I ask.

"We're coming with you, of course."

"What?" GenAK straightens. "No. No way."

"Part of the challenge is to gather a group of survivors with different skill sets. Consider it a resource collection."

Babysitters. Five of them.

"No," he repeats. "We go alone."

The female steps out of her troop of feminists. If I found myself where GenAK stands now, I'd have the urge to step back, which would result in falling down the elevator shaft. He resists stepping back. His neck muscles twitch. I know he doesn't like her proximity.

"We all go or you stay," she says.

GenAK twitches his nose, almost like he's about to sneeze. "How can we trust you?"

"I gave you the map. If that's not enough validation, I don't know what is."

"How did you know we were here?" he asks.

"You weren't exactly quiet hanging from the bottom of the elevator we were in."

I bite my lip, then remember they could have come to the door below, not lift the elevator and then come back down to get us. "Why did you send the elevator back up before opening the door?"

"My associates went down, but there's a Mord on the other side of those doors. I'm surprised you didn't know that…"

I smack my forgetful head. "The kid, right. I forgot."

GenAK kicks the back of my knee, buckling it.

"The kid?" the woman asks.

"I mean, that's right. I forgot some random, young-looking Mord managed to climb up after us."

The main speaker narrows her eyes at me. I almost shrug my shoulder, but opt to pull my left sleeve tight over my wrist, allowing no opportunity to notice my tatless skin.

"Suit up," one of the feminists says.

"You have names, or are we supposed to call you fem-one and fem-two?" I ask.

One of them opens its mouth, but isn't permitted the chance to answer before the woman speaks. "No one gets a real name. Not here." She's not the first person to spout that response. She adds more to the spiel along with a bunch of pomp and importance. "Names are reserved for those assigned to AI. It's an honor."

"I dozed off when they explained honor during the rules. You know, pushed A before I finished reading the dialogue." I smile because it's funny. No one else smiles, especially not GenAK.

"We've been distinguishing by source code," I say, still not apologizing for their apparent lack of humor. "I'm Gen—"

"She's GenS and I'm an AK." I'm cut off before I say GenE, having forgotten about the hunt for all E code mandate.

"I'm GenB," says the woman in the nice suit. "My associates are also B's. And the two staying behind are S."

"Wait, they're staying behind? I thought we were all going together," I say.

"They've agreed to lure the Mord in a different direction. It's up to them to find us if they survive."

The guides don't look like they have much choice in the plan. S are obviously a lower class Gen according to these Bs, who *are* a bunch of bitches as far as I can tell. Not the kind of people I want on my team.

"If you're all the same Gen, then what do we call you? QueenB and your dogs?" I chuckle.

GenAK clenches his jaw and closes his eyes longer than a blink. He has no patience for humor. No one cracks even half a smile, though the GenS designated to stay behind look on the verge of appreciating my joke.

"I'd prefer the AK in charge of security, and you," she nods to me, "are lead scavenger and navigator." She makes no effort to hide her distaste for me once she hears I'm GenS.

"Am I?" I say. "Lucky me."

"Would you rather stay behind?"

"Actually—" I step forward, pushing my way into her bubble. By how far she leans away from me I know it's working to make her uncomfortable.

"Those assignments suit us fine," GenAK says, pulling me back toward him.

"Good to know one of you understands your place."

I mime mimicking him. I think we could take all these gamers, even with our limited ammo. If I could shake his arm off, I'd, I'd... do something stupid, but feel great about it.

"We'll need to keep an eye out for health containers. I understand Mord cure can be found or created from contents inside the syringes," GenAK says.

Creator of virus and manipulator of code. All he needs is TECH-chick's engineering know-how and this posse would be set to reprogram the entire Mord host to go against the Commander. I doubt there is such a thing as 'Mord cure'. More likely an update to old programming. "You chose your team well," I say.

"What does that mean?" FemOne asks.

GenAK answers for me. "She's having a difficult time coming down from escaping the Mord on the lower levels. Specifically, her mouth has failed to recover."

"So stop talking," QueenB instructs me.

I'm about to spit out some choice words, but a familiar large, salty palm, covers the entire lower half of my face. "We can do that," GenAK answers.

"Let's move out." QueenB motions for the GenS pair to head down to the lower levels. She presses the button for the elevator and we wait. It's not long before the five of us enter the dangling box. QueenB depresses the highest button on the panel.

"Roof?" I ask. "What's on the roof?"

"Our ride."

What? A helicopter? I have no desire to fly in another one of those things, the last time being such a fun experience. Also, how do we scavenge supplies by way of chopper?

The lift stops. I'm the last out. There's no helicopter in sight on the wide-open roof space. Buildings spread out in every direction. Tall ones stab the sky wherever they can. Shorter buildings, close ones, on the alley sides, and distant buildings with highways between them. I feel the need to stab something, similar to the most reaching structures. The closest thing to me is FemTwo. My eyes must give me away because GenAK steps back to where I stand. His hands nestle in the crook of my elbow, locking me from locating anything sharp. The move restricts the reach I would need to slide through FemTwo's code tat if I did happen to have anything sharp. The stab-rage passes and my muscles relax. GenAK's grip does not.

He mumbles through clenched teeth. "Play it cool. We want to make it out of this without alerting the Commander."

FemOne holds a leather belt, conveniently discarded near the cable line. "Take a belt, loop it over this cable, and slide down to the connecting roof. If the building is clear, we can scavenge it. If not, we'll have to continue a roofline descent until we can use an external fire escape."

"Mord tend to stay in the buildings on overcast days," FemTwo explains. "It's like they know about the rain and are trying to avoid it. Not that they can."

Please let the 'rain' she speaks of be normal rain and the Mord have some weird aversion to water, not that acid nightmare from the previous level. "Is there something we should know about this level?"

"Rain eats code," QueenB says. Her face flashes warnings at

the Fems. Clearly, she wants to keep information as far from us as possible, only permitting us to know what she chooses, whether or not it's the truth.

I look at the map QueenB put me in charge of. How much don't I know? Things she can tell me, but isn't.

She extends a leather belt toward me and one to GenAK. "You first."

29

"What if there's a Mord at the other end of the line?" I ask.

The three new members of our team shift their weight, answering my curiosity. It also explains why I'm going first. I'm expendable.

"Shouldn't we be armed, just in case?" I throw the belt over the cable and pull down on both sides testing buoyance and whether I believe it will hold me. I press my lips together and double-check the drop. "How do you know if this line is secure?" I keep pulling on the belt. "Have you tested it?"

"I'll go first," GenAK says.

QueenB's hand twitches at his announcement. "I prefer to stack our members," she says. "So no one has an unfair advantage."

Her two associates exchange nervous glances. No one wants to go first. With my belt looped around the cable, I hold both ends in one hand and offer it to FemOne. Clouds overhead roll apart, revealing a sliver of sunshine along our zipline. The light illuminates a thin landing strip on the roof below. I get my first spotlight glimpse of my future. It's gray and fails at hiding a Mord dragging itself along the roofline perimeter.

FemOne slips a knife from a hidden hilt and bites the blade between its teeth. I admit, it looks cool.

"It's only one and not well fed at that. Shouldn't be a challenge to put down." QueenB's pep-talk still doesn't inspire me to volunteer to be first.

FemOne lets go. Burning leather and graphite sweat waft up from the line. I'm next. My own fear banishes the stench of FemOne, replacing the air with a rotten fruit, pencil, and foot combo—my own brand of fear. Except I'm the only one who smells it. I constantly forget GenAK can't smell, which must have something to do with the fact I'm made from this world, more a part of it than he is.

I grip the ends of a new belt, stand on the ledge, and jump off. Smoke from the belt, protest against the line, feeble white strand follows me the entire ride.

I kick, rather than dangle, my feet.

The buildings even lower down rush below, giving me a false sense of security. *If I fall from here and land on a roof I can survive, right? A few broken bones is all.* Then the roof below me is gone. The streets look like play tracks, so far down. I'm moving too fast to notice if there are people on the streets.

My line evens out as I approach the landing. Lifting my legs, I turn my head in every direction to find where FemOne and the lone Mord have gone.

"Why didn't AK go first?" The building ledge flies under my

pointed legs. I'm holding them clear of the ledge, but my behind hangs low. A solid smack against my tailbone jars my back. My hands release the belt in reflex to the surging pain. If it wasn't for momentum plunging me forward, I would fall right off the side of the building. I land flat on my back, winded, and coughing in pain.

This roof is not as high as the security building we left. That building was tall enough to survey the city all around. There are several shorter buildings still. I have no idea how many more lines we'll have to slide on in order to reach the ground again.

Standing nearby, not facing me, a Mord rocks on its feet. Its ragged breathing is aimed toward FemOne. Stupidly, I let out a relieved laugh when FemOne strikes the Mord with her short sword. The Mord's eyeless face turns to me. Drool splashes from its teeth onto my cheek.

It has me now. Its face plummets to meet mine, not aiming for my arm like they normally do. I scramble away, wiping its spittle from my face, and come away with red stains on my hands.

The knife in FemOne's hand slashes through flesh, bone, and code of the Mord's marked arm. Its mouth contorts, stretching long in a way no normal face stretches, making its face appear to melt into a sustained scream, twisting into digital white noise before the Mord falls on its side.

FemOne raises the blade above her head and brings it down against the Mord's neck. Once. Twice. Three hacks don't make a clean cut. Again and again FemOne hacks the knife against the Mord's spinal column with the resistance of using a machete to cut a steel rod.

"Here," I demand with a hand out. "Before anyone else arrives and sees the mess you've made."

FemOne hands me the long, sharp blade without hesitation. I have every intention of striking the downed Mord in the other arm or spine, finishing the job as I've been taught. I swing the blade around my head for more force, twisting like a practiced ninja specializing in short swords, and then I strike FemOne. The blade slices through its left eye. FemOne's mouth opens. I expect some sound to come out, but perhaps the shock of the moment demands too much to scream through.

What have I done?

I can't leave it like this. I strike mid-bicep as though I have thought it through and know exactly how high to go in order to cleanly detach any coded number from FemOne's digital image.

The body before me goes pale before falling, like I've turned out the light on the brightness in FemOne's complexion.

The Mord at my feet reaches for FemOne's newly severed arm with the one it still has. I bring the blade down on the Mord's arm, now gripping FemOne's coded limb. *It's getting worse—I'm getting worse.* The blade clatters to the cement roof, joining the severed limbs next to my shaking feet.

Behind me the shrill scream of FemTwo builds.

Did they see me? Do they know what I did?

The arrival of FemTwo comes with a thud, roll, and crying shriek the second I step away from FemOne.

"Those Mord will pay," FemTwo says and steps closer to me. I back away in equal measure. FemTwo spots the knife at my feet, looks at the hackjob done on the Mord's neck, and returns soul-pained eyes to FemOne's still body. "Thank you for avenging my friend."

Who me? GenAK can't get here fast enough. I hate to admit it, but I feel more in control when he's close by.

"Please," FemTwo says. "Will you carry FemOne's code? In honor of losing a valiant teammate."

Why can't you carry it? I'm already on map duty. Instead of voicing my opinion, I search the ground for the knife again.

"We can't leave it for the Mord." FemTwo separates the Mord's head from its body. "You have to disassemble the Mord. Both arms and the head. No honor for them."

"Maybe that's why they want to kill you."

Not what FemTwo wants to hear.

Death should be honored because to have death, there must have been life. All lives deserve to be honored.

FemTwo nods, leaving me to collect the heavy limb only moments ago attached to FemOne.

GenAK's arrival comes with nothing more than the solid landing of his feet together, a stomp.

I bend over to collect my burden. The blade strokes my fingers. Or more accurately, my fingers dance along the sharp edge of the sword while I stare wide-eyed at FemTwo's back. Three inches in front of my fingers lays the severed arm I need to collect, yet... three feet away sways another arm. And I am certain I can wield the knife in total silence. My fingers step their way toward the grip.

The sword clatters out of reach, kicked from my clutches before I can wrap my palm around the hilt. GenAK's boot stomps the place he clears.

"What's taking so long? Pick it up," FemTwo says.

I look at GenAK. His eyes move from me to the gash through FemOne's face, to the arms on the roof, to FemTwo, and back to me. "I understand," he says without going into any explanation. "I'm here to help." He grabs FemOne's arm before I do. "Don't be too hasty."

QueenB lands as lightly as GenAK. She stops for a second to look down her nose at the body of FemOne without interrogating about what happened. "Follow."

She could mean to follow her, or the map. It's unclear. But since she's walking away, I follow her. GenAK quicksteps ahead of me, wedging his body between myself and the two people we met on this level.

I keep my eyes on the spot in front of me where his feet lift, matching my steps to where he's been. Distractions, such as stray nails, glass shards, and discarded cord draw my eye from GenAK's footfalls. I keep switching my attention to different objects until I find myself staring at his arm and the number sticking out the cuff of his sleeve.

Tapping the numbers out with my fingertips against my own arm causes QueenB to turn back. She looks at me, narrowing her eyes. I don't stop tapping my fingers. I have GenAK's number down to a soulful rhythm. I smile without showing teeth. "You have a high number or a low number?" I nod toward her arm.

"I'm important," she says.

"It's different ends of the spectrum to different groups," I say, still tapping out GenAK's long string of importance with my fingers.

"Not extensive." QueenB shows me her back. Rigid as we walk to the building's stairwell.

"Health pack," GenAK announces. "There. At the edge of the roof."

FemTwo runs to retrieve the white case with the red cross. It's partially obscured by the stairwell door jutting up. It's nestled in a bag, like there's the possibility it's a bomb and not a row of syringes packed in Styrofoam.

"Now we're getting somewhere," QueenB says. She stops with her hand on the door. "We don't risk going through the building." It's like she's monitoring the building's heart for signs of Mord instead of life.

A belt snaps in GenAK's grip as he preps for another fun ride on a high cable zipline. Then he pauses. "We go first."

QueenB is obviously uncomfortable with our new sand-wiched arrangement. She likes having us stacked between her own people.

"I'll go first," FemTwo offers.

"No." GenAK grabs my wrist, shoves me toward the rope he's prepped, slaps my palms against the ends, and shoves me off.

"AK?" I scream. It takes me half a second to secure my hold. For a second I'm certain I'll plummet to my death before I grip so fiercely no amount of leather burn can entice me to let go.

I know why he did it. While QueenB busied herself deter-mining the most efficient sandwich, GenAK did the math. He can't leave me with anyone. When I turn, it's no shock to see the massive military boots GenAK wears.

This time I land much more fluidly. I now know to raise my

legs and tuck my tuckus. I roll away from the strip of roof where GenAK is inbound.

"You maniac!" I holler the second GenAK makes contact with the roof. "I could have fallen."

"We need a group right now. I can't have you going AWOL on me, drawing attention before I work out a plan."

I choke when what I want to do is scream. "Do you know how ridiculous you sound?"

"You're not my first trial," he admits. "But I'm pretty sure you're my last shot."

It feels like a slap in the face. Worse. What happened to the other 'trials'?

"It's no good if I can't get you to the end. Which means you have to control yourself for a little longer."

Rage muddies explanations of things. Right now, rage burns like desire to rip GenAK's eyeballs out of his head with my bare hands. Then call in the Mord to sniff him out, putting him on the same playing field when I tell him to run. Blind.

QueenB lands next, followed by FemTwo. "What was that?" she asks.

"Wasting too much time deliberating," he answers.

Almost as a response for all of us, the shuffling drag of feet draws our attention. Mord. Lots of them. I hardly notice thick clouds roll in overhead. The sun is completely excluded from our roof party, bringing out the Mord in high numbers.

"Throw an arm!" FemTwo commands.

"Do what?"

"Throw an arm at them. It'll distract them while we escape."

The arm GenAK carries fills the sling at his back, like he's growing a third hand out of his back. He grips the fingers like a handshake. I almost expect him to cock the thing in a bow and shoot it with how graceful he makes the motion.

"Wait!" Everyone jolts at my exclamation, including the Mord. I take a closer look. One of them has a familiar quality—a childlike way of searching. Though eyeless, it has a sense of being afraid and in the dark. Not only that, it's tall and lanky. And wearing ED's green uniform. "We can cure him."

GenAK steps close enough to me. When he speaks only I can hear him. "You can't."

I point to FemTwo, who still carries the white and red health pack. "It could work, right? I mean…" I lower my voice while the words tumble out faster than my tongue can enunciate everything. "How long do you want to be looping these levels, tucked out of the Commander's way, completing throwaway missions?" I don't wait for him to answer. "We're supposed to cure a Mord. Probably impossible, but who knows? Maybe it's a thing now. Like troubleshooting for a corrupted program. Who says it has to be green dotted targets only?" I pull out the electronic map with its glowing green dot shaking on the screen as though the person to whom the dot belongs is walking repeatedly into a wall.

While we're arguing, the number of Mord doubles, triples, quadruples… We crowd together with our backs to each other and our feet tapping the roof in unease.

"He's been reprogrammed. There is nothing of him in there." GenAK raises his hand. The gun he's pointing at me clicks to ready.

30

I stand in front of GenAK, my hand over his, forcing him to point the gun down. "Then we can re-reprogram him."

"It's not ED."

"Who is ED?" QueenB raises a blade.

I can't prevent the group from attacking ED. FemTwo has the boosters. If I move from in front of GenAK he's likely to shoot. The Mord advance in the time I debate what my best move is. QueenB pulls her blade through the air on top of an outstretched Mord limb. When she moves a second time, I rush FemTwo and retrieve the white and red pack. I flip the lid open. Five syringes, like the previous level, but the color of the liquid inside differs from previous vials.

Ripping the plastic cover, I shove GenAK to the side. The gun fires into the crowd of Mord, exciting them to a frenzy of snapping jaws and ripping arms. I lunge for ED. His head twists when I touch him. The no-eye thing is pretty disturbing, especially up close. A pause for mutual shock ticks before we both lash out at each other—me with the vial and ED with his gnarly teeth.

ED has me pinned. Dripping saliva hits my cheek, like it's the Mord signature pre-death move. It takes all my strength to raise my arm under his weight. GenAK has his gun aimed for ED's arm.

"No!" I shout to GenAK.

ED battles the syringe like he can see it coming. I'm never going to get it in his arm at this rate. Using ED's momentum, I change direction, plunging the needle deep into his forehead. The liquid filled tube sticks out of his skull. I press until the vial empties into him.

Fighting him reminds me how he stole the key off me without me knowing. Before I shot him, of course. Part of me knows I've romanticized his place in my existence here. Yet, I want to bring him back. Nothing happens. It doesn't even slow him down.

A bullet shatters the cement to my right. Little roof chunks fly toward my head. I grab ED by the shoulders and roll toward where I dropped the health pack. Meanwhile I puzzle through the dilemma of how to get hold of and unwrap a new needle with ED snapping at my shoulder.

I manage to get my elbow up and slam it into the side of his head, giving me only a second to grab a needle. It sticks inside the pack. "You owe me," I holler, not bothering to take the plastic off. I've done this before. I force the capped tip into ED's arm. It's a difficult angle and the needle doesn't pierce the packaging or his skin.

Another bullet bursts at my side.

"Are you trying to hit me?" I roll ED with me so now I'm above him. Unsure what to do, I punch him in the face. It does little to give me time. I still can't rip the packaging off the needle. I jam the whole thing into his marked arm and throw my weight against it and the plunger. I feel the plastic splinter under my weight. The plunger slides down, liquid going somewhere. "This better work."

ED stiffens.

QueenB stands over me with her short sword raised high over her head. She looks like she stepped out of a Viking fairytale, but in a tailored suit.

Mord cover the roof. Shots fire from GenAK. FemTwo pulls a knife through arm after tattooed arm. Under me, ED codes.

"Crap." Green and black strings of digital information disappear from my grip. "No, no, no." I scramble to retrieve the glasses from my pocket. One lens busted, I straighten the stems and throw the spectacles on top of the fast disappearing mess who once was ED. In seconds I'm bending over nothing. Even the glasses are gone.

"Did it work?" FemTwo asks, still slashing against the Mord mob.

"No," I say. Not how I'd hoped. ED didn't become a lump, but he's gone. Not cured. Gone.

"Good work." QueenB's compliment throws me off. I'm not working for her. "Now we know that method's useless. We'll have to find a different strategy before we arrive at the target. How far are we?"

I lost ED for the second—maybe third—time, and the entitled donor chick in a suit has the nerve to boss me right now? I pull a syringe from the case, slide the plastic off the needle, palm it, and get to my feet.

GenAK and FemTwo are occupied holding off Mord. They keep coming.

"Consult the map. Has our direction changed? Did the target move?" QueenB looks over the city. She doesn't see me coming. My steps pound into the roof. Slowing, I consider every part of my process.

I can't kill everyone.

Watch me. I argue internally. *I'm performing my programmed task. GenAK made me a killer. He's a murder*—"er," I say out loud. My voice draws the attention of QueenB.

She looks at the needle in my hand. "What're you doing with that?"

I step closer.

QueenB wriggles behind her wrinkled suit, smoothing her lapel. "You can't go on without me," she says.

GenAK lobs three arms off an onslaught of Mord at the same time and turns his attention my way. "GenE, we need her."

"GenE?" FemTwo asks, not half as effective as GenAK at keeping the Mord back. One of them manages to bite FemTwo's right hand. The scream that follows joins the shrieks of background noise on my path to QueenB.

"You're a GenE?" QueenB faces me directly, speaking in a low growl. "I should have known."

"Some intelligence quiz, huh? Prove your loyalty, demonstrate your worth and earn a walking metal casket." I say, like mocking QueenB's life's objective is going to win me some 'hey don't assassinate me like the billboard told you to' points.

"A GenE would say anything to save itself," QueenB says, stepping away from me, close to the edge of the roof. "We've seen the ads."

"We have to get out of here now." GenAK slaps my shoulder, injured FemTwo at his side. "Deal with the rest later."

"I'm not going anywhere with a GenE." QueenB folds her arms across her chest, standing her ground.

My belt is still in hand. I throw the buckle over the closest zipline with a downward grade. We're not far from ground level now. One more roof and I bet I could survive a fall to the street. I pull once to test the weight and jump. Before I'm out of earshot, I hear GenAK speaking to QueenB. "We need you. I take full responsibility for the E, when we complete our task..."

What? Then what? They can chop off my arm? He and I both know I lack the code required to drop me lifeless to the dirt. Would GenAK really let them take my arm to ease their mind? And what would he expect from me? I'm not going to play possum and lie dead to get some stuck-up, suit-wearing, GenB from depriving me of a limb. Not if I can drop her first.

The city below me is nothing more than narrow alleys, depressed streets of gray with tumble weeds made of trash, and tightly packed buildings. This level mimics a Brazilian metropolis, so tightly packed with high rises a person could possibly parkour from the highest point to the lowest without jumping a span of more than three feet. Except here, the buildings are purposely jagged in relative height based on proximity. There's no jumping from one to the next without impact damage. Hence the ziplines.

An upcoming roof looks both close enough to drop to

without sustaining injury and it's free of Mord. Once I've cleared the ledge, I drop. GenAK follows me, cursing. My shins jar from the angle I land. Can my digital bones splinter? I stand to test weight on it, my leg holds fine. It hurts, but I can walk.

GenAK tumbles forward toward the far edge of the building. His arms flail for balance as he nears the lip. The belt whips the air, his leg, and the brick guardrail GenAK balances on at the top point of this roof, as he tries to stop himself from tipping the rest of the way over the building.

I still hold a vial of booster in my fist. Needle exposed, I rush over to GenAK. He hops backward, away from the building's cliff as I arrive, fist in the air.

"I'm on your side," he says, hands up like I'm holding a gun to his head.

"No. I'm on your side. You. Made. Me." Why did he kiss me on the fear level? It's like nerds who want to build a sexy girl-friend robot because they have no one else.

I feel dirty.

"One more level, I promise. One more and we can accomplish the thing we set out to do." GenAK says 'the thing we set out to do' as if it's different than 'the thing everyone else set out to do'.

"Which is what?"

He stammers. His words spill on themselves, fighting his mouth for something already formed on his tongue, but he won't let out. "Live forever. To be free."

I hear the 'every goal'. It's wide and thin. It covers everything and everyone, offers no protection, promises no safety. "Not me. I don't want to kill for your freedom."

"What else are you going to do?" GenAK steps away from the needle, keeping his hands up. "You can't let them win. It's a war in here, but it's a war out there too." He checks the line above. No QueenB backup yet. "You don't know because you don't come from there." His hands slowly drop to his sides. "If there was a different road to freedom, I'd take it. I would. But this is it. You're it."

"You assume a lot," I say.

That's when I feel the cold edge of steel serrating the flesh of my left arm. I scream, dropping the needle to the ground where it clatters before cracking. The glass tube shatters and so does any residual trust for GenAK. The whole time GenAK was stepping back, he was merely avoiding the slice radius.

My face twists, eyes turned down at the place where my elbow used to be. I can still feel it, but it's not there. I'm certain it hurts, but I'm so angry and betrayed. I feel murder rushing through my body where blood should pulse. It pumps into my arm and gushes killing aspirations all over my shoes and down my side.

I turn to GenAK. He reflects the look in my eyes back at me through a sudden paleness. Fear. The great and powerful GenAK, creator of me, can see his end coming. Probably from my right hand, since my left lays at my feet.

His head shakes side to side like a spasm. No, he's telling me no. Urging me to play along? Is he insane? QueenB and FemTwo are both armed and ready to finish the job of taking me out. But then again, I'm outnumbered and weaponless. Playing along wins.

I let my body go limp, closing my mouth seconds before

permitting my head to slap cheek against the floor. My body lands over my remaining arm, protecting it from any 'just to be sure' slashes crossing their minds. "She held out," FemTwo says. "Disloyalist."

I want to pop up like a jack-in-the box and slap FemTwo right this second. Or maybe rise and declare, *"I'm the reason FemOne isn't here."* I do neither.

"I've never seen anyone last long after dismembering their tattoo," QueenB says. The volume of her voice rises as her steps tap closer. She bends down to me. Her breath against my ear sends shivers through my spine. *Calm. She'll notice. Stay cool.*

"The E's... they're barely worth your time," GenAK says. He'd better take it back next chance he gets.

"Aren't you the one who told us she was an S?" QueenB asks.

"No. That was the two GenS, the ones we left in the building. They said she was an 'S'." Why or how QueenB doesn't call him on that is beyond me, but she doesn't. Those S didn't know me from GenSHIT. No way would they have been the ones to supply what code I am. Besides, they're all wrong. I'm no code.

Silence after he speaks sets my nerves on high alert. *Do they believe him?* Every rustle of trash on the sandpaper roof grates my nerves. My guts shake like tremors large enough to measure on the Richter scale.

"Didn't the ad say to cut off E's head and both arms?" FemTwo sucks with ideas right now.

"That's Mord protocol," QueenB answers.

"It's the same though, right?" FemTwo just wants revenge for FemOne's death. So help me, I'm going to jump up and lob her arm off and then slap her face with it if she suggests taking me apart in pieces again.

Please no, please no. I am going to kill *GenAK.*

"Not if they go down. We're good. We're fine," GenAK sounds like he's convincing himself. I almost bet he'd let them butcher me if I refused to go along with his endgame plans.

"No time to debate. Look," QueenB says.

I open my eyes, searching for the dragging feet of the sight-less Mord. No feet. The roof is as bare as before, except for us.

"They're using tools?" FemTwo asks.

"I'd hardly call employing a zipline a tool," QueenB answers.

Without moving my head, or at least trying not to, I stare above. The line is bowed under too much weight. Strain on the cord, body after body, utilizing their own arms—the non-coded ones—the way we use belts. Except their arms are still attached. The rope burns into the crook at their elbows. The barbeque scent of seared flesh fills my mind. The smell of them coming and it's not as horrible an arrival as I fear.

The thuds start. Mord drop like sacks of flour. It takes them time to roll to their hands and knees and stand. As more Mord come, they drop exactly over the top of those who've already landed, slowing their group's progress. It's a beautiful show of blindness and stupidity as one of their own crushes a previously landed Mord.

GenAK shouts to clear the roof. His voice sounds far away already.

I twist, risking movement, tracking their escape. My team-mates run for a service door. *They're going inside?*

Creatures mow one another down, falling from above. The

roof door closes behind FemTwo. I stand. Panic and adrenaline fight before combining forces to make me totally useless. There's no defending myself from the Mord surrounding me.

Stepping toward the ledge, I consider dropping the five stories to the next closest building, but it's too high. Darkness clouds the sky. The night program rolls in, as if it's programmed to plummet game-life into darkness at the most inopportune times.

None of the monsters drag their feet toward me. Their mouths sucking in the air, they follow an invisible line toward the service door. My attention goes to my injury. My head swims. I shouldn't have looked at my stub.

Dang it. I need to stop my arm from gushing. I search the ridge of the roof, but there are no health packs or abandoned shirt scraps. Nothing to wrap, tie, or cauterize my wound. The left-behind broken vial, with the majority of its contents already absorbed into the porous cement, leaves a grease stain near me. I remember it sort of worked for GenAK to swallow a booster back on the car level.

"I hope this works." I kneel, three limbed, over the puddle and lick the dirty surface. Balancing on my knees, I push some small glass shards away, and continue to lick. I can't tell if the liquid has a flavor over the other roof crud. Shoe-sole tar, rotten oranges, and the scent before rain flavor. Yum. Not to mention the cat tongue roughness of the roof's surface scrapes away skin cells with every pass.

Green-tinted clouds roll in, covering the low sun.

The Mord all lumber for the door, following the three survivors of our rag-tag group. Wait, I'm a survivor. So…

The three deserters, turncoats, traitors.

My stump bleeds on, the lapped-up liquid not enough to stop it. I see my arm. It's weird staring at a part of myself, now not a part of myself. I pat my pockets with my right arm. No map. It's not like I really thought we could cure Mord anyway.

The blood from my wound slows to a drip.

Now what?

I take inventory. Missing: one arm. Assets: one key, ED's glasses—no, those are gone—sucked away when ED coded. My head hangs forward, straining my shoulders. I don't have much.

A thunder clap wakes me from my funk. The sun disappearing into darkness wasn't enough. They have to send programed death clouds as well. The Mord leave, too.

The rain. Acid burn-your-life-away rain.

I need to find shelter. Fast.

31

My arm marks my trail. A bronze line of fire-copper, pointing me out to anyone who dares look for me. But no one looks.

The roof door sticks. *What if I'm locked out?* Pull, maybe push. I throw my weight into it. I lunge, dig my shoulder into the metal door. I can't make it budge.

I pound, jarring my shoulder against the metal again and again and again. The sky rolls with threats. The door clicks. I fall sideways through the dark space, over lumps of torso and other parts—all Mord.

"AK?" My face is inches from a flight of stairs I almost fall down as well. "Thanks for waiting for m—oh." It's not AK holding the handle.

Piles of dead Mord form a type of barricade on the landing. TECH-chick holds the door, pushing the mound to one side of the landing.

"I didn't know you leveled-up," I say. The girl knows how to navigate programs better than the rest of us. She's scary smart with the attitude to match. And right now, she looks ready to end me.

"I bet," she says without smiling. "You know how to survive this rain? The indoor sprinklers spray it, too, so I hear."

I don't bother to ask where she gets her information. It doesn't matter. Maybe she designed this level. There isn't time for it to matter. "We need to get to a maintenance space."

Forget elevator rides and escape hatches. We opt for service access and maintenance gangways. A white access panel catches my eye. I hope for some kind of access within the walls, between places. We get lucky.

"No time to be picky," she says. "By my watch, we have less than a minute before this place turns acid fountain."

"So much for a safe zone."

"A what?" TECH-chick asks.

"When AK and I got here, the people told us we were headed to the safe zone." I leave the ladder and crawl into the tight space already claimed by cables, pipes, wires, and lint.

TECH-chick has her fingers around my neck, over my windpipe, impressive maneuvering in this limited space and she's crushing those fingers as far as she can, back toward her palm. "*Shh.*"

Like I have another option.

Spurting sounds rumble through pipes at our side. The acid. It's piped in? I mean, it has to be, to get into the sprinklers, but still... how sick is that? Air gurgles as the pipes fill, sputtering in the far distance. An exit point for the liquid.

TECH-chick lightens her grip, but doesn't let go of my neck.

"It doesn't eat through the pipes." She sounds impressed. I need her upset, angry, ready to take arms and fight The Man. Literally. The Man being the Commander. Or the other enemy… GenAK? It's a dude for sure. "Someone's messing with the elements in this place."

Lights flicker and go out. Spraying sprinklers sound above a screaming, gasping, clawing roar of death beyond our cable-web sanctuary.

"Looks like you found the safe zone," TECH-chick says in my ear, releasing my throat. She pats my bloody stump. "What're friends for?"

I rub my neck, but can't rub away the feeling of her hand there. "There are no friends here. It's a single winner game."

"Whatever the Commander needs," TECH-chick mumbles. She slides a firearm from her pants. TECH-chick has a magical gift for being the worst.

"If you're here now, there's something wrong with you. Shouldn't you be dead already?"

"Come on." She pulls the chamber so a bullet drops inside. "You, of all of us, should know about cheating death."

I'm a one-armed freak. Only Mord walk around without a code arm. Will it help me if I accuse her of being one of the Commander's sheep or get me more dead?

"For being all sciencey, you suck at engineering if you need me to show you where to take cover during an acid rain raid."

"We can't all be good at everything." TECH-chick aims the gun above my left eye. "I bet I know something you don't."

Behind her, a Mord navigates the maze of dangling cables, giving me the upper hand. I've never been happier so near Mord.

And one that's been previously shot. A black stain stares back at me from its forehead, with a long-crusted drip down across the space a nose should be and into its mouth.

"Kid?" I say out loud. I wish I hadn't. How does he keep finding me? Does he have some vengeance tracking secret?

Two things happen at once. First, and the best thing, TECH-chick twists toward the approaching kid, providing me the distraction I need to knock the gun free of her hand. Second, and the much worse part, she stabs the side of my head with a knife she holds in her other hand. It lodges between my ear and jaw. If that's what she aims for, I'm impressed.

And in pain.

My entire system feels like I've been hotwired full of torture bombs. A zing shoots out from my jaw affecting my entire body with electric volts saying *'knife in the jaw'*, like I don't know already.

"I know where your code is buried. I know how to kill you," TECH-chick hisses at me. "You may have fooled GenAK and the rest of the morons who let you live, but not me. You're an E, and no amount of skin grafting can hide your disloyalty."

Skin grafting? She thinks I cut out my arm code and grafted it somewhere else? Ew. Dang.

"I saw the ads the second I spawned this level. And you're an E."

"I lied." At least, that's what I try to say. Talking with a knife wedged at the spot where my jaw hitches makes speaking impossible. Gurgles come out as my tongue tries to do all the work of speaking, while swallowing my own blood.

"Any last words?" She laughs, knowing I've been trying to

speak, to explain myself, but can't. She's made it impossible. "I finally figured out how to win this thing, thanks to my advanced engineering and science know-how. The Commander was keen to learn all the crap you and AK were up to, which I figured out right away when we met." She taps her arm. "No code, baby girl." She laughs at my missing limb, like it's the best trick she's ever seen. "Which is how we hijacked AK's method. That hack ain't going nowhere." TECH-chick is with the Commander, and we're all screwed. *Yay.* "Did I fail to mention, I'm a super nerd back home? Yeah. I'm awesome smart."

'Can't fly a chopper' isn't easy to hand signal, but a few swooshes with one finger and a shoulder lift gets my point across despite my impaired squelching voice.

She turns her head to the side, and I think she might backhand me. "See, that's why I don't like you. You're smart enough, but one hell of an ass."

The sprinklers stop. Instead of a flush of water, background noise returns to the hum and buzz of electricity. Lights flicker outside the crawlspace we're in. An eerie glow catches every object not securely attached to the floor or headspace. A shadow still covers the area directly around TECH-chick. She doesn't notice. "Nice try with the distraction, but we all know the kid was a fool to trust you. That's why he's dead, and now, so are you."

The gun comes up, held in a left-hand grip. TECH-chick's forearm raises level with my nose directly in front of Mord kid's wide open mouth, like she's offering it to him. All he has to do is bite down, which he does. High on her bicep, far above the numbers, preserving her battery-like code.

Past experience indicates the Mord can't see me, smell me, or find me, as long as I don't move, breathe, or generally act alive while around them. Except of course when it comes to this particular one. I try to remain invisible as Mord-kid gnaws through the bone of TECH-chick's arm. Her screaming covers a lot of my gagging reflex.

My feet push against the floor the second TECH-chick's other hand releases its grip on the knife in my head. There's not enough distance between me and the Mord. Sure he saved my life, but it's not like we're buds in our current conditions.

The arm drops to the floor with a thud. TECH-chick looks at it, her face remains frozen with disgust and shock at seeing her number stare up at her, disconnected from the rest of her. I know that feeling.

Mord kid lifts the arm. I expect him to fit the whole thing in his mouth like a cream-stuffed éclair. Instead he holds it out in front of him, toward me. His head bent and blood dripping mouth closed. He nods once toward his bloody offering.

It's stupid of me to touch it. I won't do that. This has to be a trap, because he can't find where I am. My reaching for the thing he's holding will give away my position. I don't move. Don't blink. I'm a freaking statue.

He tosses the arm forward. Or drops it, I guess. He nods again with his head bent low. *What is this?* Mord-kid mimes holding the severed limb, and fitting it to his own arm like he's attaching a vacuum hose to his arm, but in mime.

My right hand reaches for TECH-chick's limb. Mord-kid nods again, re-demonstrating 'the hose goes here' by cupping one hand and jamming the imaginary limb to his other arm. I lift the thing. It's heavy.

Every part of me tenses, preparing for Mord kid to attack, to spring a trick, a trap. *They use spare code like batteries.* I drag it closer to me, away from him. His mouth stays closed. No movement to jump me. Doesn't he work for the Commander? We don't get along.

I slide the knife from my head. More blood pours out. I'm pretty sure I'd scream if my jaw wasn't already gushing blood from where I've been stabbed in the face. I'm weak. The arm in front of me isn't separated in the same spot as my own stump. If I'm supposed to replace my missing part with this, it won't look right. I'll have two elbows.

Still, Mord kid isn't attacking me. A partly-squished tube rolls from where he sits along the floor. I still can't talk because of the damage done by the knife. What is this, glue? I unscrew the cap and dump the liquid over the limb I'm about to shove at my raw, sore, aching stump. It's not like I'm transplanting the thing, connecting nerve endings or arteries. There is no way this can possibly work.

It occurs to me the Mord will attack the moment I shove this thing at my own bleeding stalk limb. Still, I hold TECH-chick's detached arm inches from my stump, trying to perfectly align things as much as possible.

Not far away, TECH-chick remains nothing more than a paperweight. It's a weird feeling—her there, me having a moment with Mord-kid, and this limb growing heavy in my single hand. Staring at the eyeless monster cramped beside me, I shrug my shoulders and touch the arm to mine.

At first nothing happens. It's like blood snot clinging to the two pieces when I pull it apart to check if anything happens. Since I'm still bearing the weight of TECH-chick's arm in my right hand, I know it doesn't work.

Strings of green and black numbers swirl between the body parts. The strands wrap around each other, sucking the limb back against my arm. I strain to speak, but only gurgle and choke on my tongue. There's a problem. The strings of code don't stop at my stump or TECH-chick's severed arm. It keeps braiding its way up my shoulder, connecting the limb to me.

I can't scream. Eyes wide, I search for Mord-kid. If I could read the expression by his mouth only, I'd say he's smiling. I fell for whatever vengeance he plans without hesitation like the idiot fool I am.

I strain my neck away from the advancing numbers dancing, twining, seeping their way in through my skin. There's nothing I can do. It climbs up to my mouth, entering through clenched teeth, choking its way down my throat. Then it's green and black seeping in through the corners of my eyes.

For a second I suspect I'm leveling up, but no. This level requires a platform advancement and I'm trapped in a maintenance crawlspace with the enemy. I've leveled up enough times to recognize the difference. This is so much worse.

32

Nothing makes sense. A fuzzy-buzz hums against my brain chords. Someone plays my thoughts like a stringed instrument. Nothing comes into focus. I close my eyes.

Shuffling surrounds me. Dragging, scraping, gurgling.

Oh, hell no. Where am I?

I force my eyes open. *Please, oh please have eyes.* The world still shakes. Trembling and buzzing, still visible. I'm surrounded by closed mouth, eyeless creatures. None of them trying to bite my arms off. All of them too close.

My arms!

With my right hand I reach across my body and feel for... *yes*! It's there. A left arm. I have a left arm! So, why aren't the Mord attacking me? TECH-chick had source code on her forearm. Turning my head makes everything hurt, but not the way I expect. It's not a splitting headache because I got face speared with a knife. My neck is tight, raw, like when a blister pops and the shiny pink skin underneath is exposed to air.

On my arm, smooth rosy flesh. In the dim light it's difficult to distinguish the raw shiny quality. I'm guessing my whole self looks like I grew a fresh new skin. Excited at being alive and fully restored, I jump. Mouths drop open as Mord heads snap my direction.

"Okay, okay," I say, hands in the air. "No sudden moves, I get it." I'm a prisoner? Is that it?

Resting my head in my hands, I process information. *Think, cursed brain.* One good sign, I don't have the overwhelming urge to slash my captors across the face with a knife or even kill them in other, less horrible, ways.

Non-homocide's not enough to solve the problem of this level, but way to not be a murderous tool. I still need to level up. I somehow know where the platform is now. I don't even need QueenB and her posse. That's weird.

I turn to the nearest Mord. "Hey, did you tell me where the platform is?"

They don't talk.

"Did you show me on a map or something? How do I all of a sudden know that?"

No response, but all their mouths are closed again. I search the crowd, looking between and over the hoard surrounding me. Shadow dominates the space. There is a cover overhead, a warehouse or other large cavernous room without many walls or other rooms. The Mord at the edge of the swarm, of which I'm center, have their mouths open and chins up, like they're tasting the air coming into the room.

"Do you guys have source code on your arms?" I ask.

I reach out to try to slip the nearest Mord's sleeve high

enough to peek and get a flash of teeth and a puff of sour breath in my face. "Sorry, curious."

I see enough, however. The Mord are loaded with code. The more I look around, some have code on both arms. I rub my eyes —glad I have eyes. "None of this makes sense."

A bell dings in the distance. My head turns side to side, trying to figure out what it means. Are we supposed to be on the platform already? How do I get out of here and race to it? My internal map tells me there are seven platforms in a small gamescape, nothing more than a well-paced jog to any exit.

I remember what GenAK said about this level being a back-door-type access to other levels so the Commander can jump or send his soldiers.

The Mord at the perimeter of the room drag their feet to the edge of the shadows. They can't see. They use heat from daylight to judge the edge of darkness. More Mord amble in, missing limbs, beaten and broken. So many Mord. The crowd of code-heavy creatures surrounding me drag themselves away, moving toward the light. Long foot tracks streak in and out revealing this cavernous underground parking structure.

The new Mord don't guard me the same as those who leave. Doing my best to mimic them, I drag my own feet toward the exit gates. Peering into the darkness behind me reveals what the newcomers are set on. Piles and piles of arms, legs, torsos, even heads line the back wall.

Except these are piles of body parts being reattached to other people in a twisted version of build-a-body. Broken Mord amble in while freshly assembled Mord leave the building, like it's a changing of the guard.

So… "Mord shift equals repairs." My hands go up as an apology, or surrender, whichever works. "Sorry."

"GenE?"

I look up.

"What are you doing on this level? Don't you know they're hunting all E's?"

"ED?" The figure in front of me wears ED's glasses, cracked lens and all. "It can't be you."

"You have got to get to a platform before someone else finds you. Here, follow me." He reaches for my arm, but I pull back away from his touch.

"It's not really you," I say. "It can't be." He looks like ED, like a person with a personality and everything normal I hope a person will look like. You know, with a face. His hands are moving even faster than his mouth, fingers folding in, twisting around one another, trying to visually depict all the science-y terms he's keeping fairly understandable. The sign of a true genius, speaking in terms I can understand. Which isn't easy considering ED probably knows more large-unintelligible words than simple ones.

ED pauses, tilting his head as if a memory's been triggered. "I almost forgot. You *shot* me," he says. His hand falls to his side.

Crud, it really is him.

"After I told you not to, you still shot me. Right in front of army idiot." He refers to GenAK.

"I'm less of a fan of him lately," I say.

"If you would have given me a chance to explain. The elixir they're making is like spiking the punch. It has encrypted data to reprogram or delete neuro-code depending on the batches. The only way to tell the vials apart is to look under a microscope. I noticed they had different colors, but that's a decoy. It's a virus."

I already know all this.

"Both colors serum have both versions in different vials. I'm not even sure they can tell the difference unless they know what to look for and where. Whoever is putting together their medical supply is either intentionally sabotaging the vials or ignorantly, but the deletion mix is more opaque at the surface. The data particles are heavier than the other code."

"ED, ED…"

His hands are still moving as if he's explaining things before words make it out of his mouth. "Yeah?"

"Stop talking."

He looks confused. "I leveled here. And there are ads to kill GenE everywhere. Good thing it's a simple level. Our only objective is to make it to a game pad to advance. I'm guessing we have to fight the full abled versions of that—" ED points to the wall where hoards of Mord have their backs to us, too busy plugging in arms, legs, and other parts to bother attacking us.

"Can I see your arm?"

"My what?" ED covers his left arm with his right hand. Like he knows something's different.

I push my sleeve up to reveal pink-raw flesh void of numbers.

"How is that possible?" he asks. "You're not an E?" He takes several steps away from me. "You're not GenE. You're an imposter. Stay away." His fingers form a cross.

Come on! I'm not a vampire.

"Look at your arm, ED," I say. "Look at it."

His hands shake. Behind his frames are those same scared eyes I met all those levels ago. Desperate to trust, rely on others, follow. ED. A fine sheep.

Keeping his left hand in prime 'finger-cross' position, ED slides his sleeve toward his shoulder with his right hand. His arm jiggles with terror. Then it happens. The instant stillness of shock and confusion.

"What's happening?" he asks me, like I have all the answers. I decidedly do not, still ED hopes I do. "Where's my code? That's who I am, that's me! I can't be a donor without my code."

He's right. Maybe that's part of it. Without a serial number or source code, we don't qualify for AI placement. "I don't know what's happening," I say.

ED's arms shield his face from me, doing no good.

"But you didn't just get here," I tell him.

ED puts his arms down.

"You came like them." I point to the Mord.

"Because you shot me?"

Wow. He went from listening to me to blaming me again, real fast. I slap my arm. "I'm without code, too."

"You could have done that to yourself. With all the 'kill GenE' propaganda, you probably did."

I shake my head to negate his words.

"Survivors, they'll do anything," ED says like a tantruming grad student.

Why is he still whining? "I don't have a code!" I also do not mean to scream because of all the Mord attention it attracts. Like now. The dragging sound I hate so much. I turn to check if I'm right. Yep. I'm right. The barely-abled bunch behind us scrape themselves toward us. Some even carry their spare parts with them. I whisper to make up for the predicament we're now in. "I'm as stuck as you are and we have to move." I point behind us. "During their repair shift they don't seem too bent on killing us again, but I don't want to risk it." I motion toward the open streets. "Run for it?"

Both of us start at a backward walk out of the underground garage. When one of the repaired Mord picks up pace in pursuit, we turn and run.

"You were one of those, too?" ED asks as we both run side by side, neither of us leading the other. "We must have been shot with the deletion booster."

"Uh…" Like I have a clue what a deletion booster is. To be clear, I have no clue. "You're right."

"And you can remember?" ED asks. "I don't remember anything except for waking up in that garage." He stops talking to catch his breath while continuing to run at my pace. "I ran out, saw the ads about corrupted GenE…" Breathing. "It's then I wondered if the rest of our group leveled up in the garage, too, and I needed to warn you before you stepped out. You being an E, and all. The ads are disturbing."

Do I remember anything? "Remember is a relative term," I say.

"But you know stuff about this level, and those *things*," he says.

"The Mord." I state. "You were one of them for a while."

"Is there a way to gain our source code back?" ED asks.

"If anyone would know that…" My turn to gasp for breath. "It'd be you. You studied the program blueprints, right?"

We both adjust our speed to round a corner. Before we blind ourselves to the street behind us, I look back. The Mord no longer follow. I put a hand out to slow ED. "They've stopped."

Hands on knees, we crouch, sucking in air as if we're real people.

ED stretches his back, filling his digital lungs with fake air. "I didn't see anything indicating losing source code like this, but I guess it makes sense. Deletion kind of says it all."

"And getting it back?" I prod.

"No idea."

Voices echo from a cross street around a building we haven't passed. They get louder, heading our way. "This way. The map has our Mord materializing in a parking garage south of the safe zone."

I can recognize GenAK's voice anywhere.

From the look on ED's face, so can he. "You've got to be kidding me," he says.

Avoiding GenAK, QueenB, and FemTwo, I pull ED toward a tall building with an open doorway. The black entrance has "stay away—this place is foreboding, you idiot" written all over it. But I'll take ominous entrance over facing GenAK at the moment.

33

The second we pass through the entryway of the dark building, I know we've made a mistake. Mord rock side to side, bending their knees, their feet never leaving the ground. I suck in my breath before ED realizes what we've done.

His hand reaches out to grab me. They don't make a move toward us, but a number of the Mord closest to us lift their chins and open their mouths toward the door.

"Wait. I can smell," ED says looking at them and back toward the street where the GenAK posse runs toward the garage from which we recently left. "It's like... wow, I remember smell?"

"Metallic and acrid at the same time?" I say.

ED nods.

"That's how gamers smell."

The Mord drag their feet forward, mouths opening wider as they catch the scent of the gamers beyond. It's too thick a pack for us to dare walk through the crowd.

ED grabs my arm and pulls me out to the street, revealing our presence to the group with QueenB and GenAK. I feel like we've made a grand entrance at a ball, except we don't want to be at this event. All eyes scrutinize us like party crashers—ones that're dead already.

"Gen... ED?" GenAK stammers. "How did you?"

Mord shuffle from the building. Once in the street, their speed picks up with one goal—attack the gamers. QueenB falls backward on her nice-suited-bottom as more and more Mord filter out of the building and turn their mouths toward the trio in the street.

"We know where the platform is," I say.

ED backhands my shoulder. "We're not one of them. Why should we help?" He continues to pull me through the thinner side of the Mord crowd, increasing the space between us and GenAK. I reach into my vest pocket. Yeah, I'm still wearing the crappy vest thing. No booster vials. *Dang it.* I thought I might have stored some, but I used them all.

"Look for a health pack," I whisper to him.

ED joins me, most likely without a clue why. Otherwise, I seriously doubt he'd help me. "See anything?"

"No, you?"

"You know where to go?" GenAK screams from the other side of the Mord mob. Blades slicing and guns firing, they're fighting their way through the pack. *Ha!* Good luck.

"We need health boosters," I yell back.

"How many?" QueenB's voice rises over the hoard. "We have three total."

"Three," I say, shrugging to ED.

"Did you boost?" QueenB asks. "there' not enough for every-one." Like I'm asking her to sacrifice her shot for me. Even though she already witnessed my arm being chopped off. What-ever she thinks, I don't believe I still need health packs to survive here.

"Don't need one. Three is perfect." ED's eyebrows flinch together. His gaze darts to me, then the Mord, then back to me—too smart to have overlooked the fact I have to turn the gamers into the thing they're running from in order to save them. At least, that's my plan. "We're coming for you," I say. "We'll get you out safe."

I run through the tightly packed host of Mord. The narrow street, fenced in by tall buildings, inhibits maneuvering. Their teeth clamp shut at air rushing past like Venus flytraps ready to spring by the smallest vibration. Admittedly, running through their midst isn't my brightest idea. I'm unarmed, which, for my plan to work, poses a problem.

"Throw me a knife," I shout.

"Throw it? Like at you?" GenAK asks.

Smart mouth. "Just throw it!"

Steel catches a glint of streetlight high above the snapping crowd. I swallow back reluctance at extending my arm through the mix of snarling and grinding. By some miracle I jump up, wrap my fingers around the rubber grip, and land on my feet, without anything being bitten by Mord.

My next move, for this plan to work, is slightly trickier. I'll only have the element of surprise on my first strike. I need to take my most challenging opponent out first.

"Hurry, B's unarmed," GenAK says.

So QueenB's unarmed? That's helpful to know. I throw my elbow to the side in order to knock some uncomfortably close teeth out of my face. The distance to QueenB feels so much farther running through a sightless mesh of bared teeth.

At the edge of the crowd where the hoards thin, on the other side of their group are two blocks of road. After that, a garage packed with even more Mord. Hungrier and more desperate to stay alive than the ones we now face. Nice of the fake objective the Commander assigned to GenAK and me to make it nearly impossible to survive. Sending us into the heart of Mord-ville in order to retrieve the location of the level-up pad. Nice one.

Pushing my feet off the pavement, I leap into the air, shoving one last Mord aside to clear my aim. "I hope this works," I scream and plunge the blade deep into GenAK's skull, slicing as far down as I can to be sure.

QueenB bellows, "She's an E! I told you!" Stomping one foot, she turns and runs, leaving her teammates behind in an effort to put as much space between me and her as possible. She acts like E are more feared than Mord.

A sticky sucking sound holds the knife inside GenAK's head when I try to pull it back out. I have to lift one foot, placing it squarely on GenAK's chest, for leverage. Once free, I hack the bloodied blade against GenAK's extended left arm. Both of his hands shake, even the one now lying separated from the rest of him on the pavement. "Now we're even."

FemTwo, in obvious shock, stammers and coughs. "You killed One? D-didn't you?"

Finally figuring out what happened to FemOne, I see. "Now you know the truth. FemOne is probably in this mix right now."

ED pushes his way through the Mord pack. Someone grabs GenAK's arm and sidles off with it, probably to add it to the stockpiles in the garage.

"QueenB ran for the stockpiles," I tell ED.

He looks at me with his hands in the air like 'what do you want me to do about it?'

I raise my eyebrows and shoulders in reply, because I have no idea. But, I still want him to do something. "I need the booster pack," I say to FemTwo.

"I don't have it."

There's a bulge in FemTwo's vest pocket. "Your lies are showing." I point my knife at FemTwo's jacket.

"You're going to rob us for health packs?"

"I'm saving your ass." My blade comes down as hard and fast as I can pull it, gravity not doing enough to increase the force against FemTwo's elbow. I have to strike a second time because I stupidly picked a joint to target. Once the code is no longer connected to FemTwo's body, its head drops forward against its chest and the whole body falls to the right.

The mass of Mord behind me stop and wait, as if they're readying themselves for my command. One lunges and pulls back, going for FemTwo's arm. I point to the parking garage, but then remember they're sightless. "The one in the stockyards," I say. "All yours." They part around me, following my command and giving me space, like I'm a rock in the current. I like the feeling of control.

Holding my blade in the air, dripping with the blood of both GenAK and FemTwo, I declare, "I'm the friggin Queen of the Mord, that's what I am."

Remembering ED, I turn. The expression on his face is not awe. Surprising, since he's the same as me now. He stops meeting my gaze before I expect him to break the stare, and looks instead at the crowd of Mord obeying my direction to go after QueenB. "I thought we were saving them," he says, referring to the group I've almost completely demolished.

"Get the shots."

There are exactly three shots in the pack. They didn't lie about that. I don't know the most effective method for injecting pre-Mord in order to cure them. ED had been full Mord when I shot him. Twice. I hope once is enough, if I'm going to follow through on my promise to save these guys.

"What if it's deletion code?" ED asks.

"They use different stuff here." Do I tell him about trying to fix my mistake? Killing him and then saving him? "Tried this earlier. It took two shots. No idea if one would have done it over time or if it was a different mix in the tube."

"Do something," ED says. "The longer we wait, the more of himself he'll lose."

Why would ED care if GenAK loses his identity? They hate each other, don't they? "Not necessarily." ED catches my eye before I strip the plastic from the needle and uncap it with my teeth. "Here goes nothing." I shoot GenAK in his right arm. Nothing happens. We wait thirty seconds, which is forever when something needs to happen. Full nothing.

"Now what?" ED asks. "Waste another on this guy?"

"It's not wasting." I look at the ground. The arms. "Attach his arm."

"The one you cut off like an Amazon Warrior?" He pushes his broken glasses up the bridge of his nose.

"Has anyone ever told you you're a nerd, ED?"

"Every day of my once and glorious life," he says.

Holding the needle over GenAK, I'm unable to make myself stab him. Here's the thing—I only now realize I have no evidence I can turn regular gamers into Mord on this level. The only person I'm certain was cured from being Mord is ED. He spawned this level Mordified. So... GenAK might never come back from what I've done to him. I could have made a critical miscalculation.

34

"Why isn't he coding?" ED asks, pacing the sidewalk. He prefers the shadows to the hot sun. "And why haven't any of those creatures who chased down other Gen come back?"

"Why would they?"

ED stares at the dark garage-type doors in the distance. "Something should happen."

I agree with that. Something should happen. All our efforts to get a limb to attach to GenAK have been useless. The dang thing thunks to the earth the second I let go.

"I need something down there." I point to the parking structure, ED follows my finger and shakes his head no. "You don't have to go. Stay with AK."

"Oh, he's AK, now?"

"I'm trying to tell you, you don't have to go down there."

ED looks behind us toward the black door where we originally hid and the Mord, too. "Nothing feels safe," he says. "I keep calculating our risk and I can't determine our best course of action."

"It's designed to be incalculable." I'm surprised he hasn't figured that out yet, being a smart guy. "No-win situation."

"Impossible. There's something..." ED's fingers dance in the air, doing calculations in nervous bends and twitches. "There has to be options."

Let him count his fingers. "I'll be five minutes."

ED's fingers stop twitching. He doesn't look at me. His eyes are trained on his own feet.

"Whatever happens—try to remember it happened before we uploaded in this game..." We're nothing more than a failed tissue transfer if we lose.

He looks up. Our eyes lock. What decisions we make, it's impossible to tell the consequences. "And you're okay with that?"

"No." I turn my back and walk down the hill with two vials still in my hand. I won't waste any on FemTwo or QueenB until I know for sure whether I can save GenAK or not.

Before I reach the opening, Mord-kid blocks my path like he's a big shot among the rest of them. Waiting for him to identify my movement, odor, something, I stand in the open.

"E? Don't look behind you," ED's voice muffles.

I turn to find a mass of Mord between him and me. And the Mord-kid is blocking my forward progress. I'm boxed in. Something tells me the mass of Mord wait for the kid to motion a response. So much for me being queen of the Mord. Apparently, king is the thing to be.

"It's curable," I say to the kid, which I suspect he already knows. The only information he doesn't have is the cost of the cure. "The only side effect to the cure is the loss of code." I show my arm like he can distinguish the flawless pink flesh with his eyeless face.

Whether Mord understand spoken language or have a means of communicating themselves, I still don't know. A buzz, shuffle, and rustle takes over the air. The garage hums with movement.

"Vials." I hold up the boost shots.

The kid instantly recoils. How could he see them? I lower my hand, then lift a tube under my nose and inhale deeply. A sweet scent like sugar water comes back to me. The second vial I lift and smell. It's sour, like citric acid. How did I not notice this before? And which scent did I use to inject GenAK? I turn back toward ED, but there's no way I'm getting through the Mord crowd unless they permit me. Nothing in their demeanor communicates, "sure, pass on through."

"ED?" I shout.

"Yeah?"

"Did you notice any scent when I injected AK? Any smell at all?"

Silence.

"Do you hear me?"

"I'm thinking, give me a minute. I'm trying to be accurate."

Sometimes ED gets on my nerves. Facts don't need laboring over. He either smelled something or he didn't. How much time does he need to say 'yes' or 'no'?

"Something like rotten oranges?" ED stops talking. I open my mouth to say 'yes, that's exactly what I'm talking about, jeez' when he adds, "Or like sweet limes, or something, but like they've gone bad? Fermented maybe? Yeah. Like a fermented lemonade..."

He's definitely trying too hard with the accuracy thing. "That's—it's fine. Thanks." I only have one rot-sugar smelling vial, which lacks any sour or acrid tones. I turn back to the kid. "Come with me. I'll show you."

Behind me, the Mord army parts, allowing a path for me to take as long as Mord-kid trails me. I walk back to ED and the bodies of GenAK and FemTwo with their arms missing. The Mord kid follows at a safe distance. Safe being, he can smell us.

I kneel next to GenAK with ED above me. "What are you doing? Did you find what you were looking for?"

"No..."

ED looks past me to where the Mord-kid observes. "Is that the kid?" He steps back. "Oh my word. He's like a...a...."

"He's dead, ED."

"Does he understand you?" His fingers count out probabilities in his anxious way.

"Of course he doesn't understand me."

"Right." ED nods. I uncover a second needle. "So why isn't he killing us now?"

I can feel the tension in ED's muscles rise. His feet step side to side while he assesses the situation.

"I can cure them." I flick the needle. Two drops of liquid run down the side. Still not knowing where to jab the thing, I decide to go for the arm. Holding GenAK's limb up so it matches, I carry the weight of it against my leg and jam the needle sideways so both the attached limb and severed limb are pierced.

The serum injects into the cold body of GenAK. I continue to hold the limb up, hoping those tendrils of code, which regrew my arm, will claim it. GenAK's entire body jolts, minus the arm I'm holding over my leg. Then he turns to strings of code, which fly through the air down inside the parking garage.

I stand to run where I believe GenAK will spawn, but Mordkid stands in my path. His chin points in the air, inhaling the scents around me. I sniff to determine what he might detect on me. Fear's the only thing I taste. It's in the salt of my sweat, evaporating like a beacon of falseness all around my brave stance.

Unsure what I need to do, I hold out the last vial. Inside is the foul scent of its liquid. Mord kid neither reaches for it, nor backs away. I open the plastic, then kneel. Next to me lays dismembered FemTwo. Mord kid's chin drops so the air he sucks in has my flavor in it. He's tracking my every move.

Behind me, ED kicks gravel. "We have to get to the platform. Time won't last forever."

Unsure what more I can do, I depress the plunger, outside of FemTwo's skin. The rotten liquid sizzles on the asphalt, running between cracks and disappearing into the earth. The burning scent rises like gaseous storm clouds.

No.

I look up to the sky.

Too close, heavy yellow-lined clouds roll in. I look at Mord kid, "Another storm is coming."

All Mord lift their chins skyward and suck in the humidity.

Against my skin, the dew in the air burns like a chemical peel. "We need cover."

ED leaves the dissolving shadow of the building to grab my

shoulder. "Let's move." Instinctively he runs with the Mord toward the parking garage. "Once the storm passes, we wait for no one. Getting to the platform is our only concern."

"You're wrong," I say.

Raindrops burn the earth behind us. The storm tracks our progress like there's a string linking the clouds to us.

"What's with the killer rain?" ED screams, covering his head with both arms.

I copy his move and run harder, even though I know covering my head with my arms won't do any good. There's no longer a chance to bring back FemTwo. We clear the edge of the parking structure as the downpour splashes against the roof. A few Mord still outside the building howl as their skin melts in the shower, steam rising from the chemical reaction, once a form of digital life.

The gruesome fate of those not fast enough to reach safety lies in our path. I trip backwards, scrambling to get as far away from the pooling rain as I can. Storm drains guzzle the excess acid-water. I recognize the smell as being part of the fermented scent inside one of the vials.

"GenE?" GenAK stands behind me. "What are you doing here?" He looks around, not recognizing the environment. "Where are we?" Thank heaven he doesn't remember the street scene moments ago when I sank a machete into his skull.

ED lowers his arms from his head. "So it worked?" One finger circles the air in mock celebratory enthusiasm. "Yippee."

"Why aren't the Mord attacking?" GenAK asks, staring suspiciously at the creatures all around us.

"Check your arm," ED says pointing to his own, once source-coded, skin.

GenAK looks to me. He knows about blank arms. The fact I've been without code doesn't surprise him. "You did this to me?" Excitement crumbles from his face. Betrayal, distrust, hurt all take over. Doubtful he worships me as his savior. But I totally am.

As if to confirm what he already knows, GenAK lifts the edge of his cuff. Unblemished flesh, pink with newness, stares back at him. He pulls his sleeve low, hiding the truth from himself, knowing he can't go back.

ED steps in front of me and gets in GenAK's face. "She saved you. You would have been torn to shreds by these monsters..." The Mord drag their feet closer to ED, shuffling with their knees, side-to-side. "Sorry." He pushes his hands out like he's holding back the walls of Mord who can't comprehend his motions anyway. "It's true though. You were on the menu before GenE got there. She saved your butt."

"By killing me?" GenAK spits the words to the ground. I can almost hear them sizzle like the rain outside. "That was not the plan, GenE."

ED chews his lip. "She also brought you back," he says eventually.

"I'm out of the game," GenAK says. "We all are. And you're happy about that?" He turns away from ED to face me. "We might as well be dead."

"We're working on that," ED says.

"There's no work-around." GenAK pushes his hair back. "There isn't any other way to get out of this hell-hole." He takes an angry step toward me, causing the Mord to close in protectively. After all, I'm the one who promised them a cure. GenAK stops and points a finger at me. "You sentenced me to this!"

No matter how hard I press my lips together, I can't stifle the grin playing at the edge of my mouth. "I guess you have a vested interest in all of our success then?" I want him to feel what it's like to be me, the thing he made. With no hope of counting in this stupid world.

"Your success?" GenAK asks, contempt dripping from his words in the way saliva drips from the nearest Mord mouths.

"We're Mord. All of us." I point to the three of us first, then to the crowd around me. "And we're going to create an army."

"What the hell are you talking about?" He stops caring about the threatening closeness of the Mord and grabs my shirt collar. I slap my hand over his like I'm not threatened, even though I so totally am. He pulls me close to his mouth. "This is not what you were designed for. It's not how it works." He drops his volume further, ensuring I'm the only one who can hear him. "I made you." Even quieter, like he's sharing a secret. "There are limits."

"You made me. Now I made you like me. As in, we're the same now."

He pushes me back. "You don't get it."

The storm outside stalls over our hideout. Thank goodness for the gutters. "This storm isn't letting up anytime soon." I speak as if the community of Mord understands me. "We need to locate health packs in safe zones. Only the vials with the sugar water scent to them."

"You've guaranteed the Commander will win. You know that, don't you?"

None of us respond to GenAK. There's no need.

ED has taken post at a pillar on the safe side of the storm drains. His eyes study the rainfall. I bet he's calculating the space between each drop. I'm tempted to dare him to run between a sheet of death to find a gap in gravity to carry him to the platform. He'll disappear the second the skies clear. His goal is to save himself. I say nothing, even though I know deep inside 'saving' isn't for us, despite all my bold words. We're cheats. Our only recourse is to change the game.

To do that, we have to cheat the cheaters.

35

The underground raid for packs bearing red crosses yields only ten cases. Each case carries a different variation of sweet scented vials. In all we have twenty-five usable tubes. After sniffing so many vials, everything smells like cantaloupe melon rot.

Mord-kid stands at the front of far more than twenty-five eyeless beasts. I hesitate in my eagerness to cure him. I've wanted to redeem myself from his death for a long time, but now don't know what the result will be. What version of him comes back if I stick him?

I risk curing the kid first.

His tongue runs across jagged teeth as he waits. GenAK sulks near a large cement pillar not too far from ED. I expect them both to run for a platform once the rain lifts. Part of coming back includes knowledge of platform location, including the fact one platform currently shuts down operations. I don't know why. I only know it's offline. Since it's the farthest away from our location, it doesn't worry me.

I rub a kink in my neck before sticking Mord kid with the first dose, leaving an opening in the lead position when he codes. Whoever steps up next gets the second, and so on, until all twenty-five tubes clink empty against the floor.

"We'll find more," I promise the waiting crowd. They rock as a unit from side to side, waiting for whatever it is I'm offering. "Once the storm lifts." I have no idea if there are more out there. Ten cases of shots seem like an awful lot.

The bigger conundrum is will twenty-eight cured Mord be enough for whatever waits for us?

It doesn't take long for the coded Mord to materialize with full faces and no trace of source code. Whatever new concoction is in the vials, I guess it's a reincarnation of AKs method to create fake players. No numbers on any of us.

The kid doesn't walk up to me when he has his memories back. He's been on my tail every move on this level and now he's distant, which probably goes with not remembering his time as a Mord. It sets me on edge. Trusting the kid isn't in my programming.

The kid obviously holds some level of significance. He retained an intelligence even in his monstrosity, shadowing me through this world. The rest of the mob mimicked his actions as if they sensed his authority. Or is his distance from me because he remembers how he became one of the sightless beasts?

Leaving the recovering non-Gens to rehash their lost time, I find GenAK. He leans against a pillar offset from where ED stares at the rainwater disappearing through the storm drain.

"AK?" I avoid getting too close. "Is it okay if I call you AK? I mean, we're not Gen anymore, are we?"

"Technically, you never were."

That doesn't help the moment. "I'm trying to understand you right now. You're making it difficult."

"Am I?" He pushes his back off the pillar. Staring me down like a challenge. "I'm making it difficult for *you*?" He leans into me. I expect him to yell. Instead he lowers his voice and speaks with such control it's more terrifying than a roar. "Would you like me to apologize?"

"I would." I fake brave and bold well, holding my ground and not letting my spine wilt the way it wants to. "You programmed me to take care of the Commander just so you could take his place. You're the same as him."

ED looks back at us. "Wait, what?"

GenAK throws his hands into the air. "You planned this didn't you?" He motions ED. "Gang up on me, why don't you?"

I'm so sick of him right now. I can't believe I used to tremble at the sound of his voice. "You're honestly accusing me of figuring out I'm made of scraps?" I point to the stockpiles. My birthplace, I guess. It's where I come from. It's who I am.

"How does that work?" ED asks. His need to be informed outweighing the moral issue at hand. *Damnit ED, be on my side for once.*

Fine. I dip my head, shadowing my eyes by my brow, feeling like I might be pulling off the 'intimidating' look. Knowing I was created to appear unintimidating, so I could get close to my target. "I was programmed to assassinate the Commander. At worst, I take out anything in arm's length."

ED steps back three steps like I'm still on 'kill' mode. I'm satisfied.

GenAK scoffs at ED, "She's being dramatic."

"Am I?"

GenAK opens his mouth, then closes it. When he speaks next his shoulders roll into soldier position, his back straight and his feet align perfectly straight forward. "Do you want me to leave?" he asks. "I will, if that's what you want."

Now who's being dramatic?

"I thought I finally did it—made something new and sustainable to fight back against the code manipulation." I feel like I could join his side when he talks about 'fighting back' and taking on the system.

"You did," I say. "And you're invested now." I slap his bare arm.

All the glory in his face falls away. GenAK hollers a growl of frustration. "I can't do anything like this!" He says 'like this' coated with disgust at what we all are.

"Hypocrite," ED says.

"Another platform shut down," the kid announces as he walks up behind us. The cured Mord, as well as the uncured, shuffle in behind him.

ED adds. "What if this rain doesn't let up?" Every head turns to him, even the eyeless ones. "What if the rain is holding us here, like a barrier, while they systematically shut us out from any other level?" ED adds.

"That's assuming a whole lot," GenAK says.

"The programmers don't know where we are," the kid says. "The two platforms are nowhere near each other. The first to go down is farthest from here. Next was mid-average distance from this yard."

The kid refers to the stock-pile body-parts parking garage as a 'yard'. That's almost cute.

"What if ED's right?" I ask. The low buzz growing within the crowd dies out. "Let's assume they consider us a threat." I have their attention. "What kind of threat can we really be?"

"We need names," ED says.

"How is that relevant?" GenAK asks. I'm pretty sure by the way those two look at each other, ED could have said anything and GenAK would have retorted 'idiot'.

"Because gamers associate names with winners," ED says. "If we name ourselves, we're declaring ourselves the true and rightful winners, in a way."

"That's no threat," AK says.

"He's right," the kid says, cutting off AK with a finger pointed to ED. "We need names. Real names."

GenAK pushes his buzzed hair back, tugging his scalp high on his forehead. "This is ridiculous. You're going to name yourselves?" He kicks the dirt. "Come on. Who is going to take you seriously?"

"You seem like a John," the kid says. "John Doe. Who isn't going to last long in this company if you don't get on board real soon." He indicates the swaying mob behind him. "They'll still rip you to shreds if I let them."

GenAK narrows his eyes at the kid.

I step in between them. "Or if AK has any ideas, we can take those into consideration, too."

"Ace," he says through clenched teeth. "Call me Ace." His

finger extends over my shoulder to the kid. "Don't you ever threaten me again."

"Okay, so Ace has some temper issues, which is good for us to know about." I place my hand over Ace's tense, pointed finger. "ED? Any requests for your name?"

"I'm kind of fond of Ed, come to think of it."

"If he gets to stick with Ed, I vote GenE keeps the name version of how her name sounds. Jennie. It fits her, you know," the kid says.

"She's definitely Jennie," Ed says.

Moving on. "Kid?" I ask.

"Tony. I'm a Tony," he says. He's absolutely a Tony. Like a spawn-of-Godfather type of Tony, but built entirely of stabby joints and long bones.

The rest of the group pick names. Mike, Bridget—who died on a bridge and claims it defines her new outlook on her second, second chance—Sawyer, Joe, Fran, George, Play'a, Yosef, Krissy, Doug, Nora, and all those who can speak for themselves now, all pick names significant to them for one reason or another, not all of which are gender indicative.

"Another platform down," Tony says.

We all turn to face the rainfall. "We're trapped," I say.

Ed licks his lips. "Not necessarily."

"You can't outthink acid rain." Ace taps his skull like Ed is some kind of idiot with an advanced degree. "You need armor or something, which we don't have. Most likely, *they* do." We all know by *they,* he means the Commander and his army in military blue suits.

"I've been observing the rain for hours. Like in Ace's level, it only dissolves animate code. I threw things into the rain, and it didn't dissolve." ED points to the buildings, trees, vehicles, all outside the parking garage, and undamaged by the falling rain. "We need mobile cover."

"Does that mean you also threw independently animate items into the rain? To test your theory? Like what? One of us?" Tony asks. The remaining eyeless hoard behind him advances toward Ed.

"Rodents," Ed says, hands in the air. "Some bugs."

Tony waves the Mord back. "This is a parking garage, right?" He still leans his small frame menacingly toward Ed. "There's got to be vehicles."

"Spread out, find something we can use for cover, it doesn't have to be a vehicle, so long as it's portable and large enough to cover our skins," Tony announces. He may look like he's thirteen, but the kid can command a room. "Move fast. Platforms are closing."

We're down to three open platforms with time against us.

"Got something," Yosef calls from deep in the underground structure. "More than one thing."

We all come running. The area Yosef found is behind a half wall, filled with what looks like the crumpled remains of 'crash-and-kill' world's vehicle graveyard. Everything looks rusted out, skeletal, and a huge risk to drive in the rain.

"We can work with this," Ace says.

Those of us with eyes stare at Ace in wide, dry doubt.

"Find as many as we can hotwire. We'll peel coverings from anything we can't get moving."

"Hurry," Tony says, jumping on board.

It takes less time than I expect to rip paneling off rusted vehicles and use them to patch holes or open spots on other cars. In all, we find seven working vehicles, which means not all the Mord are coming with us.

"We'll find more vials. We'll come back for you," Tony announces, standing atop a Humvee hood with a door wired to the roof where a massive hole had been blasted through.

Depending on the vehicle, we average five people per ride. Some of the larger vehicles fit seven to ten. Of course, we're disregarding seatbelts so our average increases by two per vehicle and still maintains a little room to maneuver, if we have to.

We can take forty-six to the platforms in cars. Twenty-eight cured and eighteen Mord. Mord aren't high-functioning enough to drive a vehicle on their own, so they have to divide up among those who can.

"I'm not driving with them." Ed points at the uncured Mord. "I don't even know why we're bringing them."

"They're the same as us," I say.

"Not you," Ace points out.

"What does that mean?" I ask.

"It means Jennie is the only wildcard." His words cause Tony to look on me with doubt again. This rollercoaster of trust never stabilizes. "She should be in my car. I created her. It's my responsibility if she loses control."

What I hear is 'I'm going to try to salvage my original mission and screw the rest of you.' I turn to him, one hand on my hip. He's going to kill me the first chance he gets. Eliminate a mistake he feels responsible for. "Blame yourself," I say, dead set on killing him before he has the chance to end me.

The Mord buzz at a higher level, or maybe it's my head panicking because my clock is ticking and the chances of making it out of this are about as good as the rusted metal we patched to these cars. The best I can do is plan to take out Ace with me. Dead, if it comes to that.

Billboards on every building gleam a golden list of ten codes. All codes start with GenAK. I recognize the Commander's long ID by its length more than the individual numbers following the Gencode. Ace's former string of identity isn't listed. I don't point it out. His expression as he stares out from the garage says he knows he's disqualified from life or any semblance of it.

If I had to guess his goal, it's being the harbinger of death.

36

The seatbelts securing the metal coverings of the vehicles slide when the vehicles move. Ace and I stare at the roof as if our unblinking eyes can weld the metal into place.

"Take it slow," I say.

"Gonna be a challenge with the platforms closing down all around us."

We're in the lead, the first vehicle to test its rain resistance out of the lot. Tony pulls behind us and the rest follow. I'm sure if our vehicle holds up, Tony will break rank and race for the closest functioning platform.

"If we get ten feet, don't head for the most obvious location," I say.

Ace gives me a sideways glance, followed by a smile. "You're smarter than I give you credit for." He takes credit, like the fact he programmed spare parts means every one of my accomplishments he gets to claim, yet every failure I own. "Here goes nothing."

We inch over the storm drains. Rain pelts the hood. Nothing looks like it's leaking. Everyone stills as the windshield becomes a sheet of yellow-green liquid. Ace flips the wipers. We extend our exposure to the acid rain. My shoulders tense when the hood of the vehicle enters the downpour. It holds. No leaks. Still, no one speaks. It's too soon to declare a victory in our pursuit of survival.

As predicted, once we're fully submerged in the storm, Tony takes the lead. I nod to Ace to head toward a new course. When we come to a crossroads, our vehicle turns left. Behind us, other cars follow Tony with a few taking the same side road as us. Worse, the Mord not in vehicles drag themselves into the rain following the cars. The Mord in our vehicle become agitated. I choose not to say anything, turning in my seat to stare straight ahead.

"How close are we?"

"Over five miles."

Our speed crawls at less than thirty miles per hour. "And the other route?"

"Less than two miles."

We exchange a look. Have we made the right choice? Two vehicles chose to follow us. The rest trail Tony. I wish they all went with Tony. The larger the party, the more attention we bring and we have farther to travel before we're even close to our destination.

An explosion rips through buildings behind us. "Whoa, what was that?"

Ace presses the gas closer to the floor. The straps securing our roof cover shift sideways with the increased speed. "Company."

I twist in my seat. Sure enough, a military vehicle without any scrap-parts holding it together turns down the street we're on. They're close enough to see the passengers inside the armored vehicle have protective yellow suits on, biohazard style. It's like they know our plans before we do and they've assembled to prevent us from doing the thing we're still trying to figure out.

"Tony made it?" I ask.

"The kid'll be fine. I'm more worried about us."

The armored car rear-ends the truck at the back of our pack. Ace pushes the gas pedal to the floor. Our car complains at the increased speed. Worse than the engine grinding, a gap tears in the roof—thin, but present. It's near the front of the first patch, right in front of me. One drop of rain hits my skin. The single drip eats through pink flesh and doesn't stop. It's like a bullet digging slowly through every layer of me until it reaches the cushion I sit on. Luckily, it's different than the yellow ooze in the trenches. This stuff doesn't keep eating my skin. It only digs a horribly painful hole through my arm.

I shift so the rain falls onto the cushion directly. Contorting myself out of its path takes all my concentration. "How close are we?"

"Not close enough. Taking a detour." He turns right.

The drip angles closer to me and the gap in the roof widens. "Watch it!"

We lurch faster. I'm basically a window curtain at this point. My seat soaks in splashing acid rain. The passengers behind the front seat huddle together in a heap. Little burn marks bore their way through me with every splish—like acidic shrapnel. "Ace!" I scream.

"Trying," he says without looking at what I'm hollering about.

Behind us, the car in the rear has been run off the road. The military vehicle pulls to the side of it. Suited persons get out and slice the seatbelt bands holding the patchwork metal covering on the car. Rain pours in on those passengers.

"Step on it," I say, less worried about splash-back than getting a forced acid shower.

"We're blocks away."

Ace shifts and the engine grinds. The car never promised long-term function. Accelerating our speed pushes the vehicle's limits. "Come on, a little farther."

"What about Tony?" I press as if guilt is something I'm familiar with.

"Ask me later." Red lights fill the dash display. More warnings join every minute.

I nod. No time to worry about anyone else. We have to survive. "Move back, I'm driving."

Ace pushes his lips up toward the bottom of his nose in some gruff guffaw of my suggestion, until I leap around the dripping roof, utilizing as much dashboard as I can. But even my small frame can't completely avoid the leak. "Ah!" My skin melts in angry red scars.

It's enough of a shock to force Ace to move. He doesn't want the death rain to touch him and it's all over me. I'm committed now. The military vehicle closes fast, less concerned with the car stuck in the middle. I expect it ramming us accordion-style any second. "Which way?"

"If you don't know where you're going, why take the wheel?" Ace screams right in my ear. If I weren't trying to save our lives, I'd slap him with my acid-damaged hand. With any luck it'd leave a big handprint acid-burn on his too-handsome face.

Failure rattles with the straps holding our roof on. Everything feels close to the skin. "Why'd you kiss me?"

He doesn't say anything. He doesn't even look at me.

"Back on the fearscape. Why'd you kiss me?" Now I feel even lamer and there are witnesses to hear it too.

"Turn left here," Ace shouts.

I yank the wheel. Rain angles the opposite direction my hands move, away from me for once.

"There," I say.

The platform sprawls right in front of us and the bio-hazard wearing enemy is directly behind. We missed when the second vehicle in our caravan drives off the road. They might still be alive. I never saw the military vehicle stop to finish the job like they did the last time.

The hole in the roof widens. My right arm shreds in the back-splash. I need to get to the platform. A hundred yards, seventy-five, fifty...

The yellow haz-mats slam our bumper. Screams from the back seat gurgle under a compromised shield.

"Ace?" I holler, still staring straight ahead with my foot all the way on the floor. We sail over a bump in the road, hitting hard. The makeshift paneling slides again. My right arm is useless now—rain eating through digital bone and all.

"The Mord took the brunt of it," Ace says. "Not much cover left."

Twenty-five yards farther, a crack in the road flattens our tire. The flap, slap of rubber against pavement cripples our speed. We get rear-ended a second time—harder. The military vehicle pulls to the side.

"They're going to try to cut us off," Ace yells.

"Almost there."

Sideswiped with less than ten yards to the platform, we drift over the edge of the rubber-ribbed surface. I gun the engine, smoke curling into rain creating a sizzling fog out the front view. "Come on, come on…"

"Do we have to get out?" One of the passengers I'm less familiar with asks from way in the back.

"For it to work, we have to be out there to level up." Another passenger says.

"Make contact with the mat…" I say.

"You first," the guy in the back says.

"You want me to be the guinea pig?"

"From what I gather, you're used to it." *Smart-mouth.* They've been privy to the entire conversation between Ace and me.

"Fine, I'm already down one arm. I'm the best choice for experimental procedure."

"Wait," Ace says, one hand on my shoulder. "I'm coming with you." The cramped passengers shift to the back with the smart-mouth. "Count of three, we open our doors and jump."

"Okay."

Faceless Mord passengers push their way in front of the passengers behind. They're panting on Ace's neck. I want to warn him not to make any sudden moves, in case they turn on him and try to take a bite. They keep panting in time. I count to their panting, hoping it will calm whatever rhythm they run on.

"One… Two… Three…" The second I pull the handle and push the door out, acid bubbles through the top layer of my skin. Ace grunts while I scream into the pain, jumping as far from the car as I can and fully exposing myself to drenching liquid.

A muffling blanket falls on top of me. Mord. Right on top of me. I can't breathe. *Some new attack measure?* "Ace," I call, but little sound makes it through the Mord body. The weight of the Mord like lead, pinning me beyond any possibility of rolling it off. "Help."

My burns sooth the longer the Mord stays over me. I'm surprised the rain hasn't eaten through its body yet. My remaining arm is severely damaged in the time it spent in direct contact with the rain. Yellow-clothed feet rush past my line of sight.

A low holler pounds against my eardrums. How long have I been pinned? It feels like forever. And then everything goes streaky, synthesized, and my stomach pulls out through my throat.

"Please, let this be a good thing," I chant. Everything stings, so much I seriously doubt I'm going anywhere better.

37

The times I prefer wrongness are when the condition in which I find myself superiorly outweigh my predictions. I don't spawn one of those times.

"If it isn't GenE, come to bite me in the ass," the Commander says.

His overbearing silhouette stands over me, his voice unmistakably arrogant. His movements are calculated, making me feel childish and behind, which I definitely am at the moment.

"I thought I took care of you back at base. I guess you figured out the blue shirt thing all on your own?"

"Thanks for that," I say with a grunt. Trying to sit-up proves a problem. I'm strapped or limbless. Who knows which limbs came with me or didn't after lying in the rain. The light shining down from above blinds me to my surroundings.

I have no idea what terrain this level hides, if I'm inside or outside.

No sound of naturally moving air. A whirr of machinery.

I'm inside. What floor am I on? Can't tell. How many people in the room? "Ace?" No answer. Maybe no one else made it.

Listening again, I hear the out-of-sync breathing of more than one spectator. Most likely the Commander's men. He isn't one to go into a situation without a crowd.

"What's your plan?" I thrash one shoulder, but the restraint holds my wrist. *I have arms! Sweet mercy, I'm whole at least.* "If you wanted to kill me you'd have done it already."

"I'm surprised at you," he says, not what I'm expecting. "How does killing you serve my purpose?" The silhouette morphs into a lurching beast with a dragon head. Long sharp tongue lapping out, liquid spurting from the tip of it—but no, that's my imagination. All he has is a needle filled with liquid code. I'd rather face the dragon beast of my imagination. "I'm always starting over with you. It gets old, you know. Assuming the identity of GenE... now don't you feel bad about that? Of course, I knew who you really were. So did AK. But why ruin the real girl's chance to shine, to star in her own ad?"

"What is that?" I nod to the syringe.

"We came together, he and I. And you, in a way. But only one of us can advance. That's the trick, isn't it? Whoever you arrive with becomes the real competition. Only one of us gets the prize and it ain't Ace. If that's what he's calling himself now."

Liquid from the pointed hypodermic needle hits my bicep, cold like ice in contrast to the burning rain. "He's not like you. He doesn't have a code anymore." The needle hovers less than an inch from my quivering arm. "I've never had a code," I say. I can't move away no matter how hard I try to lean, roll, dodge the thing.

"Even still... better safe than sorry."

The tip slides into my forearm, a pocket of ice pools under my skin for seconds before spreading up my arm, crawling over my shoulder, rolling into my neck. Stretching my head, turning away from the localizing blob under my skin, does nothing to prevent its presence inside me.

"What're you doing?" I squirm, hoping to break it up, or disperse it somehow.

"Reminding you who you work for."

"Ace said you're making an army," I wriggle, hoping information can save me from a fate of being liquid-programmed again. "The only AI to make it out of here will answer to you." It's so close to my chin. "Not if I can help it."

"I'm a mere shepherd keeping the sheep in line."

The blob rises, tapping into where spine and brain make an opening for it to ascend. My eyes go wide. I'd rather suffer this without an audience. It's humiliating.

The Commander lifts both hands in the air. "I can't stop it now." He sets the empty syringe on an operating cart at his side. "Who else did he share information with?"

I spit in his face. Icy fingers of the Commander's influence spindle outward like tendrils to all corners of my mind.

He grabs a rag from the table of surgical looking tools to wipe his face and throws it back down before bending his close-shaven chin back toward me. "This game we play, it's over now."

The Commander leaves the room. His back to me, he nods at the guy holding the door, closing me in the dim lit room alone. It's a small space. They don't even have a guard over me. Have I been poisoned? I worked so hard to get here, and it ends with a needle in the arm.

38

Waiting to die bores me the most. Especially when it takes For. Freaking. Ever. After what feels like hours, more likely twenty-minutes, I test the strength of the bindings. Rocking my shoulders forward and back, some side-to-side action, torso thrusting… Tight restraints… Still holding strong.

I push with my feet and get somewhere. The rig I'm secured to isn't bolted to the floor. I scrape-hop toward the door the Commander left through. I get close, having no means to open it. Now what?

I resort to slamming myself, and the restraining rig, against the door. Metal is super not fun to body slam. I continue to ram-rod the tin coffin I'm inside with my head and shoulders until something clicks.

Oh my heck, I've cracked it! All on my own, I made it open.

"Jennie." Tony stands outside the door. So I don't save myself. Tony opens the dang door for me. "You made it."

Don't sound so shocked, kid. Or is he excited? "Help me with this." I twist to show him the contraption I'm bound to.

"You spawned like that?" he asks.

"No idea. How long have you been wandering around?"

"One, maybe two hours."

Way to estimate like a truly unhelpful person, I don't say out loud. "Have you seen anyone?"

"Take a look." He pulls a switchblade from his back pocket and slices the straps holding me bound. He motions to the metal door with rounded edges and one of those submarine handles that look like a car wheel. I half expect an ocean to await me.

I lean outside, holding onto the top rim of the doorway for stability. Only to find a sea of metal containers, like bomb shelters have been dropped on top of a gray-sand ocean spread out over a huge landscape. The dirty grains of earth rise and rearrange with the shifting wind, erasing the footprints where Tony came from.

"What is this place?" I ask.

"Some of these metal pods have food, some supplies, some are empty." He wipes his brow, leaving a muddy streak across his forehead. "I've been raiding mostly."

Not surprising.

"One was huge. I would have gone in, but didn't have backup. Not sure what I'd find."

"Good call." I'd have gone in. What a pansy, Tony. "No sign of Ace or Ed?"

"I thought they were with you."

"Ace was, but Ed followed your group."

"No, he didn't. He was behind you."

Ed, no. Please don't be dumb. If he followed us, he was in the car whose coverings failed, exposing passengers to a downpour of flesh-eating acid.

"It's worse," Tony says stepping around me. I guess we're exploring.

"How is it worse?"

"The Mord all followed out of the garage. They all walked into the rain like puppies following their masters." He speaks as though they're his pets.

I really need Tony to stop talking right now. The landscape is pissing me off, with its sandness only broken by the hundreds of metal pods that look to me like steel traps spring-loaded with Commander-shaped threats behind every wheeled door handle.

"None of the viral Mord made it, even if they were on the platform. None of them arrived on this end." If that's true, then maybe the rain serves to clear the levels of virus so the donor batch doesn't have to be rebooted. Does that mean this game terminates and a new debugged version populates with all new donors?

"Did they disappear from the platform?"

"I was one of the first to transition. I didn't see."

I can't hold it against him, no matter how much I want to hold every little thing up to Tony, pin it on him and then point so everyone knows it's his fault. All of it. Anything not right? Blame Tony. "Who did make it?" I ask.

"There's you..."

I nod and brush dust off my pants. Sand blows right back over the clean spots.

"And me..."

"Yeah," I nod. "Who else?"

"I don't know. I was in one of these pods, too."

"How do you know for sure the viral Mord didn't make it if you don't know about anyone else who *did* make it?"

"Because two of them were right next to me. I could feel their skin hot against my arm. And then they were gone and I was here."

"That doesn't mean anything. I was next to Ace."

Tony the kid lifts his eyebrows. It's not surprise below those bushy brows. It's condolences and awkward avoidance of eye contact.

"What's with all the metal pods anyway?" I ask, avoiding the subject of who did or didn't make it to this level. And the fact the Commander shot something into me

"Bomb shelters. Something happened here. It's like this is the aftermath."

"That explains the landscape." Evidence of which pod we came from melts into the shifting sand. "You haven't seen anyone? I don't mean from the previous level, but anyone-anyone?" Like the Commander for instance?

"No one."

Tony trudges through the sand. Whether he knows where he's going or not doesn't seem to matter. I walk a little behind him, familiar distrust rising between us. A few hundred feet ahead another metal box with a hatch door protrudes. The sky turns red on the horizon in front of us. "What's that?"

Tony runs, not demonstrating having heard me, definitely aware of what is happening with the bleeding horizon. Dangit. He's holding out information. I can never trust him.

The sand slows me. The kid moves fast over the foot sucking grains. He reaches the hatch almost a full thirty seconds before me. He wastes his lead to turn the submarine style latch, a wheel he keeps spinning until it finally releases and the seal puffs out with a hiss as it sucks in the outside air.

We put our shoulders into swinging the metal on its hinges. Rust makes the action nearly impossible. Once the gap opens enough for Tony to fit through, he stops pushing and slides inside. I'm petite, but not like a thirteen-year-old boy. Following, I get stuck mid-chest, sucking in as much as I can I manage to clear all but my hips.

"I'm stuck." Wriggling moves me an inch. One more and I'm past the widest part of my body. Tony's hand clamps over my forearm and he pulls me clear.

"Pull it closed. Hurry!"

Arching my back in the effort to defy rusted hinges, we get the hatch close enough to engage the seal when we turn the circular handle.

"What was that out there?" I ask about the red sky.

"Don't know." Tony shrugs. "Didn't want to find out."

His answer puts me at ease toward him for now. He's not withholding information about this level. He doesn't want to gamble with weird colored skies. I have to admit, he's right.

"Take stock. Anything useful?" A rucksack hits me in the chest. "That's for you. Fill it."

"How do we know when it's clear out there?" I shove a rope to the bottom of my pack. A flashlight across the room is my next target.

"No idea. I'm still figuring this place out, same as you."

"Someone there?" a voice calls from a shadowed corner. "Get this off me."

Tony steps in front of me when I move toward the voice. "We're on a different level, but it's the same game." I know he's telling me not to trust the voice.

I've heard the same warning so many times, I don't care anymore. Trust, blah, blah, blah… "We can't leave someone."

"Can't trust anyone," he whispers. Tony moves his foot, sliding his toes along the floor with a rasping scrape reminiscent of Mord dragging their feet when they walk.

"Get over yourself, Tony. Get this off me already," the voice says.

"Ace?" I ask.

"You know, Ace is a…" Ed stops before saying what Ace is, probably unable to find the right quality insult. "I get it. You and Ace. Okay."

Ed? I rush to the corner where a metal cabinet has him pinned. "You didn't make it to a platform."

"Get this off." Ed huffs to lift the cabinet. "I expected a warzone, not this weird office space."

He's right. With our exit from the Mord realm, we should have been greeted with guns to our heads. Since no one else mentions the same 'hello, captain needle' experience, I keep information to myself, not making eye contact with Tony. I can't let either of them know I've already encountered the Commander. Trying not to draw attention to myself, and probably drawing attention by the act of trying not to, I turn my head to observe Tony the kid. His posture demonstrates lack of concern with Ed's predicament.

"How long have you been like this?" Tony joins the rescue effort, though he doesn't appear too invested.

"Forever. Get me out of here."

"The cabinet made of lead, or something?" Tony asks.

The cabinet doors face up. Why not empty it so it's lighter to move? No lock prevents me from pulling on the handle. The catch sounds and the door swings wide. "Ah—my hell!" I let go.

My outburst causes Tony to drop his portion of the cabinet. Ed yelps upon impact, the cabinet, with all its weight, lands back on top of him.

"Dead?" Tony asks staring at the thing inside the box. The door hangs wide, covering Ed from reading our expressions.

"What is it?" Ed asks.

I shrug. Ed can't see. "It's TECH-chick," I explain. "That's what she gets for teaming up with the Commander."

"I guess the only person we're missing is Ace," Tony says.

"I'm here. No way I'm helping whining geek over there." Ace speaks from deeper in the darkness where none of us can see. We all jump. "Grow some muscles and help yourself. Think we all landed in a field of daisies?"

My chest tightens and lifts at the same time. It's all very confusing. The weird clicking sound chirps again. "You guys hear that?" I ask.

"Ed's yammering? Yeah, he hasn't shut up for three hours," Ace says.

"You've been there three hours and never bothered to say anything?" Ed strains to ask. His legs thrash, kicking air and the leg of one upturned chair, which he probably knocked over three hours ago.

"You seriously don't hear that?" I ask.

The ticking doesn't get louder or quieter. It stays steady, at regular intervals. Not exactly like a clock ticks, more like a wind-up toy—the kind with a little white knob to twist until it can't twist anymore. It tightens as it winds.

"First, move TECH-chick out of there." Ace steps from the shadows to join the fiasco.

"Wait, shouldn't she get a real name? You know, like the rest of us?" Tony asks.

"Is she like the rest of us?" Ace pushes his sleeve up his arm. Blue-ish yellow light reveals an unblemished forearm.

"I'm not checking," Tony says.

Ace reaches down, lifts TECH-chick's left arm, which I recall was forcibly taken from her one level ago, twisting to expose the marked portion.

GenTECH993421179579.

The number doesn't end there. We all stare. Tony leans in closer, presses one finger into her tattooed skin.

"That shouldn't be there," I say stepping back.

"Grab her other arm." Ace takes charge without Tony's permission.

The kid's face pulls tight. He chews the inside of his bottom lip for a second before complying.

"So?" Ed asks, still pinned under the cabinet. "Is she one of us?" No one answers him.

TECH-chick weighs a heck of a lot more than she looks like she'd weigh. If I had to guess, I'd say she was made out of steel. With Ace and Tony each lifting her arm and shoulder, I manage to wedge around behind the closed cabinet door side and pull up at her mid-section.

To be honest, I would have been happy grabbing a handful of her rainbow-spiked hair and yanking. Probably a disrespectful move on my part.

Ed doesn't repeat himself. He's too smart for that. He knows when people are ignoring him intentionally.

Once TECH-chick lies on the ground, the cabinet moves. Ed scrambles over to TECH-chick and examines her arm for himself.

"Why is she here?"

"ECHO team, back together again," Ace says under his breath.

Ed gets to his feet, brushes off his knobby knees and stands with his chin meeting Ace's nose. "What is that supposed to mean?"

"E is the fifth letter in the alphabet. E…Echo. It's a team name based on the five of us. The original group."

"Well, that's not intellectual at all," Ed says, crossing his arms.

"Who says I'm trying to be intellectual?" Ace says as he bats at Ed's head. "Right now, we're enemy number one."

Ed swerves out of the way before getting his ear boxed. He turns his face so it's right in Ace's face, looking down his nose into Ace's eyes.

Ace leans in further, forcing Ed back. "I don't need you." Ace pivots on his heels.

"You hear that? He knows more about what's going on than

he's saying. He doesn't need me? Like he knows what to expect?" Ed asks.

My left arm burns in rhythm to the clicking chords ringing in my ears. I slap a hand over the stinging portion, hoping the red sky situation outside isn't connected to what's happening to me. Radiation poisoning crosses my mind. "But, there's nothing out there. It's like *post* war."

"Not all war is fought with guns and disease," Ed says.

"Piss off, Ed," Ace shouts, knocking over a desk with half-rolled papers, a pen, and a long dried-up coffee mug. The mug shatters against the metal floor before any of us move. "We all know you're the smart one."

"Dude, chill," Tony says. Both words sound forced coming from his youthful mob demeanor.

"I won't," Ace picks up a roll of papers and throws them sideways, catching air and scattering inches after they leave his grip. "You know why?"

The rest of us exchange a look. Does he expect us to answer?

"Because we're screwed," Ace says. "We wouldn't be here unless we'd already lost."

"That doesn't make any sense," Ed says.

Ace pulls back his arm, looking ready to throw punches any second. Ed takes two steps, placing me between him and Ace.

"They had us." Venom accompanies every word out of Ace's mouth. "We shouldn't have made it out of there." He uncocks his arm, punching the air so a whoosh of stale bomb shelter rushes past us, to where TECH-chick lays. "She's the kicker though. Putting her where they knew we'd find her. To say, *'You're all dead. See, this is what it looks like'* before they pull the trigger."

"What if you're wrong?" Tony asks.

Ace bends down real low, getting in Tony's face, emphasizing he's nothing but a foolish child. "What does your gut tell you, kid?"

"I watched her lose her arm," I say. Tony flits his gaze my direction, but doesn't back me up.

"She's whole now." Ace opens his arms wide. "A whole lotta dead."

A table bumps behind me. Ed curses and grabs his foot, hopping on the other leg.

"Did you kick the table?" I ask. "On purpose? It's bolted to the floor, idiot."

Ace bursts into laughter. It's sick and twisted, this situation we're in. None of us knows what's going on. I laugh as well, as if delight in the absurdity of our fate is contagious.

"I can't believe I'm stuck with you bunch of morons," Ed says, still hopping around on one leg.

Tony doesn't laugh with us. "Ace is right. We're already dead."

Way to totally ruin the moment.

39

The metal bunker has cabinets and drawers full of files and blueprints. None of us have a clue what they're for. In a world covered in sand and littered with half-exposed bomb shelters, what's the point of building stuff? Survival of the elements seems like a more pressing concern. A cabinet full of protective gear would have been nice. Even a hazmat suit, in case there's radiation fallout.

"Ah!" I scream. My arm hangs like a weight on fire. The guys' heads rise from what they're doing to look at me. I press my right hand over my left arm where angry, red boils are visible. "We can't stay here or I'll go insane." I cover my outburst pretty well. Any normal person would scream being stuck in a bunker with three incompatible males bickering at each other the whole time.

"Too bad you're not in charge here, Jennie," Tony says.

"You still need zit cream. Get over yourself," I say.

Tony rolls the blueprints he's examining while keeping his eyes on me.

"Anyone find anything we can actually use?" Ed asks, ever the subject changer when things get tense. Unless, of course, it's going down between him and Ace.

Ace pats a roll of papers in his hand. "Schematics."

"You know where we're going?" Tony asks, tripping over himself.

"No." Ace pulls the pages higher, out of reach of the kid. "I know what it looks like when I get there."

"It's dead out there. I have no idea how to navigate wasteland," I say. "We won't make it one mile before we get turned around."

Tony holds up a handful of permanent black markers. "We mark every bunker we pass. Up high, where the sand won't cover."

"That still doesn't give us a starting direction," Ed says.

"What's all this 'we' crap? I'm going alone." Ace grabs the rucksack Tony threw at me when we first arrived in this bunker and shoves the papers he's holding inside so the tube of papers bends in the middle.

"We're all in this together. If we're going to outplay this thing, you need us," Ed says, putting a hand on the exit.

"You mean, you need me," Ace counters.

"That's not what I said."

"If you don't need me, let me leave." Ace motions for Ed to move his hand off the door.

"We should stay together," Tony says.

The burning in my arm flares. I press my lips together, but a moan still escapes my mouth. Folding my arms against my chest does nothing to insulate the pain. A sharp jab digs into my inflamed arm, breaking one of the sores open. Dark puss stains the front of my shirt. The liquid soaking into my shirt turns cold and sends chills over my skin, reminding me of another discomfort—the key stashed under my clothes.

"You okay over there?" Ace asks.

I'm too busy trying to figure out what jabbed me to listen to Ace. He wants to leave anyway. He's not allowed to abandon us and care whether or not I'm okay too.

Key. I'd forgotten about it. I can't believe it's stayed with me this long. I slide the metal from under my shirt and hold it up to examine it. It still has a flat bottom edge, hasn't changed a bit. Wish I could say the same about myself. I'm more serrated since finding the key.

"What'd you find?" Ace asks, giving up on getting out the door while Ed's standing guard. It's not going to happen without a fight.

"The key," I say.

Ace recognizes it. He stops getting closer, holding his satchel tight in one hand. He takes a step closer to the door, apparently less concerned about Ed blocking his path.

"Isn't that what you used to cut me out of the SUV when we met?" Tony asks.

"Yeah," I say, sliding a finger over the flat bottom edge. "I almost forgot that."

Ed pats his own pockets, like he lost something. He had the

key, my key, on him when I shot him at the military bunker. He must not have realized I took it back.

"What does it go to?" Tony asks.

"I don't know." Everyone's eyeing my key. I'm suddenly aware of how close the guys are and return the key to where it came from. "Maybe nothing."

Pink light from outside stretches across the floor, climbing turned over desks, cabinets and chairs to reach us.

"Ace is gone," Tony says.

Without conferring what each other are doing, we grab our respective loot and rush out the door. The blowing wind fast erases Ace's tracks. Luckily, he's not far enough away to be out of sight.

"There," Tony shouts over the scratching sound of shifting sand. He points to a broad shouldered Ace leaning into the wind.

The sky filters everything with a red hue. Yanking my sleeve low on my arm, I press my blistered skin against my side to protect it as much as possible from exposure to the light. What if my face breaks out in the same sores? Too many other things are pressing. Like the continued clicking inside my head, which no one else seems able to hear.

"Hurry up," Ed says. He and Tony are several strides ahead of me.

I rush past a silver door to catch up with the group. No one bothers checking the bunkers we pass. "Tony," I shout.

"What?"

I have to choose my words well. "How crazy is it we picked that bunker to check?" His scrawny shoulders give away signs of increased tension. "You stumble on my hatch, and the very next one—boom—group's back together again..."

Ed looks back at me, but doesn't slow his pace. His fingers dance at his side. I can tell he's calculating odds behind sand-crusted lids. What are the odds Tony knew exactly where to find all of us?

"It's also interesting how both Ed and Ace said they'd been here nearly three hours and you'd only been around for two hours, even though the platform you jumped from was closer from the parking garage than the one we came from..."

"The game doesn't make sense, I guess," Tony says, then stops. "But, wait."

"Yeah?" I ask.

"What platform *did* Ed use?" Tony turns sideways, facing Ed. "Which lead driver did you follow? I don't remember seeing you behind me." He twists, leaving his feet pointing accusingly at Ed, but faces his head and shoulders to me. "And Jennie mentioned an attack on the other vehicles in her group..."

I stop walking.

"And I haven't even mentioned the state in which I found Jennie..." Tony faces forward again.

Ed stops walking, too. *Dang the kid.* Tony holds all the cards now.

"Alright, so everyone has reason to be suspect," Ed says.

On the plus side, I don't have an uncontrollable urge to murder anyone. Yay. Though, maybe I should. This is the one environment where not having a homicidal tendency will bite me in the butt.

"Where's Ace?" Ed asks.

I look up. The sand horizon is bare except for smooth metal pods jutting out at asymmetrical angles. The clicking in my head tightens. Not faster, but more defined in each click, click, click— like it's winding up to the end.

Ed stands with his toes buried in the sand, his ankles on the brink of being swallowed by it. Tony points his fingers, slowly being eaten by the moving ground. I don't have time for this. Running, I pass both of them and glimpse Ace on the horizon again.

"Ace!" Bunkers jut less frequent or less apparent in the distance. The red sky is bright, despite the lack of a burning ball of light illuminating the land.

My lungs burn from running as well as breathing in the glass air. I say glass because breathing in heated sand literally feels like breathing glass shards. "Ace! Where are you?"

Blowing sand picks at my face in reply. I put a hand up, expecting blistered skin like my arm. My cheek, road rash raw, is free of angry boils. I check my arm. The condition on my skin worsens. Black spots inside the boils look like rotting flesh.

"See him?" Ed approaches from behind.

I hurriedly cover my arm again and press the infected portion tight to my side, in case the puss from the bursting sores soaks through the fabric. I don't want them to know about it yet. However, I do observe them for similar behavior.

"Where is he?" Tony asks, last to catch up.

Ed's arms hang loose at his side. His face, flush from running, is blemish free. I turn to Tony. Hands on hips, he bends to catch his breath. No attempt to hide anything.

"He couldn't have gotten far," Tony pants. "Where is he?"

Sweat beads down Tony's face, a digitally designed reaction to the conditions. Tony scans the landscape frantically. He spins in a circle, corkscrewing his feet deeper into the consuming sands.

"Calm down." I put a hand on Tony's shoulder.

He shakes me off. "Don't touch me." He turns one hundred eighty degrees and squints into the red tinted landscape. "I have to find him."

Ed's left hand twitches to the beat of calculating with his fingers. His eyes fix on Tony, though not much is revealed from his collected expression. Only that Ed is adding Tony up. Ed's fingers splay, as if the equation of Tony doesn't balance. Whatever's off pulls Ed's stance more to one side than the other. He leans away from Tony while his hand stays tense. His fingers remain sharp like they could be used for a weapon, if it came to it. "You seem abnormally on edge over losing track of Ace. It's not like the two of you ever got on well."

"It's part of the deal."

Ed straightens completely, no longer leaning. Prickles rise at the back of my neck. Because I have no deal.

"Tony." Ed speaks slowly, breathing heavy, pausing, searching for optimum word choice to not set the kid any more on edge. "What deal are you referring to?"

The kid rambles, "The deal, the deal." He jumbles, stutters words. "My deal. The. Deal."

"What does *the deal* involve?" Ed asks, precise and even, careful to not upset Tony.

"All of us!" Tony screams, turning around to face us. He steps out of the pit his feet have sunk into, restarting the slow process of being claimed by the environment. "I don't get a code implanted in my arm, unless I deliver all of us—" He picks up a handful of sand and lets it drip slowly through his fingers as he continues speaking, punctuating each word. "Every. Last. One."

I step away from Tony. "Deliver us?" My bag drops to the floor. "To whom?"

"You went the other direction," Tony says. "They were right on top of us. My only chance was to pull over, raise the white flag, and cut a deal."

"You could have died," Ed offers as an alternate solution. "Like the rest of the cars."

Tony wags a finger at Ed, stepping closer to him. "Funny you bring that up, because I *know* you didn't follow my car. They all died. So you had to be behind Jennie." The wagging finger breaks from beating in Ed's face for a single beat on me before going back. Tony opens his eyes wide and forms an 'O' with his mouth, holding the expression for a second, savoring the effort it's taking Ed to keep his face stoic. "But she said the other cars were ripped open, all passengers washed away in the rain."

"The Mord." Ed stands a little taller as if on moral high ground. "They shielded me and we ran twenty yards to the platform. I had burns." Ed points to his fully intact frame. "They didn't come with me."

"My arm," I say pointing to my left arm. Remembering the boils, I switch hands and point to my right arm. What difference does it make anyway? "It was eaten away from exposure, but it's fine now."

"Let me see that." Tony reaches out for my left arm.

I pull back, holding it behind me. "I pointed to my right."

"She's hiding something. Grab her shoulders," Tony orders Ed.

Ed hesitates and I breathe a little easier until his long thin fingers clamp and his palms press me deeper into the sand. Tony reaches his scrawny arm toward me. I easily slap the side of his head with my right hand before he comes close. Stepping back, he tilts his head to the side.

Tony fakes another grab for my left arm. I swipe the air when he jumps back, unprepared for the hard crack against my jaw. He punches me.

"Tony!" Ed says.

"Hey." The kid cracks his neck, looking limber like he's ready to enter a boxing ring. "Cheap shots don't go unanswered."

Ed's fingers slide over the curve of my right shoulder. His grip maintains strength, without rushing, while caressing the dimpled muscle of my bicep before stopping above my elbow, squeezing so hard my fingers go numb. I swing, but my reach is blunted.

Tony tips his head to Ed as if he wears an invisible hat. He easily snags my left arm despite my best flails. He pushes my sleeve high, which scratches open several sores. Clear liquid runs down my skin, sizzling the second it hits the sand.

"You're already tagged." Tony throws my arm back at me so forcefully it feels like a punch to the gut. "I knew it." His wagging finger returns, this time with no particular target. "I knew they already tagged you."

"You know what this is?" I ask.

"Why don't I know what's going on?" Ed can't handle being outside the information loop.

"It's a donor code," Tony says, nervous laughter making him appear insane.

"I'm not a donor. I'm not even human."

It's Ed's turn to waggle his fingers—calculating, calculating, always calculating. "What do you mean, you're not human?"

"Made from spare parts. Remember the stockpiles?" I salute the sky. "I was supposed to kill the Commander, but the booster shots had something in them. One, maybe more than one. I used a few before I knew about the code altering inside them. It changed my programming and I went on a homicidal bender." I let my hand flop to my side. There was nothing left to hide. "Or something like that."

Both Ed and Tony take a step back from me.

"I'm better now."

They don't step closer.

"Seriously, the Mord fixed the glitch. Or killed me." I shake my head over and over. "I don't know. Maybe it's more of a reboot."

"You're not even human? You're actually AI. You're spontaneous AI, in a machine designed to prevent naturally occurring AI." Ed's fingers waggle through the air faster, stopping only to push his glasses up his sweating nose. "You can't have a code."

"She didn't. How did you not notice?" Tony asks. "She never had a code."

Ed's fingers stop moving. "What are you talking about?"

"You're such a poser," Tony says. "From your appearance to your profession."

"What does that mean?" Ed pushes me aside and looms over Tony.

"It means you're a hack. There isn't even a glasses prescription in those lenses, I can tell." Tony reaches up and flips the frames on Ed's nose. Ed moves back, his hands livid with waggling. "I knew she wasn't one of us from the moment she pulled me from the truck. That was the main reason I didn't find her a threat."

"Shouldn't that make me a bigger threat?" I ask.

Ed sticks one hand inside his jacket, seemingly calming his dangling fingers. "She killed you first." Ed laughs, negating everything Tony accused him of. Then he pulls a gun from inside his vest. "And you're not the only prick who made a deal." Ed points the barrel at Tony.

"No!" I lunge for Ed's extended arm, barely tipping his elbow. I fall to the hot sand. The grains burn at the exposed sores of my left arm, eating away the flesh to reveal black letters in an orderly line, followed by numbers.

Tony's shoulder bursts backwards, twisting his whole upper body toward the direction the bullet travels. Red rain explodes out the back of his shoulder, spraying the ground to match the sky, before Tony falls onto his own blood spatter.

Ed throws me to the ground.

"You kill her…" Tony reaches a hand up in surrender. "You won't have a deal. She's the key."

"No." Ed's hand scratches against my collarbone, sand particles clinging to the cold sweat on his skin like rough paper. He smiles as he reaches down the front of my shirt. "We've been here before," he says, coming up with the blunt-edged key, winking once.

Ed holds the item up for Tony to see, giving it one good outward shake. "This. This is the key."

I stare down the dark smoking circle of the gun. Such a simple thing, a metal tube. "And I thought Ace was the ass," I say.

Tony punches sand with his good arm. "Ed!"

The gun moves from my face, refocusing on Tony. I want to jump to my feet and wrestle the gun out of Ed's hand, but I merely exhale at not getting a bullet between the eyes.

"This is the war!" Tony screams. Blood fills the gaps between his fingers where he's holding his shoulder. "We've been pitted against each other. Don't you see? We're losing."

"We can't all win," Ed says. A bullet slides into the chamber. It clicks, like the clicking in my head. So tight. Tight like a rubberband stretched to the edge of its limits. Ready to burst if it turns one click more. Two more. Three beyond capacity…

"The Commander planned this from the start. We kill each other for him. Because if we're together… together we beat him." Tony struggles with grunts of pain and continues to loosen and tighten his grip on his shoulder, finding no balance between accidentally causing more pain and stopping the bleeding.

Click.

The sky turns blue.

Click.

I turn my head to examine it closer. Clear blue air. The sky isn't red, it's refreshing and cool. At my feet is grass. Soft blades kiss my toes, bending in a gentle breeze. Why do I remember sand?

Click.

Rolling hills lift ahead. Cresting the nearest one will reveal a brick and mortar town with a little stone cathedral in the center and a city park yawning before it.

Snap.

And at my side sits a man. Tall. Dressed in enemy red. With a gun suspended between me and his small companion, who's injured for some reason.

"Jennie?" The small injured one speaks.

I turn to confirm my assessment of no threat to the Commander here. I'm prepared for three. With only two visible persons, the third could have sustained significant injury before this point. I'm prepared for that scenario as well. *This enemy is unstable. They will turn on each other as easily as fight the Commander.* A message plays in my newly stocked memory banks.

"Look at her," the small one croaks. "Her expression… and her shoulders. Not tense and distrusting like a good Jennie should be." He coughs blood.

The small one poses no threat. Only the tall one needs dealing with.

"That's not Jennie. Not our Jennie. The Commander. He did something to her." The small one continues to speak nonsense words. No need to pay attention.

"Good thing I have the key then." The tall one swings his arm back toward me.

He postures to overpower me. Humorous. I need the key. It's good of him to inform me of its location. Lifting my hand, blade of my palm out, I jab swift with one stroke at his oncoming elbow, breaking bone with the opposing force. The tall one screams. The gun falls, enveloped soundlessly by a soft tuft of grass.

"I need to confirm the third combatant has been dealt with."

The tall one's voice bends to a high register while he rocks himself and coddles his broken arm. A burden limb? I should remove it entirely for him, so he isn't tempted to cling to things without use.

"Who? Ace?" The tall one makes the most whining sounds. It bothers me, this high tone of complaint.

"Is that the indicator of the third combatant?"

"Like we'd tell you." The small one spits into the grass. I'm uncertain of the meaning of this gesture, therefore I don't bother analyzing it.

"Tell her. Maybe she'll leave us alone." The tall one cows. He is not a worthy combatant.

"Don't say anything." The small one fights the rolling hill he's lying on. He's a lazy one to lie prone at a time like this.

"Ace is dead. He didn't make it out of the bunker." The tall coward ignores the small, lazy one.

"Thank you for your honesty. I will assist you now." I plunge my arm into the grass and bring forth the weapon. Grass blades cling to its sides, but don't impede the function of the weapon.

The tall one covers his head with his working arm. His broken limb dangles at an odd angle while he struggles to force it up over his head as well.

Walking around the tall one to the useless limb, I stow the weapon in my belt and grip the shoulder above the ball joint. I can feel where the connection holds weakest. My other hand grips below the joint. Using opposing strength, I dislocate the shoulder.

The tall one screams at a high register. It makes my ears sore. I may have to render him quiet. I twist the limb to remove it entirely. Unfavorable of me to leave it dangling. Bothersome. The process isn't clean, lines and framework refuse to part this man from his malfunctioning pieces. I lack the correct tools for a neat dissection. This man provided me with information and I owe him a freedom from burden despite his cowardice.

"Be still. I am assisting you now." I twist the arm over and over, hoping to weaken everything still holding the arm to the man. The connective tissues are more stubborn than I expect.

The sticky blood has escaped the shoulder socket location, not helping the situation. Retrieving the gun from my belt I press the nozzle against the joint I wish to remove, and pull the trigger. A good portion of the stubborn flesh disintegrates in the explosive release of the bullet.

Selecting a second location to weaken the arm's hold on the rest of the body, I aim and fire. Nearly off. The tall man has stopped screaming now. An indicator of his gratitude.

His face has gone a pale color, and his mouth lolls open. Perhaps lazy is catching among this group. Like a virus. I don't like virus. I must leave them quickly and not expose myself to infection. I continue to twist the arm until the last tendon snaps. "You are now free from your burden. I thank you for sharing with me and will let you continue in the opposite direction from where I travel."

Before leaving, I reach down and take possession of the key. "Thank you for caring for this item while out of my hands."

The small one blinks at me, but says nothing. Ungrateful in equal measure to his laziness. The tall one is so grateful for my gesture he cannot utter words. They are an odd pairing.

The grass cools my heels as I crest the hill. In the valley below, I spot the cathedral in the center of town. A light shines forth from its stained-glass windows where the Commander waits for my delivery.

40

The town crawls with fellow associates of the Commander. They stomp and scrape in loud obnoxious movements. No one knows how to remain still. Their hiding efforts are wasted by mouth breathing and itching hands. I'm embarrassed associating with the fidgeting lot of them.

A grating whisper sets my teeth on edge.

"Jennie."

These soldiers have no skill at stealth maneuvers. My fists tighten and my teeth set in the grooves of one another, pressing in on each other though there is nothing in my mouth to masticate. I would much appreciate pressing my teeth upon the shifting soldiers until they all stop being bothersome.

The whisper continues to sound. Repeating the same word over and over again. "Jennie... Jennie... *psssst*... Jennie."

I have tolerated enough incompetence. Turning hard, heel click, one hundred eighty-degree pivot, I move toward the disrespectful repetitions of the useless soldier. The Commander will do well to rid himself of such associates.

The sound proves farther away than I expect. There are no other associates of the Commander this far out from the Cathedral. What a loud and horrid soldier.

The hissing word ceases. I stop my progress. Perhaps all the soldier needed was an example on proper military behavior and has decided to shape up.

But then I hear, "Oh. Shit."

I do not understand. Checking my feet for excrement, there's nothing. The loud soldier reveals himself directly ahead of me. His eyes hold mine in a familiar stare.

My organs malfunction. The pumping device forces far too much liquid through my internal cables, given the lack of physical strain required in the situation. My eyes receive additional light, blinding me to peripheral details I previously used to assess my surroundings. The wires carrying electrical current throughout my body fire charges in all directions, causing my stomach to experience a dropping sensation, and rising at the same moment. My head is in pain. Part of my neural processor must have sustained damage from my encounter with the lazy ingrates over the hill. The sky flashes red. Unpleasant. This associate must be infectious. I dislike him immediately.

"I'm broken," I say without giving my mouth permission to speak. The traitorous sounds form between my lips without being passed through my brain.

The loud soldier moves to a crouch behind a statue. Upon hearing my plea for repair or advice he shifts to one side, revealing a red shirt. I step away. The sky flashes again and the world turns to dust and ashes. This is what the enemy does. Distorts the world to make it messy. I know this as fact.

I force my head to override whatever is malfunctioning in the rest of me. "You're the enemy." When I speak, grass soothes my feet and the land returns right and true, green and blue.

The enemy holds both his hands in the air, some gesture which signals weakness. He sidesteps and exposes himself, not at all concealed by his shielding statue. What kind of enemy teaches their soldiers such useless counter measures? This is why the enemy loses.

"Jennie, listen to me." His voice creates electricity and heat. I can't understand how he does this. "I forgive you."

"I do not know that term. Are you signaling someone?" I twist, observing the portion of the city we're in. No one to signal.

"I made you." He steps forward. His hands rise up to the sky with his palms facing me. "You s-saved me." His hands twitch. "I was upset about that because of the code wipe... But we're connected. You and I."

"I don't know you."

"I did something once because I thought I could bring someone back, but I couldn't." Hesitation spans gaps between shifting grass blades and rushing sky. "Maybe it'll work this time."

When he speaks, the world flips back to dust and ash, my organs fail to perform, and my head throbs with issues too numerous to count.

The man steps closer to me, hands still in the air. I assess he offers no threat in this position, but still do not understand its purpose.

"You're mistaken. We've never met."

He stands in front of me. How did he get so close without any warning signs activating my defensive techniques?

"Don't panic," he says. His hands hover under the sharp edge of my chin. "Don't…"

His mouth presses against mine. His lips part and mine copy the motion, perhaps in shock of the predicament in which I find myself. The closeness of him causes failure throughout my entire being.

What sort of weapon is this?

My hands find his chest and I push against him to move away. For the briefest eternity our mouths part and my hands grip his shirt, curling the fabric into my fingers and locking it in my fists. His hands move to the back of my neck.

Memory of icy tendrils stretching out from the base of my neck and up through my head flush through me like shock waves. Heat replaces the cold invasion, a welcome heat I keep pulling closer, closer…

Ace moves his hands from my neck, gripping my hair, and before I realize what I'm doing, I no longer intend to dispatch his head from his shoulders.

He pulls away first, despite my effort to bring him back to me. The world around us is blistering sand, bloodied sky, and ash dust. Sort of the opposite of magic after a kiss like that.

"Hey, hey. There's a war on." His smile reassures me he meant every second of what happened between us.

"What was that?" I ask.

"I thought it'd help. You know, history and all between us."

I know he means the fear level so long ago. This time was

much different. Like he thought someone else might materialize out of his fears. Someone he feared and missed at the same time.

Not me.

"I've been under the impression you don't trust me."

"Can you blame me?"

Ruins and rusted statues mark the places where beautiful buildings and ornate decorations stood moments before. "The Commander sure knows how to paint a pretty picture."

"What do you mean?" Ace asks.

"Nothing." I wave him off, no time to explain the whole brainwashing to a better world thing. "Now what?"

"This." Ace holds up a key, like mine.

"Where did you get that?" I pat my chest and pockets. I still have my key.

"Come on. I made you didn't I?" Ace blushes. "How hard do you think programming a key is?" Then his smile drops like he can't keep hitting the smile icon in his brain. "TECH-chick made it," he admits. His head drops and he slides one hand through his hair. "I stole it from her in the bunker when I found her. Before Ed came to, complaining up a storm." Time passes with neither of us speaking. I have to form the question in my head, like he knows I'm thinking it, but either wants me to ask or hopes I never will. Before I get the nerve to decide if I want to know for certain, he says, "She was already dead."

A relieved breath escapes me. I hadn't realized I stopped letting air out of my lungs while I wait. I can't think of what to say to knowing he didn't murder TECH-chick in the bunker. It's not like I have a shining record of dealing with people in the game. "It looks exactly like my key."

"That's the idea." He steps next to me so we're side by side, key by key. "I knew the key was traveling with you through the levels. It wasn't part of my program, but I figured it had some purpose." Ace isn't known for his loquaciousness, except for when discussing military strategy. Such topics transform him from the strong silent type to borderline chatty. I can tell this explanation might last a while, so I settle in for a monologue. "I didn't know what significance it held at the time, because you never really talked about it, brought it up, mentioned it. You get the idea. I thought of asking Ed, since he's educated and sort of okay when he's not being a total jerk, but I don't trust him. So I had to wait to learn its purpose. But that doesn't mean I had to wait to notice TECH-chick fabricated a similar item." He flips the key in his palms. "The trick revolved around figuring out she was observing you while programming her key—every moment out of your company she'd plug in and tap information to upload into this."

"It's programmed? So not like a car key?" I look at my own copy.

"It dawned on me, when we all became codeless, how I could program the key so it would only benefit us. But, I had to get my hands on it first—and TECH-chick wasn't with us. She was never on that level."

Listening to him speak, I keep to myself that I saw TECH-chick during the last gamescape. I hide my left arm behind my back, hoping he doesn't notice. I'm not the same as him anymore. Our keys might serve different purpose. Had he ever thought to ask TECH-chick what she was programming? Or... if she programmed mine to begin with?

365

"I had to gamble on the idea the Commander was the master-mind of the key you now possess. He arranged to give it to you as early as possible, undermining me from the start."

The key showed up in the same level we met TECH-chick. But, I was the one who saw it first—lying on the floormat of the burned-out vehicle where we recovered the kid. Not privy to my mental hesitation about trusting any item that can be traced back to either Tony or TECH-chick as possible sources for when and where and how the object was planted on me to begin with, Ace keeps talking.

"Whatever its purpose, it would plug into the system and change the requirements of donor matches. At least, that's my best guess. This..." Ace shakes his key in front of my face. "It makes us a match for endgame. Us—the non-code players. And the rest of those imbeciles, if they don't kill each other first." Ace looks around. "Where are the guys? Were you separated?" Ace stares at me. "Did the same thing happen to them?"

"Why did you storm ahead?" I ask, hoping he won't press too much about the other guys.

"Infiltrating a heavily guarded building isn't a group activity, especially with Ed McBickerson, the know-it-all from must-be-documented-land, and Tony the kid, Godfather of the Damned." Ace points to the statue. "I have the schematics. I work better alone."

"Why'd you call out to me?" I ask. "If you were running a solo mission..."

"I don't know. You were walking right up to the front gate all 'Robot-Barbie'. I didn't know your game plan and it seemed questionable." He raises his eyebrows. "Thought I could use you."

"And now?" I ask. "Am I still useful?"

"Better than useful." He lifts his eyebrows like he's got this thing in the bag.

But I know better.

41

A ce holds both keys in his hand. Why didn't I pay better attention to where he placed mine? Did he slide it over the top of his key or under? "Take this." He hands me the one on top. "You're going to have to pretend to be the same way you were three minutes ago."

"I don't know what that was. My processing ability was completely impaired."

Ace motions me to take note of his demonstration. "Like this. *'I am a robot. I will destroy you.'*"

"Helpful."

"Don't speak. Walk in, deliver the key," he says, serious this time.

Turning to where I entered the statue cove, cement colored sand, red sky, and death on the wind. Nothing about the direction says success. "This can't work." I close my fingers around the key in my palm and take one step, two. When I look back, I catch the fleeting image of Ace running. Roll of paper in hand, he jumps a sand-battered, crumbling stone wall before he's gone.

I'm not on my own. Sucking in the hot air so it burns my lungs, I take the final two steps, peeling away from the cover of long broken statues.

"That was unexpected," the Commander says.

Red lights trained on my skull lead back to a dozen laser sighted guns. Lifting my hands in the air in time to the release of my pointless breath, I meet my captor's eyes. It's obvious the Commander's forces control my next actions, if they let me live.

"Not too thoughtful on your part. You had to know I was tracking you." He sweeps a hand behind him, where more of his men hold a mess of a person.

No. Two persons.

The Commander smirks. "And you were performing so well."

Ed's head lags forward. Where he once had a right arm, a bloody mess of tendons dangle. Tony wears a mess of red, too, but his head isn't hanging in front of him. He stares at me with injured accusation. "What did you do?" I ask.

"You did," Tony spits at my feet.

I jump back from the feeble gesture, only to be shoved against Tony by the Commander's men, losing my balance and falling on him. With his elbow, Tony pops my jaw so that my head lunges up. My knees buckle. I rely on Tony's scrawny frame to compose myself and get my feet back under me. When I do stand, Tony rips and pulls at my shirt. I'm sure it's supposed to be some dramatic 'ripping of the shoulder seams in a jacket.' The sign of a turncoat.

"No more wasted time." At the Commander's nod, my arms are pulled to my sides and I'm forced to walk in front of Tony and Ed, who drags behind us all. His feet leave a line in the sand, unwashed over by the ashen wind.

Off to the side from where we're being led, several soldiers dressed in Commander blue approach our line. I realize how invested I've been in a never-discussed backup plan devised and implemented by the limp figure they drag toward us.

Ace.

Unconscious and useless, at the back of the pack. Any defiance I've been holding onto evaporates like sweat. Once again, I hate being right. Ace can't win this.

"You promised me," Tony wheezes at the Commander.

"You didn't deliver," the Commander answers.

The procession passes through the rusted metal frame of the grand entrance to the once mighty cathedral, now a pile of pocked stone held together more by mold than mortar. How mold managed to survive the dry environment baffles me. Admittedly, it's not my biggest concern at the moment. This game sucks and I'm going to die.

Inside the walls, red sky bleeds through decomposed roofing. A stage set back in the majestic open room stands out as the only structure not in a state of decay.

It's a platform.

New construction peppers the musty historic setting. The final level-up platform. A sophisticated podium reaches up from the stone and sand floor. The pungent scents work like smelling salts, rousing both Ace and Ed to their misfortune. Ace tests the grip of those holding him, while Ed—less dignified in his current state—whinnies and moans before catching sight of his blood-stringy shoulder and passes out again.

"There was no task. No challenge. How can you expect to advance?" I ask.

"Of course there was a challenge." The Commander laughs. "I've been working on this objective far longer than you have. I planted the key on the one person who could take items from level to level."

Me.

"Before that, brainwashing my own best soldier to create you, thinking he's outsmarting me." He turns to Ace. "*Tsk, tsk, tsk.* Did you honestly expect to outthink me? I'm your Commander. I programmed this world."

"You started the virus. You put the nail in our coffins," Ace restrains his voice, weighting his words with each period.

The skin of the Commander's face shakes in ragged flaps, visible despite the tense cut of his jaw. His age shows in more than digital years.

"Do you have any idea how many times I've been here?" He stabs his hand like a knife downward, through the air above the ground, as if the motion could pierce the threads of code holding this room in its broken state. "I'm the only person in this room who has earned advancement." Wild red lines flare out from the corners of his eyes, similar to being bloodshot, growing in spidery wear before us. "I earned this."

The red lines of his eyes divert my attention to the walls where rusted letters spell, 'failures'. Each and every failure the Commander experienced in his pursuit of glory.

Players are sheep learning to follow rules without question.

Sheep get in the way.

Glitches in system.

Rain program affects our own kind—mistake.

Virus out of hand.

Mord can be programmed to spawn in certain levels.

Code breaks mutating.

Weather programming out of control—build bunkers.

Virus out of control.

Antiviral boost wipes code.

Donors can't carry items through platforms.

I strain to read more.

Non-donors must believe they are real or won't advance.

Cure Mord.

Several more instructions regarding methods of key delivery, travel, use of Mord, and ad campaigns to manipulate other players into opening a path for the Commander's efforts. The lines crack and wave, repeating a single message.

Sheep. Trust no one.

Sheep. Trust no one.

Sheep.

Trust no one.

Maybe he deserves to win. Trapped in this game-world, shoved back to the beginning every time he reaches this point, unable to complete the requirements because of the strict process of bringing items up the levels...

"It must be frustrating," I say. I've only been living one cycle.

"Don't speak to me." The Commander cuts me off, like my words are poison. He points a finger toward Ace. "Grab his key."

Ace thrashes in the grasp of those holding him down. They remove his pack, vest, and belt in search of a small blunted computer chip disguised as a key

"There's nothing here," one of them says.

The Commander moves close to Ace. "You managed to stay young despite replaying this charade as many times as I have." They've been playing the same amount of time? "Everyone else is a traveler and infection in the code. GenA included."

Ace kicks and twists at the mention of GenA, which is a Gen I've never heard of before now.

"You know, that thing you made looks just like her." The Commander points at me. "You think GenA would be here with me now, if we hadn't injected her with the first booster? Awful how it erased her features like that. So fast." The Commander wipes the air in front of his face like he's swiping his face clean. "Maybe we shouldn't have tested our first batch on the one person you trusted most. Or maybe it was the only person we could have used." He leans toward Ace imposing himself, as if suggesting he intended to hurt the person they're discussing so that Ace only had one person to rely on after that—the Commander. He whispers his next words so that I strain against those holding me back, so I can hear. "Trust is hard to come by these days."

Ace stops fighting.

The Commander keeps talking. Louder so we can all participate in Ace's misery. "You had to learn that it's my code. Mine. I made all of this. You can't overwrite me."

"You're wrong," Ace coughs.

The Commander smiles like those words give him a world of

information. "He has the key. Look again." Searching Ace without dignity, they finally find it in a pocket in the inner lining of his vest. "And hers." He points a finger at me without bothering to face me again. I'm not an equal challenger. Not in the same way Ace gets addressed.

Two soldiers approach me.

"Someone already took it from me."

"Nice try," the Commander says, still not looking at me.

A soldier forces my fingers straight, revealing nothing. "Her hands are empty."

"She can't have hidden it," the Commander says. "Worthless puppets." He pushes one of the soldiers away from my side. "Where did you put it?" The threat of being searched in the same fashion as Ace dances across the hungry red lines filling the whites of his eyes.

"I dropped it."

He stands. Dropping his eyes from my body with all its hiding places, to the cracks of the floor, toward the swallowing sands tinged with red light from the sky without the splintered grand doors hanging on their ancient rusted hinges. "You lie."

Unfortunately, I'm not lying. The prospect of being proven truthful sends a cold sweat beneath the hot sweat already fully soaking me. I'm super sick of whoever thought to program sweat into the game.

Tony raises his hand into the air, flailing for attention like some thug school kid. "I have it," he says, waving his good arm. "I have it."

I let my head bob forward, all the disappointments of—

however the heck long this game has been being played—weigh on me like lead through my veins.

The Commander half bends with glee. His hands together, he pivots toward me, his head near my own in his disfigured pleasure. "You banked on the kid?" He laughs. Straightening his spine gives the illusion of practically throwing his head back in villainous glee.

Soldiers wrestle the key from Tony's clenched fist without needing orders. I train my eyes on the key being handed to the Commander—a key version of the ball-in-shell game. I can't tell the two items apart, but if I can keep track of which one came from Tony… The sellout.

"You owe me a code," Tony yells. "Jennie has code and she's not even human."

Ace's head lifts. His eyes are on me, moving from my eyes to my left forearm, which he hadn't bothered to check in our earlier encounter because… why would he. The skin around his eyes tightens as if he's trying to figure out which side of the line this new information places me.

Tony doesn't let it go. "I know you have a formula which implants new source code on our arms."

The Commander rubs one key over the top of the other. The grinding noise makes me cringe. Strips of software might damage by such scraping.

"Shoot me!" Tony demands of the Commander. I'm sure he's referring to being injected with code serum, but he worded his request poorly. He stares at the stage ahead, eager to claim his place in the fresh new world on the corresponding side of the platform in front of us all. It only works with all the impossible criteria met. Something the Commander has been working toward and failing at longer than Tony could possibly have the patience to survive.

"You're right." The Commander's shoulders sag. "You've definitely earned it." He pulls a gun out of the waist band of a soldier near him, aims it at Tony's blood-smeared head, and presses the trigger all the way back. Two shots fire simultaneously. He hands it back to the soldier with his finger off the sensitive trigger as Tony's body goes limp. The soldiers restraining him drop their grip, startled by the closeness of the bullets which silence Tony.

He doesn't code. Not this time. I look away from the Tony-heap. I can't stand his self-interest, but he wasn't a bad kid. I almost liked him sometimes.

Then the scraping of the keys reminds me I've taken my eyes off the shell game.

The Commander throws the keys to his associate at my left, the one holding my freshly coded arm. Following their arc through a streak of red light, I still can't tell which key is which.

"Try them both. The fake one can't hurt me." He walks to the platform. "Wait." Looking at Ace, a smile crosses the Commander's face. "No point taking chances." Grabbing Ace by the front of his neck, he forces the well-built, much younger, wounded-beyond-the-point-of-being-threatening man to the stage.

Ace trips backward when the Commander releases him. He coughs, holding his throat with one hand while the Commander continues to orate. "No code. He can't go anywhere. But if the other key is sabotaged, I'll know." He raps the textured stage with his knuckles. "We all know you're good at programming."

He steps back to where the red light of outside moves across the podium with its single key slot. "Let's see how good you really are."

A nameless soldier selects a key from his comrade at a nod from the Commander and moves his hand toward the wide hole of the podium. I suck in breaths over and over, never letting it go, as if one of those pulls of air can stop time and freeze the odds in Ace's favor. We both know he has a fifty-fifty chance of advancing now. Whichever key he programmed should let all the codeless players advance. The other one, the Commander's key, will never let the codeless through.

Trying not to shift my glance to Ace, I can't help it. I check if he acts like luck's on our side. Ace holds fatigue and failure where code once ruled. The same sagging skin hanging on the Commander is now visible in the slack around Ace's mouth.

For everything we've overcome in this stupid game, if there's some way for me to guarantee Ace moves on...

Before he can reach the platform, a different soldier in the Commander's ranks puts out his arm to halt Ace's advance and takes Ace's place at the podium.

The Commander does nothing to stop it.

The soldier slips the key into the slot. It fits perfectly. A button lights on the flat panel surface—green for go. He hits it with the heel of his palm. In the same instant his body turns red like the sky. His mouth petrifies in a scream of terror as whatever life force keeps us digitally powered, leaves his eyes. Nothing but a shape of human, burnt to a sleek black cylinder, remains.

"I thought so." The Commander pushes the charred remains

so the soldier turns to ash when his body hits the stony floor. "She has to be the one."

Nervous. I look around. What she? The room is filled with everything, except she. Other than me.

"Her arm matches the numbers on the outlet. She's the only port match."

I'm a what now? I look at my arm. GenCON1. The Podium reads 'CON'. "That doesn't mean anything," I say.

"The long con... that's you," the Commander says. "The kind of devotion it takes to win. And I was the only one who could see it through."

"In Latin 'con' means with. It's nothing—" I stare at the ashy remains of the last guy who turned the key. Then I lift my foot. Underneath is more gray ash. The room is filled with it. Swirling, falling, piling in corners. Ash. The sand covering this world is gray—ash. All of it. Ash. "I could end up just like the last guy."

"That's a chance I'm willing to take," the Commander says.

Ace looks at me. The skin around his mouth tight with determination again. "No. She deserves better. She is this game. She was born here. Don't take her away—"

Uh, don't listen to Ace. This place breeds nightmares.

"This is my life!" The Commander shouts.

"This war you're fighting is between us. No one else," Ace says.

So... it's pretty obvious I'm going to fry-crispy.

"Would you rather give it a try? I have another tester..." One snap of his fingers and an unconscious Ed gets dragged to the stage. He must have some life left in him for the Commander to bother hauling him around.

Ace stands. Every inch of the process looks painful. "I would."

"No." I'm sick of this game and not knowing who I'm a pawn for. I'm so done. I don't even care if I turn to a char statue.

With Ace still occupying the platform the Commander refers to as 'the last goodbye', I rush to the podium, and slam the key back inside the hole it automatically lifted out of, like an ejected chip forced back down the reader.

Ace chokes out some protest I don't hear. The green light blinks on once more and I slap again. It's not a small button, but I'm nervous and hyper at once and miss. I slap again and again. I know I've hit the button by now.

Slap, slap, slap. My eyes close so tight, stars and blue-white light zing through the dark of the undersides of my lids. Opening my eyes a squint, I peek toward Ace. His face is frozen in protest, the entire room frozen in white light. Not red, or blue, or green. Black strings of numbers come rushing in from all sides. I try to let go of the podium but I'm fused to it. Is this what the crispy-fried soldier experienced from his perspective?

42

The light turns yellow under the white, an ancient glow filtering its blindingness.

"What is this?" I scream. My voice doesn't carry any of the synthesized tones I'm familiar with. It's solid with weight and coarseness, like I haven't used my vocal chords in a long, long time.

The image of Ace screaming drops away along with the Commander's reaching hands. In its place, a blaring, blinding, heat-filled space. Beeps and blips assault my ears like stabbing to each nerve. The stabbing reaches up vines under my skin, connecting to my skull and crushing along the surface area like a web of pressure triggered with each stab of sound.

If auditory was the only concern, maybe I could do something, but my eyes are battered with stinging whiteness, so fierce tears flood my cornea in an attempt to shield my vision. No matter how much I try, the bitter bright won't blink away.

The air is heavy, pressing on my limbs. The atmosphere

grows in pressure and humidity. I'm being compressed and sweated together at once. Each breath is raspier, thicker with dew than the last. It also holds flavor. Salt and graphite blend in my sinuses and coat the roof of my mouth when I gasp for air.

There is so much information cocooning me from making sense of what's happening. *What's happening?* I'm drowning in sensation and information too fast and too solid to process—like being beaten with feelings made from bricks.

I can't form words because I'm dying of too much information at once. My only options are involuntary reflexes of coughing, wheezing, continuing to breathe.

It feels like lifetimes pass in this state of too muchness before a mask presses over my mouth and nose, shoving air of some kind in through my nostrils. It smells like sugar and sickness. I breathe. I can pick and decode information from the chaos. I'm not alone. There are people with white coats and white cloth covering their mouths, writing on white boards.

A sterile room with white curtains and white walls boxes me in. Cream-colored monitors pound out a rhythm pumping through my chest.

"Doctor!" I startle at the presence of a woman at my side. Why am I lying down?

I move to stand, but once again I'm restrained.

"Call the reporters. We have a qualified donor." The voice of the person in the room with me is giddy with excitement.

The white coats gather and then scatter once they confirm my blink in their direction. I turn my head, sending a thousand shooting bullets from one ear to the other. The pain rushes through me, hitting so close I might puke on the sensation. *My skin*... tingles all over. It hurts. *My eyes*... they hurt. *My tongue*... swells and my mouth sweats from the roof of my mouth down the inner lining of my cheeks and spills past my lips.

I'm drooling. Ugh.

Dipping my chin to my chest, I wipe my face against course fabric that scratches more than wicks, while lying down with arms restrained.

A man rushes into the room. He looks at me and I at him. He's old. Gray strands stick wildly out from his pepper hair. He has on a white coat and carries a bundle of note pages, but looks nothing like a medical man. He's wiry and sparse, like his bones forgot to order the meat to go on them.

"Why didn't you tell me sooner?" are the first words out of his mouth. He has an accent I'm unfamiliar with but I understand his language. "When did this happen?"

"Just now."

"There should have been alerts when one of our donors gets close to the end of the program." The wiry man flicks a nubby finger at several different screens. "Which code?"

The woman consults a screen. "Another glitch." She curses under her breath. "I'm seeing all donor codes accounted for in the system."

The doctor stands quickly, looks toward the white coats, and covers one finger over his mouth when making eye contact with the woman still consulting the screen. He lowers his voice to a whisper. "Shut it off." He reaches around her for a button.

She refuses his order, holding up one hand to deter his punchy fingers.

"If we report any more glitches..." he looks over his shoulder and nods while raising his eyebrows in an 'all's well' gesture to the white coats who compare notes from clipboards and screens, "…they'll pull our funding."

He turns his head the slightest to one side, pleading for something I'm not privy to know about in my current state of overwhelmed. The woman retrieves a handheld device. A dial tone precedes several quick sharp tones before both of them pause. The man so tense, I trust he breathes less than I do.

The woman speaks into a phone, "The program is a success," she says. "We still have to run the tests, but it's official. First upload."

"Don't tell them too much," the man warns. "This is the first after all. No telling what to expect."

"The first?" I ask, garbled through my breathing mask.

They both turn, shock on their faces, as if they expected me to speak infant and not be capable of complete sentences, much less questions.

"Oh, yes. It's impossible to predict human nature and technology coinciding." The man turns back to wipe dust from a line of monitors. "We'll have to reboot the whole system to start a second cycle. Can't run the same requirements more than once." He nods happily, punching buttons on a screen.

"What does that mean for the other donors?" I ask.

The man turns to the woman as if expecting her to translate. I'm speaking the same language they are.

"The code?" the woman offers with an unsure shrug of her shoulders.

He nods at her then returns to his screen. "They're not a match. You must realize the time and money involved in creating housing for human intelligence." He points to monitors lining three of the four walls. Names in minute block font squeeze into tight columns filling every screen, with a code listed by each one. Gen code. "Sustainable housing, body functions are required for real human thought. That's not easy to replicate." He pauses to observe the screens. "Put in a helpdesk ticket to get that glitch fixed before new applicants apply."

"Of course. Of course." The woman claps her hands together, as if business discussion is officially cleared for patting each other on the back.

"New applicants?" I ask, busting up the 'nice job, everyone' moment. "What about everyone in the game? Everyone waiting, after surviving all of that?" I nudge my head toward the screens. "Can't you reboot them?"

"Spot's taken," he says. "It's not like they're losing anything. Their organs have been reclaimed by donor programs the world over. Those people are heroes somewhere, just not here." He points to the small bright room. "Just you," he says hitting keys so fast, I can't stop him from flushing Ace and Tony and Ed into the recycle bin of scientific accolades.

"No." I shake my head slow. "They're not. They're in the program," I say.

The doctor defers to his female associate to answer.

"I'm sorry to tell you this," she says, "but they're no longer viable candidates. This whole process is the same as any other organ donation. There is a limited possibility of matches. For this housing, you're the only match. Done. The first intelligence donor in history. We've successfully uploaded human brain circuitry into a technologically advanced machine." The woman claps at her final words. "Fully human functioning in every way. Indistinguishable from any other human."

The doctor pauses to swallow and shake his head slowly side to side, his words catch in his throat, rough with mucous. "You're magnificent." Moisture glistens at the corners of his eyes.

While I remain not human. I never am nor will be.

Their perfect donor match is a machine. At best, I'm a Frankenstein made of human scrap. Slapped together and powered by losers the game over. Afraid of water and people.

"We're going to have to prep you for the press conferences," the woman says.

"Yes, yes. Thank you," the man says, shifting his tie to one side and then the other.

"No. The..." She looks at me with her head tilted down, pointing with the movement of her eyes, until the man nods and laughs to himself.

"Right. Press have heard enough from me. Sure, I made the future, but the future is..." He points to me "...you." He then turns to the woman. "The world is going to want to address it by some name. What are we calling it?"

It? If they only knew.

They both start flipping through papers for some printout with my code on it.

"Jennie," I say before they have time to find no match for me. "My name is Jennie."

The End

ACKNOWLEDGEMENTS

Somehow my youngest kid figured out how to trick me into gaming—pretending to not be able to know how to get through levels. I later caught my then four-year-old master commanding the controls like a seasoned problem solver. Thanks, Buddy, for not being super mad at all the gaming time restrictions we impose on the whole family—want you to be well rounded <3.

My whole family is amazingly supportive of my writing, revising, reading, editing, marketing, teaming, grouping, conferencing, more revision/editing, presenting, online chatting… Holy crud—I have a patient family! Thanks for being understanding when I'm in a session over the computer. Also, thank you to all the professional writing people who have been understanding when my cuties sneak on-screen.

Thank you Jessica and Rebecca for being there when anxiety was all I thought I had invested in this story.

Editor Melissa. Ha! You're a Magician and you know it. I know it. Now everyone knows it.

Jason, thanks for fighting to have me in your ranks. I like it here.

Thank you Kevin, I love your purple shirt.

Thank you Heather, Cass, Danielle, Brent, Kimberly, Krista, Jamie, Jody, Jueneke, Laura, Maura, Rachel, Serene, Shauna, Sheena, and Shelly (PCC, I love your guts).

Thank you Jamie (again from PCC) for your talents in getting this book seen. You're amazing. You do so much and you have serious skills.

Devin. You're hot. Thanks for being a geek/nerd with me forever and always. I love you.

Thanks hours between 10pm and midnight and a half—my writing time wouldn't exist without you.

6am and earlier, I never liked you. You're just embarrassing yourself at this point. It's never going to happen between us. I'm already in a committed relationship with 10pm and later. Stop already, anytime earlier than 6am.

And writer friends who support me no matter how much I demonstrate my commitment to dorkdom. Kimberly (the magic words) VanderHorst (I had to last name you, there are a lot of Kimberly's), Jolene, Mercedes (may your dark love spread across the world), Brekke (I dare readers to send in pronunciation attempts to me)—I love you girls.

Writing I love. All of you, I love more than that. <3

ABOUT THE AUTHOR

Aften Brook Szymanski, at the age of five, once fell on her bum looking out a large picture window while eating a pickle and people laughed. She thought she was funny; life has never been the same.

She's obsessed with LEGOs, cozy reading nooks, and over-the-knee socks. A graduate of the College of Southern Idaho with an Associate of Arts degree, Brigham Young University with a Bachelor of Science degree, and the University of Utah with a Master of Education degree. Learning is more fun than testing, sometimes we have to endure both.

Aften has Marfan syndrome and facial recognition disorder (unrelated conditions). She is likely to say hi to someone she doesn't know and totally miss noticing her best friend crossing paths at the grocery store. It can be awkward either way.

She lives in a very cold Wyoming valley with her husband,

three kids, and one unhappy cat, where they are being cryogenically preserved for all time—thanks to how cold it is.

For information about facial recognition disorder, quiz links, and contests visit aftenbrook.com.

facebook.com/aftenbrook

twitter.com/aftenbrook

instagram.com/aftenbrook